Praise for The Dresden Files

"What's not to like about this series? . . . I would, could, have, and will continue to recommend [it] for as long as my breath holds out. It takes the best elements of urban fantasy, mixes it with some good old-fashioned noir mystery, tosses in a dash of romance and a lot of high-octane action, shakes, stirs, and serves." —SF Site

"Jim Butcher's Harry Dresden series has consistently been one of the most enjoyable marriages of the fantasy and mystery genres on the shelves . . . a great series—fast-paced, vividly realized and with a hero/narrator who's excellent company." —Cinescape

Dead Beat

"Butcher's latest maintains the momentum of previous Dresden outings and builds the suspense right up to a rousing conclusion."
—Booklist

"Horror fans with a sense of humor will be pleased."
—Publishers Weekly

"A mix of the supernatural and bounding adventure. . . . A fun-loaded series." —Kirkus Reviews

Blood Rites

"Filled with sizzling magic and intrigue as well as important developments for Harry, the latest of his adventures will have fans rapidly turning the pages." —Booklist

continued . . .

D0058823

Fool Moon

"It's even more entertaining . . . than the first in the series, good fun for fans of dark fantasy mystery." —*Locus*

"*Storm Front* was one of the most enjoyable books I read last year, and *Fool Moon* is even better. Butcher keeps the thrills coming, with plenty of mystery, suspense, and edge-of-your-seat action."
—*SF Site*

"A fast-paced, fascinating noir thriller." —BookBrowser

"A really enjoyable read. . . . Jim Butcher strikes just the right narrative balance between wizard and wise guy, mystic and mobster."
—Lynn Flewelling, author of *Traitor's Moon*

Storm Front

"A very promising start to a new series, not to mention an unusually well-crafted first novel." —*Locus*

"Interesting characters, tight plotting, and fresh, breezy writing . . . an auspicious start to an engaging new series." —*SF Site*

"Butcher deftly blends the fantasy and detective genres in this entertaining yarn."
—*Publishers Weekly* (review of the audio edition)

"Required summer reading for anyone who likes a few laughs."
—*The Reporter* (Vacaville, CA)

"Wish I'd thought of this myself. Try it. You'll like it."
—Glen Cook, author of *Whispering Nickel Idols*

"Exciting, well-plotted, complex, an excellent read . . . amazingly good." —Chris Bunch, author of *Dragonmaster*

JIM BUTCHER

DEAD BEAT

A NOVEL OF THE DRESDEN FILES

A ROC BOOK

ROC

Published by New American Library, a division of
Penguin Group (USA) Inc., 375 Hudson Street,
New York, New York 10014, USA
Penguin Group (Canada), 90 Eglinton Avenue East, Suite 700, Toronto,
Ontario M4P 2Y3, Canada (a division of Pearson Penguin Canada Inc.)
Penguin Books Ltd., 80 Strand, London WC2R 0RL, England
Penguin Ireland, 25 St. Stephen's Green, Dublin 2,
Ireland (a division of Penguin Books Ltd.)
Penguin Group (Australia), 250 Camberwell Road, Camberwell, Victoria 3124,
Australia (a division of Pearson Australia Group Pty. Ltd.)
Penguin Books India Pvt. Ltd., 11 Community Centre, Panchsheel Park,
New Delhi - 110 017, India
Penguin Group (NZ), 67 Apollo Drive, Rosedale, North Shore 0632,
New Zealand (a division of Pearson New Zealand Ltd.)
Penguin Books (South Africa) (Pty.) Ltd., 24 Sturdee Avenue,
Rosebank, Johannesburg 2196, South Africa

Penguin Books Ltd., Registered Offices:
80 Strand, London WC2R 0RL, England

Published by Roc, an imprint of New American Library, a division of Penguin
Group (USA) Inc. Previously published in a Roc hardcover edition.

First Roc Mass Market Printing, May 2006
10   9   8

For my son.
The best thing that ever happened to me.
I love you, Short-stuff.

ACKNOWLEDGMENTS

I owe another round of thanks to the usual suspects: The inmates of the Beta Foo Asylum, both long-term and recent arrivals. The Dresden Files' new editor, the warm and gracious Anne Sowards—are you sure you actually live in NYC, Anne? My agent, Jennifer Jackson, who has been doing ten kinds of running around getting various deals put together, and for whom I am most grateful.

More thanks to my family for their continuing support and love. To Shannon for being who she is, and whose good opinion I would work ten . . . well, wait, no, maybe three times as hard to keep—okay, okay, five, tops. (Ten would be more hours than exist, babe, and besides, when could I play Halo?) Also thanks to my son JJ, whose boundless energy, enthusiasm, and love are wonderfully intimidating.

Oh, and also for my ferocious furry bodyguard, Frost, who supports my career by frightening away any bad guys long before they get near enough to actually bother me, and by helping me eat any potentially distracting snacks.

Chapter

One

On the whole, we're a murderous race.

According to Genesis, it took as few as four people to make the planet too crowded to stand, and the first murder was a fratricide. Genesis says that in a fit of jealous rage, the very first child born to mortal parents, Cain, snapped and popped the first metaphorical cap in another human being. The attack was a bloody, brutal, violent, reprehensible killing. Cain's brother Abel probably never saw it coming.

As I opened the door to my apartment, I was filled with a sense of empathic sympathy and intuitive understanding.

For freaking Cain.

My apartment isn't much more than a big room in the basement of a century-old wooden boardinghouse in Chicago. There's a kitchen built into an alcove, a big fireplace almost always lit, a bedroom the size of the bed of a pickup truck, and a bathroom that barely fits a sink, toilet, and shower. I can't afford really good furniture, so it's all secondhand, but comfortable. I have a lot of books on shelves, a lot of rugs, a lot of candles. It isn't much, but at least it's clean.

Or used to be.

The rugs were in total disarray, exposing bare patches of stone floor. One of the easy chairs had fallen over onto its back, and no one had picked it up. Cushions were missing from the couch, and the curtains had been torn down from one of the sunken windows, letting in a swath of late-afternoon sunshine, all the better to illuminate the books that had been knocked down from one of my shelves and scattered everywhere, bending paperback covers, leaving hardbacks all the way open, and generally messing up my primary source of idle entertainment.

The fireplace was more or less the epicenter of the slobquake. There were discarded clothes there, a couple of empty wine bottles, and a plate that looked suspiciously clean—doubtless the cleanup work of the other residents.

I took a stunned step into my home. As I did my big grey tom, Mister, bounded down from his place on top of one of the bookshelves, but rather than give me his usual shoulder-block of greeting, he flicked his tail disdainfully at me and ghosted out the front door.

I sighed, walked over to the kitchen alcove, and checked. The cat's bowls of food and water were both empty. No wonder he was grumpy.

A shaggy section of the kitchen floor hauled itself to its feet and came to meet me with a sheepish, sleepy shuffle. My dog, Mouse, had started off as a fuzzy little grey puppy that fit into my coat pocket. Now, almost a year later, I sometimes wished I'd sent my coat to the cleaners or something. Mouse had gone from fuzz ball to fuzz barge. You couldn't guess at a breed to look at him, but at least one of his parents must have been a wooly mammoth. The dog's shoulders came nearly to my waist, and the vet didn't think he was finished growing yet. That translated into an awful lot of beast for my tiny apartment.

Oh, and Mouse's bowls were empty, too. He nuzzled my hand, his muzzle stained with what looked suspiciously like spaghetti sauce, and then pawed at his bowls, scraping them over the patch of linoleum floor.

"Dammit, Mouse," I growled, Cain-like. "It's *still* like this? If he's here, I'm going to kill him."

Mouse let out a chuffing breath that was about as much commentary as he ever made, and followed placidly a couple of steps behind me as I walked over to the closed bedroom door.

Just as I got there, the door opened, and an angel-faced blonde wearing nothing but a cotton T-shirt appeared in it. Not a long shirt, either. It didn't cover all of her rib cage.

"Oh," she drawled, with a slow and sleepy smile. "Excuse me. I didn't know anyone else was here." Without a trace of modesty, she slunk into the living room, pawing through the mess near the fireplace, extracting pieces of clothing. From the languid, satisfied way she moved, I figured she expected me to be staring at her, and that she didn't mind it at all.

At one time I would have been embarrassed as hell by this kind of thing, and probably sneaking covert glances. But after living with my half brother the incubus for most of a year, I mostly found it annoying. I rolled my eyes and asked, "Thomas?"

"Tommy? Shower, I think," the girl said. She slipped into jogging wear—sweatpants, a matching jacket, expensive shoes. "Do me a favor? Tell him that it—"

I interrupted her in an impatient voice. "That it was a lot of fun, you'll always treasure it, but that it was a onetime thing and that you hope he grows up to find a nice girl or be president or something."

She stared at me and then knitted her blond brows into a frown. "You don't have to be such a bast—" Then her eyes widened. "Oh. *Oh!* I'm sorry—oh, my God." She leaned toward me, blushing, and said in a between-us-girls whisper, "I would *never* have guessed that he was with a *man.* How do the two of you *manage* on that tiny bed?"

I blinked and said, "Now *wait* a minute."

But she ignored me and walked out, murmuring, "He is *such* a naughty boy."

I glared at her back. Then I glared at Mouse.

Mouse's tongue lolled out in a doggy grin, his dark tail waving gently.

"Oh, shut up," I told him, and closed the door. I heard the whisper of water running through the pipes in my shower. I put out food for Mister and Mouse, and the dog partook immediately. "He could have fed the damned dog, at least," I muttered, and opened the fridge.

I rummaged through it, but couldn't find what I was after anywhere, and it was the last straw. My frustration grew into a fire somewhere inside my eyeballs, and I straightened from the icebox with mayhem in mind.

"Hey," came Thomas's voice from behind me. "We're out of beer."

I turned around and glared at my half brother.

Thomas was a shade over six feet tall, and I guess now that I'd had time to get used to the idea, he looked something like me: stark cheekbones, a long face, a strong jaw. But whatever sculptor had done the finishing work on Thomas had foisted my features off on his apprentice or something. I'm not ugly or anything, but Thomas looked like someone's painting of the forgotten Greek god of body cologne. He had long hair so dark that light itself could not escape it, and even fresh from the shower it was starting to curl. His eyes were the color of thunderclouds, and he never did a single moment of exercise to earn the gratuitous amount of ripple in his musculature. He was wearing jeans and no shirt—his standard household uniform. I once saw him in the same outfit answer the door to speak to a female missionary, and she'd assaulted him in a cloud of forgotten copies of *The Watchtower.* The tooth marks she left had been interesting.

It hadn't been the girl's fault, entirely. Thomas had inherited his father's blood as a vampire of the White Court. He was a psychic predator, feeding on the raw life force of human beings—usually easiest to gain through the intimate contact of sex. That part of him surrounded him in the kind of aura that turned heads wherever he went. When Thomas made the effort to turn up the supernatural come-hither, women literally couldn't tell him no. By the time he started feeding, they couldn't even *want* to tell him no. He was killing them, just a little bit, but he had to do it to stay sane, and he never took it any further than a single feeding.

He could have. Those the White Court chose as their prey became ensnared in the ecstasy of being fed upon, and became increasingly enslaved by their vampire lover. But Thomas never pushed it that far. He'd made that mistake once, and the woman he had loved now drifted through life in a wheelchair, bound in a deathly euphoria because of his touch.

I clenched my teeth and reminded myself that it wasn't easy for Thomas. Then I told myself that I was repeating myself way too many times and to shut up. "I know there's no beer," I growled. "Or milk. Or Coke."

"Um," he said.

"And I see that you didn't have time to feed Mister and Mouse. Did you take Mouse outside, at least?"

"Well sure," he said. "I mean, uh . . . I took him out this morning when you were leaving for work, remember? That's where I met Angie."

"Another jogger," I said, once more Cain-like. "You told me you weren't going to keep bringing strangers back here, Thomas. And on my freaking *bed?* Hell's bells, man, *look* at this place."

He did, and I saw it dawn on him, as if he literally hadn't seen it before. He let out a groan. "Damn. Harry, I'm sorry. It was . . . Angie is a really . . . *really* intense and, uh, athletic person and I didn't realize that . . ." He paused and picked up a copy of Dean Koontz's *Watchers.* He tried to fold the crease out of the cover. "Wow," he added lamely. "The place is sort of trashed."

"Yeah," I told him. "You were here all day. You said you'd take Mouse to the vet. And clean up a little. *And* get groceries."

"Oh, come on," he said. "What's the big deal?"

"I don't have a beer," I growled. I looked around at the rubble. "And I got a call from Murphy at work today. She said she'd be dropping by."

Thomas lifted his eyebrows. "Oh, yeah? No offense, Harry, but I'm doubting it was a booty call."

I glared. "Would you stop it with that already?"

"I'm telling you, you should just ask her out and get it over with. She'd say yes."

I slammed the door to the icebox. "It isn't like that," I said.

"Yeah, okay," Thomas said mildly.

"It isn't. We work together. We're friends. That's all."

"Right," he agreed.

"I am not interested in dating Murphy," I said. "And she's not interested in me."

"Sure, sure. I hear you." He rolled his eyes and started picking up fallen books. "Which is why you want the place looking nice. So your business friend won't mind staying around for a little bit."

I gritted my teeth and said, "Stars and stones, Thomas, I'm not asking you for the freaking moon. I'm not asking you for rent. It wouldn't kill you to pitch in a little with errands before you go to work."

"Yeah," Thomas said, running his hand through his hair. "Um. About that."

"What about it?" I demanded. He was supposed to be gone for the afternoon so that my housecleaning service could come in. The faeries wouldn't show up to clean when someone could see them, and they wouldn't show up ever again if I told someone about them. Don't ask me why they're like that. Maybe they've got a really strict union or something.

Thomas shrugged a shoulder and sat down on the arm of the couch, not looking at me. "I didn't have the cash for the vet or the groceries," he said. "I got fired again."

I stared at him for a second, and tried to keep up a good head of steam on my anger, but it melted. I recognized the frustration and humiliation in his voice. He wasn't faking it.

"Dammit," I muttered, only partly to Thomas. "What happened?"

"The usual," he said. "The drive-through manager. She followed me into the walk-in freezer and started ripping her clothes off. The owner walked through on an inspection about then and fired me on the spot. From the look he was giving *her,* I think she was going to get a promotion. I hate gender discrimination."

"At least it was a woman this time," I said. "We've got to keep working on your control."

His voice turned bitter. "Half of my soul is a demon," he said. "It can't be controlled. It's impossible."

"I don't buy that," I said.

"Just because you're a wizard doesn't mean you know a damned thing about it," he said. "I can't live a mortal life. I'm not made for it."

"You're doing fine."

"Fine?" he demanded, voice rising. "I can disintegrate a virgin's inhibitions at fifty paces, but I can't last two weeks at a job where I'm wearing a stupid hairnet and a paper hat. In what way is that *fine?*"

He slammed open the small trunk where he kept his clothes, seized a pair of shoes and his leather jacket, put them on with angry precision, and stalked out into the gathering evening without looking back.

And without cleaning up his mess, I thought uncharitably. Then

I shook my head and glanced at Mouse, who had lain down with his chin on his paws, doggy eyes sad.

Thomas was the only family I'd ever known. But that didn't change the truth: Thomas wasn't adjusting well to living life like normal folks. He was damned good at being a vampire. That came naturally. But no matter how hard he tried to be something a little more like normal, he kept running into one problem after another. He never said anything about it, but I could sense the pain and despair growing in him as the weeks went by.

Mouse let out a quiet breath that wasn't quite a whine.

"I know," I told the beast. "I worry about him too."

I took Mouse on a long walk, and got back in as late-October dusk was settling over Chicago. I got my mail out of the box and started for the stairs down to my apartment, when a car pulled in to the boardinghouse's small gravel lot and crunched to a stop a few steps away. A petite blonde in jeans, a blue button-down shirt, and a satin White Sox windbreaker slipped the car into park and left the engine running as she got out.

Karrin Murphy looked like anything but the head of a division of law enforcement in charge of dealing with everything that went bump in the night in the whole greater Chicago area. When trolls started mugging passersby, when vampires left their victims dead or dying in the streets, or when someone with more magical firepower than conscience went berserk, Chicago PD's Special Investigations department was tasked to investigate. Of course, no one seriously believed in trolls or vampires or evil sorcerers, but when something weird happened, SI was in charge of explaining to everyone how it had been only a man in a rubber mask, and that there was nothing to worry about.

SI had a sucky job, but the men and women who worked there weren't stupid. They were perfectly aware that there were things out there in the darkness that were beyond the scope of conventional understanding. Murphy, in particular, was determined to give the cops every edge they could get when dealing with a preternatural threat, and I was one of her best weapons. She would hire me on as a consultant when SI went up against something really dangerous or alien, and the fees I got working with SI paid the lion's share of my expenses.

When Mouse saw Murphy, he made a little huffing sound of greeting and trotted over to her, his tail wagging. If I had leaned back and kept my legs straight I could have gone skiing over the gravel, but other than that, the big dog left me with no option but to come along.

Murphy knelt down at once to dig her hands into the fur behind Mouse's floppy ears, scratching vigorously. "Hey, there, boy," she said, smiling. "How are you?"

Mouse slobbered several doggy kisses onto her hands.

Murphy said, "Yuck," but she was laughing while she did. She pushed Mouse's muzzle gently away, rising. "Evening, Harry. Glad I caught you."

"I was just getting back from my evening drag," I said. "You want to come in?"

Murphy had a cute face and very blue eyes. Her golden hair was pulled back into a ponytail, and it made her look a lot younger than usual. Her expression was a careful, maybe even uncomfortable one. "I'm sorry, but I can't," she said. "I've got a plane to catch. I don't really have time."

"Ah," I said. "What's up?"

"I'm going out of town for a few days," she said. "I should be back sometime Monday afternoon. I was hoping I could talk you into watering my plants for me."

"Oh," I said. She wanted me to water her plants. How coy. How sexy. "Yeah, sure. I can do that."

"Thanks," she said, and offered me a key on a single steel ring. "It's the back-door key."

I accepted it. "Where you headed?"

The discomfort in her expression deepened. "Oh, out of town on a little vacation."

I blinked.

"I haven't had a vacation in years," she said defensively. "I've got it coming."

"Well. Sure," I said. "Um. So, a vacation. By yourself?"

She shrugged a shoulder. "Well. That's sort of the other thing I wanted to talk to you about. I'm not expecting any trouble, but I wanted you to know where I was and with who in case I don't show up on time."

"Right, right," I said. "Doesn't hurt to be careful."

She nodded. "I'm going to Hawaii with Kincaid."

I blinked some more.

"Um," I said. "You mean on a job, right?"

She shifted her weight from one hip to the other. "No. We've gone out a few times. It's nothing serious."

"Murphy," I protested. "Are you insane? That guy is major bad news."

She glowered at me. "We've had this discussion before. I'm a grown-up, Dresden."

"I know," I said. "But this guy is a mercenary. A killer. He's not even completely human. You can't trust him."

"You did," she pointed out. "Last year against Mavra and her scourge."

I scowled. "That was different."

"Oh?" she asked.

"Yeah. I was paying him to kill things. I wasn't taking him to b—uh, to the beach."

Murphy arched an eyebrow at me.

"You won't be safe around him," I said.

"I'm not doing it to be *safe,*" she replied. Her cheeks colored a little. "That's sort of the point."

"You shouldn't go," I said.

She looked up at me for a moment, frowning.

Then she asked, "Why?"

"Because I don't want to see you get hurt," I said. "And because you deserve someone better than he is."

She studied my face for a moment more and then exhaled through her nose. "I'm not running off to Vegas to get married, Dresden. I work all the time, and life is going right by me. I just want to take the time to live it a little before it's too late." She pulled a folded index card out of her pocket. "This is the hotel I'll be at. If you need to get in touch or anything."

I took the folded index card, still frowning, and full of the intuition that I had missed something. Her fingers brushed mine, but I couldn't feel it through the glove and all the scars. "You sure you'll be all right?"

She nodded. "I'm a big girl, Harry. I'm the one choosing where

we're going. He doesn't know where. I figured he couldn't set anything up ahead of time, if he had any funny business in mind." She
made a vague gesture toward the gun she carried in a shoulder holster under her jacket. "I'll be careful. I promise."

"Yeah," I said. I didn't even try to smile at her. "For the record,
this is stupid, Murph. I hope you don't get killed."

Her blue eyes flashed, and she frowned. "I was sort of hoping
you'd say something like, 'Have a good time.'"

"Yeah," I said. "Whatever. Have fun. Leave me a message when
you get there?"

"Yes," she said. "Thanks for looking out for my plants."

"No problem," I said.

She nodded at me, and lingered there for a second more. Then
she scratched Mouse behind the ears again, got in her car, and
drove off.

I watched her go, feeling worried.

And jealous.

Really, really jealous.

Holy crap.

Was Thomas right after all?

Mouse made a whining sound and pawed at my leg. I sighed,
stuck the hotel information in a pocket, and led the dog back to the
apartment.

When I opened my door, my nose was assaulted with the scent
of fresh pine—not pine cleaner, mind you. Real fresh pine, and
nary a needle in sight. The faeries had come and gone, and the
books were back on the shelves, the floor scrubbed, curtains re-
paired, dishes done, you name it. They may have weird bylaws, but
faerie housecleaning runs a tight ship.

I lit candles with matches from a box I had sitting on my coffee
table. As a wizard, I don't get on so well with newfangled things
like electricity and computers, so I didn't bother to try to keep electric service up and running in my home. My icebox is a vintage
model run on actual ice. There's no water heater, and I do all my
cooking on a little wood-burning stove. I fired it up and heated
some soup, which was about the only thing left in the house. I sat
down to eat it and started going through my mail.

The usual. The marketing savants at Best Buy continued in their unabated efforts to sell me the latest laptop, cell phone, or plasma television despite my repeated verbal and written assurances that I didn't have electricity and that they shouldn't bother. My auto-insurance bill had arrived early. Two checks came, the first a token fee from Chicago PD for consulting with Murphy on a smuggling case for an hour the previous month. The second was a much meatier check from a coin collector who had lost a case of cash from dead nations over the side of his yacht in Lake Michigan and resorted to trying out the only wizard in the phone book to locate them.

The last envelope was a big yellow manila number, and I felt a nauseating little ripple flutter through my guts the second I saw the handwriting on it. It was written in soulless letters as neat as a kindergarten classroom poster and as uninflected as an English professor's lecture notes.

My name.

My address.

Nothing else.

There was no rational reason for it, but that handwriting scared me. I wasn't sure what had triggered my instincts, unless it was the singular lack of anything remarkable or imperfect about it. For a second I thought I had gotten upset for no reason, that it was a simple printed font, but there was a flourish on the last letter of "Dresden" that didn't match the other Ns. The flourish looked perfect, too, and deliberate. It was there to let me know that this was inhuman handwriting, not some laser printer from Wal-Mart.

I laid the envelope flat on my coffee table and stared at it. It was thin, undeformed by its contents, which meant that it was holding a few sheets of paper at the most. That meant that it wasn't a bomb. Well, more accurately, it wasn't a high-tech bomb, which was a fairly useless weapon to use against a wizard. A low-tech explosive setup could have worked just fine, but they wouldn't be that small.

Of course, that left mystical means of attack. I lifted my left hand toward the envelope, reaching out with my wizard's senses, but I couldn't get them focused. With a grimace I peeled the leather driving glove off of my left hand, revealing my scarred and ruined fingers. I'd burned my hand so badly a year before that the doctors I'd seen had mostly recommended amputation. I hadn't let them take my hand, mostly for the same reason I still drove the same junky old VW Beetle—because it was mine, by thunder.

But my fingers were pretty horrible to look at, as was the rest of my left hand. I didn't have much movement in them anymore, but I spread them as best I could and reached out to feel the energies of magic moving around the envelope once more.

I might as well have kept the glove on. There was nothing odd about the envelope. No magical booby traps.

Right, then. No more delays. I picked up the envelope in my weak left hand and tore it open, then upended the contents onto the coffee table.

There were three things in the envelope.

The first was an eight-by-ten color photo, and it was a shot of Karrin Murphy, director of Chicago PD's Special Investigations division. She wasn't in uniform, though, or even in business attire. Instead she was wearing a Red Cross jacket and baseball hat, and she was holding a sawed-off shotgun, an illegal model, in her hands. It was belching flame. In the picture you could also see a man standing a few feet away, covered in blood from the waist down. A long, black steel shaft protruded from his chest, as if he'd been impaled on it. His upper body and head were a blur of dark lines and red blobs. The shotgun was pointing right at the blur.

The second was another picture. This one was of Murphy with her hat off, standing over the man's corpse, and I was in the frame with her, my face in profile. The man had been a Renfield, a psychotically violent creature that was human only in the most technical sense—but then the camera shot of his murder was a most technical witness.

Murphy and I and a mercenary named Kincaid had gone after a nest of vampires of the Black Court led by a deadly vampire named Mavra. Her minions had objected pretty strenuously. I'd gotten my hand badly burned when Mavra herself took the field against us, and I had been lucky to get away that lightly. In the end, we'd rescued hostages, dismembered some vampires, and killed Mavra. Or at least, we'd killed someone we were meant to think was Mavra. In retrospect, it seemed odd that a vampire known for being able to render herself all but undetectable had lurched out at us from the smoke and ash of her ruined stronghold to be be-headed. But I'd had a full day and I had been ready to take it on faith.

We tried to be as careful as we could during the attack. As a re-sult, we saved some lives we might not have if we'd gone in hell-for-leather, but that Renfield had come damn close to taking my head off. Murphy killed him for it. And she'd been photographed doing it.

I stared at the photos.

The pictures were from different angles. That meant that some-one else had been in the room taking them.

Someone we hadn't even seen.

The third item that fell to the coffee table was a piece of type-writer paper, covered in the same handwriting as the address on the envelope. It read:

> *Dresden,*
>
> *I desire a meeting with you, and offer a truce for the duration, bound by my word of honor to be upheld. Meet with me at seven p.m. tonight at your grave in Graceland Cemetery, in order to help me avoid taking actions that would be unfortunate to you and your ally in the police.*
>
> *Mavra*

The final third of the letter had a lock of golden hair taped to it. I held the picture up next to the letter.

The hair was Murphy's.

Mavra had her number. With pictures of her committing a felony (and with me aiding and abetting, no less), Mavra could have her out of the cops and behind bars in hours. But even worse was the lock of hair. Mavra was a skilled sorceress, and might have been as strong as a full-fledged wizard. With a lock of Murphy's hair, she could do virtually anything she pleased to Murph, and there wouldn't be squat anyone could do about it. Mavra could kill her. Mavra could *worse* than kill her.

It didn't take me long to make up my mind. In supernatural

circles, a pledge of truce based upon a word of honor was an institution—especially among the old-world types like Mavra. If she was offering a truce so that we could talk, she meant it. She wanted to deal.

I stared down at the pictures.

She wanted to deal, and she was going to be negotiating from a position of strength. It meant blackmail.

And if I didn't play along, Murphy was as good as dead.

Chapter

Two

The dog and I went to my grave.

Graceland Cemetery is famous. You can look it up in just about any Chicago tour book—or God knows, probably on the Internet. It's the largest cemetery in town, and one of the oldest. There are walls, substantial ones, all the way around, and it has far more than its share of ghost stories and attendant shades. The graves inside range from simple plots with simple headstones to life-sized replicas of Greek temples, Egyptian obelisks, mammoth statues—even a pyramid. It's the Las Vegas of boneyards, and my grave is in it.

The cemetery isn't open after dark. Most aren't, and there's a reason for it. Everybody knows the reason, and nobody talks about it. It isn't because there are dead people in there. It's because there are not-quite-dead people in there. Ghosts and shadows linger in graveyards more than anywhere else, especially in the older cities of the country, where the oldest, biggest cemeteries are right there in the middle of town. That's why people build walls around graveyards, even if they're only two feet high—not to keep people out, but to keep other things in. Walls can have a kind of power in the spirit world, and the walls around graveyards are almost always filled with the unspoken intent of keeping the living and the unliving seated at different sections of the community dinner table.

The gates were locked, and there was an attendant in a small building too solid to be called a shack, and too small to be called anything else. But I'd been there a few times, and I knew several ways to get in and out after dark if need be. There was a portion of the fence in the northeast corner where a road construction crew just outside had left a large mound of gravel, and it sloped far enough up the wall that even a man with one good hand and a large and ungainly dog could reach the top.

We went in, Mouse and I. Mouse might have been large, but he was barely more than a puppy, and he still had paws that looked too big for his lean frame. The dog had been built on the scale of those statues outside Chinese restaurants, though—broad chested and powerful, with that same mountainous strength built into his muzzle. His coat was a dark and almost uniform grey, marked on the tips of his fuzzy ears, his tail, and his lower legs with solid black. He looked a little gangly and clumsy now, but after a few more months of adding on muscle, he was going to be a real monster. And damned if I minded the company of my own personal monster going to meet a vampire over my grave.

I found it not far from a rather famous grave of a little girl named Inez, who had died a century before. The little girl's grave had a statue mounted on it. I'd seen it often, and it looked mostly like Carroll's original Alice—a cherub in a prim and proper Victorian dress. Supposedly the child's ghost would occasionally animate the statue and run and play among the graves and the neighborhoods near the graveyard. I'd never seen her, myself.

But, hey. The statue was missing.

My grave is one of the more humble ones there. It's standing open, too—the vampire noble who bought it for me had set it up to be that way. She'd gotten me a coffin on permanent standby, too, sort of like the president gets Air Force One, only a little more morbid. Dead Force One.

My headstone is simple white marble, a vertical stone, but it's engraved in bold letters inlaid with gold: HARRY DRESDEN. Then a gold-inlaid pentacle, a five-pointed star surrounded by a circle— the symbol of the forces of magic contained within mortal will. Underneath it are more letters: HE DIED DOING THE RIGHT THING.

It's a sobering sort of place to visit.

I mean, we're all going to die. We know that on an intellectual level. We figure it out sometime when we're still fairly young, and it scares us so badly that we convince ourselves we're immortal for more than a decade afterward.

Death isn't something anyone likes to think about, but the fact is that you can't get out of it. No matter what you do, how much you exercise, how religiously you diet, or meditate, or pray, or how much money you donate to your church, there is a single hard, cold fact that faces everyone on earth: One day it's going to be over. One day the sun will rise, the world will turn, people will go about their daily routines—only you won't be in it. You'll be still. And cold.

And despite every religious faith, the testimony of near-death eyewitnesses, and the imaginations of storytellers throughout history, death remains the ultimate mystery. No one truly, definitively knows what happens after. And that's assuming there *is* an after. We all go there blind to whatever is out there in the darkness beyond.

Death.

You can't escape it.

You.

Will.

Die.

That's a bitter, hideously concrete fact to endure—but believe me, you get it in a whole new range of color and texture when you face it standing over your own open grave.

I stood there among silent headstones and memorials both sober and outrageous, and the late-October moon shone down on me. It was too cold for crickets, but the sound of traffic, sirens, car alarms, overhead jets, and distant loud music, the pulse of Chicago, kept me company. Mist had risen off of Lake Michigan like it did a lot of nights, but tonight it had come on exceptionally thick, and tendrils of it drifted through the graves and around the stones. There was a silent, crackling tension in the air, a kind of muted energy that was common in late autumn. Halloween was almost here, and the borders between Chicago and the spirit world, the Nevernever, were at their weakest. I could sense the restless shades of the graveyard, most of them too feeble ever to manifest to mortal eyes, stirring in the roiling mist, tasting the energy-laden air.

Mouse sat beside me, ears forward and alert, his gaze shifting regularly, eyes focused, his attention obvious enough to make me think that he could literally see the things I could only vaguely feel. But whatever was out there, it didn't bother him. He sat beside me in silence, content to leave his head under my gloved hand.

I wore my long leather duster, its mantle falling almost to my elbows, along with black fatigue pants, a sweater, and old combat boots. I carried my wizard's staff with me in my right hand, a length of solid oak hand-carved with flowing runes and sigils all up and down its length. My mother's silver pentacle hung by a chain around my neck. My scarred flesh could barely feel the silver bracelet hung with tiny shields on my left wrist, but it was there. Several cloves of garlic tied together in a big lump lay in my duster's pocket, and brushed against my leg when I shifted my weight. The group of odd items would have looked innocuous enough to the casual eye, but they amounted to a magical arsenal that had seen me through plenty of trouble.

Mavra had given me her word of honor, but I had plenty of other enemies who would love to take a shot at me. I wasn't going to make myself an easy target. But standing around in the haunted graveyard in the dark started to make me nervous, fast.

"Come on," I muttered after a few minutes. "What's taking her so long?"

Mouse let out a growl so low and quiet that I barely heard it—but I could feel the dog's sudden tension and wariness quivering up through my maimed hand, shaking my arm to the elbow.

I gripped my staff, checking all around me. Mouse was doing much the same, until his dark eyes started tracking something I couldn't see. Whatever it was, judging from Mouse's gaze, it was getting closer. Then there was a quiet, rushing sound and Mouse crouched, nose pointed at my open grave, his teeth bared.

I stepped closer to my grave. Patches of mist flowed down into it from the green grounds. I muttered under my breath, took off my amulet, and pushed some of my will into the five-pointed star, causing it to glow with a low blue light. I draped the amulet over the fingers of my left hand while I gripped the staff in my right, and peered down into the grave.

The mist inside it suddenly gathered, congealed, and flowed into the form of a withered corpse—that of a woman, emaciated and dried as though from years in the earth. The corpse wore a gown and kirtle, medieval style, the former green and the latter black. The fabric was simple cotton—modern manufacture, then, and not actual historic dress.

Mouse's snarl bubbled up into a more audible rumbling snarl.

The corpse sat up, opened milk-white eyes, and focused on me. It lifted a hand, in which it held a white lily, and held it toward me. Then the corpse spoke in a voice that was all rasp and whisper. "Wizard Dresden. A flower for your grave."

"Mavra," I said. "You're late."

"There was a headwind," the vampire answered. She flicked her wrist, and the lily arched up out of the grave and landed on my headstone. She followed it out with a similar, uncannily smooth motion that reminded me of a spider in its eerie grace. I noted that she wore a sword and a dagger on a weapons belt at her waist. They looked old and worn, and I was betting that they were not of modern make. She came to a halt and faced me from across my grave, her face turned very slightly away from the blue light of my amulet, her cataract eyes steady on Mouse. "You kept your hand? After those burns, I would have thought you would have amputated it."

"It's mine," I said. "And it's none of your business. And you're wasting my time."

The vampire's corpse lips stretched into a smile. Flakes of dead flesh fell down from the corners of her mouth. Brittle hair like dried straw had mostly been broken off to the length of a finger, but here and there longer strands the color of bread mold brushed the shoulders of her dress. "You're allowing your mortality to make you impatient, Dresden. Surely you want to take this opportunity to discuss your assault on my scourge?"

"No." I slipped my amulet on again and rested my hand on Mouse's head. "I'm not here to socialize. You've got dirt on Murphy and you want something from me. Let's have it."

Her laugh was full of cobwebs and sandpaper. "I forget how young you are until I see you," she said. "Life is fleeting, Dresden. If you insist on keeping yours, you ought to enjoy it."

"Funny thing is, trading insults with an egotistical superzombie just isn't my idea of a good time," I said. Mouse punctuated the sentence with another rumbling growl. I turned my shoulders from her, starting to turn away. "If that's all you had in mind, I'm leaving."

She laughed harder, and the sound of it spooked the hell out of me. Maybe it was the atmosphere, but something about it, the way that it simply *lacked* anything to do with the things that should motivate laughter . . . There was no warmth in it, no humanity, no kindness, no joy. It was like Mavra herself—it had the withered human shell, but underneath it all was something from a nightmare.

"Very well," Mavra said. "We shall embrace brevity."

I faced her again, wary. Something in her manner had changed, and it was setting off all my alarm bells.

"Find The Word of Kemmler," she said. Then she turned, dark skirts flaring, one hand resting negligently upon her sword, and started to leave.

"Hey!" I choked. "That's it?"

"That's it," she said without turning.

"Wait a minute!" I said.

She paused.

"What the hell is The Word of Kemmler?"

"A trail."

"Leading to what?" I asked.

"Power."

"And you want it."

"Yes."

"And you want me to find it."

"Yes. Alone. Tell no one of our agreement or what you are doing."

I took in a slow breath. "What happens if I tell you to go to hell?"

Mavra silently lifted a single arm. There was a photo between two of her desiccated fingers, and even in the moonlight I could see that it was of Murphy.

"I'll stop you," I said. "And if I don't, I'll come after you. If you hurt her, I'll kill you so hard your last ten victims will make miraculous recoveries."

"I won't have to touch her," she said. "I'll send the evidence to the police. The mortal authorities will prosecute her."

"You can't do that," I said. "Wizards and vampires may be at war, but we leave the mortals out of it. Once you get mortal authorities involved, the Council will do it as well. And then the Reds. You could escalate matters into global chaos."

"If I intended to employ the mortal authorities against you, perhaps," Mavra said. "You are White Council."

My stomach twisted with sudden, sickened understanding. I

was a member of the White Council of Wizards, a solid citizen of the supernatural realms.

But Murphy wasn't.

"The protector of the people," Mavra all but purred. "The defender of the law will find herself a convicted murderer, and her only explanation would make her sound like a madwoman. She is prepared to die in battle, wizard. But I won't merely kill her. I will unmake her. I will destroy the labor of her life and her heart."

"You bitch," I said.

"Of course." She looked at me over her shoulder. "And unless you are prepared to unmake mortal civilization—or at least enough of it to impose your will upon it—there is nothing you can do to stop me."

Fury exploded somewhere in my chest and rolled out through my body and thoughts in a red fire. Mouse rolled forward toward Mavra a step, shaking the mist around us with a rising growl, and I didn't realize at first that he was following my lead. "Like hell there isn't," I snarled. "If I hadn't agreed to a truce I would—"

Mavra's corpse-yellow teeth appeared in a ghastly smile. "Kill me in my tracks, wizard, but it will do you no good. Unless I put a halt to it, the pictures and other evidence will be sent to the police. And I will do so only once I am satisfied with your retrieval of The Word of Kemmler. Find it. Bring it to me before three midnights hence, and I will turn over the evidence to you. You have my word."

She dropped the photo of Murphy, and some kind of purple, nauseating light played over it for a second as it fell to the ground. There was the acrid smell of scorched chemicals.

When I looked back up at Mavra there was no one there.

I walked slowly over to the fallen photo, struggling to slap my anger aside quick enough to reach out with my supernatural senses. I didn't feel any of Mavra's presence anywhere near me, and over the next several seconds my dog's growls died down to low, wary sounds of uncertainty—and then to silence. While I wasn't quite certain of the all the details, Mouse wasn't your average dog, and if Mouse didn't sense lurking bad guys, it was because there weren't any bad guys lurking.

The vampire was gone.

I picked up the photo. Murphy's picture had been marred. The dark energy had left scorch marks in the shape of numbers over Murphy's face. A phone number. Cute.

My righteous fury kept on fading, and I missed it. Once it was gone, there was going to be only sick worry and fear left in its place.

If I didn't work for one of the worst of the bad guys I've ever dealt with, Murphy would get hung out to dry.

Said bad guy was after power—and was on a deadline to boot. If Mavra needed something that soon, it meant that some kind of power struggle was about to go down. And three midnights hence meant Halloween night. Aside from ruining my birthday, it meant that black magic was going to be brought into play sometime soon, and at this time of year that could mean only one thing.

Necromancy.

I stood there in the boneyard, staring down at my grave, and started shivering. Partly from the cold.

I felt very alone.

Mouse exhaled a breath that was not quite a whimper of distress, and leaned against me.

"Come on, boy," I told him. "Let's get you home. No sense in more than one of us getting involved with this."

Chapter

Three

I needed some answers.

Time to hit the lab.

Mouse and I returned to my apartment in the Blue Beetle, the beat-up old Volkswagen Bug that is my faithful steed. "Blue" is kind of a metaphorical description. The car has had various doors and panels replaced with white, yellow, red, and green. My mechanic, Mike, had managed to pound the hood more or less back into its original condition, which I'd bent out of shape while ramming a bad guy, but I hadn't had the money to repaint, so now the car had primer grey added to its ensemble.

Mouse had been growing too quickly to be very graceful about getting out of the car. He filled up most of the backseat, and when climbing from there to the front and then out the driver's-side door he reminded me of some footage I've seen of an elephant seal flopping through a New Zealand parking lot. He emerged happily enough, though, panting and waving his tail contentedly. Mouse liked going places in the car. That the place had happened to be a clandestine meeting in a freaking graveyard didn't seem to spoil anything for him. It was all about the journey, not the destination. A very Zen soul, was Mouse.

Mister hadn't come back yet, and neither had Thomas. I tried not to think too hard about that. Mister had been on his own when I found him, and he frequently went rambling. He could take care of himself. Thomas had managed to survive for all but the last several months of his life without me. He could take care of himself too.

I didn't have to worry about either of them, right?

Yeah, right.

I disarmed my wards, the spells that protected my home from various supernatural intrusions, and slipped inside with Mouse. I built up the fire a bit, and the dog settled down in front of it with a pleased sigh. Then I ditched my coat, grabbed my thick old flannel robe and a Coke, and headed downstairs.

I live in a basement apartment, but a trapdoor underneath one of my rugs opens up on a folding wooden stair ladder that leads down to the subbasement and my lab. It's cold down there, year-round, which is why I wear the heavy robe. It's one more drop of romance sucked out of the wizarding mystique, but I stay comfortable.

"Bob," I said as I climbed down into the pitch-dark lab. "Warm up the memory banks. I've got work to do."

The first lights in the room to flicker on were the size and golden-orange color of candle flames. They shone out from the eye sockets of a skull, slowly growing brighter, until I could see the entire shelf the skull rested upon—a simple wooden board on the wall, covered in candles, romance novels, a number of small items, and the pale human skull.

"About time," the skull mumbled. "It's been weeks since you needed me."

"'Tis the season," I said. "Most of the Halloween jobs start looking the same after a few years. No need to consult you when I already know the answers I need."

"If you were so smart," Bob muttered, "you wouldn't need me now."

"That's right," I told him. I pulled a box of kitchen matches out of my robe's pockets and began lighting candles. I started with a bunch of them on a metal table running down the center of the small room. "You're a spirit of knowledge, whereas I am only human."

"Right," said Bob, drawing out the word. "Are you feeling all right, Harry?"

I continued on, lighting candles on the white wire shelves and workbenches on the three walls in a C shape around the long steel table. My shelves were still crowded with plastic dishes, lids, coffee cans, bags, boxes, tins, vials, flasks, and every other kind of small container you can imagine, filled with all kinds of substances as mundane as lint and as exotic as octopus ink. I had several hundred pounds' worth of books and notebooks on the shelves, some arranged neatly and some stacked hastily where they'd been when last I left them. I hadn't been down to the lab for a while, and I don't allow the faeries access, so there was a little bit of dust over everything.

"Why do you ask?" I said.

"Well," Bob said, his tone careful, "you're complimenting me, which is never good. Plus lighting all of your candles with matches."

"So?" I said.

"So you can light all the candles with that stupid little spell you made up," Bob said. "And you keep dropping the box because of your burned hand. So it's taken you seven matches now to keep lighting those candles."

I fumbled and dropped the matchbox again from my stiff, gloved fingers.

"Eight," he said.

I suppressed a growl, struck a fresh match, and did it too forcefully, snapping it.

"Nine," Bob said.

"Shut up," I told him.

"You got it, boss. I'm the best at shutting up." I lit the last few candles, and Bob said, "So did you come down here to get my help when you start working on your new blasting rod?"

"No," I said. "Bob, I've only got the one hand. I can't carve it with one hand."

"You could use a vise grip," the skull suggested.

"I'm not ready," I said. My maimed fingers burned and throbbed. "I'm just . . . not."

"You'd better get ready," Bob said. "It's only a matter of time before some nasty shows up and—"

I shot the skull a hard look.

"All right, all right," Bob said. If he had hands, the skull would have raised them in a gesture of surrender. "So you're telling me you still won't use any fire magic."

"Stars and stones." I sighed. "So I'm using matches instead of my candle spell and I'm too busy to get the new blasting rod done. It's not a big deal. There's just not much call for blowing anything up or burning it to cinders on my average day."

"Harry?" Bob asked. "Are your feet wet? And can you see the pyramids?"

I blinked. "What?"

"Earth to Dresden," Bob said. "You are standing knee-deep in de Nile."

I threw the matchbook at the skull. It bounced off halfheartedly, and the few matches left in tumbled out at random. "Keep your inner psychoanalyst to your damned self," I growled. "We've got work to do."

"Yeah," Bob said. "You're right, Harry. What do I know about anything?"

I glowered at Bob, and pulled up my stool to the worktable. I got out a notebook and a pencil. "The question of the hour is, what do you know about something called The Word of Kemmler?"

Bob made a sucking sound through his teeth, which is fairly impressive given that he's got no saliva to work with. Or maybe I'm giving him too much credit. I mean, he can make a B sound with no lips, too. "Can you give me a reference point or anything?"

"Not for certain," I said. "But I have a gut instinct that says it has something to do with necromancy."

Bob made a whistling sound. "I hope not."

"Why?" I asked.

"Because *that* Kemmler was a certifiable nightmare," Bob said. "I mean, wow. He was sick, Harry. Evil."

That got my attention. Bob the skull was an air spirit, a being that existed in a world of knowledge without morality. He was fairly fuzzy on the whole good-evil conflict, and as a result he had only vague ideas of where lines got drawn. If *Bob* thought someone was evil, well . . . Kemmler must have really pushed the envelope.

"What'd he do?" I asked. "What made him so evil?"

"He was best known for World War One," Bob said.

"The whole *thing?*" I demanded.

"Mostly, yeah," Bob said. "There were about a hundred and

fifty years of engineering built into it, and he had his fingers into all kinds of pies. He vanished at the end of hostilities and didn't show up again until he started animating mass graves during World War Two. Went on rampages out in Eastern Europe, where things were pretty much a nightmare even without his help. Nobody is sure how many people he killed."

"Stars and stones," I said. "Why would he do something like that?"

"A wild guess? He was freaky insane. Plus evil."

"You say 'was,'" I said. "Past tense?"

"Very," Bob said. "After what the guy did, the White Council hunted him down and wiped his dusty ass out in 1961."

"You mean the Wardens?"

"I mean the White Council," Bob said. "The Merlin, the whole Senior Council, the brute squad out of Archangel, the Wardens, and every wizard and ally the wizards could get their hands on."

I blinked. "For one man?"

"See above, regarding nightmare," Bob said. "Kemmler was a *necromancer,* Harry. Power over the dead. He had truck with demons, too, was buddies with most of the vampire Courts, every nasty in Europe, and some of the uglier faeries, too. Plus he had his own little cadre of baby Kemmlers to help him out. Apprentices. And thugs of every description."

"Damn," I said.

"Doubtless he was," Bob said. "They killed him pretty good. A bunch of times. He'd shown up again after the Wardens had killed him early in the nineteenth century, so they were real careful the second time. And good riddance to the psychotic bastard."

I blinked. "You *knew* him?"

"Didn't I ever tell you?" Bob asked. "He was my owner for about forty years."

I stared. "You worked with this monster?"

"I do what I do," Bob said proudly.

"How did Justin get you, then?"

"Justin DuMorne was a Warden, Harry, back at Kemmler's last stand. He pulled me out of the smoldering ruins of Kemmler's lab. Sort of like when you pulled me out of the smoldering ruins of

Justin's lab when you killed him. Circle of life, like that Elton John song."

I felt more than a little tiny bit cold. I chewed on my lip and laid my pencil down. I had the feeling the rest of this conversation was not going to be something I wanted to create a written record of. "So what is The Word of Kemmler, Bob?"

"Not a clue," Bob said.

I glowered. "What do you mean, not a clue? I thought you were his skull Friday."

"Well, yeah," Bob said. His eyelights flickered suddenly, a nervous little dance. "I don't remember very much of it."

I snorted out a laugh. "Bob. You never forget anything."

"No," Bob said. His voice shrank into something very small. "Unless I want to, Harry."

I frowned and took a deep breath. "You're saying that you chose to forget things about Kemmler."

"Or was compelled to," Bob said. "Um. Harry, can I come out? Just inside the lab? You know, while we talk."

I blinked a couple of times. Bob was full of mischief on the best of days. I didn't let him out except on specific intelligence-gathering missions anymore. And while he often pestered me to let him out on one of his perverted minirampages, he had never asked permission to leave his skull for the duration of a chat. "Sure," I told him. "Stay inside the lab and be back in the skull at the end of this conversation."

"Right," Bob said. A small cloud of glowing motes of light the size of campfire sparks came sailing out of the skull's eyes and darted to the far corner of the lab. "So anyway, when are we going to work on the new blasting rod?"

"Bob," I said. "We're talking about The Word of Kemmler."

The lights shot restlessly over to the other side of the lab, swirling through the steps on my stair ladder in a glowing helix. "*You're* talking about The Word of Kemmler," Bob said. The glowing cloud stretched, motes now spiraling up and down the stairs simultaneously. "*I'm* working on my Vegas act. Lookit, I'm DNA."

"Would you stop goofing around? Can you remember anything at all about Kemmler?"

Bob's voice quavered, the motes becoming a vague cloud again. "I can."

"Then tell me what you know."

"Is that a command?"

I blinked. "Do I have to make it one?"

"You don't want to command me to remember, Harry."

"Why not?" I demanded.

The cloud of lights drifted in vague loops around the lab. "Because knowledge is what I am. Losing my knowledge of what I knew of Kemmler took away a . . . a big piece of my existence. Like if someone had cut off your arm. What's left of what I know of Kemmler is close to the missing pieces."

I thought I started to understand him. "It hurts."

The lights swirled uncertainly. "It also hurts. It's more than that."

"If it hurts," I said, "I'll stop, and you can forget it again when we're done talking."

"But—" Bob said.

"It's a command, Bob. Tell me."

Bob shuddered.

It was a bizarre sight. The cloud of lights shivered for a second, as if in a trembling breath of wind, and then abruptly just *shifted*, flickering to one side as quickly as if I had been looking at it with one eye closed and suddenly switched to the other.

"Kemmler," Bob said. "Right." The lights came to rest on the other end of the table in the shape of a perfect sphere. "What do you want to know, wizard?"

I watched the lights warily, but nothing seemed all that wrong. Other than the fact that Bob was suddenly calm. And geometric. "Tell me what The Word of Kemmler is."

The lights pulsed scarlet. "Knowledge. Truth. Power."

"Uh," I said, "a little more specific?"

"The master wrote down his teachings, wizard, so that those who came after him could learn from him. Could learn about the true power of magic."

"You mean," I said, "so that they could learn about necromancy."

Bob's voice took on the edge of a sneer. "What you call magic is nothing but a mound of parlor tricks, beside the power to master life and death itself."

"That's an opinion, I guess," I said.

"More than that," Bob said. "It is a truth. A truth that reveals itself to those who seek it out."

"What do you mean?" I said slowly.

There was a flash, and a pair of white eyes formed in the glittering cloud of red points of light. They weren't pleasant. "Shall I show you the start of the path?" Bob's voice said. "Death, Dresden, is a part of you. It is woven into the fabric of your being. You are a collection of pieces, each of them dying and in turn being reborn and remade."

The white lights were cold. Not mountain-spring cold, either. Graveyard-mist cold. But I'd never seen anything quite like them before. And there was no sense interrupting Bob when he was finally spilling some information.

Besides. Fascinating light.

"Dead flesh adorns you even now. Nails. Hair. You tend them and caress them like any other mortal. Your women decorate them. Entice with them. Death is not a thing to be feared, boy. She is a lover who waits to take you into her arms. You can feel her, if you know what her touch is like. Cold, slow, sweet."

He was right. A cold, tingling nonfeeling was glittering over my fingernails and my scalp. For a second I thought that it hurt, but then I realized that it was only a shivering sensation where that cold energy brushed close to the blood pulsing beneath my skin. It was where they met that it felt uncomfortable. Without the blood, the cold would be a pure, endless sweetness.

"Take a little of death inside, boy. And it will lead you to more. Open your mouth."

I did. I was staring at the light in any case, and it was amazing enough to merit a bit of gaping. I barely noticed a frozen mote of dark blue light, like the corpse of a tiny star, that appeared from one of the spirit's white eyes and began drifting toward my mouth. The cold sensation grew, and it hit my tongue like a thermonuclear peppermint, freezing hot, searingly bitter and sweet and—

—and *wrong.* I spat it out, recoiling, throwing my arms up in front of my face. I fell to the floor, numbness spreading.

"Too late!" crowed the spirit. It shot into the air, swirling around over me, gloating. "Whatever you have done to my thoughts, the master will not be pleased that you have meddled with his servant."

The cold started spreading, and it wasn't purely physical. There was an empty, heartless void to it, a starless, frozen quality that raked at me—not just my body, but *me*—with a mindless hunger. And I could feel it sending tendrils out through me, slowing my heartbeat, making it impossible to breathe.

"Do you know how long I've been waiting for that?" the spirit purred, drifting back and forth over me. "Sitting there locked behind my own thoughts? Waiting for the chance to fight free? Finally, you thick-witted ogre, I get to leave your stupidity behind."

"Bob," I choked out. "This conversation is over."

The spirit's scarlet lights flared to sudden, incandescent rage and it screamed, a wailing sound that rattled my shelves and felt like it was splitting my head. Then the cloud was ripped backward across the room, sucked into the eyeholes of the skull as though down a hellish drain.

Once the last of the motes went flickering back into the skull, the horrible cold faltered a little, and I curled up, focusing my will and trying to push it away. It took me a while, and that hideous void-presence lingered against my fingernails, even after I could feel my fingers again, but after a little while I was able to sit up.

After that I just curled up my knees against my chest, shocked and scared half out of my mind. I had always known that Bob was an incredibly valuable asset, and that no spirit with as much knowledge as he had could be weak. But I had not been at all prepared for the sheer power he had wielded, or for the malice with which he did it. Bob wasn't supposed to be a sleeping nightmare waiting to wake up. Bob was supposed to be my wisecracking porta-geek.

Good Lord, I couldn't remember the last time I'd confronted a demon with that much raw psychic power. If I'd been a second slower, or—stars and stones—if I hadn't remembered the condition that would banish Bob back to the skull and once again remove the dark memories, I'd be dead now. Or maybe dead and then some.

.

And it would have been my own stupid fault, too.

"Harry?" Bob said.

I flinched and let out a small squeaking sound. Then I got hold of myself and blinked up at the skull. It rested on its shelf, and its orange-gold eye lights were back to their usual color. "Oh. Hey."

Bob's voice was very quiet. "Your lips are blue."

"Yeah."

"What happened?" Bob asked.

"It got kind of cold in here."

"Me."

"Yeah."

"I'm sorry, Harry," Bob said. "I tried to tell you."

"I know," I said. "I had no idea."

"Kemmler was bad, Harry," Bob said. "He . . . he took what I was. And he twisted it. I destroyed most of my memories of my time with him, and I locked away everything I couldn't. Because I didn't want to be like that."

"You won't," I told him quietly. "Now hear this, Bob. I command you never to recover those memories again. Never to let them out again. Never to obey any command to unleash them again. From here on out they sleep with the fishes. Understand me?"

"If I do," Bob said carefully, "I won't be able to do much to help you, Harry. You'll be on your own."

"Let me worry about that," I said. "It's a command, Bob."

The skull let out a slow sigh of relief. "Thank you, Harry."

"Don't mention it," I said. "Literally."

"Right," he said.

"Okay. Let's see," I said. "Can you still remember general information about Kemmler?"

"Nothing you couldn't find in other places. But general knowledge I learned when Justin was with the Wardens, yes."

"All right, then. You—that is, that other you—said that Kemmler had written down his teachings, when I asked him what The Word of Kemmler was. So I figure it's a book."

"Maybe," Bob said. "Council records stated that Kemmler had written three books: *The Blood of Kemmler*, *The Mind of Kemmler*, and *The Heart of Kemmler*."

"He published them?"

"Self-published," Bob said. "He started spreading them around Europe."

"Resulting in what?"

"Way too many penny-ante sorcerers getting their hands on some real necromancy."

I nodded. "What happened?"

"The Wardens put on their own epic production of *Fahrenheit 451*," Bob said. "They spent about twenty years finding and destroying copies. They think they accounted for all of them."

I whistled. "So if *The Word of Kemmler* is a fourth manuscript?"

"That could be bad," Bob said.

"Why?"

"Because some of Kemmler's disciples escaped the White Council's dragnet," Bob said. "They're still running around. If they get a new round of necro-at-home lessons to expand their talents, they could use it to do fairly horrible things."

"They're wizards?"

"Black wizards, yes," Bob said.

"How many?"

"Four or five at the most, but the Wardens' information was very sketchy."

"Doesn't sound like anything the Wardens can't handle," I said.

"Unless what's in the fourth book contains the rest of what Kemmler had to teach them," Bob said. "In which case, we might end up with four or five Kemmlers running around."

"Holy crap," I said. I plunked my tired ass down on my stool and rubbed at my head. "And it's no coincidence that it's almost Halloween."

"The season when the barriers between the mortal realm and the spirit world will be weakest," Bob said.

"Like when that asshole the Nightmare was hunting down my friends," I said. I peered at Bob. "But for him to do that, he had to weaken the barriers even more. He and Bianca had tormented all those ghosts to start making the barriers more unstable. Would it have to be ghosts to stir up the kind of turbulence you'd need for big magic?"

"No," Bob said. "But that's one way. Otherwise you'd have to use some rituals or sacrifices of one kind or another."

"You mean deaths," I said.

"Exactly."

I frowned, nodding. "They'd have to invest some energy early to get things moving for a big necromantic working. Like bouncing on a diving board a couple of times before you jump."

"An accurate, if crude aphorism," Bob said. "You'd have to do a little prework if you wanted to start working Kemmler-level necromancy, even on Halloween." He sighed. "Though that doesn't really help you much."

I got up and headed for the stepladder. "It helps more than you know, man. I'm getting you new romances."

The skull's eye lights brightened. "You are? I mean, of course you are. But why?"

"Because if someone's setting up for big bad juju, they'll have left bodies. If they've done that, then I have a place to start tracking them and finding out what's going on."

"Harry?" Bob called up as I left the lab. "Where are you going?"

I stuck my head back down the trapdoor and said, "The morgue."

Chapter

Four

Chicago has a bitchin' morgue. You can't call it a "morgue" anymore because it's the Forensic Institute now. It isn't run by a "coroner" either, because now it's a medical examiner. It's on West Harrison Street, which is located in a fairly swanky industrial park, mostly specializing in various biotech industries. It's pretty. There are wide green lawns, carefully kept and trimmed, complete with sculpted trees and bushes, a fantastic view of the city's skyline, and quick access to the freeway.

It's upscale, sure. But it's also very quiet. Despite the gorgeous landscaping and a more antiseptic naming scheme, it's where they bring the dead to be poked and prodded.

I parked the Blue Beetle in the visitor's parking lot—of the complex next door. The morgue had more than average security, and I didn't want to advertise my presence. I grabbed my bribe from the backseat and headed for the front door of the Office of the Medical Examiner. I knocked, flashing my little laminated card I got from the police that makes me look like an official policelike person. The door buzzed, and I went in, nodding to a comfortably heavyset security guard reading a magazine behind a nondescript desk to one side of the entry area.

"Phil," I said.

"Evening, Dresden," he said. "Official?"

I held up the wooden box packed with McAnally's microbrew. "Unofficial."

"Hosannah," drawled Phil. "I like unofficial better." He put his feet back up on the desk and opened up his magazine again. I left the beer on the floor next to the desk, where it would be out of sight from the door. "How come I never heard of this bar?"

"Just a little local tavern," I said. I didn't add, *that caters to the supernatural community and doesn't exactly try to attract the attention of locals.*

"I'll have to get you to take me by sometime."

"Sure," I said. "Is he here?"

"Back in the slabs," he said, reaching down for one of the ales. Phil opened the lid with a thumb and took a swig, eyes on his magazine again. "Ahhhhh," he said, his tone philosophical. "You know, if anyone had come through that door, I'd tell him to get his ass going before someone drives up or something."

"Gone," I said, and hurried back into the hallways behind the entry area.

There were several slabs—I mean, examination rooms—in the morgue—that is, in the Forensic Institute. But I knew that the guy I was looking for would be in the smallest, crummiest room, the one farthest away from the entrance.

Waldo Butters, other than having the extreme misfortune of being born to parents with little to no ability to bestow a manly name upon their son, had also been cursed with a sense of honesty, a measure of integrity, and enough moral courage to make him act on them. When he'd examined the corpses of a bunch of things I'd burned mostly to briquettes, he'd pronounced them "humanlike, but definitely nonhuman," in his report.

It was a fair enough description of the remains of a bunch of batlike Red Court vampires, but since everyone knew that there were no such things as "humanlike nonhumans," and the remains were obviously human corpses that had been horribly twisted by intense heat, Butters wound up sitting in a psych ward for ninety days for observation. After that, he had been forced to wage a legal battle just to keep his job. His superiors didn't want him around, and they handed him the worst parts of the job they could come up with, but Butters stuck it out. He mostly worked the overnight shift and weekends.

It had the happy side effect of producing an ME who regarded the establishment with the same sort of cheerful disrespect I myself occasionally indulged in. Which was damned handy when, for example, one needed a bullet removed from one's arm without intruding upon the law enforcement community's busy schedule.

The doctor was in. I heard polka music oompahing cheerfully through the hall as I approached the room. But the music was off, somehow. Butters normally played his polka records and CDs loud, and I had gotten used to hearing the elite performers of the polka universe. Whoever he was playing now sounded admirably energetic, but lumpy and uneven. There were odd jerks and breaks in the music, though the whole of it somehow managed to hang on the rhythm of a single bass drum. On the whole, it made the music happy, lively, and somehow misshapen.

I opened the door and regarded the source of the Quasimodo Polka.

Butters was a little guy, maybe five-foot-three in his shoes, maybe 120 pounds soaking wet. He was dressed in blue hospital scrubs and hiking boots. He had a shock of wiry black hair that gave him a perpetual look of surprise that stopped just short of being a perpetual look of recent electrocution. He was wearing Tom Cruise sunglasses and had transformed himself into Polkastein.

A bass drum was strapped to his back, and a couple of wires ran to his ankles from a pair of beaters mounted on the frame. The drum beat in time to stomps of his feet. A small but genuine tuba hung from his slender shoulders, and there were more strings attached to his elbows, which moved back and forth in time to "oom" and "pah" respectively. He held an accordion in his hands, strapped to the harness on his chest. A clarinet had been clamped to the accordion so that the end was near his mouth, and there was, I swear to God, a cymbal on a frame held to his head.

Butters marched in place, red-faced, sweating, and beaming as he thumped and oompahed and blared accordion music. I just stood there staring, because while I have seen a lot of weird things, I hadn't ever seen that. Butters wrapped up the polka and energetically banged his head against the tuba, producing a deafening clash from the cymbal. The motion brought me into his peripheral vision and he jumped in surprise.

The motion overbalanced him and he fell amidst a clatter of

cymbal, a honk of tuba, a fitful stutter of drum, and then lay on the floor while his accordion wheezed out.

"Butters," I said.

"Harry," he panted from the pile of polka. "Cool pants."

"I can see you're busy."

He missed the sarcasm. "Heck, yeah. Gotta get set. Oktoberfest Battle of the Bands tomorrow night."

"I thought you weren't going to enter after last year."

"Hah," Butters said, sneering defiantly. "I'm not going to let the Jolly Rogers laugh at me like that. I mean, come on. Five guys named Roger. How much polka can be in their souls?"

"I have no freaking clue," I answered truthfully.

Butters flashed me a grin. "I'll get them this year."

I couldn't help it: I started smiling. "Need any help getting out of there?"

"Nah, I got it," he said brightly, and started unstrapping himself. "Surprised to see you. Your checkup isn't until next week. Hand bothering you?"

"Not really," I said. "Wanted to talk to you about—"

"Oh!" he said. He hopped up from the stuff and left it on the floor so that he could scamper toward a desk in the corner. "Before you get started, I found something interesting."

"Butters," I said, "I'd like to chat, man, but I'm in a pretty big hurry."

He paused, crestfallen. "Really?"

"Yeah. It's a case, and I need to find out if you know anything that could help me."

"Oh," he said. "Well, you have cases all the time. *This* is important. I've been doing a lot of research since you started seeing me about your hand, and the conclusions I've been able to extrapolate from—"

"Butters." I sighed. "Look, I'm in a huge hurry. Five words or less, okay?"

He leaned his hands on his desk and regarded me, eyes sparkling. "I know how wizards live forever." He paused for a thoughtful second and then said, "Wait, that's six words. Never mind, then. What did you want to talk about?"

My mouth fell open. I shut it and glared at him. "No one likes a wiseass, Butters."

He grinned. "I told you it was important."

"Wizards don't live forever," I said. "Just a really long time."

Butters shrugged and kept pulling out file folders. He flicked on a backlight for reading X-ray films, and started pulling them from the folders and putting them on the light. "Hey, I'm still not sure I buy into this whole hidden-world-of-magic thing. But from what you've told me, wizards can live five or six times as long as the average human. That's closer to forever than anyone I know. And what I've seen makes me think there must be something to it. Come here."

I did, frowning at the X-rays. "Hey. Aren't these mine?"

"Yep," Butters confirmed. "After I switched to one of the older machines, I got about fifteen percent of them to come out," he said. "And there are three or four from your records that managed to survive whatever it is about you that screws up X-rays."

"Ugh. This is that gunshot wound I got in Michigan," I said, pointing at the first. It showed a number of fracture lines in my hip bone, where a small-caliber bullet had hit me. I had barely avoided a shattered pelvis and probable death. "They got this one after they got the cast off."

"Right," Butters said. "And here, this is one from a couple of years ago." He pointed at a second shot. "See the fracture lines? They're brighter, where the bone re-fused. Leaves that signature."

"Right," I said. "So?"

"So," Butters said. "Look at this one." He flipped up a third X-ray. It was much like the others, but without any of the bright or dark lines. He flicked it with a finger and looked at me, eyes wide.

"What?" I asked.

He blinked, slowly. Then he said, "Harry. This is an X-ray I took two months ago. Notice the lack of anything wrong."

"So?" I asked. "It healed, right?"

He made an exasperated sound. "Harry, you are dense. Bones don't *do* that. You carry marks where they re-fused for the rest of your life. Or rather, I would. *You* don't."

I frowned. "What's that got to do with wizard life span?"

Butters waved his hand impatiently. "Here, here are some more." He slapped up more X-rays. "This is a partial stress fracture to the arm that didn't get shot. You got it in that fall from the train a couple nights after we met," he said. "It was just a crack. You didn't even know you had it, and it was mild enough that it just needed a splint for a few days. It was off before you were ambulatory."

"What's so odd about that?"

"Nothing," Butters said. "But look, here it is again. There's a fuse marker, and in the third one, poof, it's gone. Your arm is back to normal."

"Maybe I just drink too much milk or something," I said.

Butters snorted. "Harry, look. You're a tough guy. You've been injured a lot." He pulled out my medical file and thumped it down with a grunt of effort. Granted, there are phone books smaller than my hospital file. "And I'm willing to bet you've had plenty of boo-boos you never saw a doctor about."

"Sure," I said.

"You're at least as battered as a professional athlete," Butters said. "I mean, like a hockey player or football player. Maybe as much as some race-car drivers."

"They get battered?" I asked.

"When you go around driving half a ton of steel at a third the speed of sound for a living, you get all kinds of injuries," he said seriously. "Even the crashes that aren't spectacular are pretty vicious on the human body at the speeds they're going. Ever been in a low-speed accident?"

"Yeah. Sore for a week."

"Exactly," Butters said. "Multiply that. These guys and other athletes take a huge beating, right? They develop a mental and physical toughness that lets them ignore a lot of pain and overcome the damage, but the damage gets done to their bodies nonetheless. And it's cumulative. That's why you see football players, boxers, a lot of guys like that all beat to hell by the time they're in their thirties. They regain most of the function after an injury, but the damage is still there, and it adds up bit by bit."

"Again I ask, what's that got to do with me?"

"You aren't cumulative," Butters said.

"Eh?"

"Your body doesn't get you functional again and then leave off," Butters said. "It continues repairing damage until it's *gone*." He stared at me. "Do you understand how *incredibly significant* that is?"

"I guess not," I said.

"Harry, that's probably *why* people age to begin with," he said. "Your body is a big collection of cells, right? Most of them get damaged or wear out and die. Your body replaces them. It's a continual process. But the thing is, every time the body makes a replacement, it's a little less perfect than the one that came before it."

"That copy-of-a-copy thing," I said. "I've heard about that, yeah."

"Right," Butters said. "That's how you're able to heal these injuries. It's why you have the potential to live so long. Your copies are perfect. Or at least a hell of a lot closer to it than most folks."

I blinked. "You're saying I can heal any injury?"

"Well," he said, "not like mutant X-factor healing. If someone cuts an artery, you're gonna bleed out. But if you survive it, given enough time your body seems to be able to replace things almost perfectly. It might take you months, even several years, but you can get better when other people wouldn't."

I looked at him, and then at my gloved hand. I tried to talk, but my throat wouldn't work.

"Yeah," the little doctor said quietly. "I think you're going to get your hand back at some point. It didn't mortify or come off. There's still living muscle tissue there. Given enough time, I think you'll be able to replace scar tissue and regrow the nerves."

"That . . ." I said, and choked up. I swallowed. "That would be nice."

"We can help it along, I think," Butters said. "Physical therapy. I was going to talk to you about it next visit. We can go over it then."

"Butters," I said. "Uh. Wow, man. This is . . ."

"Really exciting," he said, eyes gleaming.

"I was going to say amazing," I said quietly. "And then I was going to say thank-you."

He grinned and twitched a shoulder in a shrug. "I calls them like I see them."

I stared down at my hand and tried to twiddle my fingers. They sort of twitched. "Why?" I asked.

"Why what?"

"Why am I able to make good copies?"

He blew out a breath and pushed his hand through his wiry hair, grinning. "I have no freaking clue. Neat, huh?"

I stared down at the X-ray film for a moment more, then put my hand in my duster's pocket. "I hoped you could help me get some information," I said.

"Sure, sure," Butters replied. He went to his polka suit and started taking it apart. "Is something going on?"

"I hope not," I said. "But let's just say I've got a real bad feeling. I need to know if there have been any odd deaths in the area in the past day or two."

Butters frowned. "Odd how?"

"Unusually violent," I said. "Or marks of some kind of murder method consistent with a ritual killing. Hell, I'll even take signs of torture prior to death."

"Doesn't sound like anyone I've met," Butters said. He took off his sunglasses and put on his normal black-rimmed glasses. "Though I'm not done for tonight. Let me check the records and see who's in the hiz-ouse."

"Thank you," I said.

Butters knocked a few flyers off his chair and sat down. He dragged a keyboard out from under a medical magazine and gave me a significant look.

"Oh, right," I said. I backed away from his desk to the far side of the room. Proximity to me tended to make computers malfunction to one degree or another. Murphy still hadn't forgiven me for blowing out her hard drive, even though it had happened only the once.

Butters got on his computer. "No," he said, after a moment's reading and key thumping. "Wait. Here's a guy who got knifed, but it happened way up in the northwest corner of the state."

"No good," I said. "It would have to be local. Within a county or three of Chicago."

"Hmph," Butters said. "You investigative types are always so picky about this kind of thing." He scanned over the screen. "Drive-by shooting victim?"

"Definitely no," I said. "For a ritual killing it would be a lot more intimate."

"Think you're out of luck then, Harry," he said. "There were some high-profile stiffs that came in, and the day crew took them all."

"Hmm."

"Tell me about it. I got stuck with a wino and some poor bastard who got caught under a tractor and had to be tested for drugs and booze earlier tonight, but that's . . ." He paused. "Hello."

"Hello?"

"*That's* odd."

That perked up my ears, metaphorically speaking. "What's odd?"

"My boss, Dr. Brioche, passed over one of his subjects. It got moved to my docket, but I didn't get a memo about it. Not even an e-mail, the bastard."

I frowned. "That happen a lot?"

"Attempts to make it look like I'm neglecting my job so he can fire me?" Butters said. "That one's new, but it's in the spirit of my whole history here."

"Maybe he was just busy today."

"And maybe Liv Tyler is waiting in my bedroom to rub my feet," Butters responded.

"Heh. Who's the stiff?"

"A Mr. Eduardo Anthony Mendoza," Butters read. "He was in a head-on collision with a Buick on the expressway. Only he was a pedestrian." Butters scrunched up his nose. "Looks like it will be a nasty one. No wonder high-and-mighty Brioche didn't want to handle it."

I mused. It wasn't what I was looking for, but there was something about the situation around that corpse that set off my internal alarm bells. "Mind if I ask you to indulge an intuition?"

"Sure. I'm as polka empowered as I'm going to get, anyway. Lemme break out my gear and we'll take a look-see at the late Eddie Mendoza."

"Cool," I said. I leaned against the wall and folded my arms, preparing to settle in for a while.

The door to the examination room slammed open, and Phil the security guard walked in with a businesslike stride.

Except Phil's throat had been slit open from ear to ear, and blood covered his upper body in a sheet of ugly splatters. His face was absolutely white. There was no chance whatsoever that poor Phil was alive.

That didn't stop him from striding into the room, seizing Butters's desk, and throwing it, computer, heavy file cabinet, and all, into the far wall of the room, where it shattered with a thunderous sound of impact. Butters stared at Phil with horror, then let out a somewhat rabbitlike shriek and scurried back from him.

"Don't move!" thundered a deep, resonant voice from the hallway outside. Dead Phil froze in his tracks. A big man in a khaki trench coat and, I swear to God, a dark fedora strode into the room, intent on Butters, and he didn't see me against the wall. I hesitated for a second, still shocked at the suddenness of it all. Three other men in coats, all grey of face and purposeful of motion, flanked him.

"Don't hurt the little coroner, gentlemen," the man said. "We'll need him. For a little while."

Chapter

Five

The man in the fedora took a step toward Butters, drumming a slender book against his thigh with one hand. "Stand aside," he muttered, and dead Phil sidestepped.

Butters had scrambled back into a corner, his eyes the size of glazed doughnuts behind his glasses. "Wow," he babbled. "Great entrance. Love the hat."

The guy in the fedora took a step forward and reached out with his other hand, at which point I decided to act. A raised hand isn't much in the regular world, but from a guy in a long coat with his own flock of zombies it had to be at least as menacing as pointing a gun.

"That will be enough," I said, and I said it loud enough to hurt ears. I stepped away from the wall with my left hand extended. My silver bracelet of heat-warped shields hung on my wrist, and I readied my will, pushing enough power into the bracelet to prepare a shield to leap up immediately. The bracelet was still pretty banged-up from the beating it had taken the last time I'd used it, and I'd only barely gotten it working again. As a result, it channeled the energy pretty sloppily, and blue-white sparks leaped out and fell to the floor in a steady drizzle. "Put your hand down and step away from the coroner."

The man turned to face me, book thumping steadily against his leg. For a second I thought he was another dead man himself, his face was so pale—but spots of color appeared high on his cheeks, faint but there. He had a long face, and though it was pale it was leathery, as if he'd spent years in the blowing desert wind and sand without seeing the sun. He had dark eyes, thick grey sideburns, no beard, and a scar twisted his upper lip into a perpetual sneer.

"Who," said the man, his accent thick and British, "are you?"

"The Great Pumpkin," I responded. "I've risen from the pumpkin patch a bit early because Butters is just that nifty. And you are?"

The man studied me in silence for a long second, eyes focused on my sparking wrist, then on my throat, where my mother's silver pentacle amulet was probably lying outside my shirt. "You may call me Grevane. Walk away, boy."

"Or what?" I said.

Grevane gave me a chilly little smile, thumping his book, and nodded at his unmoving companions. "There's room in my car for one more."

"I've got a job already," I said. "But there's no reason for this to get nasty. You're going to stand right there while Butters and me leave."

"And *I*," he said, his voice annoyed.

"What's that?"

"Butters and *I*, fool. Do you seriously think that a defensive shield barely held together by a clumsy, crude little focus will intimidate me into allowing you to leave?"

"No," I said, and drew my .44 revolver from my duster's pocket. I pointed it at him and thumbed back the trigger. "That's why I brought this."

He lifted his eyebrows. "You intend to murder me *in cruor gelidus?*"

"No, I'll do it right here," I said. "Butters, get up. Come over here to me."

The little guy hauled himself to his feet, shaking, and edged around the empty, staring gaze of the late Phil.

"Good," I said. "This is moving along nicely, Grevane. Keep it up and I won't need to make Forensics pick your teeth out of that wall behind you."

Butters scuttled over to me while Grevane thumped his book on his leg. The necromancer stared at me, barely sparing a glance for Butters. Then a slow and fairly creepy smile spread over his face. "You are not a Warden."

"I flunked the written."

His nostrils flared. "Not one of the Council's guard dogs. You are, in fact, more of my own persuasion."

"I really doubt that," I said.

Grevane had narrow, yellow teeth and a crocodile's smile. "Don't play games. I can smell the true magic on you."

The last person to talk about "true magic" had been necro-Bob. I had to fight off a shiver. "Uh. I guess that's the last time I buy generic deodorant."

"Perhaps we can make an arrangement," Grevane said. "This need not end in bloodshed—particularly not now, so close to the end of the race. Join me against the others. A living lieutenant is far more useful to me than a dead fool."

"Tempting," I told him in the voice I usually reserved for backed-up toilets. Butters got to me, and I bumped him toward the door with my hip. He took the hint instantly, and I sidestepped to the door of the room with him. I kept my eyes and my gun on Grevane, my readied bracelet drizzling heatless sparks to the floor. "But I don't think I like your management technique. Butters, check the hall."

Butters bobbed his head out and looked nervously around. "I don't see anyone."

"Can you lock that door?"

Keys rattled. "Yes," he said.

"Get ready to do it," I said. I stepped out in the hall, slammed the door shut, and snapped, "Lock it. Hurry."

Butters fumbled with a key. He jammed one in the door and turned it. Heavy security bolts slid to with a comfortably weighty snap an instant before something heavy and solid hit the door hard enough for me to feel the floor rattle through my boots. A second later the door jumped again, and a fist-sized dent mushroomed half an inch out of its center.

"Oh, God," Butters babbled. "Oh, God, that was Phil. What is that? What is happening?"

"Right there with you, man," I said. I grabbed him and started walking down the hall as quickly as I could drag the little guy. "Who else has keys to the door?"

"What?" Butters blinked for a second. "Uh. Uh. The other doctors. Day security. And Phil."

The door rattled again, dented again, and then went silent.

"Grevane's figured that out too," I said. "Come on, before he finds the right key. Do you have your car keys with you?"

"Yes, yes, wait, oh, yes, right here," Butters said. His teeth were chattering together so loudly that he could barely speak clearly, and he stumbled every couple of steps. "God. Oh, God, it's *real.*"

In the halls behind us, metal clicked and scraped on metal. Someone was trying keys in a lock. "Butters," I said. I grabbed his shoulders and had to resist the urge to slap him in the face, like in the movies. "Do what I tell you. Stop thinking. Think later. Move now or there won't *be* a later."

He stared at me, and for a second I thought he was going to throw up. Then he swallowed, nodded once, and said, "Okay."

"Good. We run to your car. Come on."

Butters nodded and took off for the front of the building at a dead sprint. He accelerated a lot faster than I did, but I have long legs and I caught up pretty quickly. Butters stopped to hit the buzzer at the guard station, and I held the door open wide enough to let him out first. He turned right and ran for the parking lot, and I was only a couple of feet behind him.

We rounded the corner of the building, and Butters dashed toward a pint-sized pickup truck parked in the nearest space. I followed him, and after the silence of the morgue, the night sounds of the city were a blaring music. Traffic hissed by in an automotive river on the highway. Sirens sounded in the distance, ambulance rather than patrol car. Somewhere within a two-hundred-mile radius, one of those enormous, thumping bass stereos pounded out a steady beat almost too low to hear.

The light in the parking lot was out, making everything dark and hazy, but the scent of gasoline came sharp to my nose, and I seized Butters's collar and pulled. The little guy choked and all but fell down, but stopped.

"Don't," I said, and slipped my fingers under the pygmy truck's hood. It flipped up, already open.

The engine had been torn apart. A snapped drive belt hung out like the tongue of a dead steer. Wires were strewn everywhere, and finger-sized holes had been driven into plastic fluid tanks. Coolant and windshield cleaner still dribbled to the parking lot's concrete, and from the smell of it they were mixing with whatever gasoline had been in the tank.

Butters stared at it with wide eyes, panting. "My truck. They killed my truck."

"Looks like," I said, sweeping my gaze around.

"Why did they kill my truck?"

That heavy bass stereo kept rumbling through the October night. I paused for a second, focusing on the sound. It was changing, getting a little bit higher pitched with each beat. I recognized what that meant, and panic slammed through my head for a second.

Doppler effect. The source of the rumbling bass was coming toward us.

In the darkness of the industrial park's lanes a pair of headlights flashed on, revealing a car accelerating toward the Forensic Institute. The lights were spaced widely apart—an older car, and judging by the sound of the engine some kind of gas-guzzling dinosaur like a Caddy or a big Olds.

"Come on," I snapped to Butters, and started running to the lot next door, back to the Blue Beetle. We'd already been spotted, obviously, so I fired up my shield bracelet again, so that my hand looked like it had been replaced with a small comet. Butters followed, and I had to give the little guy credit—he was a good runner.

"There!" I shouted. "Get to my car!"

"I see it!"

Behind us the rumbling Cadillac swerved into the Institute's parking lot and lurched over a concrete-encased grassy median, sparks flying from its undercarriage. The car roared up onto the grass and skidded to a broadside stop. The door flew open and a man got out.

I got a half-decent glance at him in the backwash of the Caddy's headlights. Medium height at most, long, thinning hair, and pale, loose skin with a lot of liver spots. He moved stiffly, like someone with arthritis, but he hauled a long shotgun out of the car with him and raised it to his shoulder with careful deliberation.

I juked to one side so that I was directly between the driver and Butters, twisted at the hips, extended my arm behind me, and raised my shield. It flickered to life in a ghostly half dome just a second before one barrel of the shotgun bloomed with light and thunder. The shield flashed and sent off a cloud of sparks the size of a small house. I felt it falter through the damaged bracelet on my wrist, but it solidified again in time to catch the second blast from the gun's other barrel. The old man with the shotgun howled in wordless outrage, broke the barrel, and started loading in fresh shells.

Butters was screaming, and I was yelling right along with him. We got to the Beetle and piled in. I stomped the engine to life, and the Beetle sputtered once and then gamely took off at its best clip. I screeched out of the parking lot and onto the road, started to skid, turned into it, fishtailed once, and then shot off down the street.

"Look out!" Butters screamed, pointing.

I snapped a glance over my shoulder and saw Phil and the other three dead men from the examination room sprinting across the grounds at us. I don't mean they were running. It was a full-out sprint, faster than Phil could have done even in the prime of his life. I stomped on the gas and kept my eyes on the road.

The Beetle lurched, and Butters cried out, "Holy crap!"

I looked back again and saw Dead Phil clinging to the back of the car. He had to have been standing on the rear bumper. The other three dead men weren't far behind him, keeping up with the car. Dead Phil drove his hand down at the back of the Beetle, and there was a wrenching sound of impact, then a series of snaps and squeals as he tore the back cover from the car, exposing the engine.

"Take the wheel!" I shouted to Butters. He reached over and seized the steering wheel. I twisted and thrust my right hand at Dead Phil. I focused my attention on the plain silver ring on my middle finger. It was another focus, like the shield bracelet, one designed to store back a little kinetic energy every time I moved my arm. I focused on the ring, clenched my hand into a fist, and shoved it directly at Dead Phil, releasing the energy within.

Dead Phil had raised his arm again, this time to tear apart the Beetle's engine, but I beat him to the punch. The unseen force unleashed from the ring hit him at the top of his thighs, kicking his whole lower body out straight. The force tore his grip loose from the car, and he tumbled away, hitting the street with heavy, crunching sounds of impact, arms and legs splayed. The other dead men ran past him, one leaping clear over, and Dead Phil lay twitching on the ground like a broken toy.

I got back to the wheel and shifted the car into the next gear. In my rearview mirror I saw the leading dead man spring at us again, but he missed the car by a couple of feet, and I left the rest of them behind in the darkness, scooting out of the industrial park and onto public streets.

I drove for a while, taking a lot of unnecessary turns. I didn't think anyone was pursuing us, but I didn't want to take the chance that the old man might have gotten back into his Caddy and onto our tails. Maybe ten minutes went by before I started breathing easier, and I finally felt safe enough to pull over into a well-lit convenience-store parking lot.

I started shaking as soon as I set the parking brake. Adrenaline does that to me. I usually get along just fine when the actual crisis is in progress, but after it's over, my body makes up for the lost terror. I closed my eyes and tried to keep my breathing slow and calm, but it was a fight to do it. There wasn't anything I could do about the trembling.

It had been getting harder and harder to maintain my composure ever since the battle where I nearly lost my hand. The emotions I'd always felt seemed to be hitting me harder and harder lately, and sometimes I had to literally close my eyes and count to ten to keep from losing control. Right then I wanted to scream and howl—partly in joy at being alive, and partly in rage that someone had tried to kill me. I wanted to call up my power and start laying waste with it, to feel the raw energy of creation scorching through my thoughts and body, mastered by raw will. I wanted to cut loose.

But I couldn't do that. Even among the strongest wizards on the planet, I'm no lightweight. I don't have the finesse and class and experience that a lot of the older practitioners do, but when it comes to raw metaphysical muscle, I rank in the top thirty or forty wizards alive. I had a ton of strength, but I didn't always have the fine control to go with it—that's why I had to use specially prepared articles such as my bracelet and my ring to focus that power. Even with them, it wasn't always easy to be precise. The last time I had surrendered my self-control and really cut loose with my power, I burned as many as a dozen people to scorched skeletons.

I had a responsibility to keep that destructive strength in check; to use it to help people, to protect them. It didn't matter that I still felt terrified. It didn't matter that my hand was screaming with pain. It didn't matter that my car had been mutilated yet again, or that someone had tried to kill one of the few people in town I considered a real friend.

I had to hold back. Be careful. Think clearly.

"Harry?" Butters asked after a minute. "Are you okay?"

"Yeah. Just give me a minute."

"I don't understand this," he said. His voice didn't sound any too steady either. "What just happened?"

"You don't want to know," I said.

"Yes, I do."

"Trust me," I said. "You don't want to be involved in this kind of business."

"Why not?"

"You'll get hurt. Or killed. Don't go looking for trouble."

He let out a frustrated neighing sound. "Those people came for me. I didn't go looking for them. *They* were looking for *me.*"

He had a point, but even so, Butters was not someone I would want to see involved in a conflict between people like Grevane and his dead men and his liver-skinned partner. Mortals usually didn't fare too well when it came to tangling with preternatural bad guys. In my day I'd seen dozens of men and women die from it, despite everything I did to help them.

"This is unreal," Butters said. "I know you and Murphy have talked about this black-magic supernatural stuff a lot. And I've seen some things that are tough to explain. But . . . I never imagined something like this could happen."

"You're happier that way," I said. "Hell, if I could do it, I might want to forget I ever found out about any of it."

"I'm happier being scared?" he asked almost timidly. "I'm happier wondering if maybe my bosses were right the whole time, and I really am insane? I'm happier being in danger, and having no idea what to do about it?"

I didn't have a quick answer for that one. I stared at my hands. The trembling had almost stopped.

"Help me understand this, Harry," he said. "Please."

Well, dammit.

I raked the fingers of my right hand through my hair. Grevane had been after Butters, specifically. He had backup waiting outside, and he trashed Butters's truck to make sure the little guy couldn't escape. He openly said that he needed Butters, and needed him in one piece to boot.

All of which meant that Butters was in very real—and very serious—danger. And by now I've learned that I can't always protect everyone. I screw up sometimes, like everyone else. I make stupid mistakes.

If I kept quiet, if I forced Butters to wear blinders, he wouldn't be able to do jack to protect himself. If I made a bad call and something happened to him, it would be my fault that he didn't have every chance to survive. His blood would be on my hands.

I couldn't take that choice away from him. I wasn't his father or his guardian angel or his sovereign king. I wasn't blessed with the wisdom of Solomon, or with the foresight of a prophet. If I chose Butters's path for him, in some ways it would make me no different from Grevane, or any number of other beings, human and nonhuman alike, who sought to control others.

"If I tell you this," I said quietly, "it could be bad for you."

"Bad how?"

"It could force you to keep secrets that people would kill you for knowing. It could change the way you think and feel. It could really screw up your life."

"Screw up my life?" He stared at me for a second and then said, deadpan, "I'm a five-foot-three, thirty-seven-year-old, single, Jewish medical examiner who needs to pick up his lederhosen from the dry cleaners so that he can play in a one-man polka band at Oktoberfest tomorrow." He pushed up his glasses with his forefinger, folded his arms, and said, "Do your worst."

The words were light, but there was both fear and resolve just under the surface of them. Butters was smart enough to be scared. But he was also a fighter. I could respect him for both.

"Okay," I said. "Let's talk."

Chapter

Six

Butters hadn't taken time to collect his coat when he left, and the last time the Beetle's heater had worked was before the demolition of the Berlin Wall. I ducked into the store, got us each a cup of coffee, then untwisted the wire that holds down the lid of the storage trunk. I dug out a worn but mostly clean blanket that I kept in the trunk to cover the short-barreled shotgun I stored in the event that I would ever need to give Napoleon's charging hordes a taste of the grape. Given the way the night was going, I got the shotgun, too, and slipped it into the backseat.

Butters accepted the blanket and the coffee gratefully, though he shivered hard enough to slop a little of the drink over the side of the cup. I sipped a little coffee, slipped the cup into the holder I'd rigged on the car's dashboard, and got moving again. I didn't want to wait around in the same place for too long.

"All right," I told Butters. "There are two things you have to accept if you want to understand what's going on."

"Hit me."

"First the tough one. Magic is real."

I could feel him looking at me for a moment. "What do you mean by that?"

"There's an entire world that exists alongside the everyday life of mankind. There are powers, nations, monsters, wars, feuds, alliances—everything. Wizards are a part of it. So are a lot of other things you've heard about in stories, and even more you've never heard of."

"What kind of things?"

"Vampires. Werewolves. Faeries. Demons. Monsters. It's all real."

"Heh," Butters said. "Heh, heh. You're joking. Right?"

"No joke. Come on, Butters. You know that there are weird things out there. You've seen the evidence of them."

He pushed a shaking hand through his hair. "Well, yes. Some. But, Harry, you're talking about something else entirely here. I mean, if you want to tell me that people have the ability to sense and affect their environment in ways we don't really understand yet, I can accept that. Maybe you call it magic, and someone else calls it ESP, and someone else calls it the Force, but it's not a new idea. Maybe there are people whose genetic makeup makes them better able to employ these abilities. Maybe it even does things like make them reproduce their DNA more clearly than other people so that they can live for a very long time. But that is not the same thing as saying that there's an army of weird monsters living right under our noses and we don't even notice them."

"What about those corpses you analyzed?" I said. "Humanoid but definitely not human."

"Well," Butters said defensively, "it's a big universe. I think it's sort of arrogant to assume that we're the only thinking beings in it."

"Those corpses were the bodies of vampires of the Red Court, and you don't want to meet a living one. There were a lot of them in town at one point. There aren't so many now, but there are plenty more where they came from. They're only one flavor of vampire. And *vampires* are only one flavor of supernatural predator. It's a jungle out there, Butters, and people aren't anywhere near the top of the food chain."

Butters shook his head. "And you're telling me that nobody knows about it?"

"Oh, lots of people know about it," I said. "But the ones who are in the know don't go around talking about it all that much."

"Why not?"

"Because they don't want to get locked up in a loony bin for three months for observation, for starters."

"Oh," Butters said, flushing. "Yeah. I guess I can see that. What about regular people who see things? Like sightings and close encounters and stuff?"

I blew out a breath. "That's the second thing you have to understand. People don't want to accept a reality that frightening. Some of them open their eyes and get involved—like Murphy did. But most of them don't want anything to do with the supernatural. So they leave it behind and don't talk about it. Don't think about it. They don't want it to be real, and they work really hard to convince themselves that it isn't."

"No," Butters said. "I'm sorry. I just don't buy that."

"You don't need to buy it," I said. "It's true. As a race, we're an enormous bunch of idiots. We're more than capable of ignoring facts if the conclusions they lead to make us too uncomfortable. Or afraid."

"Wait a minute. You're saying that a whole world, multiple civilizations of scientific study and advancement and theory and application, all based around the notion of observing the universe and studying its laws is . . . what? In error about dismissing magic as superstition?"

"Not just in error," I said. "Dead wrong. Because the truth is something that people are afraid to face. They're terrified to admit that it's a big universe and we're not."

He sipped coffee and shook his head. "I don't know."

"Come on, Butters," I said. "Look at history. How long did the scholarly institutions of civilization consider Earth to be the center of the universe? And when people came out with facts to prove that it wasn't, there were riots in the streets. No one wanted to believe that we all lived on an unremarkable little speck of rock in a quiet backwater of one unremarkable galaxy. The world was supposed to be flat, too, until people proved that it wasn't by sailing all the way around it. No one believed in germs until years and years after someone actually saw one. Biologists scoffed at tales of wild beast-men living in the mountains of Africa, despite eyewitness testimony to the contrary, and pronounced them an utter fantasy—right up until someone plopped a dead mountain gorilla down on their dissecting table."

He chewed on his lip and watched the streetlights.

"Time after time, history demonstrates that when people don't want to believe something, they have enormous skills of ignoring it altogether."

"You're saying that the entire human race is in denial," he said.

"Most of the time," I replied. "It's not a bad thing. It's just who we are. But the weird stuff doesn't care about that—it keeps on happening. Every family's got a ghost story in it. Most people I've talked to have had something happen to them that was impossible to explain. But that doesn't mean they go around talking about it afterward, because everyone knows that those kinds of things aren't real. If you start saying that they are, you get the weird looks and jackets with extra-long sleeves."

"For everyone," he said, voice still skeptical. "Every time. They just keep quiet and try to forget it."

"Tell you what, Butters. Let's drive down to CPD and you can tell them how you were just attacked by a necromancer and four zombies. How they nearly outran a speeding car and murdered a security guard who then got up and threw your desk across the room." I paused for a moment to let the silence stretch. "What do you think they'd do?"

"I don't know," he said. He bowed his head.

"Unnatural things happen all the time," I said. "But no one talks about it. At least, not openly. The preternatural world is everywhere. It just doesn't advertise."

"You do," Butters said.

"But not many people take me seriously. For the most part even the ones who accept my help just pay the bill, then walk out determined to ignore my existence and get back to their normal life."

"How could someone do that?" Butters asked.

"Because it's terrifying," I said. "Think about it. You find out about monsters that make the creatures in the horror movies look like the Muppets, and that there's not a damned thing you can do to protect yourself from them. You find out about horrible things that happen—things you would be happier not knowing. So rather than live with the fear, you get away from the situation. After a while you can convince yourself that you must have just imagined it. Or maybe exaggerated it in the remembering. You rationalize whatever you can, forget whatever you can't, and get back to your life."

I glanced down at my gloved hand and said, "It's not their fault, man. I don't blame them."

"Maybe," he said. "But I don't see how things that hunt and kill human beings could be there among us without our knowing."

"How big was your graduating class in high school?"

Butters blinked. "What?"

"Just answer me."

"Uh, about eight hundred."

"All right," I said. "Last year in the U.S. alone more than nine hundred thousand people were reported missing and not found."

"Are you serious?"

"Yeah," I said. "You can check with the FBI. That's out of about three hundred million, total population. That breaks down to about one person in three hundred and twenty-five vanishing. Every year. It's been almost twenty years since you graduated? So that would mean that between forty and fifty people in your class are gone. Just gone. No one knows where they are."

Butters shifted uncomfortably in his seat. "So?"

I arched an eyebrow at him. "So they're missing. Where did they go?"

"Well. They're missing. If they're missing, then nobody knows."

"Exactly," I said.

He didn't say anything back.

I let the silence stretch for a minute, just to make the point. Then I started up again. "Maybe it's a coincidence, but it's almost the same loss ratio experienced by herd animals on the African savannah to large predators."

Butters drew his knees up to his chest, huddling farther under the blanket. "Really?"

"Yeah," I said. "Nobody talks about this kind of thing. But all those people are still gone. Maybe a lot of them just cut their ties and left their old lives behind. Maybe some were in accidents of some kind, with the body never found. The point is, people don't *know.* But because it's an extremely scary thing to think about, and because it's a lot easier to just get back to their lives they tend to dismiss it. Ignore it. It's easier."

Butters shook his head. "It just sounds so insane. I mean, they'd believe it if they saw it. If someone went on television and—"

"Did what?" I asked. "Bent spoons? Maybe made the Statue of Liberty disappear? Turned a lady into a white tiger? Hell, I've *done* magic on television, and everyone not screaming that it was a hoax was complaining that the special effects looked cheap."

"You mean that clip that WGN news was showing a few years back? With you and Murphy and the big dog and that insane guy with a club?"

"It wasn't a dog," I said, and shivered a little myself at the memory. "It was a loup-garou. Kind of a superwerewolf. I killed him with a spell and a silver amulet, right on the screen."

"Yeah. Everyone was talking about it for a couple of days, but I heard that they found out it was a fake or something."

"No. Someone disappeared the tape."

"Oh."

I stopped at a light and stared at Butters for a second. "When you saw that tape, did you believe it?"

"No."

"Why not?"

He took a breath. "Well, because the picture quality wasn't very good. I mean, it was really dark—"

"Where most scary supernatural stuff tends to happen," I said.

"And the picture was all jumpy—"

"The woman with the camera was terrified. Also pretty common."

Butters made a frustrated sound. "And there was an awful lot of static on the tape, which made it look like someone had messed with it."

"Sort of like someone messed with almost all of my X-rays?" I shook my head, smiling. "And there's one more reason you didn't believe it, man. It's okay; you can say it."

He sighed. "There's no such things as monsters."

"Bingo," I said, and got the car moving again. "Look, Butters. You are your own ideal example. You've seen things you can't explain away. You've suffered for trying to tell people that you *have* seen them. For God's sake, twenty minutes ago you got attacked by the walking dead. And you're *still* arguing with me about whether or not magic is real."

Seconds ticked by.

"Because I don't want to believe it," he said in a quiet, numb voice.

I exhaled slowly. "Yeah."

Dead silence.

"Drink some coffee," I told him.

He did.

"Scared?"

"Yeah."

"Good," I said. "That's smart."

"Well, then," he murmured. "I m-must be the smartest guy in the whole world."

"I know how you feel," I said. "You run into something you totally don't get, and it's scary as hell. But once you learn something about it, it gets easier to handle. Knowledge counters fear. It always has."

"What do I do?" Butters asked me.

"I'm taking you somewhere you'll be safe. Once I get you there, I'll figure out my next move. For now, ask me questions. I'll answer them."

Butters took a slower sip of his coffee and nodded. His hands looked steadier. "Who was that man?"

"He goes by Grevane, but I doubt that's his real name. He's a necromancer."

"What's a necromancer?"

I rolled a shoulder in a shrug. "Necromancy is the practice of using magic to muck around with dead things. Necromancers can animate and control corpses, manipulate ghosts, access the knowledge stored in dead brains—"

Butters blurted out, "That's impos—" Then he stopped himself and coughed. "Oh. Right. Sorry."

"They can also do a lot of really freaky things involving the soul," I said. "Even in the weird circles, it isn't the kind of thing you talk about casually. But I've heard stories that they can inhabit corpses with their consciousness, possess others. I've even heard that they can bring people back from the dead."

"Jesus," Butters swore.

"I kinda doubt they had anything to do with that one."

"No, no, I meant—"

"I know what you meant. It was a joke, Butters."

"Oh. Right. Sorry." He swigged more coffee, and started looking around at the streets again. "But bringing the dead to life? That doesn't sound so bad."

"You're assuming that what the necromancer brings them back to is better than death. From what I've heard, they don't generally do it for humanitarian reasons. But that might be a load of crap. Like I said, no one talks about it."

"Why not?" Butters asked.

"Because it's forbidden," I told him. "The practice of necromancy violates one of the Laws of Magic laid down by the White Council. Capital punishment is the only sentence, and no one wants to even come close to being suspected by the Council."

"Why? Who are they?"

"They're me," I said. "Sort of. The White Council is a . . . well, most people would call it a governing body for wizards all over the world, but it's really more like a Masonic lodge. Or maybe a frat."

"I've never heard of a fraternity handing out a death sentence."

"Yeah. Well the Council has only seven laws, but if you break them . . ." I drew my thumb across my neck. "By the way, they aren't fond of regular folks knowing about them. So don't talk about them to anyone else."

Butters swallowed and touched the fingers of one hand to his throat. "Oh. So this guy, Grevane. He was like you?"

"He's not like me," I said, and it came out in a snarl that surprised even me. Butters twitched violently. I sighed and made an effort to lower my voice again. "But he's probably a wizard, yeah."

"Who is he? What does he want?"

I blew out a breath. "He's most likely a student of this badass black magic messiah named Kemmler. The Council burned Kemmler down a while back, but several of his disciples may have escaped. I think Grevane is looking for a book his teacher hid before he died."

"A magic book?"

I snorted. "Nah. Trinkets aren't too hard to come by. If my guess is correct, this book contains more of the knowledge and theory Kemmler used in his most powerful magics."

Butters nodded. "So . . . if Grevane gets hold of the book and learns, he gets to be the next Kemmler?"

"Yeah. And he mentioned that there were others involved in this business too. I think word of the presence of Kemmler's book came up, and his surviving students are showing up to grab it before their fellow necromancers do. For that matter, just about anyone involved in black magic might want to get their hands on it."

"So why doesn't the Council just grab them and . . . ?" He drew his thumb across his throat.

"They've tried," I said. "They thought the disciples had all been accounted for."

Butters frowned. Then he said, "I guess wizards can go into denial about uncomfortable things too, huh?"

I barked out a laugh. "People are people, man."

"But now you can tell this Council about Grevane and this book, right?"

My stomach quivered a little. "No."

"Why not?"

Because if I did, Mavra would destroy my friend. The thought screamed across my brain in a blaze of frustration that I tried to keep concealed. "Long story. The short version is that I'm not real popular with the Council, and they're pretty busy right now."

"With what?" he asked.

"A war."

He scrunched up his nose and tilted his head, studying me. "That's not the only reason you aren't calling them, is it?" Butters said.

"Egad, Holmes," I told him. "No, it isn't. Don't push."

"Sorry." He finished the coffee, then made a visible effort to cast around for a new conversational thread. "So. Those were actual zombies?"

"Never seen one before," I said. "But that seems like a pretty good guess."

"Poor Phil," Butters said. "Not a saint or anything, but not a bad guy."

"He have a family?" I asked.

"No," Butters said. "Single. That's a mercy." He was silent for a second, then said, "No. I guess it isn't."

"Yeah."

"If those guys were zombies, how come they didn't want

brains?" Butters said. He held both arms stiff out in front of him, rolled his eyes back in his head, and moaned, "Braaaaaaaaaaaaains."

I snorted. He gave me a weak smile.

"Seriously," Butters said. "These guys were more like the Terminator."

"What's the use of a foot soldier who can't do anything but hobble along and moan about brains?"

"Good point," Butters said. He scrunched up his nose in thought. "Don't I remember something about sewing a zombie's lips shut with thread to kill them? Does that work?"

"No clue," I said. "But you saw those things. If you want to get close enough to find out, be my guest, but I'll be observing it through a freaking telescope."

"No, thank you," Butters said. "But how do we stop them?"

I sighed. "They're tough, but they're still flesh and bone. Massive trauma will do it sooner or later."

"How massive?"

I shrugged. "Run them over with a truck. Chop them to bits with an ax. Burn them to ashes. A gun or a baseball bat won't do it."

"This may come as a shock to you, Harry, but I don't have an ax with me. Is there something else? Maybe something that isn't so Bunyan-esque?"

"Plenty," I said. "If you can cut off the flow of energy into them, they'll drop."

"How do you do that?"

"You'd have to ground them out. Running water is the best way, but there needs to be a lot of it. A small stream, at least. I could also probably trap one in a magic circle and cut off any energy from getting to it. Either way, they'd just fall over, plop."

"Magic circles," Butters shook his head. "And nothing else?"

"Keep in mind that they aren't intelligent," I said. "Zombies follow orders, but they don't have much more intellect than your average animal. You have to outthink them—or the necromancer who is giving them orders. You could also cut off the necromancer's control of them."

"How?"

"Kill their drum."

"Uh, what?"

I shook my head. "Sorry. A zombie . . . well, it isn't really a person with thoughts and feelings and such, but the corpse is *used* to being a person. To eating, breathing—and to a beating heart. That's how the necromancer controls them. He plays a beat or some kind of rhythmic music, and uses magic to substitute his beat for the zombie's heartbeat. He links himself to the beat, the beat to the zombie's heart, and when the necromancer gives a command, as far as the zombie is concerned it's coming from inside him and he wants to do it. That's how they can control them so completely."

"That book," Butters said. "Grevane kept drumming it against his leg. And then outside, that huge bass woofer in that Cadillac."

"Exactly. Make the beat stop or get the zombies out of earshot, and he loses control of them. But that's really dicey."

"Why?"

"Because it won't destroy the zombie. It just frees it from the necromancer's control. Anything could happen. It could just shut down, or it could start killing everyone it sees. Totally unpredictable. If I'd stopped him from drumming in the exam room, they might have killed us all. Or run off in different directions to hurt other people. We couldn't afford to take the chance."

Butters nodded, absorbing this for a minute. Then he piped up with, "Grevane said you weren't a Warden. What is a Warden?"

"Wardens are the White Council's version of cops," I said. "They enforce the Laws of Magic, bring criminals in for a trial, and then they chop off their heads. Sometimes they get enthusiastic and just skip to the chopping."

"Well. That doesn't sound so bad."

"In theory," I said. "But they're so paranoid that next to them, Joe McCarthy looks like a friendly puppy. They don't ask many questions, and they don't hesitate to make up their minds. If they *think* you've broken a law, you might as well have."

"That's not fair," Butters said.

"No. It isn't. I'm not real popular with the Wardens. I'm not sure they'd come out to help me if I asked them."

"What about other wizards on the Council?"

I sighed. "The White Council is already at the limits of its resources. Even if they weren't, the Council really, really likes to not get involved."

He frowned. "Could the cops stop Grevane?"

"No way," I said, "Not a chance in hell are any of them prepared to handle him. And if they tried, a whole lot of good people would die."

Butters sputtered. "They'll just *sit* there and let people like Phil get killed?" he demanded, his voice outraged. "If regular people can't do it, and the Council won't get involved, who the hell is going to stop him?"

"I am," I said.

Chapter

Seven

We went back to my apartment, and I wasted no time getting Butters inside and behind the protection of my wards. Mouse loomed up from little kitchen alcove and padded over to me, tail wagging.

"Holy crap," Butters said. "You have a pony."

"Heh," I said. Mouse sniffed at my hand and then walked over to snuffle around Butters's legs with a certain solemn ceremony. Then he sneezed and looked up at Butters, wagging his tail.

"Can I pet him?" Butters said.

"If you do, he won't leave you alone." I went into my room to pick up a few things from my closet, and when I came back out Butters was sitting on the hearth, poking the fire to life and feeding it fresh wood. Mouse sat nearby, watching with patient interest.

"What breed is he?" Butters asked.

"Half chow and half wooly mammoth. A wooly chammoth."

Mouse's jaws opened in a doggy grin.

"Wow. Some serious teeth there," Butters said. "He doesn't bite, does he?"

"Only bad guys," I told him. I grabbed Mouse's lead and clipped it to his collar. "I'm going to take him outside for a bit. I'll bring him back in; then I want you to lock up and stay put."

He hesitated in midpoke. "You're leaving?"

"It's safe," I said. "I've got measures in place here that will prevent Grevane from finding you by magical means."

"You mean with a spell or something?"

"Yeah," I said. "My spells should counter Grevane's and keep him from locating you while I get some things done."

"You won't *be* here?" Butters said. He didn't sound too steady.

"Grevane won't find you," I said.

"But what if he does it anyway?"

"He won't."

"Sure, sure, he won't. I believe you." Butters swallowed. "But what if he *does?*"

I tried to give him a reassuring smile. "There are more wards in place to stop someone from coming in. Mouse will keep an eye on you, and I'll leave a note for Thomas and ask him to stay home tonight, just in case."

"Who's Thomas?"

"Roommate," I said. I dragged a piece of paper and a pen out of a cabinet in the base of the coffee table and started writing the note.

Thomas,

Bad guys from my end of the block are trying to kill the little guy in the living room. His name is Butters. I brought him here to get him off the radar while I negotiate with them. Do me a favor and keep an eye on him until I get back.

Harry

I folded the note and stuck it up on the mantel. "He's smart, and fairly tough. I'm not sure when he'll get back. When he does, tell him I brought you here and give him the note. You should be okay."

Butters exhaled slowly. "All right. Where are you going?"

"To the bookstore," I said.

"Why there?"

"Grevane was reading a copy of a book called *Die Lied der Erlking.* I want to know why."

Butters stared at me for a second and then said, "In all of that, with threats and guns and zombies and everything, you noticed the title of the book he was holding?"

"Yeah. Damn, I'm good."

"What do I do?" he asked.

"Get some sleep." I waved a hand at my bookshelves. "Read. Help yourself to anything in the kitchen. Oh, one more thing: Do not open the door for any reason."

"Why not?"

"Because the spells on it might kill you."

"Oh," he said. "Of course. The spells."

"No joking, Butters. They're meant to keep things out, but if you open the door you could get caught in the backwash. Thomas has a talisman that will let him in safely. So do I. Anyone else will be in for a world of hurt, so stand clear."

He swallowed. "Right. Okay. What if the dog has to go?"

I sighed. "He can't mess the place up any worse than Thomas. Come on, Mouse. Let's make sure you'll be settled."

Mouse seemed to have a sixth sense about when not to take his time making use of the boardinghouse's yard, and we went to our little designated area and back with no delays. I got him back inside with Butters, revved up the Beetle, and headed for Bock Ordered Books.

Artemis Bock, proprietor of Chicago's oldest occult shop, had been a fixture near Lincoln Park for years before I had ever moved to town. The neighborhood was a bizarre blend of the worst a large city had to offer marching side by side with the erudite academia of the University of Chicago. It wasn't the kind of place I wanted to walk around after dark, wizard or no, but there wasn't much choice.

I parked the Beetle a block down from the shop, across the street from cheap apartments that were flying gang colors on the windows nearest the doors. I wasn't too worried that someone was going to steal the Blue Beetle while I was in the shop. The car just wasn't sexy enough to warrant stealing. But to be on the safe side, I made no pretense whatsoever of hiding my gun as I left the car and slipped it into a shoulder holster under my duster. I had my staff with me, too, and I took it firmly into my right hand as I shut the car door and started down the street with a purpose, my expression set and cold. I didn't have a concealed-carry permit for the gun, so I could wind up in jail for toting it along with me. On the other hand, this part of town was a favorite spot for some of the nastier denizens of the supernatural community. Between them and the very real prospect of your everyday urban criminal, I could wind up in my grave for *not* toting it. I'd err on the side of survival, thank you very much.

On the short walk to the store, I stepped over a pair of winos and tried to ignore a pale and too-thin woman with empty eyes who staggered by in leopard-print tights, a leather coat, and a bra. Her pupils had dilated until her blue eyes looked black, and she was nearly too stoned to walk. She probably wasn't old, but life had used her hard. She saw me and for a second looked like she was going to display her wares. But she got a closer look at my face and skittered to one side and tried to become invisible. I went by her without comment.

The night was very cold. In a few more weeks it would get cold enough that people like the two drunks and the stoned girl would start freezing to death. Someone would see a body, and eventually someone would call the police. The cops would show up and fill out on the police report that the body had been found and presumed accidentally frozen to death. Sometimes it wasn't an accident. The weather was a convenient way for a dealer or for the outfit to kill someone who had gotten on their nerves. Something to knock them out, a removal of a bit of clothing, and leave them for the night to devour. Most of those bodies were found within a few blocks of where I was walking.

Maybe thirty yards short of the shop, I crossed some kind of invisible line where the oppressive, dangerous atmosphere of the bad part of town lessened by several degrees. A few steps later I caught my first glance of a U of C campus building, far down the block. I felt myself relax a little in response, but that unspoken promise of safety and the rule of law was only an illusion. The closer you got to campus, the less crime occurred, but there was nothing other than convention and slightly more frequent police patrols to keep the darker elements of the city from pushing the boundaries.

Well, there was one more thing. But I couldn't afford to get involved with it. Mavra's prohibition against involving anyone else meant that even if I wanted extra help, I didn't dare ask for it. I was on my own. And if trouble came looking, I'd have to handle it alone.

Predators respond to body language. I walked like I was on my way to rip someone's face off, until I made it to the shop and entered the store.

Artemis Bock, proprietor, sat behind a counter facing the door. He was a bear of a man in his late fifties, broad-shouldered, unshaven, and heavyset with weathered muscle under a layer of comfortable living. He had knuckles the size and texture of golf balls, marked with old scars from whatever career he'd pursued before he'd become a storekeeper. He wasn't anything so strong as a wizard, but he knew his way around Chicago, around basic magical theory, and his shop was protected with half a dozen subtle wards that did a lot to encourage people looking for trouble to look elsewhere.

The door chimes tinkled as I came in, and there was a deeper chime from somewhere behind the counter. Bock had one arm on the counter and one out of sight under it until he peered over his reading glasses at my face, and nodded. He folded his arms onto the counter again, hunched over what looked like an auto magazine, and said, "Mister Dresden."

"Bock," I replied with a nod.

His eyes flickered over my staff, and I got the impression that he noticed or sensed the gun under the jacket.

"I need to get into the cage," I told him.

His shaggy eyebrows drew together. "The Wardens were here not a month ago. I run a clean shop. You know that."

I lifted my gloved hand in a pacifying gesture. "This isn't an inspection tour. Personal business."

He made a rumbling sound in his throat, something halfway between a sound of acknowledgment and one of apology. He reached behind him without looking and snagged a key from where it hung on a peg on the wall behind him. He flicked it at me. I had to let my staff fall into the crook of my left arm so that I could use my right hand to catch the key. I doubt it looked graceful, but at least I didn't drop the staff and the key both, which would have been more my speed.

"You want to come along?" I asked him. Bock didn't let customers peruse the books in the cage without supervision.

"What am I going to tell you?" he said, and turned the page in his magazine.

I nodded and started for the back of the store.

"Mister Dresden," Bock said.

"Hmm?"

"Word is on the street that there's dark business afoot. Will was through here today. Said things were getting nervous."

I paused. Billy Borden was the leader of a gang of genuine werewolves who called themselves the Alphas and lived in the neighborhood around campus. About four years before, the Alphas had learned how to shapeshift into wolves and had declared the campus area a monster-free zone. They backed it up by ripping monsters to shreds, and they did it well enough that the local underworld of vampires, ghouls, and various other nasties found it easier to hunt elsewhere.

The magical community of Chicago—of people, I mean—was centered around a number of different neighborhoods in town. The clump around campus was the smallest, but probably the most informed of them. Word has a way of getting around the occult crowd when something vicious is on the warpath, and sends them hurrying to seek shelter or keep their heads down. It was a survival instinct on behalf of those who were blessed with one form or another of talent for magic, but who didn't have enough power to be a credible threat, and one that I heartily encouraged. Things were bad enough without some amateur one-trick Willy deciding he was going to hat up and take on the bad guys.

Of course, that was precisely what Billy Borden had done. Billy and company were not up to taking on people on Grevane's level. Don't get me wrong: They were a real threat to your average dark whatever, especially working together, but they weren't used to dealing with someone in Grevane's weight class. Billy needed to keep his head down, but I couldn't contact him to tell him that. Hell, even if I did, he'd just stick his jaw out at me and tell me he could handle it. So I had to play another angle to get him to lie low.

"If you see him again," I told Bock, "let him know that I'd

appreciate it if he'd keep his head down, his eyes open, and to get in touch with me before he moves on anything."

"Something's happening," Bock said. His eyes flickered over to his calendar.

I suddenly became conscious of the eyes of three or four other customers in the store. It was late, true, but the occult community doesn't exactly keep standard hours, and Halloween was only two days off. Scratch that, it was almost one A.M. *Tomorrow* was Halloween. That meant trick-or-treating for some people, but it meant sacred Samhain for others, and there were a number of other beliefs attached to the day in the occult circles. There was shopping to be done.

"It might be," I told Bock. "You might want to be behind a threshold after dark for the next day or two. Just to be careful."

Bock's expression told me that he thought I wasn't telling him everything. I gave him a look that told him to mind his own damned business, and headed for the back of the store.

Bock's shop was bigger than you'd have expected from the outside. It had been a speakeasy back in the day, fronting as a neighborhood grocery. The front of the store offered a browsing area for customers interested in purchasing everything from crystals to incense to candles to oils to wands and other symbolic instruments of ritual magic—your typical New Agey stuff. There were various statues and idols for personal shrines, meditation mats, bits of furniture and other decoration for any alternative religion you'd care to name, including some figures of Buddha and Ghanesh.

Behind the occult area were several rows of bookshelves holding one of the largest selections in town of books on the occult, the paranormal, and the mystical. Most of the books were chock-full of philosophy or religion—predominantly Wiccan of one flavor or another, but there were several texts slanted toward Hindu beliefs, drawn from the kabbalah, voodoo, and even a couple grounded in ancient beliefs in the Norse or Greek gods. I steered clear of the whole mess, myself. Magic wasn't something you needed God, a god, or gods to help you with, but a lot of people felt differently than I did. Even some wizards of the Council held deep religious convictions, and felt that they were bound intricately to their magic.

Of course, if they believed it, it was as good as true. Magic is closely interwoven with a wizard's confidence. Some would say that it is bound up with a wizard's faith, and it would mean practically the same thing. You have to believe in the magic for it to work—not just that it *will* happen, but that it *should* happen.

That's what makes people like Grevane so dangerous. Magic is essentially a force of creation, of life. Grevane's necromancy made a mockery of life, even as he used it to destroy. Besides being murderous and extremely icky, there was something utterly profane about using magic to create a rotting semblance of a human life. My stomach turned a little, just thinking about what it might be like to work a spell like that. And Grevane *believed* in it.

Which really seemed to make him look more and more like some kind of wacko. A deadly, powerful, calm, and intelligent lunatic. I shook my head. How do I get myself into this kind of crap?

I walked through the bookshelves to a door in the back wall. While it wasn't precisely hidden, the door had no frame and was set flush with the wall around it, and was covered with the same paneling as the wall. Once it had opened to allow customers to slip into a private area to drink illegal booze. Now it was locked. I used Bock's key to open it and let myself into the back of the store.

The rear area wasn't large—nothing more than a single room with an office built into one corner, and a pair of long bookshelves set behind a heavy iron grille on the wall opposite. The room was full of boxes, shelves, tables, where Bock would keep his spare inventory, if any, and where he handled his mail-order business. There were a couple of safety lights glowing on outlets on the walls. The office door was partly open, and the light was on. I heard the office radio playing quietly on a classic-rock station.

I went to the door set in the iron grille and unlocked it, then rolled open the cage door. Bock kept all of his valuable texts in the cage. He had an original first printing of *Through the Looking Glass* by Lewis Carroll, autographed, on the highest shelf, carefully sealed in plastic, and several dozen other rare books, some of them even more valuable.

The remaining shelves were filled with serious texts on magic theory. A lot of them were almost as occluded with opinion and philosophy as their more modern counterparts on the shelves in the front of the store. The difference was that most of them were written by members of the Council at one time or another. There were very few volumes that addressed magic in its most elemental sense, as a pure source of energy, the way I'd been taught about it. One of the notable exceptions was *Elementary Magic* by Ebenezar McCoy. It was the first book most wizards ever handed an apprentice. It dealt with the nuts and bolts of moving energy around, and stressed the need for control and responsibility on behalf of the wizard.

Though now that I thought about it, Ebenezar hadn't handed me a copy of the book when he'd been teaching me. He hadn't even lectured me more than a couple of times. He told me what he expected, and then he lived it in front of me. Damned effective teaching method, to my way of thinking.

I drew out a copy of his book and stared at it for a moment. My stomach fluttered a little. Of course, he'd been lying to me, too. Or at least not telling me the whole truth. And the whole time he'd been teaching me, he'd been under orders from the Council to execute me if I wasn't perfectly behaved. I hadn't been perfect. The old man didn't kill me, but he didn't trust me enough to come clean, either. He didn't tell me that he was in charge of dirty jobs for the Council. That he was their wetworks man, the one who broke the Laws of Magic with their blessing, who betrayed the same responsibility he wrote about, talked about, and had apparently lived.

He was trying to protect you, Harry, I told myself.

That didn't make it right.

He never tried to be your hero, your role model. You did that.

That didn't change a damned thing.

He never wanted to hurt you. He had the best intentions.

And the road to hell is paved with them.

You need to get over it. You need to forgive him.

I slammed the book back onto the shelf. Hard.

"Hello?" called a woman's voice from behind me.

I nearly jumped out of my skin. My staff clattered to the ground, and when I spun around my shield bracelet was up and spitting sparks, and my .44 was in my right hand, pointing at the office.

She was young, midtwenties at most. She was dressed in a long wool skirt, a turtleneck, and a cardigan sweater, all in colors of grey. She had hair of medium brown, held up into a bun with a pair of pencils, wore glasses, and had a heart-shaped face that was more attractive than beautiful, her features soft and appealing. She had a smudge of ink on her chin and on the fingers of her right hand, and she wore a name tag that had the store logo at the top and HI, MY NAME IS SHIELA below it.

"Oh," she said, and stiffened, becoming very pale. "Oh. Um. Just take what you want. I won't do anything."

I let out my breath between my teeth, and slowly lowered the gun. For crying out loud, I had nearly started shooting. Tense much, Harry? I let go of the energy running through the shield bracelet, and it dimmed as well. "Excuse me, miss," I said as politely as I could manage. "You startled me."

She blinked at me for a second, confusion on her features. "Oh," she said, then. "You aren't robbing the store."

"No," I said.

"That's good." She put a hand to her chest, breathing a little quickly. It had to be a fairly generous chest, given that I could notice the curves of her breasts even through the cardigan. Ah, trusty libido. Even when I am up to my ears in trouble, you are there to distract me from such trivial matters as survival. "Oh. Then you're a customer, I suppose? May I help you?"

"I was just looking for a book," I said.

"Well," she said with businesslike cheer, "flick on that lamp next to you, to begin with, and we'll find what you're looking for." I did, and Shiela smoothed her skirts and walked over to me. She was average height, maybe five-six, which made her approximately a foot shorter than me. She paused as she got closer, and peered up at me. "You're him," she said. "You're Harry Dresden."

"That's what the IRS keeps telling me," I said.

"Wow," she said, her eyes bright. She had very dark eyes that went well with skin like cream, and as she got closer I saw that her outfit did a lot to conceal some pleasant curves. She wasn't going to be modeling bikinis anywhere, but she looked like she'd be very pleasant to curl up with on a cold night.

Man. I needed to date more or something. I rubbed at my eyes and got my mind back on business.

"I've wanted to meet you," she said, "ever since I came to Chicago."

"You new in town? I haven't seen you here before."

"Six months," she said. "Five working here."

"Bock works you pretty late," I said.

She nodded and brushed a curl of hair away from her cheek, leaving a smudge of dark ink on it. "End of the month. I'm doing books and inventory." Then she looked stricken and said, "Oh, I didn't even introduce myself."

"Shiela?" I guessed.

She stared at me for a second, and then flushed and said, "Oh, right. The name tag."

I stuck out my hand. "I'm Harry."

She shook my hand. Her grip was firm, soft, warm, and tingled with the energy of someone who had some kind of minor talent to practice.

I'd never really considered what it might be like for someone to sense my own aura. Shiela drew in a sharp breath, and her arm jumped. Her ink-stained fingers squeezed tight for a second and smudged my hand. "Oh. Sorry, sorry."

I rubbed my hand on my fatigue pants. "I've seen worse stains tonight," I said. "Which brings me to the books."

"You stained a book?" she said, her face and voice distressed.

"No. That was just a bad segue."

"Oh. Oh, right," she said, nodding. She absently rubbed her hands together. "You're here for a book. What are you looking for?"

"A book called *Die Lied der Erlking*."

"Oh, I've read that one." She scrunched up her nose, eyes distant for a second, then said, "Two copies, right-hand shelf, third row from the top, eighth and ninth books from the left."

I blinked at her, then went to the shelf and found the book where she'd said. "Wow. Good call."

"Eidetic memory," she said with a pleased smile. "It's . . . sort of my talent." She gestured vaguely with the hand she'd touched me with.

"Must come in handy during inventory." I checked the shelf. "There's only one copy, though."

She frowned, then shrugged. "Mister Bock must have sold one this week."

"I bet he did," I said, troubled. It bothered me to think about Grevane standing in a store, speaking to people like Bock or Shiela. I pulled the cage closed and started slowly for the front of the store.

I opened the book. I'd heard it referenced before, in other works. It was supposed to deal with the lore around the Erlkoenig, or Elfking. He was supposed to be a faerie figure of considerable power, maybe a counterpart to the Queens of the Faerie Courts. The book had been compiled by Wizard Peabody early last century from the collected notes of a dozen different crusty wizards, most of them dead at the time, and was considered to be a work of nearly pure speculation.

"How much?" I asked.

"Should be on an index card inside the cover," Shiela said, walking politely beside me.

I looked. The book was worth half a month's rent. No wonder I'd never bought a copy. Business hadn't been bad lately, but between handling all of Mouse's licensing and shots and the trucks of food he ate, and Thomas's job troubles, I didn't have anything to spare. Maybe Bock would let me lease it or something.

Shiela and I walked out of the back room and started toward the front of the store. As we came out of the book areas, she said, "Well, I think you know the way from here. It was a pleasure meeting you, Harry."

"You too," I said, smiling. Hey, she was a woman, and pretty enough. Her smile was simply adorable. "Maybe I'll bump into you again sometime."

"I'd like that. Only next time without the gun."

"One of those old-fashioned girls, huh?" I said.

She laughed and walked back toward the rear of the store.

"Find what you needed?" Bock asked. There was an edge to his voice, something I couldn't quite place. He was definitely uncomfortable.

"I hope so," I said. "Uh. About the price . . ."

Bock looked at me hard from under his thick eyebrows.

"Uh. Would you take a check?"

He looked around the store and then nodded. "Sure, from you."

"Thanks," I said. I wrote out a check, hoping it wouldn't bounce before I got to the door, and sneaked my own glance around the shop. "Did I run out your customers?"

"Maybe," he said uncomfortably.

"Sorry," I said.

"It happens."

"Might be better for them to be home. You too, in fact."

He shook his head. "I have a business to run."

He was an adult, and he'd been in this town longer than I had. "All right," I said. I handed him the check. "Did you sell the other copy you had in inventory?"

He put the check in the register, and put the book into a plastic bag, zipped it shut, then put that in a paper sack. "Two days ago," he said after a moment's thought.

"Do you remember to whom?"

He puffed out a breath that flapped his jowls. "Old gentleman. Long hair, thinning. Liver spots."

"Real loose skin?" I asked. "Moved kind of stiff?"

Bock looked around again, nervous. "Yeah. That's him. Look, Mister Dresden, I just run the shop, okay? I don't want to get involved with any trouble. I had no idea who the guy was. He was just a customer."

"All right," I told him. "Thanks, Bock."

He nodded and passed over the book. I folded the sack, book and all, into a pocket on my duster, and fished my car keys out of my pocket.

"Harry," came Shiela's voice, low and urgent.

I blinked and looked up at her. "Yeah?"

She nodded toward the front of the store, her face anxious.

I looked out.

On the street outside the shop stood two figures. They were dressed more or less identically: long black robes, long black cape, big black mantles, big black hoods that showed nothing of the faces inside. One was taller than the other, but other than that they simply stood on the sidewalk outside, waiting.

"I told these guys last week I didn't want to buy a ring," I said. I glanced at Shiela. "See that? Witty under pressure. That was a Tolkien joke."

"Ha," said Bock, more than a little uneasy. "I don't want any trouble here, Mister Dresden."

"Relax, Bock," I said. "If they wanted trouble, they'd have kicked down the door."

"They're here to talk to you?" Shiela asked.

"Probably," I said. Of course, if they were more of Kemmler's knitting circle, they might just walk up and try to kill me. Grevane had. I drummed my fingers thoughtfully along the solid wood of my wizard's staff.

Bock looked at me, his expression a little queasy. He wasn't an easy man to frighten, but he was no fool, either. I had wrecked three . . . no wait, four. No . . . at *least* four buildings during my cases in the last several years, and he didn't want Bock Ordered Books to be appended to the list. That hurt a little. Normals looked at me like I was insane when I told people I was a wizard. People who were in the know didn't look at me like I was insane. They looked at me like I was insanely dangerous.

I guess at least four buildings later, they've got reason to think so.

"Maybe you'd better close up shop for the night," I told Bock and Shiela. "I'll go out and talk to them."

Chapter

Eight

I paused just before I opened the shop's door and walked outside. It was one of those moments that would have had dramatic music if my life were a movie, but instead I got a radio jingle for some kind of submarine sandwich place blaring over the store's ambient stereo. The movie of my life must be really low-budget.

The trick was to figure out which movie I was in. If this was a variant on *High Noon,* then walking outside was probably a fairly dangerous idea. On the other hand, there was always the chance that I was still in the opening scenes of *The Maltese Falcon* and everyone trying to chase down the bird still wanted to talk to me. In which case, this was probably a good chance to dig for vital information about what might well be a growing storm around the search for *The Word of Kemmler.*

But just in case, I shook out my shield bracelet to the ready. I took my staff in hand and settled my fingers around it in a solid grip, curling them to the sigil-carved surface of the wood one by one.

Then I called up my power.

Like I said, magic comes from life, and especially from emotions. They're a source of the same intangible energy that everyone can feel when an autumn moon rises and fills you with a sudden sense of bone-deep excitement, or when the first warm breeze of spring rushes past your face, full of the scents of life, and drowns you in a sudden flood of unreasoning joy. The passion of mighty music that brings tears to your eyes, and the raw, bubbling, infectious laughter of small children at play, the bellowing power of a stadium full of football fans shouting "Hey!" in time to that damned song—they're all charged with magic.

My magic comes from the same places. And maybe from darker places than that. Fear is an emotion, too. So is rage. So is lust. And madness. I'm not a particularly good person. I'm no Charles Manson or anything, but I'm not going to be up for canonization either. Though in the past, I think maybe I was a better person than I am today. In the past I hadn't seen so many people hurt and killed and terrorized by the same kind of power that damn well should have been making the world a nicer place, or at the least staying the hell away from it. I hadn't made so many mistakes back then, so many shortsighted decisions, some of which had cost people their lives. I had been sure of myself. I had been whole.

My stupid hand hurt like hell. I had half a dozen really gut-wrenchingly good reasons to be afraid, and I was. Worst of all, if I made any mistakes, Murphy was going to be the one to pay for it. If that happened, I didn't know what I would do.

I drew it all in, the good, the bad, and the crazy, a low buzz that coursed through the air and rattled the idols and candles and incense holders on their shelves in the store around me. In the glass door of the shop I saw my left hand vanish, replaced with an irregular globe of angry blue light that trailed bits of heatless fire to the floor. I pulled in the energy from all around me, readying myself to defend, to attack, to protect, or to destroy. I didn't know what the two cloaked figures wanted, but I wanted them to know that if they'd come looking for a fight, I'd be willing to oblige them.

I held my power around me like a cloak and slipped out to face the pair waiting for me on the sidewalk. I took my time, every step unhurried and precise. I kept an eye on them, but only in my peripheral vision. Otherwise I left my eyes on the ground and walked slowly, until the blue glow of my shield light fell on their dark robes, making the black look blue, darkening the shadows in the folds to hues too dark to have names. Then I stopped and lifted my eyes slowly, daring them to meet my gaze.

It might have been my imagination, but I thought the pair of them rocked back a little, swaying like reeds before an oncoming storm. October wind blew about us, freezing-cold air that took its chill from the icy depths of Lake Michigan.

"What do you want?" I asked them. I borrowed frost from the wind and put it in my voice.

The larger of the pair spoke. "The book."

But which book? I wondered. "Uh-huh. You're a Schubert fan boy, aren't you? You've got the look."

"Goethe, actually," he said. "Give it to me."

He was definitely after a copy of *Der Erlking,* then. His voice was . . . odd. Male, certainly, but it didn't sound quite human. There was a kind of quavering buzz in it that made it warble, somehow, made the words slither uncertainly. The words were slow and enunciated. They had to be, in order to be intelligible.

"Bite me," I answered him. "Get your own book, Kemmlerite."

"I have nothing but disdain for the madman Kemmler," he spat. "Have a care what insults you offer. This need not involve you at all, Dresden."

That gave me a moment's pause, as they say. Taking on arrogant, powerful dark wizards is one thing. Taking on ones who have done their homework and who know who you are is something else entirely. It was my turn to be rattled.

The dark figure noted it. His not-human voice swayed into the night again in a low laugh.

"Touché, O dark master of evil bathrobes," I said. "But I'm still not giving you my copy of the book."

"I am called Cowl," he said. Was there amusement in his voice? Maybe. "And I am feeling patient this evening. Again I will ask it. Give me your copy of the book."

Die Lied der Erlking bumped against my leg through the pocket of my duster. "And again do I answer thee. Bite me."

"Thrice will I ask and done," said the figure, warning in its tone.

"Gee, let me think. How am I gonna answer this time," I said, planting my feet on the ground.

Cowl made a hissing sound, and spread its arms slightly, hands still low, by its hips. The cold wind off the lake began to blow harder.

"Thrice I ask and done," Cowl said, his voice low, hard, angry. "Give . . . me . . . the book."

Suddenly the second figure took a step forward and said, in a female version of Cowl's weird voice, "Please."

There was a second of shocked silence, and then Cowl snarled, "Kumori. Mind your tongue."

"There is no cost in being polite," said the smaller of the two, Kumori. The robes were too thick and shapeless to give any hint at her form, but there was something decidedly feminine in the gesture she made with one hand, a roll of her wrist. She faced me again and said, "The knowledge in *Der Erlking* is about to become dangerous, Dresden," she said. "You need not give us the book. Simply destroy it here. That will be sufficient. I ask it of you, please."

I looked between the two of them for a moment. Then I said, "I've seen you both before."

Neither of them moved.

"At Bianca's masquerade. You were there on the dais with her." As I spoke the words, I became increasingly convinced of them. The two figures I'd seen back then had never shown their faces, but there was something in the way that Cowl and Kumori moved that matched the two shadows back then precisely. "You were the ones who gave the Leanansidhe that *athame*."

"Perhaps," said Kumori, but there was an inclination to her head that ceded me the truth of my statement.

"That was such an amazingly screwed-up evening. It's been coming back to haunt me for years," I said.

"And will for years to come," said Cowl. "A great many things of significance happened that night. Most of which you are not yet aware."

"Hell's bells," I complained. "I'm a wizard myself, and I still get sick of that I-know-and-you-don't shtick. In fact, it pisses me off even faster than it used to."

Cowl and Kumori exchanged a long look, and then Kumori said, "Dresden, if you would spare yourself and others grief and pain, destroy the book."

"Is that what you're doing?" I asked. "Going around trashing copies?"

"There were fewer than a thousand printed," Kumori confirmed. "Time has taken most of them. Over the past month we have accounted for the rest, but for two here, in Chicago, in this store."

"Why?" I demanded.

Cowl moved his shoulders in the barest hint of a shrug. "Is it not enough that Kemmler's disciples could use this knowledge for great evil?"

"Are you with the Council?" I responded.

"Obviously not," Kumori replied from the depths of her hood.

"Uh-huh," I said. "Seems to me that if you were on the up-and-up you'd be working with the Council, rather than running around reinterpreting *Fahrenheit 451* from a Ringwraith perspective."

"And it seems to me," Kumori answered smoothly, "that if you believed that their motives were as pure as they claim, you would already have notified them yourself."

Hello. Now *that* was a new tune, someone suggesting that the Council was bent and I was in the right. I wasn't sure what Kumori was trying to do, but it was smartest to play this out and see what she had to say. "Who says I haven't?"

"This is pointless," Cowl said.

Kumori said, "Let me tell him."

"Pointless."

"It costs nothing," Kumori said.

"It's going to if you keep dawdling," I said. "I'm going to start billing you for wasting my time."

She made a weird sound that I only just recognized as a sigh. "Can you believe, at least, that the contents of the book are dangerous?"

Grevane had seemed fond enough of his copy. But I wouldn't know for sure what the big stink was about until I had time to read the book myself. "For the sake of expediency, let's say that I do."

"If the knowledge inside the book is dangerous," Cowl said, "what makes you think that the Wardens or the Council would use it any more wisely than Kemmler's disciples?"

"Because while they are a bunch of enormous assholes, they always try to do the right thing," I said. "If one of the Wardens thought he might be about to practice black magic, he'd probably cut off his own head on pure reflex."

"All of them?" Kumori asked in a quiet voice. "Are you sure?"

I looked back and forth between them. "Are you telling me that someone on the Council is after Kemmler's power?"

"The Council is not what it was," said Cowl. "It has rotted from the inside, and many wizards who have chafed at its restrictions have seen the war with the Red Court reveal its weakness. It will fall. Soon. Perhaps before tomorrow night."

"Oh," I drawled. "Well, gee, why didn't you say so? I'll just hand you my copy of the book right now."

Kumori held up a hand. "This is no deception, Dresden. The world is changing. The Council's end is near, and those who wish to survive it must act now. Before it is too late."

I took a deep breath. "Normally I'm the first one to suggest we t.p. the Council's house," I said. "But you're talking about necromancy. Black magic. You aren't going to convince me that the Council and the Wardens have suddenly gotten a yen to trot down the left-hand path. They won't touch the stuff."

"Ideally," Cowl said. "You are young, Dresden. And you have much to learn."

"You know what young me has learned? Not to spend too much time listening to the advice of people who want to get something out of me," I said. "Which includes car salesmen, political candidates, and weirdos in black capes who mug me on the street in the middle of the night."

"Enough," Cowl said, anger making his voice almost unintelligible. "Give us the book."

"Bite my ass, Cowl."

Kumori's hood twitched back and forth between Cowl and me. She took three steps back.

"Just as well," Cowl murmured. "I have wanted to see for myself what has the Wardens so nervous about you."

The cold wind rose again, and the hairs on the back of my neck rose up stiffly. A flash of sensation flickered over me as Cowl drew in power. A *lot* of power.

"Don't," I said. I lifted my shield bracelet, weaving defensive energy before me with my thoughts. I solidified my hold on my own power, wrapping my fingers tight around my staff, and then slammed it down hard on the concrete. The cracking sound of it echoed back and forth from darkened buildings and the empty street. "Walk away. I'm not kidding."

"*Dorosh,*" he snarled in reply, and extended his right hand.

He hit me with raw, invisible force—pure will, focused into a violent burst of kinetic energy. I knew it was coming, my shield was ready, and I braced myself against it in precisely the correct way. My defense was perfect.

It was all that saved my life.

I've traded practice blows with my old master Justin DuMorne, himself at one time a Warden. I fought him in earnest, too, and won. I've tested my strength in practice duels against the mentor who succeeded him, Ebenezar McCoy. My faerie godmother, the Leanansidhe, has a seriously nasty right hook, metaphysically speaking, and I've even gone up against the least of the Queens of Faerie. Throw in a couple of demons, various magical constructs, a thirteen-story fall in a runaway elevator, half a dozen spellslingers of one amount of nasty or another, and I've seen more sheer mystic violence than most wizards in the business. I've beaten them all, or at least survived them, and I've got the scars to show for it.

Cowl hit me harder than any of them.

My shield lit up like a floodlight, and despite all that I could do to divert the energy he threw at me, it hit me like a professional linebacker on an adrenaline frenzy. If I hadn't been able to smooth it out and take the blow evenly across the whole front of my body, it might have broken my nose or ribs or collarbone, depending on where the energy bled through. Instead it felt like the Jolly Green Giant had slugged me with a family-sized beanbag. If there had been any upward force on it, it would have thrown me far enough to make me worry about the fall. But the blow came head-on, driving me straight back.

I flew several yards in the air, hit on my back, scraped along the sidewalk, and managed to turn the momentum into a roll. I staggered to my feet, leaning hard against a parked car. I must have clipped my head at some point, because stars were swirling around in my vision.

By the time I got myself upright again, the panic had set in. No one had ever thrown power like that at me. Stars and stones, if I hadn't been absolutely prepared for that blow . . .

I swallowed. I'd be dead. Or at best broken, bleeding, and utterly at the mercy of an unknown wizard. One who was still nearby, and probably getting ready to hit me again. I forced thoughts and doubts from my mind and readied my shield, my bracelet already grown so warm that I could feel it through the ugly scars on the skin of my wrist. I couldn't even think about hitting back, because if my shield wasn't back up and ready for another blow, I wouldn't live long enough to get the chance.

Cowl walked slowly toward me down the sidewalk, all cloak and hood and shadows. "Disappointing," he said. "I hoped you were ready for the heavyweight division."

He flicked his wrist, and the next blow howled at me in the freezing wind blowing off the lake. This one came in at an angle, and I didn't even try to stop it cold. I sidestepped like a nervous horse, angling my shield to deflect the blow. Again energy leaked through, but this time it only shoved me across the sidewalk.

My shoulder hit the building, and it drove the breath out of me. I've had shoulder injuries before, and it probably made it feel worse than it was. I bounced off the building and kept my feet, but my legs wobbled—not from the effort of holding me up, but from the energy I'd had to expend to survive the attacks.

Cowl kept walking toward me. Hell's bells, it didn't even look like he was trying all that hard.

I got a cold feeling in my chest.

This man could kill me.

"The book, boy," Cowl said. "Now."

What rose up in me then wasn't outrage or terror. It wasn't righteous wrath. It wasn't confidence, or surety, or determination to protect a loved one. It was 100 percent pure, contrary stubbornness. Chicago was my town. I didn't care who this joker was; he wasn't going to come gliding down the streets of *my* town and push in my teeth for my milk money.

I don't get pushed around by anyone.

Cowl was strong, but his magic wasn't inhuman. It was huge, and it was different from what I worked with, but it didn't have that nauseating, greasy, somehow empty feel that I'd come to associate with the worst black magic. No, that wasn't entirely true. There was a lingering sense of black magic involved in his power. Then again, there's a little of it in mine, too.

The point being that Cowl wasn't some kind of demon. He was a wizard. Human.

And, behind the magic, just as fragile as me.

I poured power down my arm, whirled my staff, pointed it at the car on the street beside him, and snarled, "*Forzare!*"

The sigils on the staff burst into sudden, hellish scarlet light, as bright as the blaze of my shield, and shimmering waves of force flowed out from me. They flooded out over the sidewalk, under the Toyota parked on the street nearest Cowl. I snarled with effort, and the Hellfire force abruptly lashed up, underneath the street side of the car. The car flipped up as lightly and quickly as a man over-turning a kitchen chair. Cowl was under it.

There was a crash, and Hell's bells, it was loud. Glass shattered everywhere, and sparks flew out in every direction. The car's alarm went off, warbling drunkenly, and alarms started going off all up and down the street. In apartment windows, lights started blinking on.

I fell to one knee, suddenly exhausted, the light from staff and shield both dwindling to nothing and vanishing. I had never moved that much mass before, that quickly, with nothing but raw kinetic energy, and I could hardly find enough energy to focus my eyes. If I hadn't had the staff to lean on, I'd have been hugging the sidewalk.

There was the sound of metal grating on concrete.

"Oh, come on," I said panting.

The car shuddered, then slid a few inches to one side. Cowl straightened slowly. He'd gotten back to the very rear of the car's impact area somehow, and he must have been able to shield him-self from the partial impact. As he straightened he wavered, then braced himself against a streetlight with one black-gloved hand. I felt a surge of satisfaction. *Take that, jerk.*

A low growling sound came warbling out of the black hood. "The book."

"Bite," I panted, "me."

But he hadn't been talking to me. Kumori stepped out of the shadows of a doorway and gestured with a whispered word.

I felt a sudden, strong tug at my duster's pocket. The flap cov-ering it flew up, and the slender book in its paper bag started slid-ing out.

"Ack," I managed, which was all the repartee I was up for at the moment. I rolled and trapped the book between my body and the ground.

Kumori extended her hand again, and more forcefully. I slid two feet over the concrete, until I braced a boot against an uneven joint in the sidewalk and saw movement behind the two figures. "Game over," I said. "Stop it."

"Or what?" Cowl demanded.

"Ever see *Wolfen?*" I spat.

Wolves appeared, just freaking *appeared* out of the Chicago night. Big wolves, refugees from a previous epoch, huge, strong-looking beasts with white fangs and savage eyes. One was crouched on the wrecked Buick, within an easy leap of Cowl, bright eyes fastened on him. Another had appeared behind Kumori, and a third leapt lightly down from a fire escape, landing in a soundless crouch in front of her. One appeared on either side of me, and snarls bubbled out of the night.

More lights were coming on. A siren wailed in the night.

"What big teeth they have," I said. "You want to keep going until the cops show up? I'm game."

There wasn't even a pause for the two cloaked figures to look significantly at each other. Kumori glided to Cowl's side. Cowl gave me a look that I felt, even if I couldn't see his face, and he growled, "This isn't—"

"Oh, shut up," I said. "You lost. Go."

Cowl's fingers formed into a rigid claw and he snarled a word I couldn't quite hear, slashing at the air.

There was a surge of power, darker this time, somehow more nebulous. The air around them blurred, there was the sudden scent of mildew and lightless waters, a sighing sound, and as quickly as that, they were simply gone.

"Billy," I said a second later, angry. "What the *hell* are you doing? Those people could have killed you."

The wolf crouching on the wrecked car looked at me, and dropped its mouth open into a lolling grin. It leapt over the broken glass to land beside me, shimmered, and a second later the wolf was gone, replaced by a naked man crouching beside me. Billy was a little shorter than average, and had more muscle than a Bowflex commercial. Medium brown hair, matching eyes, and he wore a short beard now that made him look a lot older than when I'd met him years ago.

Of course, he *was* older than when I'd met him years ago.

"This is my neighborhood," he said quietly. "Can't afford to let anyone make me look bad here." He moved with quick efficiency, getting a shoulder under one of mine and hauling me to my feet by main strength. "How bad are you hurt?"

"Bruises," I said. The world spun a little as he hauled me up, and I wasn't sure I could have stood on my own. "Little wobbly. Out of breath."

"Cops will be here in about seventy seconds," he said, like someone who knew. "Come on. Georgia's in the car at the other end of this alley."

"No," I said. "Look, just get me to my car. I can't be . . ." I couldn't be seen with him. If Mavra was watching me, or having me tailed, it might mean that she would release the dirt she had on Murphy. But I damn sure couldn't just explain everything to him. Billy wasn't the sort to stand by when he saw a friend in trouble.

And I was damned lucky he wasn't. I hadn't had much left in me but some hot air when Cowl had stood up again.

"No time," Billy said. "Look, we'll get you back here after things calm down later. Christ, Harry, you crushed that car like a beer can. I didn't know you were that strong."

"Me neither," I said. I couldn't get to my car on my own. I couldn't afford to be seen with Billy and the Alphas. But I couldn't allow myself to get detained or thrown into jail, either. Never mind that if Cowl and his sidekick had found me, there might be other interested parties after me, too. If I kept showing my face on the streets, someone would tear it off for me.

I had to go with Billy. I would cut things as short as I could. I didn't want them involved in this business any more than they already were, anyway, as much to protect them as Murphy. Dammit, Mavra would just have to show some freaking understanding. Maybe if I said please.

Yeah, right.

I might already have blown it and doomed Murphy, but I didn't have much choice.

I leaned on Billy the werewolf, and did the best I could to hobble along with him down the alley and off the street.

Chapter

Nine

Billy probably could have picked me up and carried me at a flat run if he needed to, but we had to cross only about fifty yards of alley and darkened street before an expensive SUV, its lights out, cut over to the curb and made a swift stop in front of us.

"Quick," I said, still panting, "to the Woofmobile."

Billy helped me into the backseat, followed me in, and before the door was even shut the SUV began accelerating smoothly and calmly from the scene. The interior smelled like new-car-scented air freshener and fast food.

"What happened?" asked the driver. She was a willowy young woman about Billy's age, somewhere around six feet tall. Her brown hair was pulled into a severe braid, and she wore jeans and a denim jacket. "Hello, Harry."

"Evening, Georgia," I replied, slumping back against the headrest.

"Are you all right?"

"Nothing a nice long nap won't fix."

"He was attacked," Billy supplied, answering the first question. He tugged sweats and a T-shirt out of an open gym bag and hopped into them with practiced motions.

"The vampires again?" Georgia asked. She turned on the headlights and joined other traffic. Reflected streetlights gleamed off the diamond engagement ring on her left hand. "I thought the Reds were staying out of town."

"Not vampires," I said. My eyelids started increasing their mass, and I decided not to argue with them. "New friends."

"I think they must have been other wizards," Billy said quietly. "Big black cloaks and hoods. I couldn't see their faces."

"What set the police off?" she asked.

"Harry flipped a car over on top of one of them."

I heard Georgia suck in her breath through her teeth.

"Yeah, and I'm the one who *lost* the fight," I muttered. "Barely even rattled his cage."

"My God," Georgia said. "Is everyone all right?"

"Yeah," I replied. "The bad guys got away. If the Alphas hadn't come along when they did, I'm not sure I would have."

"Everyone else scattered, and they'll meet us back at the apartment," Billy said. "Who were those guys?"

"I can't tell you that," I said.

There was an empty second, and then Billy's voice turned cautious. "Why? Is it some kind of secret, need-to-know wizard thing?"

"No. I just have no freaking clue who it was."

"Oh. What did they want?" Billy asked. "I only showed up at the end."

"I picked up a rare book at Bock's. Apparently they wanted it."

I could have sworn I heard his brow furrow. "Is it valuable?"

"Something in it must be," I answered. I fumbled at my pocket and drew out the book to make sure it was still there. The slender volume looked innocent enough. And at least it wouldn't take too long to read through. "I appreciate the assist, but I can't stay."

"Sure, sure," Billy said. "What can we do to help?"

"Don't take me to your apartment, for one," I said. "Somewhere you don't go as much."

"Why not?" Billy asked.

"Please, man. Just do it. And let me think for a minute," I said, and closed my eyes again. I tried to work out how best to keep the Alphas from getting involved in this business, but my weary, aching body betrayed me. I dropped into a sudden darkness too black and silent to allow for any dreams.

When I jerked awake, my neck was aching from being bent forward, my chin on my chest. We weren't driving anymore, and I was alone in the SUV. The hollow weariness had abated significantly, and I didn't feel any trembling in my limbs. I couldn't have been out for very long, but even a little sleep can do wonders sometimes.

I got out and found myself in a garage big enough to house half a dozen cars, though the SUV and a shiny black Mercury were the only two vehicles in it. I recognized the place—Georgia's parents' house, an upper-end place on the north side of town. The Alphas had brought me here once before, when they helped rescue me from the lair of a gang of psychotic lycanthropes. Susan had been with me.

I shook my head, took up my staff and the little book, and walked toward the door to the house. I paused just before I opened it, and heard voices speaking in quiet tones. I closed my eyes and focused on my sense of hearing, head tilted to one side, and the sound of the voices became clear and distinct enough for me to understand. It's a useful skill, Listening, though I couldn't tell you exactly how to do it.

There was the sound of a phone being returned to its cradle. "They're all fine," Billy said.

"Good," Georgia replied. "Something's going on. Did you see his face?"

"He looked tired," Billy said.

"He looked more than just tired. He's afraid."

"Maybe," Billy said, after a second of hesitation. "So what if he is?"

"So how bad must things be if *he* is afraid?" Georgia asked. "And there's more."

Billy exhaled. "His hand."

"You saw it then?"

"Yeah. After he nodded off."

"He's not supposed to have any movement in it," she said, her voice growing more worried. "You've seen him on gaming nights. He can barely cup his fingers to hold chips. I heard the wood of his staff creaking under them tonight. I thought he would crush it."

I blinked at that news and looked down at my gloved hand. I tried to wiggle my fingers. They sort of twitched.

"He's been a little different since he got burned," Billy said.

"It's been longer than that," Georgia said. "It's been since the year before. Remember when he showed up to gaming with all those bandages under his sweater? He never would talk about what happened. It was a week after that murder at the docks, and that big terrorist scare at the airport. It's been since then. He's been distant. More all the time."

"You think he had something to do with that murder?" Billy asked.

"Of course not," Georgia said. "But I think he might have been working on a case and gotten involved with the victim in some way. You know how he is. He probably blames himself for her death."

I swallowed and tried not to think of a pretty, dark-haired woman bleeding to death while the hold of her boat slowly filled with water. She'd made enough bad choices to get herself into trouble. But I hadn't been able to protect her from the creature that had taken her life.

"If he's in trouble we're going to help him," Billy said.

"Yes," Georgia replied. "But think about this, Billy. Getting involved might not be the best way to do it."

"What do you mean?"

"I mean that he didn't want us to take him to the apartment," Georgia said. "Do you know why?"

"No, I don't. Neither do you."

She made a disgusted sound. "Billy, he's afraid the apartment is being watched."

"By who?"

"By *what*," Georgia said. "We haven't seen or heard or scented anything. If there's magic at work here, it could be more than we know how to handle."

"So what are you saying?" Billy said. "That we should just abandon him if he's in trouble?"

"No." She sighed. "But, Billy, you saw what he was capable of doing. We saw him mow through an army at the faerie battleground. And you tell me tonight that he flipped a car onto one of these other wizards, and that the man blew it off. I don't think we're weak, but running off ghouls and trolls and the occasional vampire is one thing. Mixing it up with wizards is something else. You've seen what kind of power they have."

"I'm not afraid," Billy said.

"Then you're stupid," Georgia replied, her voice blunt but not cruel. "Harry isn't what he used to be. He's been hurt. And I don't care what he says, his injured hand bothers him more than he lets on. He doesn't need any more handicaps."

"You want to just leave him alone?" Billy asked.

"I don't want to weigh him down. You know him. He'll protect other people before he takes care of himself. If he's operating so far out of our league, we might not be anything but a distraction to him. We have to understand our limits."

There was a long silence.

"I don't care," Billy said then. "I'm not just going to stand by if he's in trouble."

"All I want," Georgia said, "is for you to listen to him. If he doesn't want our support, or if he thinks it is too dangerous for us to be involved, we have to trust that he knows what he's doing. He knows things that we don't. He's trusted us before, and he's never led us wrong. Just promise me that you'll return the compliment."

"I can't just . . . turn away," Billy said.

"I wouldn't want you to," Georgia said. "But . . . sometimes you think with your fangs and not with your head, Will." There was the soft sound of a kiss. "I love you. We'll help him however we can. I just wanted you to consider the idea that he might not need us for violence."

Billy took a couple of heavy steps. One of the kitchen chairs creaked. "I don't know what else we can do."

"Well," Georgia said. She opened the fridge. "What about these masked wizard types. Did you get close enough to scent them?"

"I tried," Billy said. "And I was closest to them. But . . ."

"But?"

"I couldn't get a scent. Harry did something. He flipped the car over. There was a flash of red light and after that all I could smell was . . ."

I heard Georgia take a couple of steps, maybe to touch him. "What did you smell?"

"Sulfur," Billy said, his voice a little weak. "I smelled brimstone."

There was silence.

"What does it mean?" Georgia asked.

"That I'm worried about him," Billy said. "You should have seen the look on his face. The rage. I've never seen anyone look that angry."

"You think he's . . . what? Unstable?" Georgia asked.

"You're the psych grad," Billy said. "What do you think?"

I put my hand on the door. I hesitated for just a second and then pushed it open.

Billy and Georgia both sat in a rather roomy kitchen at a small table, with two bottles of beer set open but untouched on the table. They blinked and straightened, staring up at me in surprise.

"What do you think?" I asked Georgia quietly. "I'd like to know, too."

"Harry," Georgia said, "I'm just a grad student."

I went to the fridge and got myself a cold beer. It was an American brand, but I've got no palate in any case. I like my beer cold. I twisted the cap off, then walked over to the table and sat down with them. "I'm not looking for a therapist. You're a friend. Both of you are." I swigged beer. "Tell me what you think."

Georgia and Billy traded a look, and Billy nodded.

"Harry," Georgia said, "I think you need to talk to someone. I don't think it's important who it is. But you have a lot of pressures on you, and if you don't find some way to let them out, you're going to hurt yourself."

Billy said, "People talk to their friends, man. No one can do everything alone. You work through it together."

I sipped some more beer. Georgia and Billy did, too. We sat in silence for maybe four or five minutes.

Then I said, "About two years ago I exposed myself to a demonic influence. A creature called Lasciel. A fallen angel. The kind of being that turns people into . . . into real monsters."

Georgia watched me, her eyes focused intently on my face. "Why did you do that?"

"It was in a silver coin," I said. "Whoever touched it would have been exposed. There was a child who had no idea what it was. I didn't think. I just slapped my hand over it before the child could pick it up."

Georgia nodded. "What happened?"

"I took measures to contain it," I said. "I did everything I could think of, and for a while I thought I'd been successful." I sipped more beer. "Then last year, I realized that my magic was being augmented by a demonic energy called Hellfire. That's what you smelled tonight, Billy, when I flipped the car."

"Why do you use it?" Billy asked.

I shook my head. "It isn't my choice. It just happens."

Georgia frowned. "I'm not an expert on magic, Harry, but from what I've learned that kind of power doesn't come for free."

"No. It doesn't."

"Then what was the price?" she asked.

I drew in a deep breath. Then I started peeling the leather glove off my scarred hand. "I wondered that too," I said. I slid the glove off and turned my hand over.

The scarring was the worst on the insides of my fingers and over my palm. It looked more like melted wax than human flesh, all white with flares of blue where some of the veins still survived—all except for the exact center of my palm. There, three lines of pink, healthy flesh formed a sigil vaguely suggestive of an hourglass.

"I found this there when I got burned," I said. "It's an ancient script. It's the symbol for the name of Lasciel."

Georgia drew in a slow breath and said, "Oh."

Billy looked back and forth between us. "Oh? What, oh?"

Georgia gave me a be-patient look and turned to Billy. "It's a demon mark. Like a brand, yes?" She looked at me for confirmation.

I nodded.

"He's worried that this demon, Lasciel, might be exerting some kind of control on him in ways that he cannot detect."

"Right," I said. "Everything I know tells me that I should be cut off from Lasciel. That I should be safe. But the power is still there somehow. And if the demon is influencing my thoughts, pulling my strings, I might not even be able to feel it happening."

Georgia frowned. "Do you believe that to be a probability?"

"It's too dangerous to assume anything else," I said. I held up a hand. "That's not hubris. It's just a fact. I have power. If I use it unwisely or recklessly, people could get hurt. They could die. And if Lasciel is somehow influencing me . . ."

"Who knows what could happen," Billy finished, his tone sober.

"Yeah."

"Damn," Billy said.

We all took a sip of beer.

"I'm worried," I said. "I haven't been able to find any answers. I've gone through spell after spell. Rites, ceremonies, I've tried everything. It won't go away."

"Jesus," Billy breathed.

"An influence like this is detectable, and against the Laws of Magic. If the Wardens found out and pushed a trial on me, it might be enough to get me executed. And if I get near the Knight of the Cross I told you about, he'll be able to feel it on me. I don't know how he'd react. What he would think." I swallowed. "I'm scared."

Georgia touched my arm briefly, then said, "You shouldn't be so hard on yourself, Harry. I know you well enough to know that you would never want that kind of power, much less abuse it."

"If some part of me didn't want it," I asked, "why didn't I pick up the kid instead of Lasciel's coin?"

A heavy silence settled over the kitchen.

"You've been friends to me. Stuck it out by me when times were rough," I said a moment later. "You've made me welcome in your home. In your life. You're good people. I'm sorry I haven't been more open with you."

"Is that what tonight was about?" Billy asked. "The demon?"

"No," I said. "Tonight was different. And I can't tell you about it."

"If you're trying to protect us . . ." Billy began.

"I'm not protecting you," I said. "I'm protecting someone else. If I'm seen with you, it could get them badly hurt. Maybe even killed."

"I don't understand. I want to help . . ." Billy said.

Georgia put her hand over Billy's. He glanced at her, flushed, and then closed his mouth.

I nodded and finished the beer. "I need you to trust me for a little while. I'm sorry. But the faster I'm out of here, the better."

"How can we help?" Georgia asked.

"Just knowing that you want to is a help," I told her. "But that's almost the only thing you can do. For now, at least."

"Almost the only thing?"

I nodded. "If I could get something to eat, and maybe a ride back to my car, I'd be obliged."

"We can do that," Billy said.

"Thank you," I said.

Chapter

Ten

I raided the refrigerator and divested it of a small plate of cold cuts while Billy made a call to his apartment. Moments later one of the other Alphas called back, confirming that the furor around Bock Ordered Books had begun to die down.

"Only one patrol car still there," Billy reported. "Plus the guys with the wrecker."

"We shouldn't wait any longer," I said. "With cops around, any neighborhood monsters will lie low for a while to be careful. I want to be back there and gone before they get moving again."

"Eat in the car," Georgia suggested, and we all piled back into her SUV.

Georgia parked on the curb behind the Beetle and let me out. I had my keys in my hand, ready to get in and get gone. But when I saw the car, I stopped.

Someone had smashed out the remaining windows in the car. Glass littered the street and the car's interior. Parts of the windshield were missing, and the rest clung together in a mass of fracture lines that made the whole mess opaque. The back window had already been broken when I used my force ring on that zombie earlier in the evening. The doors and the hood were dented in dozens of places, and the door handles had been entirely smashed off. The tires sagged limply, and I could see long, neat slashes in them without difficulty.

I approached the car slowly.

The wooden handle of a Louisville Slugger baseball bat protruded from the gaping driver's-side window, the cardboard tag from the store still dangling from its string.

Billy leaned out the SUV window and let out a low whistle. "Wow."

"But on the upside," I said, "now all the windows match."

"What a mess," Georgia said.

I went around to the front of the car and opened the trunk. It hadn't been tampered with. My sawed-off shotgun was still in the backseat. Billy and Georgia got out and walked over to me.

"Gang?" Georgia asked.

"Gang wouldn't have left the gun," I said.

"The guys in the hoods?" Billy guessed.

"Didn't strike me as the baseball-bat type." I reached in and picked up the bat with just my forefinger and thumb, near the middle, where it wouldn't mar any fingerprints left on it. I showed it to them. "Cowl would have used his magic to smash the car up, not a club." I walked around to the back of the car and frowned down at the engine. It looked intact. I leaned in the window and tried my key. The engine turned over without any trouble.

"Huh," Billy said. "Who completely ruins a car but doesn't touch the engine?"

"Someone sending me a message," I said.

Billy pursed his lips. "What does it say?"

"That I need to rent a car, apparently," I said. I shook my head. "I don't have time for this."

Billy and Georgia traded a look, and Georgia nodded. She came over to me, took my car keys where I held them in my cupped left hand, and replaced them with her own.

"Oh, hell, no," I said. "Don't do that."

"It's not a big deal," she told me. "Look, you still take your car to Mike's Garage, right?"

"Well, yeah, but—"

"But nothing," Billy said. "We're only a couple of blocks from the apartment. We'll get your car towed to Mike's."

Georgia nodded firmly. "Just bring back the SUV whenever the Beetle is ready."

I thought it over. Seeing my car torn up was actually a hell of a lot more distressing than I had thought it would be. It was only a machine. But it was *my* machine. Some part of me felt furious that someone had done this to my ride.

My first instinct was to refuse their offer, get the Beetle to the shop, and use cabs until then—but that was the anger talking. I forced myself to apply my brain to it, and figured that, given how much running around I might need to do in the near future, I couldn't afford it. I couldn't afford the time that public transportation would cost me, either, assuming I could use it at all. Damn, but I hate to swallow my pride.

"It's a new car. Something will blow out."

"It's still under warranty," Georgia said.

Billy gave me a thumbs-up. "Good hunting, Harry. Whatever you're after."

I nodded back to him and said, "Thanks."

I got into the SUV and headed out to speak to the only person in Chicago who knew as much about magic and death as I did.

Mortimer Lindquist had done pretty well for himself over the past couple of years, and he'd moved out of the little California-import stucco ranch house he'd been in the last time I'd gone to visit him. Now he was working out of a converted duplex in Bucktown. Mort leased both halves of the duplex, and ran his business on one side, with his home on the other. There were no cars in the business driveway, though he mostly operated at night. He must have already wrapped up for the evening. He had abandoned the faux-Gothic decor that had previously graced his place of business, which was a hopeful sign. I needed the help of someone with real skill, not a charlatan with a batch of gimmicks.

I parked the SUV in the business driveway, mowing down a patch of yellow pansies as I did. I wasn't used to driving something that big. The Beetle might be small and slow, but at least I knew exactly where its tires were going to go.

The lights were all out. I availed myself of the brass knocker hung on the residential door.

Fifteen minutes later, a bleary-looking little man answered. He was short, twenty or thirty pounds overweight, and had given up trying to conceal his receding hairline in favor of shaving his scalp completely bald. He was wrapped in a thick maroon bathrobe and wore grey slippers on his feet.

"It's three o'clock in the morning," Mort complained. "What the hell do you—" He saw my face and his eyes widened in panic. He hurried to shut the door.

I stabbed my oak staff into the doorway and stopped him from closing it. "Hi, Mort. Got a minute?"

"Go away, Dresden," the little man said. "Whatever it is you want, I don't have it."

I leaned on my staff and put on an affable smile. "Mort, after all we've been through together, I can't believe you'd speak to me like that."

Mort gestured furiously at a pale scar on his scalp. "The last time I had a conversation with you, I wound up with a concussion and fifteen stitches in my head."

"I need your help," I said.

"Ha," Mort said. "Thank you, but no. You might as well ask me to paint a target on my chest." He kicked at my staff, but not very hard. Those slippers wouldn't have protected his foot very well. "Get out, before something sees you here."

"Can't do that, Mort," I said. "There's black magic afoot. You know that, don't you?"

The little man stared at me in silence for a moment. Then he said, "Why do you think I want you gone? I don't want to be seen with you. I'm not involved."

"You are now," I said. I kept smiling, but all I really wanted to do was throw a jab at his nose. I guess my feelings must have leaked through into my expression, because Mort took one look at my face and blanched. "People are in trouble. I'm helping them. Now open this damned door and help me, or I swear to God I am going to come camp out on your lawn in my sleeping bag."

Mort's eyes widened, and he looked around outside the house, nervous energy making his eyes flick back and forth rapidly. "You son of a bitch," he said.

"Believe it."

He opened the door. I stepped inside and he shut it behind me, snapping several locks closed.

The interior of the house was clean, businesslike. The entry hall had been converted into a small waiting room, and beyond it lay the remainder of the first floor, a richly colored room lined with candles in sconces, now unlit, featuring a large table of dark polished wood surrounded by matching hand-carved chairs. Mort stalked into his séance room, picked up a box of kitchen matches, and started lighting a few candles.

"Well?" he asked. "Going to show me how all-powerful you are? Call up a gale in my study? Maybe slam a few doors for dramatic effect?"

"Would you like me to?"

He threw the matches down on the table and took a seat at its head. "Maybe I haven't been clear with you, Dresden," Mort said. "I'm not a wizard. I'm not with the Council. I have no interest in attracting their attention or that of their enemies. I am not a participant in your war with the vampires. I like my blood where it is."

"This isn't about the vampires," I said.

Mort frowned. "No? Are things dying down, then?"

I grimaced and took a seat a few chairs down. "There was a nasty fight in Mexico City three weeks ago, and the Wardens bloodied the Red Court's nose pretty well. Seems to have thrown a wrench in their plans for some reason."

"Getting ready to hit back," Mort said.

"Everyone figures that," I said. "We just don't know where or when."

Mort exhaled and leaned his forehead on the heel of one hand. "Did you know I found someone they'd killed a couple of years ago? Young boy, maybe ten years old."

"A ghost?" I asked.

Mort nodded. "Little guy had no idea what was going on. He didn't even know he was dead. They cut his throat with a razor blade. You could barely see the mark unless he turned to look over his right shoulder."

"That's what they do," I said. "How can you see things like that and not want to fight them?"

"Bad things *happen* to people, Dresden," Mort said. "I'm sorry as hell about it, but I'm not you. I don't have the power to change it."

"Like hell you don't," I said. "You're an ectomancer. One of the strongest I've met. You've got access to all kinds of information. You could do a lot of good."

"Information doesn't stop fangs, Dresden. If I start using what I know against them, I'd be a threat. Five minutes after I get involved I'll be the one with his throat cut."

"Better them than you, huh?"

He looked up and spread his hands. "I am what I am, Dresden. A coward. I don't apologize for it." He folded his fingers and regarded me soberly. "What's the fastest way for me to get you away from my home and out of my life?"

I leaned my staff against the table and slouched into my chair. "What do you know about what's been happening in town lately?"

"Black magic?" Mort asked. "Not much. I've had nightmares, which is unusual. The dead have been nervous for several days. It's been difficult to get them to answer a summons, even with Halloween coming up."

"Has that happened before?" I asked.

"Not on this scale," Mort said. "I've asked, but they won't explain to me why they're afraid. In my experience, it's one way that spiritual entities react to the presence of dark powers."

I nodded, frowning. "It's necromancy," I said. "You ever heard about a guy named Kemmler?"

Mort's eyes widened. "Oh, God. His disciples?"

"I think so," I said. "A lot of them."

Mort's face turned a little green. "That explains why they're so afraid."

"Why?"

He waved a hand. "The dead are terrified of whatever is moving around out there. Necromancers can enslave them. Control them. Even destroy them."

"So they can feel their power?" I asked.

"Absolutely."

"Good," I said. "I was counting on that."

Mort frowned and arched an eyebrow.

"I'm not sure how many of them are in town," I said. "I need to know where they are—or at least how many of them are here. I want you to ask the dead to help me locate them."

He lifted both hands. "They won't. I'll tell you that for certain. You couldn't get a ghost to willingly appear within screaming distance of a necromancer."

"Come on, Mort. Don't start holding out on me."

"I'm not," he said, and held up two fingers in a scout's hand signal. "My pledge of honor upon it."

I exhaled, frustrated. "What about residual magic?"

"What do you mean?"

"Whenever these necromancers work with dark magic it leaves a kind of stain or footprint. I can sense it if I get close enough."

"So why don't you do it?"

"It's a big town," I said. "And whatever these lunatics are up to, it's got to happen by midnight Halloween. I don't have time to walk a grid hoping to get close."

"And you think the dead will?"

"I think the dead can move through walls and the floor, and that there are a whole lot more of them than there are of me," I said. "If you ask them, they might do it."

"They might attract attention to themselves, you mean," Mort said. "No. They may be dead, but that doesn't mean that they can't get hurt. I won't risk that for Council infighting."

I blinked for a second. A few years ago Mort had barely been able to crawl out of his bottle long enough to cold-read credulous idiots into believing he could speak to their dead loved ones. Even after he had gotten his life together and begun to reclaim his atrophied talents, he had never displayed any particular indication that he wanted anything more than to turn a profit on his genuine skills rather than with fraud. Mort always looked out for number one.

But not tonight. I recognized the quiet, steady light in his eyes. He was not going to be pushed on this issue. Maybe Mort wasn't willing to go to the wall for his fellow human beings, but apparently with the dead it was different. I hadn't expected the little ectomancer to grow a backbone, even if it was only a partial one.

I weighed my options. I could always try to lean harder on Mort, but I was pretty sure that it wouldn't do me much good. I could try contacting the ghosts of Chicagoland myself—but while I knew the basic theory of ectomancy, I had no practical experience with it. I had no time to waste floundering around like a clueless newbie in an area of magic totally outside my practical experience.

"Mort," I said, "look. If you mean it, I'll respect that. I'll go right now."

He frowned, his eyes wary.

"But this isn't about wizard politics," I said. "Kemmler's disciples have already killed at least one person here in town, and they're going to kill more."

He slumped a little in his chair and closed his eyes. "Bad things happen to people, Dresden. That's not my fault."

"Please," I said. "Mort, I have a friend involved in this. If I don't deal with these assholes, she's going to get hurt."

He didn't open his eyes or answer me.

Dammit. I couldn't force him to help me. If he wasn't going to be moved, he wasn't going to be moved.

"Thanks for nothing then, Mort," I told him. My voice sounded more tired than bitter. "Keep on looking out for number one." I rose, picked up my staff, and walked toward the door.

I had it unlocked and half-open when Mort said, "What's her name?"

I paused and inhaled slowly. "It's Murphy," I said without turning around. "Karrin Murphy."

There was a long silence.

"Oh," Mort said then. "You should have just said so. I'll ask them."

I looked over my shoulder. The ectomancer stood up and walked over to a low bureau. He withdrew several articles and started laying them out on the table.

I shut the door and locked it again, then went back to the ectomancer. Mort unfolded a paper street map of Chicago and laid it flat on the table. Then he set candles at each of its corners and lit them. Finally he poured red ink from a little vial into a perfume atomizer.

After watching him for a moment, I asked, "Why?"

"I knew her father," Mort said. "I know her father."

"She's a good person," I said.

"That's what I hear." He closed his eyes for a moment and took a deep breath. "Dresden, I need you to be quiet for a while. I can't afford any distraction."

"All right," I said.

"I'm going to ask them," Mort said. "You won't hear me, but they will. I'll spray the ink into the air over the map, and they'll bring it down wherever they find one of your footprints."

"You think it will work?" I asked.

He shrugged. "Maybe. But I've never done this before." He closed his eyes and added, "Shhh."

I sat waiting and tried not to fidget. Mort was completely still for several minutes, and then his lips started moving. No sound came from them, except for the quiet sighs of breathing when he inhaled. He broke out into a sudden and heavy sweat, his bald head gleaming in the candlelight. The air suddenly vibrated against my face, and flashes of cold raced over my body at random. A second later I became acutely conscious of another presence in the room. Then another. And a third. Seconds after that, though I could see or hear no one, I became certain that the room was packed with people, and an accompanying sense of claustrophobia made me long to get outside into fresh air. It was definitely magic, but different from any I had felt before. I fought the trapped, panicked sensation and remained seated, still and quiet.

Mort nodded sharply, picked up the atomizer, and sprayed a mist of red ink into the air over the map.

I held my breath and leaned closer.

The mist drifted down over the map, but instead of settling into an even spread, the fine droplets began to swirl into miniature vortexes like tiny, bloody tornadoes sweeping over the map. Scarlet circles formed at the base of the minitornadoes, until the whirling cones spiraled down into vertical lines, then vanished.

Mort let out a grunt and slumped forward in his chair, gasping for breath.

I stood up and examined the street map by candlelight.

"Did it work?" Mort rasped.

"I think it did," I said. I put my finger beside one of the larger red circles. "This is the Forensic Institute. One of them created a zombie there earlier tonight."

Mort sat up and leaned forward over the map, his eyes glazed with fatigue. He pointed at another bloody dot. "That one. It's the Field Museum."

I traced my finger to another one. "This one is in a pretty tough neighborhood. I think it's an apartment building." I moved on to the next. "A cemetery. And what the hell, at O'Hare?"

Mort shook his head. "The ink's darker than the others. I think that means it's beneath the airport, in Undertown."

"Uh-huh," I said. "That makes sense. Two more. An alley down by Burnham Park, and a sidewalk on Wacker."

"Six," Mort said.

"Six," I agreed.

Six necromancers like Grevane and Cowl.

And only one of me.

Hell's bells.

Chapter

Eleven

I clipped my old iron mailbox with the front fender of the stupid SUV as I pulled into the driveway at my apartment. The box dented one corner of the vehicle's hood and toppled over with a heavy clang. I parked the SUV and shoved the pole the mailbox was mounted on back into the ground, but the impact had bent the pole. My mailbox leaned drunkenly to one side, but it stayed upright. Good enough for me.

I gathered up my gear, including the sawed-off shotgun I'd removed from the Beetle, and got indoors in a hurry.

I set things down and locked up my wards and the heavy steel door I'd had installed after a big, bad demon had huffed and puffed and blown down the original. It wasn't until I had them all firmly secured that I let out a slow breath and started to relax. The living room was lit only by the embers of the fire and a few tiny flames. From the kitchen alcove, I heard the soft thumping sound of Mouse's tail wagging against the icebox.

Thomas sat in the big comfy recliner next to the fire, absently stroking Mister. My cat, curled up on Thomas's lap, watched me with heavy-lidded eyes.

"Thomas," I said.

"All quiet on the basement front," Thomas murmured. "Once Butters wound down he just about dropped unconscious. I told him he could sleep in the bed."

"Fine," I said. I took my copy of *Erlking,* lit a few candles on the end table, and flopped down onto the couch.

Thomas arched an eyebrow.

"Oh," I said, sitting up. "Sorry, didn't think. You probably want to sleep."

"Not especially," he said. "Someone should keep watch, anyway."

"You all right?" I asked him.

"I just don't feel like sleeping right now. You can have the couch."

I nodded and settled down again. "You want to talk?"

"If I did, I'd be talking." He went back to staring at the fire and stroking the cat.

He was still upset, obviously, but I'd learned that it was pointless to start pushing Thomas, no matter how well-intentioned I might be. He'd dig in his heels from sheer obstinacy, and the conversation would get nowhere.

"Thanks," I said, "for looking out for Butters for me."

Thomas nodded.

We fell into a relaxed silence, and I started reading the book.

A while later I fell asleep.

I dreamed almost immediately. Threatening trees, mostly evergreens, rose up around a small glade. In its center a modest, neat campfire sparked and crackled. I could smell a lake somewhere nearby, moss and flowers and dead fish blending in with the scent of mildewed pine. The air was cold enough to make me shiver, and I hunched a little closer to the fire, but even so I felt like my back was to a glacier. From somewhere overhead came the wild, honking screams of migrating geese under a crescent moon. I didn't recognize the place, but it somehow seemed perfectly familiar.

A camping rig straddled the fire, holding a tin coffee mug and a suspended pot of what smelled like some kind of rich stew, maybe venison.

My father sat across the fire from me.

Malcolm Dresden was a tall, spare man with dark hair and steady blue eyes. His jeans were as heavily worn as his leather hiking boots, and I could see that he was wearing his favorite red-and-white flannel shirt under his fleece-lined hunting jacket. He leaned forward and stirred the pot, then took a sip from the spoon.

"Not bad," he said. He picked up a couple of tin mugs from one of the stones surrounding the fire and grabbed the coffeepot by its wooden handle. He poured coffee into both cups, hung the coffeepot back over the fire, and offered me one of them. "You warm enough?"

I accepted the mug and just stared at him for a moment. Maybe I had expected him to look exactly like I remembered, but he didn't. He looked so thin. He looked young, maybe even younger than me. And . . . so very, very ordinary.

"You go deaf, son?" my father asked, grinning. "Or mute?"

I fumbled for words. "It's cold out here."

"It is that," he agreed.

He pulled a couple of packs of powdered creamer from a knapsack, and passed them over to me along with a couple of packs of sugar. We prepared the coffee in silence and sipped at it for a few moments. It filled me with an earthy, satisfying warmth that made the terrible chill along my spine more bearable.

"This is a nice change of pace from my usual dream," I said.

"How so?" my father asked.

"Fewer tentacles. Fewer screams. Less death."

Just then, out in the blackness beneath the trees, something let out an eerie, wailing, alien cry. I shivered and my heart beat a little faster.

"The night is young," my father said dryly.

There was a rushing sound out in the woods, and I saw the tops of several trees swaying in succession as something, something big, moved among them. From tree to tree, the unseen threat moved, circling the little glade. I looked down and saw ripples on the surface of my coffee. My hand was trembling.

"What is that?" I asked.

"Beware the Jabberwock, my son," he said. He took a sip of his coffee and regarded the motion in the trees without fear. "You know what it is. You know what it wants."

I swallowed. "The demon."

He nodded, blue eyes on mine.

"I don't suppose—"

"I'm fresh out of vorpal swords," my father said. He reached into the pack and tossed me a miniature candy bar. "The closest I can get is a Snickers snack."

"You call that a funny line?" I asked.

"Look who's talking."

"So," I said. "Why haven't I dreamed about you before?"

"Because I wasn't allowed to contact you before," my father said easily. "Not until others had crossed the line."

"Allowed?" I asked. "What others? What line?"

He waved a hand. "It isn't important. And we don't have much time here before it returns."

I sighed and rubbed at my eyes. "Okay, I'm done with the stupid nostalgia dream. Why don't you go back to wherever you came from and I'll have a nice soothing dream of going to work naked."

He laughed. "That's better. I know you're afraid, son. Afraid for your friends. Afraid for yourself. But know this: You are not alone."

I blinked at him several times. "What do you mean?"

"I mean that I'm not a part of your own subconscious, son. I'm me. I'm real."

"No offense, but of course the dream version of you would say that," I said.

He smiled. "Is that what your heart tells you I am? A dreamed shadow of memory?"

I stared at him for a minute and then shook my head. "It can't be you. You're dead."

He stood up, walked around the fire, then dropped to one knee beside me. He put his hand on my shoulder. "Yes. I'm dead. But that doesn't mean that I'm not here. It doesn't mean that I don't love you, boy."

The light of the fire blurred in front of my eyes, and a horrible pang went through my chest. "Dad?"

His hand squeezed tighter. "I'm here."

"I don't understand it," I said. "Why am I so afraid?"

"Because you've got more to lose than you ever have before," he said. "Your brother. Your friends. You've opened yourself up to them. Loved them. You can't bear the thought of someone taking them away from you."

"It's getting to be too much," I said. My voice shook. "I just keep getting more wounded and tired. They just keep coming at me. I'm not some kind of superhero. I'm just *me*. And I didn't want any of this. I don't want to die."

He put his other hand on my other shoulder and faced me intently. I met his eyes while he spoke. "That fear is natural. But it is also a weakness. A path of attack for what would prey upon your mind. You must learn to control it."

"How?" I whispered.

"No one can tell you that," he said. "Not me. Not an angel. And not a fallen angel. You are the product of your own choices, Harry, and nothing can change that. Don't let anyone or anything tell you otherwise."

"But . . . my choices haven't always been very good," I said.

"Whose have?" he asked. He smiled at me and rose. "I'm sorry, son, but I have to go."

"Wait," I said.

He put his hand on my head, and for that brief second I was a child again, tired and small and utterly certain of my father's strength.

"My boy. There's so much still ahead of you."

"So much?" I whispered.

"Pain. Joy. Love. Death. Heartache. Terrible waters. Despair. Hope. I wish I could have been with you longer. I wish I could have helped you prepare for it."

"For what?" I asked him.

"Shhhhh," he said. "Sleep. I'll keep the fire lit until morning."

And darkness and deep, silent, blissfully restful night swallowed me whole.

Chapter

Twelve

The next morning my brain was throbbing with far too many thoughts and worries to allow for any productive thinking. I couldn't afford that. Until I knew exactly what was going on and how to stop it, the most important weapon in my arsenal was reason.

I needed to clear my head.

I got my running clothes on as quietly as I could, but as tired as Butters looked I could probably have decked myself in a full suit of Renaissance plate armor without waking him. I took Mouse on his morning walk, filled up a plastic sports bottle with cold water, and headed for the door.

Thomas stood waiting for me at the SUV, dressed as I was in shorts and a T-shirt. Only he made it look casually chic, whereas I looked like I bought my wardrobe at garage sales.

"Where's the Beetle?" he asked.

"Shop," I said. "Someone beat it up."

"Why?"

"Not sure yet," I said. "Feel like a run?"

"Why?" he asked.

"My head's full. Need to move."

Thomas nodded in understanding. "Where?"

"Beach."

"Sure," he said. He hooked a thumb at the SUV. "What's with the battleship?"

"Billy and Georgia loaned it to me."

"That was nice of them."

"Nice and stupid. It won't last long with me driving it." I sighed. "But I need the wheels. Come on. It's after dawn, but I still don't want to leave Butters alone for long."

He nodded, and we got into the SUV. "You want to tell me what's going on?"

"God, not until I can blow off some steam running."

"I hear you," he said, and we remained silent all the way to the beach.

North Avenue Beach is one of the most popular spots in town in the summer. On a cloudy morning at the end of October, though, not many folk were about. There were two other cars in the parking lot, probably belonging to the two other joggers moving steadily on the running trail.

I parked the SUV, and Thomas and I got out. I spent a couple of minutes stretching, though it probably wasn't as thorough as it should have been. Thomas just leaned against the SUV, watching me without comment. From what I've seen, vampires don't seem to have a real big problem with pulled muscles. I nodded to him, and we both hit the running trail, starting off at the slowest jog I could manage. I ran like that for maybe ten minutes before I felt warm enough to pick up the pace. Thomas matched me the whole time, his eyes half-closed and distant. My breathing hit a comfortable stride, hard but not labored. Thomas didn't breathe hard at first, either, but my legs are a lot longer than his, and I'd developed a taste for running as exercise over the past few years. I shifted into a higher gear, and finally made him start working to keep up with me.

We ran down the beach, past the beach house—a large structure built to resemble the top few decks of an old riverboat, giving the impression that the vessel had sunk into the sand of the beach. At the far end of the beach we would turn and come back. We went all the way down and back three times before I slowed the pace a little, and said, "So you wanna hear what's going on?"

"Yeah," he said.

"Okay." There was no one nearby, and by now the sun had risen enough to touch the top of the Chicago skyline behind me. Mavra couldn't have been listening in herself, and it was unlikely any mortal accomplice could, either. It was as close to ideal privacy as I was likely to get. I started with the arrival of Mavra's package and told Thomas of the events of the entire evening.

"You know what we should do?" Thomas asked when I was finished. "We should kill Mavra. We could make it a family project."

"No," I said. "If we take her out, Murphy will be the one to suffer for it."

"Yeah, yeah," Thomas said. "I'm pretty sure I know what Murphy would have to say about that."

"I don't want it to come to that," I said. "Besides, whatever this *Word of Kemmler* is, there are some seriously nasty people after it. It's probably a good idea to make sure they don't get it."

"Right," Thomas said. "So you keep it away from the nasty people so you can give it to the nasty vampire."

"Not if I can help it," I said.

"So Murphy gets burned anyway?" he asked.

I narrowed my eyes. "Not if I can help it."

"How are you going to manage that?"

"I'm working on it," I said. "The first step is to find *The Word of Kemmler,* or the whole thing is a bust."

"How do you do that?"

"The map," I said. "I don't think these guys are running around working the major black magic for no reason. I need to check out where they've been and figure out what they were doing."

"What about Butters?" Thomas asked.

"For now we keep him behind my wards. I don't know why Grevane wanted him, and until I figure it out he's got to keep his head down."

"I doubt Grevane was looking for a polka afficionado," Thomas said.

"I know. It's got something to do with one of the bodies at the morgue."

"So why not go there?" Thomas asked.

"Because the guard was killed there. There's blood all over the place, maybe the guard's body, and God only knows what Grevane did to the place after we left. The cops will have it locked down hard by now, and they'll definitely want to have a nice long talk with anyone who might have been there. I can't afford to spin my wheels in an interrogation room right now. Neither can Butters."

"So ask Murphy to look around," Thomas said.

I ground my teeth together for a few steps. "I can't. Murphy's on vacation."

"Oh," he said.

"I'm watering her plants."

"Right."

"While she's in Hawaii."

"Uh-huh," he said.

"With Kincaid."

Thomas stopped running.

I didn't.

He caught up to me a hundred yards later. "Well, that's a bitch."

I grunted. "I think she wanted me to tell her not to go," I said. "I think that's why she came to see me."

"So why didn't you?" he asked.

"Didn't realize it until it was too late. Besides, she's not my girlfriend. Or anything. Not my place to tell her who she should see." I shook my head. "Besides . . . I mean, if it was going to be right with Murphy, it would have been right before now, right? If we got all involved and it didn't work out, it would really screw things up for me. I mean, most of my living comes from jobs for SI."

"That's real reasonable and mature, Harry," Thomas said.

"It's smarter not to try to complicate things."

Thomas frowned at me for a moment. Then he said, "You're serious, aren't you?"

I shrugged. "I guess so. Yeah."

"Little brother," he said, "I simply cannot get over how stupid you are at times."

"Stupid? You just told me it was reasonable."

"Your excuses are," Thomas said, "but love isn't."

"We're not in love!"

"Never gonna be," Thomas said, "if you keep being all logical about it."

"Like you're one to talk."

Thomas's shoes hit the trail a little more sharply. "I know what it's like to lose it. Don't be an idiot, Harry. Don't lose it like I did."

"I can't lose what I haven't ever had."

"You have a *chance,*" he said, a snarl in his words, and I had the sudden sense that he had come precariously close to violent action. "And that's more than I've got."

I didn't push him. We got to the end of the trail and moved off it, slowing to walk down the beach, winding down. "Thomas," I said, "what's wrong with you today, man?"

"I'm hungry," he said, his voice a low growl.

"We can hit a McDonald's or something on the way home," I suggested.

He bared his teeth. "Not that kind of hunger."

"Oh." We walked awhile more, and I said, "But you fed just yesterday."

He laughed, a short and bitter sound. "Fed? No. That woman . . . that wasn't anything."

"She looked like she'd just run a marathon. You took from her."

"I took." He spat the words. "But there's no substance to it. I didn't take deeply from her. Not from anyone anymore. Not since Justine."

"But food is food, right?" I said.

"No," he said. "It isn't."

"Why?"

"It isn't like that."

"Then what *is* it like?"

"There's no point in telling you," he said.

"Why not?"

"You couldn't understand," he said.

"Not if you don't *tell* me, dolt," I said. "Thomas, I'm your brother. I want to understand you." I stopped and put my hand on his shoulder, shoving him just hard enough to make him turn to face me. "Look, I know it's not working out the way we hoped. But dammit, if you just go storming off every time you get upset about something, if you don't give me the chance to understand you, we're never going to get anywhere."

He closed his eyes, frustration evident on his face. He started walking down the beach, just at the edge of what passed for surf in Lake Michigan. I kept pace. He walked all the way down the beach, then stopped abruptly and said, "Race me back. Beat me there, and I'll tell you."

I blinked. "What kind of kindergarten crap is that?"

His grey eyes flashed with anger. "You want to know what it's like? Beat me down the beach."

"Of all the ridiculous, immature nonsense," I said. Then I hooked a foot behind Thomas's calf, shoved him down to the sand, and took off down the beach at a dead sprint.

There's an almost primal joy in the sheer motion and power of running a race. Children run everywhere for a reason—it's fun. Grown-ups can forget that sometimes. I stretched out my legs, still loose from the longer jog, and even though I was running across sand, the thrill of each stride filled my thoughts.

Behind me, Thomas spat out a curse and scrambled to his feet, setting out after me.

We ran through the grey light. The morning had dawned cold, and even at the lakeside the air was pretty dry. Thomas got ahead of me for a couple of steps, looked back, and kicked his heel, flinging sand into my face and eyes. I inhaled some of it, started gasping and choking, but managed to hook my fingers in the back of Thomas's T-shirt. I tugged hard as he stepped, and I outweighed Thomas considerably. He stumbled again, and, choking and gasping, I got ahead of him. I regained my lead and held it.

The last hundred yards were the worst. The cold, dry air and sand burned at my throat, that sharp, painful dryness that only a long run and hard breathing can really do to you. I swerved off the sand toward the parking lot, Thomas's footsteps close behind me.

I beat him back to the SUV by maybe four steps, slapped the back of the vehicle with my hand, then leaned against it, panting heavily. My throat felt like it had been baked in a kiln, and as soon as I could manage it I took the keys out of my black nylon sports pouch. There were several keys on the ring, and I fumbled at them one at a time. After the third wrong guess I had a brief, sharp urge to break the window and grab the bottle of water I'd left sitting in the driver's seat. I managed to force myself to try the keys methodically until I found the right one.

I opened the door, grabbed the bottle, twisted off the cap, and lifted it to ease the parched discomfort in my throat.

I took my first gulp, and the water felt and tasted like it had come from God's own water cooler. It took the harshest edge off the burning thirst, but I needed more to ease the discomfort completely.

Before I could swallow again, Thomas batted the water bottle out of my hand. It arched through the air and landed on the sand, spilling uselessly onto the beach.

I spun on Thomas, staring at him in surprised anger.

He met my gaze with weary grey eyes and said, "It's like that."

I stared at him.

"It's exactly like that." His expression didn't change as he went around and got into the SUV on the passenger side.

I stayed where I was for a moment, trying to ignore my thirst. It was all but impossible to do so. I thought about living with that discomfort and pain hour after hour, day after day, knowing that all I had to do was pick up a vessel filled with what I needed and empty it to make me feel whole. Would I be able to content myself with a quick splash of relief now and then? Would I be able to take enough to keep me alive?

For a time, perhaps. But time itself would make the thirst no easier to bear. Time would inevitably weigh me down. It would become more difficult to concentrate and to sleep, which would in turn undermine my self-control, which would make it more difficult to concentrate and sleep—a vicious cycle. How long would I be able to last?

Thomas had done it for most of a year.

I wasn't sure I would have done as well in his place.

I got into the SUV, closed the door, and said, "Thank you."

My brother nodded. "What now?"

"We go to 7-Eleven," I said. "Drinks are on you."

He smiled a little and nodded. "Then what?"

I took a deep breath. The run had helped me clear some of the crap out of my head. Talking to my brother had helped a little more. Understanding him a little better made me both more concerned and a bit more confident. I had my head together enough to see the next step I needed to take.

"The apartment. You keep an eye on Butters," I said. "I'm hitting these spots on the map to see what I can find. If I can't turn up anything on my own, I might have to go to the Nevernever for some answers."

"That's dangerous, isn't it?" he said.

I started the car and shrugged my shoulder. "It's a living."

Chapter

Thirteen

I took a shower, got dressed, and left Thomas behind with the still-sleeping Butters. Thomas settled down on the couch with a candle, a book, and an old U.S. cavalry saber he'd picked up in an estate sale and honed to a scalpel's edge. I left the sawed-off shotgun on the coffee table within arm's reach, and Thomas nodded his thanks to me.

"Keep an eye on him?" I asked.

Thomas turned a page. "Nothing will touch him."

Mouse settled down on the floor between Butters and the door, and huffed out a breath.

I got into the SUV and got out Mort's map. I headed for the nearest magical hot spot marked in bloody ink on the map—the spot of sidewalk on Wacker.

It was a bitch to find a parking place. It's never easy in Chicago, and I had a shot at a pretty good spot on the street, but while the Beetle would have managed just fine, the SS *Loaner* would have had to smash the cars on either side a few inches apart to fit. I wound up taking out a mortgage to pay for a parking space at a garage, walked a couple of city blocks, and proceeded down the street with my wizard's senses alert, feeling for the dark energy that the city's dead had found.

I found the spot on the sidewalk outside of a corner pharmacy.

It was so small I had walked almost completely through it before I felt it. It felt almost like walking into air-conditioning. The residual magic felt cold, like the other dark power I'd touched, terribly cold, and my skin erupted in goose bumps. I stopped on the spot, closed my eyes, and focused on the remaining energy.

It felt strange somehow. Dawn had dispersed most of the energy that had been there, but even as an aftertaste of the magic that had been worked there, the cold was dizzying. I'd felt dark power similar to this before today—similar, but not identical. There was something about this that was unlike the horrible aura surrounding Grevane, or that I had sensed from wielders of black magic in my past. This was undeniably the same power, but it somehow lacked the greasy, nauseating sense of corruption I'd felt before.

That was all I could sense. I frowned and looked around. There was a spot on the sidewalk that might have been a half-cleaned bloodstain, or might have been spilled coffee. Around me, business-day commuters came and went, some of them pausing to give me annoyed glares. Cars purred by on the street.

I checked at the pharmacy, but the place had been closed the night before, and no one had been there or heard about anything out of the ordinary. I checked the neighboring places of business, but it was a part of town where not much was open after six or seven in the evening, and no one had seen or heard about anything out of the ordinary.

Most of the time the investigation business is like that. You do a lot of looking and not finding. The cure for it is to do more looking. I walked back to the SUV and went to the next spot on the map, at the Field Museum.

The Field Museum is on Lake Shore Drive, and occupies the whole block north of Soldier's Field. I felt a brief flash of gratitude that things usually went to hell during the workweek. If this had been a Sunday with the Bears at home, I'd have had to park and then backpack in from Outer Mongolia. As it was, I got a spot in the smaller parking lot in the same block as the museum, which cost me only a portion of the national gross income.

I walked to the entrance from the parking lot, and slowed my steps for a few strides. There were two patrol cars and an ambulance parked outside the Field Museum's main entrance. Aha. This stop looked like it might be a bit more interesting than the last one.

The doors had just opened for normal visiting hours, and it cost me yet more of my money to get a ticket. My wallet was getting even more anorexic than usual. At this rate I wouldn't be able to afford to protect mankind from the perils of black magic. Hell's bells, that would be really embarrassing.

I went in the front entrance. It's impressively big. The first thing my eyes landed on was the crown jewel of the Field Museum—Sue, the largest, most complete, and most beautifully preserved skeleton of a Tyrannosaurus rex ever discovered. They're the actual petrified bones, too—none of this cheap plastic modeling crap for the tourists. The museum prided itself on the authenticity of the exhibit, and with reason. There's no way to stand in Sue's shadow, to see the bones of the enormous hunter, its size, its power, its enormous teeth, without feeling excruciatingly edible.

Late October is not the museum's high traffic season, and I saw only a couple of other visitors in the great entrance hall. Museum security was in evidence, a couple of men in brown quasi-uniforms, and an older fellow with greying hair and a comfortable-looking suit. The man in the suit stood next to an unobtrusive doorway, talking to a couple of uniformed police officers, neither of whom I recognized.

I moseyed over closer to the three of them, casually browsing over various exhibits until I could get close enough to Listen in.

". . . damnedest thing," the old security chief was saying. "Never would have figured that this kind of business would happen here."

"People are people," said the older of the two cops, a black man in his forties. "We can all get pretty crazy."

The younger cop was a little overweight and had a short haircut the color of steamed carrots. "Sir, do you know of anyone who might have had some kind of argument with Mister Bartlesby?"

"Doctor," the security man said. "Dr. Bartlesby."

"Right," said the younger cop, writing on a notepad. "But do you know of anyone like that?"

The security man shook his head. "Dr. Bartlesby was a crotchety old bastard. No one liked him much, but I don't know of anyone who disliked him enough to kill him."

"Did he associate with anyone here?"

"He had a pair of assistants," the security chief replied. "Grad students, I think. Young woman and a young man."

"They a couple?" the younger cop asked.

"Not that I could tell," the security chief said.

"Names?" the older cop asked.

"Alicia Nelson was the girl. The guy was Chinese or something. Lee Shawn or something."

"Does the museum have records on them?" the cop asked.

"I don't think so. They came in with Dr. Bartlesby."

"How long have you known the doctor?" the older cop asked.

"About two months," the security chief said. "He was a visiting professor doing a detailed examination of one of the traveling exhibits. It's already been taken down and packed up. He was due to leave in a few more days."

"Which exhibit?" the young cop asked.

"One of the Native American displays," the security man supplied. "Cahokian artifacts."

"Ka-what?" the older cop asked.

"Cahokian," the security chief said. "Amerind tribe that was all over the Mississippi River valley seven or eight hundred years ago, I guess."

"Were these artifacts valuable?" asked the older cop.

"Arguably," the security chief said. "But their value is primarily academic. Pottery shards, old tools, stone weapons, that kind of thing. They wouldn't be easy to liquidate."

"People do crazy things," the young cop said, still writing.

"If you say so," the security chief said. "Look, fellas, the museum would really like to get this cleared up as quickly as possible. It's been hours already. Can't we get the remains taken out now?"

"Sorry, sir," the older cop said. "Not until the detectives are done documenting the scene."

"How long will that take?" the security chief asked.

The older cop's radio clicked, and he took it off his belt and had a brief conversation. "Sir," he told the security chief, "they're removing the body now. Forensics will be over in a couple of hours to sweep the room."

"Why the delay?" the chief asked.

The cop answered with a shrug. "But until then, I'm afraid we'll have to close down access to the crime scene."

"There are a dozen different senior members of the staff with offices off of that hallway," the security chief protested.

"I'm sure they'll finish up as quickly as they can, sir," the cop said, though his tone brooked no debate.

"Told my boss I'd give it a try." The chief sighed. "You want to come explain it to him?"

"Glad to," the cop said with a forced smile. "Lead the way." The two cops and the security chief strode off together, presumably to talk to somebody with an office, a receptionist, and an irritatingly skewed perspective on the importance of isolating a crime scene.

I chewed on my lip. I was pretty sure that the apparent murder the cops were talking about and my hot spot of dark magic had to be related to each other. But if the hot spot was located on a murder site, it would be shut away from any access. Forensics could spend hours, even days, going over a room for evidence.

That meant that if I wanted to get a look around, I had to move immediately. From what the cops had said, Forensics wasn't there yet. The men moving the body were part of the new civilian agency the city government was employing to transport corpses around town, judging from the ambulance outside. Both cops were with the security chief, which would mean that at most there was maybe a detective and a cop at the crime scene. There might be a chance that I could get close enough to see something.

It took me about two seconds to make up my mind. The minute the security chief was out of sight, I slipped through the nondescript doorway, down a flight of stairs, and into the plain and unassuming hallways meant for the Field Museum's staff instead of its visitors. I passed a small alcove with a fridge, a counter, and a coffee machine. I picked up a cup of coffee, a bagel, a newspaper, and a spiral notebook someone had left there. I piled up everything in my arms and tried to look like a bored academic on his way to his office. I had no clue where I was going yet, but I tried to walk like I knew what I was doing, reaching out with my arcane senses in an effort to feel where the remnants of the hot spot might be.

I chose intersections methodically, left each time. I hit a couple of dead ends, but tried to keep close track of where I was going. The complex of tunnels and hallways under the Field Museum could swallow a small army without needing a glass of water, and I couldn't afford to get lost down there.

It took me fifteen minutes to find it. One hallway had been marked with crime-scene tape, and I homed in on it. Even before I turned down the hall, my senses prickled with uneasy cold. I'd found my hot spot of necromantic energy, and there was a murder scene at its center. I heard footsteps and slipped to one side, remaining still as a pair of cops in suits came out, arguing quietly with each other about the shortest path outside so that they could smoke. They'd been cooped up with the body, taking pictures and documenting the scene since before anyplace had been open for breakfast, and neither one of them sounded like he was in a good mood.

"Rawlins," said one of them into his radio, "where the hell are you?"

"Talking to some administrator," came the reply, the voice of the older cop from upstairs.

"How soon can you get down here to watch the site?"

"Give me a few minutes."

"Dammit," cursed the other detective. "Bastard is doing this on purpose."

The one with the radio nodded. "Screw this. I've been on duty since noon yesterday. We've got the scene documented. It'll keep for two minutes while he walks his slow ass down here."

The other detective nodded his agreement and they left.

I set my props aside and slipped under the tape and down the hallway. There were office doors every couple of steps, all closed. At the end of the hall a door stood open, the lights on. I might have only a few minutes, and if I was going to learn anything it had to be now. I hurried forward.

There might not have been a body there anymore, but even before I saw it, the room stank of death. It's an elusive scent, something that you get as a bonus to other smells, rather than a distinctive smell of its own. The thick, sweet odor of blood was in the air, mixed in with the faint stench of offal. There was the musty, moldy smell of old things long underground, too, as well as a few traces of something spicier, maybe some kind of incense. The death scent was mixed all through it, something sharp and unnerving, halfway between burned meat and cheap ammonia-based cleaner. My stomach rolled uncomfortably, and the rising sense of dark energy didn't help me keep it calm.

The office was a fairly large one. Shelves and filing cabinets lined the walls. Three desks sat clumped together in the middle of the room. A small refrigerator sat in the corner, near an old couch and a coffee table littered with mostly empty boxes of Chinese takeout and a laptop computer. Books and boxes filled the shelves. The desks were cluttered with books, notebooks, folders, and a few personal articles—a novelty coffee mug, a couple of picture frames, and some recent popular novels.

Everything had been splattered with blood and dark magic.

The blood had dried out, and most of it was either red-black or dark brown. There was a large pool on the floor between the door and the nearest desk, dried into a sticky sludge. A sharp, almost straight line marked where the corpse had been lifted, probably peeling up the hem of a jacket or coat from where it had been stuck to the floor. Droplets had splattered the walls, the desk, the photographs, the novels, and the novelty mugs.

I hated blood. As a decorating theme it left something to be desired. And it smelled horrible. My stomach twisted again, and I fought to keep down the doughnuts I'd grabbed at the convenience store. I closed my eyes and then forced myself to open them again. To look. The only way to avoid more scenes like this was to look at this one, figure out who had done it, and then to go stop them from doing it again.

I pushed my revulsion away and focused on the scene, searching for details.

There were a few smears of blood on the floor but none on the sides, surface, or edge of the nearest desk. That meant that the victim hadn't moved much after he'd gone down. Either he'd been held down or he'd bled out so quickly that he hadn't had time to crawl toward the nearest phone, on the desk, to call for help. I looked up. There wasn't much blood on the ceiling. That didn't prove anything, but if someone had opened his throat, there would almost certainly have been blood sprayed all over it. Any other kind of bleeding wound would probably have left the victim, evidently Dr. Bartlesby, able to function, at least for a couple of minutes. He'd probably been held down.

I looked down. There was part of a footprint in blood on the floor, leading away. It looked like part of the heel of an athletic shoe—and not a large one, either. Probably a woman's shoe, or a large child's. For the sake of my ability to sleep at night, I hoped it was an adult's shoe. Children shouldn't see such things.

Then again, who should?

On an entirely different level, the room was even more disturbing. The dark power here was not the pure, silent cold I'd felt on the sidewalk on Wacker. It felt corrupt, dark, somehow mutilated. There was a sense of malicious glee to the residue of whatever magic had been worked here. Someone had used their power to murder a man—and they had loved doing it. Worse, it was a distinctly different aura than I had felt near either Cowl or Grevane. Magical workings didn't leave behind an exact fingerprint that could be traced to a given wizard, but intuition told me that this working had been sloppier and more frenetic than something Grevane would have done, and messier than Cowl would prefer.

But it was strong—stronger magic than almost anything I had ever done. Whoever was behind the spell that had been wrought here was at least as powerful as I was. Maybe stronger.

"Heh," drawled a voice from behind me. "I thought that was you."

I stiffened and turned around. The older of the two cops from upstairs stood ten feet down the hall from me, one hand resting casually on the butt of his sidearm. His dark face was wary, but not openly hostile, and his stance one of caution but not alarm. The name tag on his jacket read RAWLINS.

"Thought who was me?" I asked him.

"Harry Dresden," he said. "The wizard. The guy Murphy hires for SI."

"Yeah," I said. "I guess that's me."

He nodded. "I saw you upstairs. You didn't look like your typical museum patron."

"It was the big leather coat, wasn't it?" I said.

"That helped," Rawlins acknowledged. "What are you doing down here?"

"Just looking," I said. "I haven't gone into the room."

"Yeah. You can tell that from how I haven't arrested you yet."

Rawlins looked past me, into the room, and his expression sobered. "Hell of a thing in there."

"Yeah," I said.

"Something don't feel right about it," he said. "Just . . . I don't know. Sets my teeth on edge. More than usual. I've seen knifings before. This is different."

"Yeah," I said. "It is."

Dark eyes flicked back to me, and the old cop exhaled. "This is something from down SI's way?"

"Yeah."

He grunted. "Murphy send you?"

"Not exactly," I said.

"Why you here then?"

"Because I don't like things that put cops' teeth on edge," I said. "You guys have any suspects?"

"For someone who just happened to be walking by, you got a lot of questions," he said.

"For a beat cop in charge of securing the scene, you were asking plenty of your own," I said. "Upstairs, with museum security."

He grinned, teeth very white. "Shoot. I been a detective before. Twice."

I lifted my eyebrows. "Busted back down?"

"Both times, on account of I have an attitude problem," Rawlins said.

I gave him a lopsided smile. "You going to arrest me?"

"Depends," he said.

"On what?"

"On why you're here." He met my gaze directly, openly, his hand still on his gun.

I didn't meet his eyes for very long. I glanced over my shoulder, debating how to answer, and decided to go with a little sincerity. "There are some bad people in town. I don't think the police can get them. I'm trying to find them before they hurt anyone else."

He studied me for a long minute. Then he took his hand off the gun and reached into his coat. He tossed me a folded newspaper.

I caught it and unfolded it. It was some kind of academic newsletter, and on the cover page was a photograph of a portly old man with sideburns down to his jaw, together with a smiling young woman and a young man with Asian features. The caption under the picture read, *Visiting Professor Charles Bartlesby and his assistants, Alicia Nelson, Li Xian, prepare to examine Cahokian collection at the FMNH, Chicago.*

"That's the victim in the middle," Rawlins said. "His assistants shared the office with him. They have not been answering their cell phone numbers and are not in their apartments."

"Suspects?" I asked.

He shrugged. "Not many people murder strangers," he said. "They were the only ones in town who knew the victim. Came in with him from England somewhere."

I looked from the newsletter up to Rawlins, and frowned. "Why are you helping me?"

He lifted his eyebrows. "Helping you? You could have found that anywhere. And I never saw you."

"Understood," I said. "But why?"

He leaned against the wall and folded his arms. "Because when I was a young cop, I went running down an alley when I heard a woman scream. And I saw something. Something that . . ." His face became remote. "Something that has given me bad dreams for about thirty years. This *thing* strangling a girl. I push it away from her, empty my gun into it. It picks me up and slams my head into a wall a few times. I figured Mama Rawlins's baby boy was about to go the way of the dodo."

"What happened?" I asked.

"Lieutenant Murphy's father showed up with a shotgun loaded with rock salt and killed it. And when the sun comes up, it burns this thing's corpse like it had been soaked in gasoline." Rawlins shook his head. "I owed her old man. And I seen enough of the streets to know that she's been doing a lot of good. You been helping her with that."

I nodded. "Thank you," I told him.

He nodded. "Don't really feel like losing my job for you, Dresden. Get out before someone sees you."

Something occurred to me. "You heard about the Forensic Institute?"

He shrugged at me. "Sure. Every cop has."

"I mean what happened there last night," I said.

Rawlins shook his head. "I haven't heard of anything."

I frowned at him. A grisly murder at the morgue would have been all over the place, in police scuttlebutt if not in the newspapers. "You haven't? Are you sure?"

"Sure, I'm sure."

I nodded at him and walked down the hallway.

"Hey," he said.

I looked over my shoulder.

"Can you stop them?" Rawlins asked.

"I hope so."

He glanced at the bloodied room and then back at me. "All right. Good hunting, kid."

Chapter

Fourteen

"**W**ow," Butters said, fiddling with the control panel on the SUV. "This thing has everything. Satellite radio stations. And I bet I could put my whole CD collection inside the changer on this player. And, oh, cool, check it out. It's got an onboard GPS, too, so we can't get lost." Butters pushed a button on the control panel.

A calm voice emerged from the dashboard. "Now entering Helsinki."

I arched an eyebrow at the dashboard and then at Butters. "Maybe the car is lost."

"Maybe you're interfering with its computer, too," Butters said. "You think?"

He smiled tightly, checking his seat belt for the tenth time. "Just so we're clear, I have no problems with hiding, Harry. I mean, if you're worried about my ego or something, don't. I'm fine with the hiding. Happy, even."

I pulled off the highway. The green lawns and tended trees of the industrial park hosting the Forensic Institute appeared as the SUV rolled up the ramp. "Try to relax, Butters."

He jerked his head in a nervous, negative shake. "I don't want to get killed. Or arrested. I'm really bad at being arrested. Or killed."

"It's a calculated risk," I said. "We need to find out what Grevane wanted with you."

"And we're taking me to work . . . why?"

"Think about it. What would have happened if they'd found you missing, blood all over the place, the building ransacked, and Phil's corpse lying in the morgue or on the lawn outside?"

"Someone would have gotten fired," Butters said.

"Yeah. And they would have locked down the building to search for evidence. And they would have grabbed you and locked you away somewhere, for questioning at least."

"So?" Butters asked.

"If Grevane cleaned up what happened at the morgue, it means he didn't want too much official attention focused there. Whatever he wants from you, I'm betting it's still in the building." I pulled into the industrial park. "We have to find it."

"Eduardo Mendoza?" he asked me.

"Offhand, I can't think of any other reason for someone to want to grab your friendly neighborhood assistant medical examiner," I said. "Grevane's got to be interested in a corpse at the morgue, and that one was the only one that seemed a little odd."

"Harry," Butters said, "if this guy really is a necromancer—a wizard of the dead—then why the hell would he need a plain old vanilla science nerd like me?"

"That's the sixty-four-thousand-dollar question," I said. "And we have another reason, too."

"The museum doctor guy, right?" Butters asked.

I nodded at him and parked in the lot next to Butters's ruined little truck. "Right. I need to know what killed him. Hell, any information could be useful."

Butters exhaled. "Well. I don't know what I'll be able to manage."

"Anything is more than I have now."

He looked around warily. "Do you think . . . do you think Grevane or his buddy is out there right now? Watching for . . . you know . . . me?"

I pulled open my coat and showed Butters my shoulder holster and gun. Then I reached behind me and drew out my staff from the back of the SUV. "If they show up, I'm going to ruin their whole day."

He chewed on his lip. "You can do that, right?"

I took a look around and said, "Butters, trust me. If there's one thing I'm good at, it's ruining people's day."

He let out a nervous little laugh. "You can say that again."

"If there's one thing I'm good at—" I began. Butters punched me lightly on the arm, and I smiled at him. "We'll get in and out as quick as we can, get you back under cover. I think we've got it under control."

I killed the SUV's ignition and pulled out the key. The truck shuddered, and a warbling, wailing sound came from the dashboard. For a second I expected someone to shout, "Red alert, all hands to battle stations!" Instead there was a hiccup of sound from the truck, and then a smooth, recorded voice reported, "Warning. The door is ajar. The door is ajar."

I blinked at the dashboard. It repeated the warning several more times, getting a little slower and lower pitched each time, then droned into a basso rumble, followed by silence.

"That was not an omen," I said firmly.

"Right," Butters replied in a faint voice. "Because stuff is always messing up around you."

"Exactly," I said. I tried to think of a way to wring positive spin from that last statement, but I wasn't up to the mental gymnastics. "Come on. The sooner we get moving, the sooner we get you out of here."

"Okay," he said, and the pair of us got out of the SUV and headed for the Forensic Institute. As we approached the door, I started limping and leaning on my staff a little, as if I needed the support. Butters opened the door for me, and I hobbled in with a pained expression on my face as we approached the security desk.

I didn't know the guard on duty. He was in his mid-twenties and looked athletic. He watched us coming, squinting a little, and when we were well inside his eyebrows lifted. "Dr. Butters," he said, evidently surprised. "I haven't seen you in a while."

"Casey," Butters said, giving him a jerky nod of the head. "Hey, I like the new haircut. Is Dr. Brioche in?"

"He's working now," Casey said. "Room one, I think. What are you doing here?"

"Hoping to avoid a lecture," Butters replied dryly. He clipped his identification to his coat. "I forgot to file some forms, and if I don't get them done before the mail goes out, Brioche will scold me until my eyes bleed."

Casey nodded and looked me over. "Who's this?"

"Harry Dresden," Butters said. "He's got to sign off on the forms. He's a consultant for the police department. Harry, this is Casey O'Roarke."

"Charmed," I said, and handed him the laminated identification card Murphy had issued me to get me through police lines to crime scenes. As I did, I felt another cold pocket of dark energy. Grevane had murdered and then reanimated Phil while the poor guy was sitting at his desk.

Casey examined the card, checked my face against the picture on it, and passed it back to me with a polite smile. "You want me to tell Dr. Brioche you're here, Dr. Butters?"

Butters shuddered. "Not particularly."

"Right," Casey said, and waved us past. We were almost out of the entry hall when he spoke again. "Doctor? Did you see Phil this morning?"

Butters hesitated for a second before he turned around. "He was there at the desk the last time I saw him, but I had to leave for an early dentist appointment. Why?"

"Oh, he wasn't at the desk when I got here," Casey said. "Everything was locked down, and the security system was armed."

"Maybe he had somewhere to be, too," Butters suggested.

"Maybe," Casey agreed. There was a faint frown line between his eyes. "He didn't tell me anything, though. I mean, I'd have come in early if he had an appointment or something."

"Beats me," Butters said.

Casey squinted at Butters and then nodded slowly. "Okay. I just wouldn't want him to get in trouble over breaking protocol."

"You know Phil," Butters said.

Casey rolled his eyes and nodded, then went back to filling out some kind of paperwork. Butters and I slipped away from the entry hall and down to Butters's usual examination room. The place had been put back together. His desk rested in its usual spot, piled with papers and his computer. Whoever had cleaned up the room had done a fairly good job of it.

"Casey knows something," Butters said the minute the door was shut. "He suspects something."

"That's what they pay security to do," I said. "Don't let it rattle you."

Butters nodded, looking around the examination room. He walked over to his polka suit, still piled in the corner. "At least they didn't wreck this," he said. Then he let out a short laugh. "Man. Are my priorities skewed or what?"

"Everyone has something they love," I said.

He nodded. "Okay. So what do we do now?"

"First things first," I said. "Can you get a look at Bartlesby's corpse?"

Butters nodded and walked over to his computer. I backed up and stood against the wall.

Butters started the thing up and spent a minute or two waggling a mouse and stabbing at keys with his forefinger. Then he whistled. "Wow. Bartlesby's body got here about an hour ago, and it's been flagged for immediate examination. Brioche is doing it."

"Is that unusual?" I asked.

He nodded. "It means someone really wants to know about the victim. Someone in government or law enforcement, maybe." He wrinkled up his nose. "Plus it was pretty horrific. Brioche will get some press out of it. Of course he took this one for himself."

"Can you get to it?" I asked.

Butters frowned and tapped a few more keys. Then he looked up at the clock. "Maybe. Brioche is working in room one right now, but he's got to be almost finished with whatever he's doing. Bartlesby's corpse is in room two. If I hurry . . ." He stood up and scurried for the door. "Wait here."

"You sure?" I asked him.

He nodded. "Someone really would get suspicious if they saw you roaming around. If I need you I'll give you a signal."

"What signal?"

"I'll imitate the scream of a terrified little girl," he said with a waggle of his eyebrows. He headed out the door. "Back in a minute."

Butters wasn't gone long, and he slipped back into the room before five minutes had passed. He looked a little shaky.

"You all right?" I asked.

He nodded. "Couldn't stay there for long. I heard Brioche come out of room one."

"You see the body?"

"Yeah," Butters said with a shudder. "It was already stripped and laid out. Bad stuff, Harry. He had thirty or forty stab wounds in his upper thorax. Someone carved his face up, too. His nose, ears, eyelids, and lips were in a sandwich Baggie next to his head." He took a deep breath. "Someone had sliced off the quadriceps on both legs. They were missing. And he'd been eviscerated."

I frowned. "How?"

"A big X-shaped cut across his abdomen. Then they peeled him open like a Chinese take-out box. He was missing his stomach and most of his intestines. There might have been other organs gone, too."

"Ick," I said.

"Extremely."

"Could you see anything else?"

"No. Even if I'd wanted to, there wasn't time for more than a quick look." He walked over to a rolling stand of medical instruments. "Why would someone do that to him? What possible purpose could it have served?"

"Maybe some kind of ritual," I said. "You've seen that before."

Butters nodded. He went through the motions of pulling on an apron, mask, gloves, cap—the works. "I still don't get it. You know?"

I did know. Butters didn't have it in him to comprehend the kind of violence, hatred, and bloodlust that had fallen upon the late Bartlesby. That kind of utter disregard for the sanctity of life simply didn't exist in his personal world, and it left him at a total loss when confronted with it face-to-face.

"Or," I said, a thought occurring to me, "it might have been something else. Anthropomancy."

He walked over to one of the freezers and cracked it open. "What's that?"

"An attempt to divine the future or gain information by reading human entrails."

Butters turned to me slowly, his face sickened. "You're kidding."

I shook my head. "It's possible."

"Does it work?" he asked.

"It's extremely powerful and dangerous magic," I answered. "Anyone who does it has to kill someone and gets an immediate death sentence if the Council learns of it. If it didn't work, no one would bother."

Butters's mouth hardened into a firm line. "That's . . . really wrong." He frowned over the sentence and then nodded. "Wrong."

"I agree."

He turned back to the freezer, checked a toe tag, and then hauled a rolling exam table over to it. "This might take me a little while," he said. "An hour and a half, maybe more."

"You want a hand with that?" I asked. I hoped he didn't.

Butters, bless him, shook his head. He walked over to his desk and flicked on his CD player. Polka music filled the room. "I'd really rather do this alone."

"You sure?" I asked.

"Just listen for a girlie scream," he said. "Can you wait for me up front?"

I nodded, leaned my staff in the corner, and left him in the room. He locked the door behind me, and I wandered up to sit down in the waiting area near the front doors. I took a chair that put the wall to my back, and where I could see Casey's video monitor, the front door, and the door leading back to the examination rooms.

I leaned my head back against the wall with my eyes mostly closed and waited. Over the next hour one doctor came in and another left. The mailman showed up with the day's deliveries, as did the UPS truck. An ambulance arrived with the cadaver of an old woman that Casey rolled away, presumably into storage.

Then a young couple came in. The girl was about five-six and pleasantly pretty, even without much in the way of makeup. She was dressed in sandals, a simple blue sundress, and a wool jacket. Her hair was cut into a bob full of unruly brown curls, and her eyes were bloodshot with fatigue. The young man wore a simple, well-cut business suit. He was a little under six feet tall, had Asian features, wire-rimmed glasses, wide shoulders, and wore his hair in a long ponytail.

I recognized them: Alicia Nelson and Li Xian, from the picture on the cover of the newsletter Rawlins had given me. Dr. Bartlesby's missing assistants had come to the morgue.

I remained very still, and tried to think thoughts that would make me blend in with the wall. They walked to the security desk and stood so close to me that I didn't need to bother with Listening to them.

"Good morning," Alicia said, producing a driver's license and showing it to Casey. "My name is Alicia Nelson. I'm the late Dr. Bartlesby's assistant. I understand that his remains have been brought here."

Casey regarded her without much in the way of expression. "Ma'am, we do not make that kind of information available to the public, in order to protect the relatives of the deceased."

She nodded, drew an envelope out of her purse, and passed that to Casey as well. "The doctor had no surviving family or next of kin," she said. "But he granted me power of attorney over his estate two years ago. The paperwork is all in order."

Casey scanned it, frowning. "Mmmmph."

Alicia pushed brown curls wearily from her eyes. "Please, sir, the doctor had several personal effects which I need to take into custody as soon as possible. Passwords, credit cards, keys, that sort of thing. They were in his wallet."

"What's the rush?" Casey drawled.

"Some of his effects could potentially grant a thief access to his accounts and security boxes. As you can see in the documents, he wanted control of them to pass to me until I could arrange to have them passed on to the charities he patronized."

Casey folded up the pages again and put them back in the envelope. "Ma'am, you're going to have to speak with our director, Dr. Brioche. I'm sure he'll be happy to help you out."

"All right," Alicia agreed. "Is he available?"

"I'll go speak to him," Casey said. "If you'll wait here, please."

"Of course," the girl replied. She waited for Casey to go through the security door and then spun on her heel and stalked over to the entrance, staring out at the morning sunlight. Her posture was stiff with anger. She leaned her forearm on the glass door and pressed her forehead to it.

The tall young man, Li Xian, had remained silent the whole while. He followed her over to the door and spoke in a quiet voice I could scarcely hear. I narrowed my eyes and Listened.

". . . back at any moment," Xian murmured. "We should sit down."

"Don't tell me what to do," Alicia shot back in a heated whisper. "I'm weary, not idiotic."

"You should get some rest before you do anything more," Xian said. "I don't see why you're playing games. You should have let me follow the guard back."

"Stop thinking with your stomach," the girl growled. "It's bad enough that you lost control without adding a further lack of discipline to the situation."

"We are not here because I stopped to eat," Xian replied, anger of his own in his whisper. "If you hadn't indulged yourself we wouldn't face this problem."

The girl spun from the glass, facing Xian squarely, her face contorted with pride and anger. "Your attitude, Li, is making you part of the problem. Not part of the solution."

The long-haired man went white and cringed back from the girl. His face rippled, a sort of slithery motion just beneath the surface of his skin that stretched his features grotesquely, causing a slight sinking of the eyes, a slight elongation of the jaw. He let out a gasp, and when his mouth opened I could see the teeth of a carnivore.

It happened for only a second, but I averted my eyes before he might have noticed me watching him. If he had seen me, I would have been in immediate danger. I'd seen a flash of Li Xian's true face—he was a ghoul. Ghouls are preternatural predators who derive their primary sustenance from devouring human flesh. Fresh, cold, rotting, they don't care as long as it gets into their bellies.

My stomach turned. Butters said that someone had removed Bartlesby's quadriceps, the long, strong muscles on the front of the thigh. It had been Xian. He'd carved himself steaks from the old man's corpse. If he suspected that I knew what he was, he might decide to protect himself with extreme prejudice, and that would be bad. Ghouls are quick, strong, and harder to kill than a juicy rumor about the president. I'd fought ghouls before, and it wasn't something I wanted to repeat if I could avoid it. Especially given that I'd left my staff in Butters's office.

Xian recovered his normal appearance and lowered his eyes. He bowed his head to Alicia.

"Do I make myself clear?" the girl whispered.

"Yes, my lord," Xian replied.

Lord? I thought. My mind raced over the possibilities.

Alicia exhaled and pressed her thumb against the spot between her eyebrows. "Don't talk, Xian. Just don't talk. We'll all be happier. And safer." She breezed past him, back to the little waiting area, and sat down. She picked up a copy of *Newsweek* sitting out on an end table and began to flick through it, while Xian remained standing near the door. I pretended to be drowsing.

Casey returned a couple of minutes later and said, "Ms. Nelson, it's going to be a while before Dr. Brioche can see you."

"How long?" she asked, smiling.

"An hour or so at least," Casey said. "He says that if you'd like to make an appointment for this afternoon that he will be glad to—"

"No," she interrupted him, shaking her head firmly. "Some of his business is time-critical, and I need to recover his effects at the earliest possible opportunity. Please tell him that I will wait."

Casey lifted his eyebrows and then shrugged. "Yes, ma'am."

I blinked my eyes a few times and then sat up straight, stretching. "Oh, hey, Casey," I mumbled, standing. I feigned a limp and went to the desk. "I left my cane in Butters's office. Would it be okay to go back and grab it?"

Casey nodded. "One second." He picked up the phone, and a second later I heard polka music pumping through the little speaker. "Doctor, your consultant friend forgot something in your office. You want me to send him back?" He listened, nodding, and then waved me at the door, buzzing me through.

I hurried back to Butters's examination room and knocked. Butters unlocked the door to let me in.

"Hurry," I told him, glancing back down the hall. "We've got to go."

Butters gulped. "What's going on?"

"There are some bad guys here."

"Grevane?" he asked.

"No. New bad guys," I said.

"*More* of them?" Butters said. "That's not fair."

"I know. It's getting to be like Satan's reunion tour around here." I shook my head. "Is there a back door?"

"Yes."

"Good. Grab your stuff and let's go."

Butters gestured at the exam table. "But what about Eduardo?"

I chewed on my lip. "You find out anything?"

"Not a lot," he said. "A car hit him. He suffered some pretty massive blunt impact trauma. He died."

I frowned and took a few steps toward the corpse. "There's got to be more to it than that."

Butters shrugged. "If there is, I didn't see it."

I frowned down at the dead man. He was a painfully skinny specimen. His abdomen had been opened with a neat Y incision. There was a lot of blood and disgusting-looking greyish flesh. Broken, jagged bone protruded from the skin of one leg. One hand had been crushed into pulp. And his face . . .

Looked familiar. I recognized him.

"Butters," I said. "What was this guy's name?"

"Eduardo Mendoza."

"His full name," I said.

"Oh. Uh, Eduardo Antonio Mendoza."

"Antonio," I said. "It's him. It's Tony."

"Who?" Butters asked.

"Bony Tony Mendoza," I said, excited. "He's a smuggler."

Butters tilted his head at me. "A smuggler? Not like Han Solo, I guess."

"No. He's a ballooner."

"What's that?"

I gestured at his head. "He'd done time in a carnival as a sword swallower when he was a kid. He would fill up a balloon with jewels or drugs or whatever other small items he wanted to move around. Then he swallowed the balloon with a string tied to it. Check at the back of his mouth. He'd wedge the string between two of his back teeth and pull the balloon out when the coast was clear."

"That's silly," Butters said, but he went over to the corpse and pried its jaws open. He adjusted an overhead work lamp on a flexible stand and peered down past Bony Tony's teeth. "Holy crap. It's there."

He fished around for a few moments while I went back to the door and picked up my staff. I looked back to see Butters drag from the corpse's mouth a yellow-white condom with its end closed and a heavy piece of kite cord knotted around it.

"What's in it?" I asked.

"Hang on." Butters sliced the condom open with a scalpel and withdrew a small rectangle of dark plastic, about the size of a key chain ornament.

"What is that?" I asked him.

"It's a jump drive," he said, frowning.

"A what?"

"You plug it into your computer so you can store data on it when you want to move files around to other machines."

"Information," I said, frowning. "Bony Tony was smuggling information. Something Grevane needed to know. Maybe the two out front wanted it too. Maybe that's why he got killed."

"Ugh," Butters said.

"Can you read the information?" I asked him.

"Maybe," he said. "I can try another machine."

"Not now," I said. "No time. We need to get out of here."

"Why?"

"Because things have just become a lot more dangerous."

"They have?" Butters chewed on his lip. "Why?"

"Because," I said. "Bony Tony worked for John Marcone."

Chapter

Fifteen

Gentleman Johnnie Marcone was the most powerful figure in Chicago's criminal underworld. If there was an illegal enterprise afoot, Marcone was either in charge of it or had been paid for the privilege of its operating in his territory. Bony Tony had done most of a dime in a federal penitentiary for trafficking in narcotics, and after that he'd moved into less politically incorrect areas of the business. He mostly dealt in moving stolen goods, everything from jewels to hot furniture.

I wasn't sure exactly where Bony Tony ranked in Marcone's criminal hierarchy, but Marcone wasn't the sort of person who would take the murder of one of his people lightly—not without his approval, at any rate. Marcone would know about Bony Tony's death soon, if he didn't already. He was sure to get involved in one fashion or another, and the best way for him to get to whoever had killed Bony Tony would be to get his hands on whatever it was they wanted.

I had to get Butters somewhere safe, the quicker the better. But until I knew what was on that storage device, I couldn't judge what would be safe for him and what wouldn't.

"Harry," Butters said, as if he was repeating himself.

I blinked a couple of times. "What?"

"Do you want to hang on to this?" he said in the same tone. He stepped over to me and offered me the little slip of plastic.

"No!" I snapped, and took two steps back. "Butters, get that the hell away from me."

He froze in place, staring at me, his expression somewhere between confused and wounded. "I'm sorry."

I took in a deep breath. Where the hell was my concentration? This was no time to start spacing out on trains of thought, no matter how relevant to the circumstances. "Don't be," I said. "Look, that thing doesn't have any moving parts, right? Electronic storage?"

"Yeah."

"Then I don't dare touch it," I said. "Remember how messed up my X-rays were?"

He nodded. "You're saying that the data on here could get messed up the same way."

"I couldn't ever have cassette tapes after I started working magic," I said. "They'd just fade away into static after a while. The magnetic strips on my credit cards stopped working in a day or two."

Butters chewed on his lip and nodded slowly. "The data on the jump drive would be even more fragile than a magnetic strip. It might make sense if it was some kind of erratic electromagnetic field around you. Every human body gives off a unique field of electromagnetic energy. It could be like with your cell replication, that your field is more—"

"Butters," I said, "no time for that now. The important thing is that I don't dare touch that toy." I frowned, thinking out loud. "Or take it back to my place, either. The wards keep magic out, but they keep it in, too. It would probably fry it to hang around in there for too long. Even working any heavy energy around it could be dangerous."

"Well, that's stupid," Butters said. "I mean, storing important wizard information on something that getting close to a wizard would destroy."

"It's not stupid if you want to sell it to a wizard and you're worried the buyer might off you instead of dealing in good faith," I said.

Butters looked at the corpse and then back at me. "You think Grevane killed Bony Tony?"

"Yeah," I said. "But Grevane knew that he couldn't get to the information on that jump drive on his own."

Butters swallowed. "Which explains why he needed me."

"Yeah." I chewed on my lip for a second and then said, "Get Bony Tony back in the fridge. We're leaving."

Butters nodded and went back to the examining table. He threw the cloth over the corpse. "Where?"

"Can you read that thing here?"

"No," Butters said. "This computer is too old. It has the wrong ports. We could go to one of the other offices, maybe—"

"No. We need to get out of here—now."

"We could go to my place," Butters suggested.

"No. Grevane will definitely have it under surveillance. Dammit."

"Why dammit?"

"We're short on options, and that means we have to go someplace I didn't want to go."

"Where?" he asked.

"A friend's. Come on."

"Right," Butters said, and promptly walked over to his polka suit. He heaved up a couple of pieces. The cymbals clashed tinnily against one another.

"What are you doing?" I demanded. "We've got to go."

"I'm not leaving it here for God-knows-what to mess with," Butters said. He grunted and threw a strap awkwardly over his shoulder. The bass drum rumbled.

"Yes, you are," I said. "We are not taking it with us. We don't have time for this."

Butters turned to face me, his expression stricken.

That stupid polka suit filled up most of the back of the SUV. It was a pain to move it without making a bunch of noise, but in the end we managed to slip out the back door of the Forensic Institute and make a clean getaway. I watched the road behind us carefully, until I was sure that I wasn't being followed. Then I headed for the campus area, and Billy's apartment.

I pulled into the apartment's parking lot, leaned out, and yelled, "Hey!"

A young man with arms and legs a few sizes too large to match his body appeared from behind the corner of the building, frowning. He was dressed in sweats, a T-shirt, and boat shoes, standard easily discarded werewolf wardrobe for troubled times. He flipped an untidy mop of black hair out of his eyes and leaned against the SUV's door. "Hey, Harry."

"Kirby," I greeted him. "This is my friend Butters."

Kirby nodded to Butters and asked me, "Did you spot me?"

"No, but Billy always has someone on watch outside when times are tense."

Kirby nodded, his expression serious. "What do you need?"

"Park this beast for me. I keep running into things."

"Sure. Billy and Georgia are upstairs."

I got out of the car, and Butters hopped out with me. "Thanks, man."

"Yeah," Kirby said. He got in the SUV and frowned. He looked around at all the doors.

"The door is ajar," the dashboard said.

"It won't shut up," I explained to him.

"It gets sort of Zen after a while," Butters said brightly. "Life is a journey. Time is a river. The door is a jar."

Kirby gave him a skeptical look. I grabbed Butters by the shoulder and hauled him into the building and up to the apartment.

Billy opened the door before we even got to it, and looked out expectantly. He stepped a bit to one side, holding the door open for us, watching up and down the hallway. "Heya, Harry."

The apartment was a typical college place—small, a couple of bedrooms, nothing permanent on the walls, furniture that wasn't too expensive or hard to move, and equipped with an expensive entertainment center. Georgia sat on the couch reading from one of a small mountain of medical books. I walked in and introduced everyone.

"I need a computer," I told Billy.

He arched an eyebrow at me.

I waved a hand in a vague motion. "Tell him, Butters."

Butters pulled the jump drive from his pocket and showed it to Billy. "Anything with a USB port."

Georgia frowned and asked, "What's on it?"

"I'm not sure," I said. "I need to know."

She nodded. "Better let him use the one on the far wall of the computer room, Will. The farther from Harry the better."

"Feel the love." I sighed. I pointed at the little table next to the door and asked, "Can I make a few calls while I wait?"

"Sure." Billy turned to Butters. "Right this way."

They went into one of the bedrooms. Georgia went back to her book. I picked up the phone.

The phone at my place rang a dozen times before it rattled, and then Thomas slurred, "What?"

"It's me," I said. "You all right?"

"I was all right. I was asleep. Stupid Mouse woke me up to get the phone."

"Any sign of visitors? Calls?"

"No and no," he said.

"Get some more sleep," I said.

He made a grunting noise and hung up.

I called my answering service next. They had recently phased over to stored voice mail. I was suspicious of it on general principles. From a purely logical standpoint, I knew my issues with technology wouldn't extend all the way across town over the phone lines, but all the same I didn't trust it. I would much rather have dealt with an actual person taking messages, but it cost too much now to keep someone manning the phones when voice mail could do all the work. I punched the buttons and had to go through all the menus only twice to get it to work.

Beeeeeep. "Harry, it's Murphy. We got into Hawaii all right, and there was no problem with the hotel, so you can reach me at those contact numbers. I'll call in again in a couple of—" Her voice broke off into a sudden high-pitched noise. "Would you *stop* that?" she demanded, with a lot more laughter than anger in her voice. "I'm on the phone. In a couple of days, Harry. Thanks for taking care of my pants. Er, plants, *plants.*" *Beeeeeep.*

I wondered what had caused Murphy to make a high-pitched noise and a big old Freudian slip. And I wondered what to read into the fact that she had left me a message instead of calling me at home. Probably nothing. She probably didn't want to wake me up or something. Yeah. She was probably only thinking of me.

Beeeeep. "Harry. Mike. The Beetle will be ready at noon." *Beeeeep.*

God bless Mechanic Mike. If I heard a car complaining about

its closed doors being open one more time, I would have to disintegrate something.

Beeeeep. "Oh," said a young woman's voice. "Mister Dresden? It's Shiela Starr. We met at Bock Ordered Books last night?" There was the sound of her taking an unsteady breath. "I wondered if I could ask for a few minutes of your time. There have been . . . I mean, I'm not completely certain but . . . I think something is *wrong.* Here at the store, I mean." She let out a snippet of laughter that was half anxiety and half weariness. "Oh, hell, I probably sound crazy, but I would really like to speak to you about it. I'll be at the shop until noon. Or you can call my apartment." She gave me the number. "I hope you can come by the store, though. I would really appreciate it." *Beeeep.*

I found myself frowning. Shiela hadn't said it outright, but she had sounded pretty scared. That wasn't terribly surprising, given what she'd probably seen happening right outside Bock's shop the night before, but it made me feel uncomfortable to hear fear in her voice. Or maybe it's more correct to say that I'm not comfortable with fear in any woman's voice.

It's not my fault. I know it's sexist and macho, and it's retrograde social evolution, but I hate it when bad things happen to women. Don't get me wrong; I hate bad things to happen to anyone—but when it's a woman that's in danger, I hate it with a reflexive, bone-deep, primal mindlessness that borders on insanity. Women are beautiful creatures, and dammit, I enjoy making sure that they're safe and treating them with old-fashioned manners and courtesy. It just seems right. I'd suffered for thinking that way more than once, but it still didn't change the way I felt.

Shiela was a girl, and she was scared. Therefore, if I wanted to have any peace of mind, I was going to have to go talk to her.

I checked the clock. Eleven. She was still at the store.

I dialed one more number, and got an answering machine with no message, only a tone. "This is Dresden," I told the machine. "And we need to talk."

Butters and Billy reappeared. I hung up the phone and asked them, "Well?"

"Numbers," said Billy.

"More specific?" I asked.

Butters shook his head. "It's hard to be any more specific than that. There was only one file on the jump drive, and it was empty. The only information on it was the file name, and it was just a number." He offered me a piece of white paper with a string of numerals printed on it in his spidery scrawl. I counted. There were sixteen of them. "That's it."

I took the paper and frowned at the numbers. "That is spectacularly useless."

"Yeah," Butters said quietly.

I rubbed at the bridge of my nose. "Okay. Let me think." I tried to prioritize. Grevane was out there looking for Butters. Maybe Marcone was looking for him too. Maybe the dead professor's two assistants to boot. "Butters, we have to get you behind my wards again."

He blinked at me. "But why? I mean, they wanted me so that they could get to the information. I'm useless to them now."

"You and I know that. They don't."

"Oh."

"Billy," I said, "could you please take Butters over to my place?"

"No problem," he said. "What about you? Won't you need wheels?"

"The Beetle is ready. I'll take a cab."

"I can drop you off," Billy offered.

"No. It's the opposite way from my apartment, and Butters needs to get there yesterday. Go around the block once or twice before you pull in. Make sure no one is watching the door."

Billy smiled. "I know the drill."

"Don't try to open the door yourself, Butters. Knock and wait for Thomas to do it."

"Right." Butters fretted at his lip a little. "What are you going to be doing?"

"Detective stuff. I have places to go and people to see."

And with a little luck, none of them would kill me.

Chapter

Sixteen

Billy's apartment was only a couple of blocks from Bock Ordered Books, and while I could have taken a couple of alleys to make the trip even shorter, I kept on the open streets, where there were plenty of people. I didn't see anyone following me, but if there was a good enough team on me—or if they were using veils to hide their presence, of course—I might miss them. I kept my staff in my right hand and made sure my shield bracelet was ready, in case anyone tried some kind of variant on the old drive-up assassination. I'd survived them before, but the classics never go out of style.

I got to Bock's in one piece, and no one so much as glared at me. I felt sort of rejected, but comforted myself with the knowledge that there were at least half a dozen people in town who were sure to keep making my life dangerous. More if you counted Mavra, who technically wasn't a person.

Bock didn't open the doors of his store until eleven, so when I went in I was probably the first one to show up for the day. I paused outside the door. Two of the store windows and the glass panel of the door were all gone, replaced by rough sheets of plywood. Bock had gotten off better than the boutique next door—all the glass was gone, doubtless shattered by one kind of flying debris or another during my conversation with Cowl and his sidekick. I went inside.

Bock was at his place behind the counter, and looked tired. He glanced up at the sound of his door chimes. His expression became something closed and cautious when he saw me.

"Bock," I said. "You here all night?"

"End-of-the-month inventory," he said, his voice careful and quiet. "And repairing the windows. What do you need?"

I looked around the inside of the store. Shiela appeared from behind one of the shelves at the back of the store, looking anxious. She saw me and exhaled a little, then gave me a quiet smile.

"Just here to talk," I told Bock, nodding toward Shiela.

He glanced at her, then back at me, frowning. "Dresden. There's something I need to say to you."

I arched an eyebrow at him. "What's wrong?"

"Look. I don't want to make you upset."

I leaned on my staff. "Bock, come on. You've known me ever since I came to town. If something's wrong, you aren't going to upset me by telling me about it."

He folded his thick forearms over his paunch and said, "I don't want you coming into my store anymore."

I leaned on my staff a little more. "Oh."

"You're a decent enough man. You've never jumped down my throat like the other folks from the Council. You've helped people around here." He took a deep breath and made a vague gesture toward the plywood patches on his shop. "But you're trouble. It follows you around."

Which was true enough. I didn't say anything.

"Not everyone can drop a car on someone who attacks them," Bock went on. "I've got a family. My oldest is in college. I can't afford to have the place wrecked."

I nodded. I could understand Bock's position. It's terrifying to feel helpless in the face of a greater power—more so than it is painful to be told you aren't wanted somewhere.

"Look. If you need anything, give me a call. I'll order it or pull it off the shelves for you. Will or Georgia can come pick it up. But . . ."

"Okay," I said. My throat felt a little tight.

Bock's face got red. He looked away from me, at the ruined door. "I'm sorry."

"Don't be," I said. "I understand. I'm sorry about your shop."

He nodded.

"I'm just here for a minute. After that I'll go."

"Right," he said.

I walked down the aisles back to Shiela, and nodded to her. "I got your message."

Shiela was wearing the same clothes as the night before, only more rumpled. She'd pulled her hair back and held it in place with a pair of ballpoint pens thrust through a knot at right angles. With her hair like that, it showed the pale, clean lines of her jaw and throat, and I was again struck by the impulse to run my fingers over her skin and see if it was as soft as it looked.

She glanced at Bock, then smiled up at me and touched my arm with her hand. "I'm sorry he did that. It isn't fair of him."

"No. It's fair enough. He has the right to protect himself and his business," I said. "I don't blame him."

She tilted her head to one side, studying my face. "But it hurts anyway?"

I shrugged. "Some. I'll survive." The chimes rung at the front of the store as another customer came in. I glanced back at Bock, and sighed. "Look, I don't want to be here very long. What did you need?"

She brushed back a few strands of hair that had escaped the knot. "I . . . well, I had a strange experience last night."

I lifted my eyebrows. "Go on."

She picked up a small stack of books and started shelving them as she spoke. "After all the excitement, I went back to the inventory in the back room, and Mr. Bock had gone to get the plywood for the windows. I thought I heard the chimes ring, but when I looked no one was there."

"Uh-huh," I said.

"But . . ." She frowned. "You know how when you go into an empty house, you *know* it's empty? How it just *feels* empty?"

"Sure," I said. I watched her stretch up onto the tips of her toes to put a book away on the top shelf. It drew her sweater up a little, and I could see muscles move under a swath of the pale skin of her lower back.

"The store didn't feel empty," she said, and I saw her shiver. "I never saw anyone, never heard anyone. But I was sure someone was here." She glanced back at me and flushed. "I was so nervous I could hardly think straight until the sun came up."

"Then what?" I asked.

"It went away. I felt a little silly. Like I was a scared little kid. Or one of those dogs that's staring at something growling when nothing is there."

I shook my head. "Dogs don't just stare and growl for no reason. Sometimes they can perceive things people can't."

She frowned. "Do you think something was here?"

I didn't want to tell her that I thought a Black Court vampire had been lurking unseen in the shop. Hell, for that matter I didn't particularly want to *think* about it. If Mavra had been here, there wouldn't have been anything Shiela or Bock could do to defend themselves against her.

"I think you wouldn't be foolish to trust your instincts," I said. "You've got a little talent. It's possible you were sensing something too vague for you to understand in any other way."

She put the last book away and turned to face me. She looked tired. Fear made her expression one of sickness, an ugly contortion. "Something was here," she whispered.

"Maybe," I said, nodding.

"Oh, God." She tightened her arms across her stomach. "I . . . I might be sick."

I leaned my staff against the shelf and put a hand on her shoulder, steadying her. "Shiela. Take a few deep breaths. It's not here now."

She looked up at me, her expression miserable, her eyes wet and shining. "I'm sorry. I mean, you don't need this." She squeezed her eyes tightly shut, and more tears fell. "I'm sorry."

Oh, hell. Tears. Way to go, Dresden—terrify the local maiden you showed up to comfort. I drew Shiela a little toward me, and she leaned against me gratefully. I put my arm around her shoulders and let her lean against me for a minute. She shivered with silent tears for a little bit and then pulled herself together.

"Does this happen to you a lot?" she asked in a quiet voice, sniffling.

"People get scared," I murmured. "There's nothing wrong with that. There are scary things out there."

"I feel like a coward."

"Don't," I told her. "All it means is that you aren't an idiot."

She straightened and took a step back. Her face looked a little blotchy. Some women can cry and look beautiful, but Shiela wasn't one of them. She took off her glasses and wiped at her eyes. "What do I do if it happens again?"

"Tell Bock. Get somewhere public," I said. "Call the cops. Or better yet, call Billy and Georgia. If what you felt really was some kind of predator, they won't want to stick around if they know they've been spotted."

"You sound as if you've dealt with them before," she said.

I smiled a little. "Maybe a time or two."

She smiled up at me, and it was a grateful expression. "It must be very lonely, doing what you do."

"Sometimes," I said.

"Always being so strong when others can't. That's . . . well, it's sort of heroic."

"It's sort of idiotic," I replied, my voice dry. "Heroism doesn't pay very well. I try to be cold-blooded and money-oriented, but I keep screwing it up."

She let out a little laugh. "You fail to live up to your ideals, eh?"

"Nobody's perfect."

She tilted her head again, eyes bright. "Are you with someone?"

"Just you."

"Not with them. *With* them."

"Oh," I said. "No. Not really."

"If I asked you to come have dinner out with me, would it seem too forward and aggressive?"

I blinked. "You mean . . . like a date?"

Her smile widened. "You do . . . you know . . . like women? Right?"

"What?" I said. "Oh, yes. Yes. I'm down with the women."

"By coincidence I happen to be a woman," she said. She touched my arm again. "And since it seems like I might not get a chance to flirt with you a little more while I'm at work, I thought I had better ask you now. So is that a yes?"

The prospect of a date seemed to me like a case of bad timing in several ways. But it also seemed like a good idea. I mean, it had been a while since a girl had been interested in me in a nonprofessional sense.

Well. A human girl, anyway. The only one who even came close was in Hawaii with someone else, giggling and thinking about pants. It might be really nice just to be out talking and interacting with an attractive girl. God knows it would beat hanging around my crowded apartment.

"It's a yes," I said. "I'm kind of busy right now, but . . ."

"Here," she said. She took a black marker out of a pocket in her sweater and grabbed my right hand. She wrote numbers on it in heavy black strokes. "Call me here, maybe tonight, and we'll figure out when."

I let her do it, amused. "All right."

She popped the cap back on the marker and smiled up at me. "All right, then."

I picked up my staff. "Shiela, look. I might not be around this place. I'll respect Bock's wishes. But let him know that if there's any trouble, all he has to do is call me."

She shook her head, smiling. "You're a decent person, Harry Dresden."

"Don't spread that around too much," I said, and started for the door.

And froze in my tracks.

Standing in the little entry area of the bookstore, facing Bock at his counter, were Alicia and the ghoul, Li Xian.

I stepped back to Shiela and pulled her around the corner of a shelf.

"What is it?" she asked.

"Quiet," I said. I closed my eyes and Listened.

". . . a simple question," Alicia was saying. "Who bought it?"

"I don't keep track of my customers," Bock replied. His voice was polite, but it had an undertone of granite. "I'm sorry, but I just don't have that information. A lot of people come through here."

"Really?" Alicia asked. "And how many of them purchase rare and expensive antique books from you?"

"You'd be surprised."

Alicia let out a nasty little laugh. "You really aren't going to volunteer the information, are you?"

"I don't *have* it to volunteer," Bock said. "Both copies of the book were bought yesterday. Both were men, one older and one younger. I don't remember anything more than that."

I heard a couple of footsteps, and Li Xian said, "Perhaps you need help remembering."

There was the distinct, heavy click of a pair of hammers on a shotgun being drawn back. "Son," Bock said in that same voice, "you'll want to step away from the counter and leave my shop now."

"It would appear that the good shopkeeper has taken sides on this matter," Alicia said.

"You're wrong, miss," Bock said. "I run this shop. I don't give information. I don't take sides. If I had a third copy, I'd sell it to you. I don't. Both of you leave, please."

"I don't think you understand," Alicia said. "I'm not leaving here until I have an answer to my question."

"I don't think you understand," Bock replied. "There's a ten-gauge shotgun wired under this counter. It's loaded, cocked, and pointing right at your bellies."

"Oh, my," Alicia said, her voice amused. "A shotgun. Xian, whatever shall we do?"

I ground my teeth. Bock had asked me to stay away, but even so he was standing there protecting my identity, even though he knew damned well that the two in front of him were dangerous.

I checked. The door to the back room of the shop was open. "The back door," I said to Shiela in a whisper. "Is it locked?"

"Not from this side."

"Go into the back room and get in the office," I said. "Get on the floor and stay there. Now."

She looked up at me with wide eyes and then hurried back through the open door.

I gripped my staff and closed my eyes, thinking. I patted my duster's pocket. The book was still there, riding along with my .44. Ghouls were hard to kill. I had no idea what Alicia was, but I was willing to bet she wasn't a mere academic assistant. For her to command the respect of a creature like Li Xian, she had to be major-league dangerous. It would be an extremely foolish idea to assault them.

But that didn't matter. If I didn't do something, they were going to get unpleasant at Bock. Bock might not have been a stalwart companion who stuck through thick and thin, but he was what he was: an honest shopkeeper who wanted neither to become involved in supernatural power struggles nor to compromise his principles. If I did nothing, he was going to get hurt while protecting me.

I stepped around the shelf and started walking toward the front of the store.

Bock sat in his spot behind the counter, one hand gripping its edge in a white-knuckled grasp, the other out of sight below it. Alicia and Li Xian stood in front of it. She looked relaxed. The ghoul was slouched into an eager stance, knees bent a little, arms hanging loosely.

"Shopkeeper, I will ask you one last time," Alicia said. "Who purchased the last copy of *Die Lied der Erlking*?" She lifted her left hand and faint heat shimmers rose from her fingers along with a whisper of dark power. "Tell me his name."

I drew in my will, lifted my staff, and snarled, "*Forzare!*"

The runes on the staff burst into smoldering scarlet light. There was a thunderstorm's roar, and raw power, invisible and solid, lashed out of the end of my staff. It whipped across the shop, knocking books from the shelves on the way, and hit the ghoul in the chest. It lifted him off his feet and sent him smashing into the plywood-covered door. He went through the wood without slowing down, out over the sidewalk, and into the wall of the building across the street, where he hit with a crunch.

Alicia spun toward me, her eyes wide and shocked.

I stood with my feet spread. My shield bracelet was on my left hand, thrumming with power and drizzling blue-white sparks. My staff smoldered with the scent of fresh-burned wood, and the scarlet runes shone in the darkness at the back of the store. I pointed it directly at Alicia.

"His name," I snarled, "is Harry Dresden."

Chapter

Seventeen

"**Y**ou," I snarled, gesturing at Bock with the end of my staff. "You little weasel. You were gonna sell me out. I ought to kill you right here."

From his vantage point above Alicia's curly-haired head, Bock blinked at me in confusion. I stared at him, hard, not daring to leave anything in my expression that the girl would see. If I'd tried to protect Bock, it would only have made it more likely that she would do something to him. By appearing to threaten him, it would make him seem more unimportant to the necromancer and her henchman. It was the best thing I could do to protect him.

Bock got it. His expression flickered through several subtle shades of comprehension, fear, and guilt. He twitched his head at me in a nod of thanks.

"Well, well," Alicia said. She hadn't moved, other than to turn toward me. "I've never heard of you, but I must admit that you know how to make an entrance, Harry Dresden."

"I took lessons," I said.

"Give me the book," she said.

"Ha," I said. "Why?"

"Because I want it," she said.

"Sorry. It's the hot Christmas present this year," I said. "Maybe you can find a scalper in a parking lot or something."

She tilted her head, the fingers of her hand still flickering with little shimmers, like heat rising from asphalt. "You refuse?"

"Yes, moppet," I told her. "I refuse. I deny thee. No, already."

Her eyes narrowed in anger and . . . well, something happened that I hadn't ever seen before. The store got darker. I don't mean that the lights went out. I mean everything got darker. There was a low, trembling sensation that seemed to make my eyeballs jiggle a little, and the shadows simply expanded up out of the corners and dim areas of the store like time-lapse photography of growing molds. As they slid over portions of the store, that nasty, greasy sensation of cold came with them. When the shadows washed over an outlet that housed the power cords to a pair of table lamps, the lamps themselves went dim and then died out. They covered the old radio, and Aretha Franklin's voice faded away to a whisper and vanished. The shadows got to the register and its lights went out, and when they brushed the old ceiling fan it began to whirl down to a stop. The shadows crept over Bock and he went pale and started shaking. He thrust one hand down onto the counter as if he had to do it to keep himself upright.

The only place the darkness didn't spread was over me. The shadows stopped in a circle all around me, maybe six inches away from me and the things I was carrying. The Hellfire smoldering in the runes of my staff glowed more brightly in the darkness, and the tiny sparks falling in a steady rain from my damaged shield bracelet seemed to burn away tiny pockets of the darkness where they fell, only to have it slide back in once they had burned away.

This was a kind of power I hadn't felt before. Normally when someone who can sling major mojo around draws their stuff up around them, it's something violent and active. I'd seen wizards who charged the air around them with so much electricity it made their hair stand on end, wizards whose power would gather light into nearly solid gem-shaped clouds that orbited around them, wizards whose mastery of earth magic literally made the ground shake, wizards who could shroud themselves in dark fire that burned anyone near them with the raw, emotional rage of their magic.

This was different. Alicia's power, whatever it was, didn't fill the store. It *emptied* it in a way that I didn't think I fully understood. Utter stillness spread out from her—not peace, for that would have been something tranquil, accepting. This stillness was a horrible, hungry emptiness, something that took its power from being *not*. It was made of the emptiness at the loss of a loved one, of the silence between the beats of a heart, and of the inevitability of the empty void that waited patiently for the stars to grow cold and burn out. It was power wholly different from the burning fires of life that formed the magic I knew—and it was strong. God, it was so *strong*.

I began to tremble as I realized that everything I had wasn't enough to go up against this.

"I don't like your answer," Alicia said. She smiled at me, a slow and evil expression. She had a dimple on one cheek. Hell's bells, an evil dimple.

My mouth felt dry, but my voice sounded steady when I spoke. "That's too bad. If you're so upset about not getting a copy, I suggest you take it up with Cowl."

She stared at me with no expression for a moment and then said, "You are with Cowl?"

"No," I told her. "I was, in fact, forced to drop a car on him last night when he tried to take the book from me."

"Liar," she said. "Had you truly fought Cowl, you'd be dead."

"Whatever," I replied, my tone bored. "I'll tell you what I told him. My book. You can't have it."

She pursed her lips thoughtfully. "Wait a moment. You were at the mortuary. In the entryway."

"We call it the Forensic Institute now."

Her eyes glittered. "You found it. You succeeded where Grevane failed, didn't you?"

I turned up one corner of my mouth, and said nothing.

Alicia took in a deep breath. "Perhaps we can reach an understanding."

"Funny," I said. "Grevane said the very same thing."

Alicia took an eager step toward me. "You denied him?"

"I didn't like his hat."

"You have wisdom for one so young," she said. "In the end he is nothing but a dog mourning his fallen master. He would turn on you in a moment. The gratitude of the Capiorcorpus, by contrast, is an eternal asset."

Capiorcorpus. Roughly translated, the taker of corpses, or bodies. I suddenly had a better idea of why Li Xian had referred to Alicia as "my lord."

"Assuming I want that gratitude," I said, "what price would it carry?"

"Give me the book," she said. "Give me the *Word*. Stand with me at the Darkhallow. In exchange I will grant you autonomy and the principality of your choice when the new order arises."

I didn't want her to know that I had no freaking clue what she was talking about, so I said, "That's a tempting offer."

"It should be," she said. She lifted her chin, and her eyes glittered with something bright and utterly confident. "The new order will change many things in this world. You have the opportunity to help shape it to your liking."

"And if I turn you down?" I asked.

She met my eyes directly. "You are young, Harry Dresden. It is a great tragedy when a man with your potential dies before his time."

I shied away from her gaze at once. When a wizard looks into another person's eyes for an instant too long, he sees into them in a profound and unsettling kind of vision called a soulgaze. If I'd left my gaze on Alicia's eyes, I would get an up-close and personal look at her soul—and she at mine. I didn't want to see what was going on behind that dimpled smile. I recognized that perfect surety in her manner and expression as something more than rampant ego or fanatic conviction.

It was pure madness. Whatever else Alicia was, she was calmly and horribly insane.

My mouth felt a lot drier. My legs were shaking, and my feet were advising the rest of me to let them run away. "I'll have to think about it."

"By all means," Alicia said. Her face took on an ugly expression and her voice hardened. "Consider it. But take a single step from where you stand and it will be your last."

"Killing me might get you a copy of the book, but it won't get you the *Word*," I said. "Or did you think I was carrying both of them around with me?"

Her right hand clenched into a slow fist and the room got a couple of degrees colder. "Where is the *Word*?"

Wouldn't I like to know? I thought.

"Wouldn't you like to know," I said. "Kill me now and there's no *Word*. No new order."

She uncurled her hand. "I can make you tell me," she said.

"If you could do that, you'd have done it by now, instead of standing there looking stupid."

She started taking slow steps toward me, smiling. "I prefer to attempt reason before I destroy a mind. It is a somewhat taxing activity. Are you sure you wouldn't rather work with me?"

Gulp. Mental magic is a dark, dark, dark grey area of the art. Every wizard who makes it to the White Council has received training in how to defend against mental assaults, but that was perfunctory at best. After all, the Council made it a special point to wipe out wizards who violated the sanctuary of another's mind. It's one of the Laws of Magic, and if the Wardens caught someone doing it, they killed them, end of story. There was no such thing as an expert at that kind of magic on the White Council, and as a result the defense training was devised by relative amateurs.

Something told me that Alicia the Corpsetaker wasn't an amateur.

"That's close enough," I said in a cold voice.

She kept walking, very slowly, a sort of sinuous enjoyment in her stride. "Last chance."

"I mean it," I said. "Stay ba—"

Before I could finish the word, she made a rippling gesture with the shimmering fingers of her left hand.

There was a whirling sensation, and I was suddenly caught in a gale, a whirlwind that tried to carry me toward the girl. My feet started sliding across the floor. I leaned back with a cry, lifting my shield bracelet, and it blazed into a dome of solid blue light before me. It did nothing—nothing at all. The vicious vortex continued to draw me to her outstretched hand.

I started to panic, and then realized what was happening. There was no wind—not physically, anyway. The books on the shelves were not stirring, nor was my long leather duster. My shield offered me no protection from a wholly nonphysical threat, and I released it, saving my strength.

The hideous vacuum wasn't meant for my body. It was targeting my thoughts.

"That's right," Alicia said.

Holy crap. She'd heard me thinking.

"Of course, young man. Give me what I want now and I may leave you enough of your mind to feed yourself."

I gritted my teeth, marshaling my thoughts, my defenses.

"It's too late for that, boy."

Like hell it was. My thoughts coalesced into a unified whole, an absolute image of a wall of smooth, grey granite. I built the image of the wall in my mind and then filled it with the power I'd been holding at the ready. I felt a nauseating confusion for a second, and then the mental gale ceased as abruptly as it had begun.

Alicia's head jerked as if she'd been slapped across the cheek.

I glared at her, teeth gritted, and asked, "Is that all you got?"

Corpsetaker snarled out a spiteful curse, lifted her left arm, and twisted her fingers into a raking claw.

There was a hideous pressure against the image of the granite wall in my mind. It wasn't a single, resounding blow, as I had expected from my training, a kind of psychic battering ram. Instead it was an enormous, steady weight, as if a sudden tide had flooded in to wash the wall away completely.

I thought that pressure would ease in a moment, but it only became more and more difficult to bear. I struggled to hold the image of the wall in place, but despite everything I could do, dark and empty cracks began to appear and spread through it. My defenses were crumbling.

"Delicious," Corpsetaker said, and her voice didn't sound strained at all. "After a century, they're still teaching the young ones the same tripe."

I saw movement beyond Corpsetaker, and Li Xian appeared in the shattered plywood doorway. Half of his face was lumpy and purpled with bruising, and one shoulder had been smashed grossly out of shape. He was bleeding a thin, greenish-brown fluid, and moved as if in great pain, but he came in on his own power, and his eyes were alert.

"My lord," Xian said. "Are you well?"

"Perfectly," Corpsetaker purred. "Once I have his mind, the rest is yours."

His misshapen face twisted into a smile that spread too wide for human features. "Thank you, lord."

Holy crap. It was time to leave.

But my feet wouldn't move.

"You needn't bother, young wizard," Corpsetaker said. "If you take the attention you would need to free your feet, your wall will fail. Just open to me, boy. You will feel less pain."

I ignored the necromancer and tried to think of other options. My mental defenses were indeed crumbling, but any strength of will I spent to move my legs would collapse the defenses entirely. I had to get the pressure off of me for a moment—only time enough to distract Corpsetaker, to give me time to get the hell away. But given that I could barely move at all, my options were severely limited.

Part of the wall began to crumble. I felt Corpsetaker's will begin pouring in, the first trickle from a dark sea.

If I wanted to live, I had little choice.

I reached my thoughts down into the smoldering Hellfire burning in the runes of my staff, and sent it flooding into my mind, into the failing wall that protected me. The cracks in the cold grey granite filled with crimson flame, and where the dark sea of Corpsetaker's will pressed against it there was a screaming hiss of freezing water boiling into a cloud of steam.

Corpsetaker let out a sudden, hollow gasp, and the pressure on my thoughts vanished.

I spun, wobbled, got my balance, and then ran for the back door.

"Take him!" Corpsetaker snarled behind me. "He has the book and the *Word!*"

There was a sickly ripping, crackling sound, and Li Xian let out a bestial and inhuman howl.

I dashed through the back room of the bookstore, and to the back door. I slammed its opening bar and sprinted through it, out into the alley behind the shop. I heard two sets of feet following me, and Corpsetaker began chanting in a low, growling voice. That hideous pressure began to surge against my thoughts again, but this time I was ready for it, and my defenses fell into place more quickly, more surely. I was able to keep running.

I ran down the alley, and made it maybe thirty yards before a sudden fire exploded through my right calf. I crashed down to the ground, barely holding on to my mental defenses. I dropped my staff and reached down to my calf, to feel something metal and sharp protruding from it. I cut my fingers on an edge and jerked them back. I couldn't get a good look, but I saw a flash of steel and a lot of blood—and Corpsetaker and the ghoul were still coming.

There was no way I could have whipped up any magic to stop them—not with all of my power focused on keeping Corpsetaker from invading my mind. I wouldn't be able to overcome the ghoul physically—even wounded, Xian was quick on his feet, and closing the distance fast.

I drew the .44 and sent three shots back down the alley. Corpsetaker darted to one side, but the ghoul never even slowed down. He flung one too-long arm through an arc, and there was a glitter of steel in the gloomy alley. Something hit me in the ribs nearly hard enough to knock me down, but the spell-covered leather of my duster stopped it from piercing through. A triangle of steel fell to the ground, each point sharpened and given a razor's edge.

"All I needed," I muttered. "Ninja ghouls." I emptied the revolver at Xian. He wasn't ten feet from me on the last shot, and I must have hit him. He jerked, careened off a wall, and stumbled, but he was a long way from down.

Corpsetaker's will continued to erode my defenses. I had to get away from her, or she'd open up my brains like a tin of sardines— and then Xian would eat them.

The three-pointed shuriken still in my calf, I forced myself to my feet through the screaming pain. I seized my staff, hobbling in earnest this time, and struggled toward the end of the alley. My only chance was to make it to the street, to flag down a cab, somehow beg a ride from a passing car, or maybe get some help. I knew there wasn't much hope of any of those things happening, but it was all I had.

I almost got to the end of the alley, the pain in my leg growing steadily worse—and then I abruptly lost track of what was going on.

One moment I'd been busy, I knew. I was doing something important. The next I was just standing there, sort of floundering. Whatever I'd been doing, it was right on the tip of my tongue. I knew that if I could just focus for a second, I'd be able to remember it and get back on track. My leg hurt. I knew that. And my head felt jumbled, the thoughts there, but in disarray, as if I'd gone through a drawer of folded laundry, pulled out something from the bottom, and then slapped the drawer shut again without straightening anything up.

I heard a snarl behind me, and realized that whatever I'd been doing, it was too late to get back on track now. I tried to turn around, but for some reason I couldn't remember how.

"I have it," panted a woman's voice behind me. "Numbers. It's only . . . He only has *numbers*."

"My lord," snarled a thick, deformed voice. "What is your command?"

"He doesn't know where the *Word* is. He is useless to me. The book is in the right pocket of his coat. Take it, Xian. Then kill him."

Chapter

Eighteen

I was pretty sure that Corpsetaker was talking about me, and I knew for sure that getting killed was a bad thing. I just couldn't figure out how to go about doing something to stop it. Something about my mind. That it wasn't working right.

A battered-looking man entered my field of view, and I was able to turn my head enough to watch him. Oh, crap, it was Li Xian, the ghoul. I had a bad feeling that he was going to do something unpleasant, but he just stuck his hand in my coat pocket and pulled out the slender copy of *Erlking*.

The ghoul turned away from me and offered the book to someone out of my field of view.

There was the sound of flipping pages. "Excellent," Corpsetaker said. "Take him back from the street and finish him. Hurry. He's stronger than most. I'd rather not hold him all day."

Oh, right. Corpsetaker was holding my mind captive. That meant that she was in my head. That meant she had beaten my defenses down. Just pulling those thoughts together made me feel stronger. My head started clearing, and as it did the pain in my wounded leg grew more intense.

"Hurry," she said, her voice now strained.

Rough hands seized the back of my coat. I wanted to run, but I still couldn't get everything to respond together. An inspiration seized me. If Corpsetaker was in my head, it meant that she could feel everything I was feeling—such as the burning pain in my leg.

When the ghoul started pulling me backward, I couldn't struggle, but I managed to twist my hips a little and bend my good knee. I fell over sideways, onto the wounded leg. The fall drove the shuriken a little harder into my calf, and the world went white with pain.

Corpsetaker shrieked. I heard a metallic clatter, as if she had stumbled into a trash can, and I felt my arms and legs come all the way back under my command. The ghoul stumbled on his mangled leg. He pushed off the wall and came at me. I spun on the small of my back and kicked out hard and straight at his good knee.

That's a nasty defensive technique Murphy taught me, and one that doesn't rely upon raw physical power. The ghoul's weight was all on that leg, and the kick connected hard. There was a grinding pop, and he let out a spitting snarl of pain.

I scrambled away from him on one leg and the heels of my hands. I could see my blood on the floor of the alley, smeared in a trail from my wounded leg. There were little stars fluttering through my vision, and I felt as weak as a starved kitten. Everything was spinning around so much that I didn't even bother to get to my feet. I crawled out of the cold shadows of the alley, onto the sidewalk, and into broad daylight.

I heard someone shout something. There were police sirens a block or two away. They were doubtless heading for Bock's place, after someone had seen me throw the ghoul out through the plywood-covered door. Give them two minutes to sort out what was going on, and I'd have men with silver shields and a strong desire to speak to the dead professor's missing assistants all around me.

Of course, by then I'd probably have been dead for a minute and a half.

The wounded ghoul, his face twisted, jaws lolling open wide to show yellowed fangs, came shambling out of the alley after me.

I heard a woman shout, the sound high and furious and totally unafraid. There was a whooshing sound, a spinning shape, and then an ax—a freaking double-bladed *ax*—buried itself to the eye in the ghoul's flank. Just as it hit, there was a flash of light from a spot on the blade, so bright that it left a red mark in the shape of a single rune burned into my vision. There was a loud bark of sound as the ax hit the ghoul. The creature was thrown forcefully to the sidewalk, and thin, greenish-brown fluid sprayed everywhere in a disgusting shower.

A woman in a dark business suit stepped into my line of sight. She was better than six feet tall, blond, and coldly beautiful. Her blue eyes burned with battle-lust and excitement as she drew a sword with a straight, three-foot blade from the scabbard at her side. As I watched, she took several smooth steps to place herself between the ghoul and me. Then she pointed the tip of the sword at him and snarled, "Avaunt, carrion."

The ghoul tore the ax from his side and staggered into a crouch, holding the weapon in both hands with a panicked desperation. He took a pair of awkward, shuffling steps back.

An engine roared and a grey sedan swerved up onto the sidewalk.

"Avaunt!" cried the woman; then she raised the sword and glided toward the ghoul.

Li Xian didn't want any part of it. His inhuman face twisted in recognizable fear. He dropped the ax and fled back down the alley.

"Coward." The woman sighed, clearly disappointed. She snatched up the ax, then said to me, "Get in."

"I know you," I said. "Miss Gard. You work for Marcone."

"I work for Monoc Securities," the woman corrected me. Her hand clamped down on my arm like a slender steel vise, and she hauled me to my feet without effort. My wounded calf clenched into a nasty cramp, and I could feel the steel blades continuing to cut at my muscles. I clenched my teeth, snarling my defiance at the pain. Gard gave me a quick glance of approval and tugged me toward the grey sedan. I still had to hobble on my staff, but with her help I made it to the car and fumbled my way into the backseat. More hands pulled me in.

The whole time Gard kept her sharp, cold blue gaze on the alley and the street around us. Once I was in, she shut the door, sheathed the sword, and unclipped the scabbard from her belt before getting into the passenger's seat. The grey sedan pulled out into the street again, and started away from the scene.

The driver turned his head just enough to catch me in his peripheral vision. His neck was too thick for any more movement than that. He had red hair clipped into a close buzz, shoulders wide enough to build a deck on, and he'd had to get his business suit at the big-and-tall store.

"Hendricks," I greeted him.

He looked up into the rearview mirror with his beady eyes and glowered.

"Nice to see you again, too," I said. I settled back into the seat as much as I could, trying to ignore my leg, and refusing to look at the man sitting beside me.

I didn't really need to look at him. He was a man a little over average height, somewhere in the late prime of his life, his dark hair flecked with grey. He had skin that had seen a lot of time out in the weather, leaving him with a perpetual boater's tan, and eyes the color of wrinkled old dollars. He'd be wearing a suit that cost more than some cars, and making it look good. He looked handsome and wholesome, more like the coach of a successful sports team than a gangster. But John Marcone was the most powerful figure in Chicago's criminal underworld.

"Isn't that a little childish?" he asked me, his voice amused. "Refusing to look at me like that?"

"Indulge me," I said. "It's been a long day."

"How serious is your injury?" he asked.

"Do I look like a doctor to you?" I asked.

"You look more like a corpse," he answered.

I squinted at him. He sat calmly in his seat, mirroring me. "Is that a threat?" I asked.

"If I wanted you dead," Marcone said, "I would hardly have come to your aid just now. You must admit, Dresden, that I have just saved your life. Again."

I closed my eye again and scowled. "Your timing is improbable."

He sounded amused. "In what way?"

"Coming to my rescue just as someone was about to punch my ticket. You must admit, Marcone, that it smells like a setup."

"Even I occasionally enjoy good fortune," he replied.

I shook my head. "I called you less than an hour ago. If it wasn't a setup then how did you find me?"

"He didn't," said Gard. "I did." She looked over her shoulder at Marcone and frowned. "This is a mistake. It was his fate to die in that alley."

"What is the point of having free will if one cannot occasionally spit in the eye of destiny?" Marcone asked.

"There will be consequences," she insisted.

Marcone shrugged. "When aren't there?"

Gard turned her face back to the front and shook her head. "Hubris. Mortals never understand."

"Tell me about it," I said. "Everyone makes that mistake but me."

Marcone glanced at me, and his eyes wrinkled at the corners. It was very nearly a smile. Gard turned her head slowly and gave me a cold glare that wasn't anywhere close to smiling.

"Let's get to the part of the conversation where you tell me what you want," I said. "I don't have time for any more banter."

"Ah," Marcone said. "I suspected you would somehow become involved in the events at hand."

"What events would those be?" I asked.

"The situation concerning the death of Tony Mendoza."

I scowled at him. "What do you want?"

"Unless I miss my guess," Marcone said, "I want to help you."

"Yeah," I said. "Right."

"I'm quite serious, Dresden," he told me. "I allow no one to harm those in my employ. Whoever murdered Mendoza must be chastised immediately—whether or not they happen to be necromancers."

I blinked. "How did you know what they were?"

"Miss Gard," he replied serenely. "She and her colleagues have outstanding resources."

I shrugged. "Good for you. But I'm not interested in helping you maintain your empire."

"Naturally. But you *are* interested in stopping these men and women before they accomplish whatever goal it is that they are pursuing."

I shrugged. "You don't know that."

"Yes, I do," he said, his tone growing distant and cool. He met my eyes and said, "Because I know you. I know that you would oppose them. Just as you know that I will not permit them to take one of mine from me without punishment."

I glared back at him. I wasn't worried about a soulgaze. Those happened only once between any two people, and Marcone had already gotten a look at me. When he said that he knew me, that's

what he was talking about. I'd seen his soul in return, and it had
been a cold and barren place—but one of order, as well. If Marcone gave his word, he kept it. And if someone came for one of his
people, he would go after them without hesitation, fear, or pity.

That didn't make him noble. Marcone had the soul of a tiger, of
a predator protecting his territory. It only made him more resolved
and more dangerous.

"I'm not a hit man," I told him. "And I don't work for you."

"Nor am I asking you to," he said. "I simply want to give you information that might help you in your efforts."

"You aren't listening. I am not going to kill anyone for you."

His teeth suddenly showed, very white against the tan. "But you
will go up against them."

"Yes."

He settled back in his seat. "I've seen what you do to the people
who get in your way. I'm willing to take my chances."

That thought, that attitude, was a little creepier than I was comfortable with. I wasn't a killer. I mean, sure, sometimes I fought.
Sometimes people and not-people got killed. But it wasn't as
though I was some kind of Jack the Ripper. From time to time matters got desperately dangerous between me and various denizens
of the preternatural world, but I had only killed . . .

I thought about it for a minute.

I'd killed more of them than I hadn't.

Quite a few more.

I felt a little sick to my stomach.

Marcone watched me from behind hooded eyes and waited.

"What do you want to tell me?" I asked him.

"I don't want to waste your time," he said. "Ask me questions.
I'll answer whichever I can."

"How much do you know about the deal that got Mendoza
killed?"

He drummed the fingers of his right hand on his thigh for a moment. "Mendoza was getting ready to retire," Marcone said. "He
had a final scheme to complete. I owed the man for loyalties past,
and at his request I allowed him certain liberties."

"He was selling something independently?"

Marcone nodded. "The contents of an old storage locker. Mendoza had come across the key to it in an estate sale."

That was criminal-speak for purchasing hot merchandise from a mugger or burglar. "Go on."

"The key opened a storage locker that had been sealed since 1945. It contained a number of works of art, jewelry, and similar cultural artifacts."

I arched an eyebrow. "Loot from World War Two?"

"So Mendoza presumed," Marcone said. "He offered me my selection of the contents, and in return I allowed him to dispose of the rest in whatever manner he saw fit."

"What did you get out of it?" I asked.

"Two Monets and a Van Gogh."

"Holy crap." I shook my head. "What happened then?"

"Mendoza went about liquidating his cache. It had been in process for several weeks when he reported that one of the people he had approached regarding an antique book seemed to have access to resources that were well beyond the ordinary."

"Did he give you a name?" I asked.

"A man named Grevane," Marcone said. "Mendoza asked for my advice on the matter."

"And you told him about how wizards are technologically challenged."

"Among other things," he said, nodding.

"But the deal went south."

"So it would seem," Marcone said. "Since Mendoza's death, I have asked Miss Gard to collect information on recent events in the local supernatural community."

I glanced at the woman and nodded. "And she told you there were necromancers running around."

"Once that had been established, we attempted to narrow down the location of these individuals, particularly Grevane, but met with very limited success."

"I'm able to find where they've been," Gard said without turning around. "Or at least where they've been weaving their spells."

"And there are a number of hot spots of necromantic energy around town," I said. "I know that already."

Marcone placed his fingers in a steeple before him. "But what I suspect you do not know is that last night at the location on Wacker, a member of my organization had an altercation with representatives of a rival interest from out of town. There was a gunfight. My man was mortally wounded and left for dead."

"That doesn't add up to necromancy," I said, frowning. "What caused the hot spot?"

"That is the question," Marcone said. He took a folded piece of paper from his breast pocket and passed it to me. "These are the names of the responding EMTs," he said. "According to my man, they were the first on the scene."

"Did he talk to you before he died?" I asked.

"He did," Marcone replied. "In point of fact, he did not die."

"Thought you said he was mortally wounded."

"He was, Mister Dresden," Marcone said, his features remote. "He was."

"He survived."

"The surgeons at Cook County thought it a bona fide miracle. Naturally I thought of you at once."

I rubbed at my chin. "What else has he said?"

"Nothing," Marcone said. "He has no memory of the events after he saw the ambulance arriving."

"So you want me to talk to the EMTs. Why haven't you done it yourself?" I asked.

He arched his brows. "Dresden. Try to keep in mind that I am a criminal. For some reason it's quite difficult to get people in uniforms to open their hearts to me."

I gritted my teeth at another agonizing twinge from my leg. "Right."

"So," he said, "we're back to my original question. How serious is your injury?"

"I'll make it," I said.

"Do you think you'll need to see a doctor? If it's too mild a wound, I'll be glad to have Miss Gard make it look more authentic."

I looked at him for a moment. "I'm heading for an emergency room whether I need it or not, eh?"

"As luck would have it, we are near a hospital. Cook County, in fact."

"Yeah. The cut's pretty deep." I looked at the piece of paper and then stuck it in my pocket. "There's bound to be an EMT or two there. Maybe you should drop me off at the emergency room."

Marcone smiled, and it didn't touch his eyes. "Very well, Dresden. You have my deepest sympathies for your pain."

Chapter

Nineteen

Marcone and company dropped me off a hundred yards from the emergency entrance to the hospital, and I had to hobble in alone. It was hard, and I was tired, but I'd been hurt worse before. It wasn't like I wanted to do this every day or anything, but after a certain point of ridiculous discomfort, the pain all feels pretty much the same.

Once I made it to the emergency room, I was a big hit. When you drag yourself inside panting and leaving a trail of bloody footprints behind you, it makes a certain impression. I had an orderly and a nurse helping me onto my stomach on a gurney within a few seconds while the nurse examined the wound.

"It isn't life-threatening," she reported after she cut away my pant leg and took a look. She glanced at me almost in accusation. "From the way you came in here, you'd think this almost killed you."

"Well," I said, "I'm kind of a wimp."

"Nasty," commented the burly orderly. He produced a clipboard layered in forms and a ballpoint pen and handed them both to me. "They'll have to cut this out."

"We'll let the doctor decide that," the nurse said. "How did this happen, sir?"

"I have no clue," I said. "I was walking down the street and all of a sudden I thought my leg was on fire."

"You walked here?" she asked.

"A helpful Boy Scout brought me most of the way," I said.

She sighed. "Well, it's been a slow day. They should be able to see to you shortly."

"That's super," I said. "Because it hurts like hell."

"I can get you some Tylenol," the nurse said primly.

"I don't have a headache. I have a four-inch piece of steel in my leg."

She passed me a paper cup and two little white tablets. I sighed and took them.

"Heh," the orderly said after she left. "Don't worry too much. They'll get you something when the doctor sees to you."

"With this kind of loving care, I probably won't need it."

"Don't be too hard on her," the orderly said. "You should see what people try so that they can get to some painkillers. Vicodin, morphine, that kind of thing."

"Yeah," I said. "Hey, man, can I ask you something?"

"Sure." He had brought a bowl of ice with him, and he started sealing it into plastic bags, which he started packing around my leg. "This should numb it a little, and maybe take down some of the swelling. It ain't a local, but it's what I've got."

The ice didn't actually burst into steam upon touching me, even though it felt like it should have. The pain didn't exactly lessen, but it did suddenly feel a little more distant. "Thanks, man. Hey, I was hoping I could talk to a couple of guys I know while I was here," I said. "They're EMTs. Gary Simmons and Jason Lamar."

The orderly lifted his eyebrows. "Simmons and Lamar, sure. They drive an ambulance."

"I know. Are they around?"

"They were on shift last night," he said. "But it's the end of the month and they might be on their swing shift. I'll ask."

"Appreciate it," I said. "If Simmons is there, tell him a school buddy is here."

"Sure. If I do that, though, you gotta do something for me and fill out these forms."

I eyed the clipboard and picked up the pen. "Tell the doc to sign me up for carpal tunnel surgery when he gets that thing out of me. Two birds with one stone."

The orderly grinned. "I'll do that."

He left me to fill in forms, which didn't used to take terribly long to fill out since I didn't have any kind of insurance. One of these days, when I had the money, I was going to have to get some. They say that when you pay for insurance you're really buying peace of mind. It might make me feel peaceful to think of how much money the company was probably going to lose on me in the long run. If I lived my whole life in the open, as I had been since I'd come to Chicago, they might be dealing with me for two or three centuries. I wondered what the yearly markup would be for a two-hundred-and-fifty-year-old.

A young doctor came in after I was finished with the forms, and true to the orderly's prediction, he had to cut the shuriken out of me. I got a local, and the sudden cessation of pain was like a drug all by itself. I fell asleep while he was cutting and woke up as he was wrapping my leg up.

". . . the sutures dry," he was saying. "Though from the looks of your file I suppose you know that."

"Sure, Doc," I said. "I know the drill. Do you need to take them out or did I get the other kind?"

"They'll dissolve," he said. "But if you experience any swelling or fever, get in touch. I'm giving you a prescription for something for the pain and some antibiotics."

"Follow all the printed instructions and be sure to take them all," I said, in my best surgeon-general-slash-television-announcer voice.

"Looks like you've done this as often as I have," he said. He gestured to the steel tray where the bloodied shuriken lay. "Did you want to keep the weapon?"

"Might as well. I'll have to get a souvenir in the gift shop otherwise."

"You sure you don't want the police to look at it?" he said. "They might be able to find fingerprints or something."

"I already told you guys it must have been some kind of accident," I said.

He gave me a look of extreme skepticism. "All right. If that's the way you want it." He dropped the little weapon into a metal tray of alcohol or some other sterilizer. "Keep your leg elevated. That will ease the swelling. Stay off of it for a couple of days, at least."

"No problem," I said.

He shook his head. "The orderly will be by in a minute with your prescriptions and a form to sign." He departed.

A minute later there were footsteps outside the little alcove they'd put me in, and a large young man drew the curtain aside. He had skin almost as dark as my leather duster, and his hair had been cropped into a flat-top so precise that his barber must have used a level. He was on the heavy side—not out of shape or ripped out, but simply large and comfortable with it. He wore an EMT's jacket, and the name tag on it read LAMAR. He stood there looking at me for a minute and then said, "You're the wrong color to have been in my high school. And I didn't do college."

"Army medic?" I asked.

"Navy. Marines." He folded his arms. "What do you want?"

"My name is Harry Dresden," I said.

He shrugged. "But what do you want?"

I sat up. My leg was still blissfully numb. "I wanted to talk to you about last night."

He eyed me warily. "What about it?"

"You were on the team who responded to a gunshot victim on Wacker."

His breath left him in a long exhale. He looked up and down the row, then stepped into the little alcove and closed the curtain behind him. He lowered his voice. "So?"

"So I want you to tell me about it," I said.

He shook his head. "Look, I want to keep my job."

I lowered my voice as well. "You think telling me is going to endanger that?"

"Maybe," he said. He pulled open his jacket and then unbuttoned two buttons on his shirt. He opened it enough to show me a Kevlar vest beneath it. "See that? EMTs have to wear them around here, because people shoot at us sometimes. Gangbangers, that kind of thing. We show up to try to save lives and people shoot at us."

"Must be tough," I said cautiously.

He shook his head. "I can handle it. But a lot of people don't. And if it looks like you're starting to crack under the pressure, they'll pull you out. Word gets around that I'm telling fairy tales about things I've seen, they'll have me on psychiatric disability by tomorrow." He turned to go.

"Wait," I said. I touched his arm lightly. I didn't grab him. You don't go unexpectedly grabbing former marines if you want your fingers to stay in the same shape. "Look, Mr. Lamar. I just want to hear about it. I'm not going to repeat it to anyone. I'm not a reporter or—"

He paused. "You're the wizard," he said. "Saw you on *Larry Fowler* once. People say you're crazy."

"Yeah," I said. "So it isn't as if they'd believe me, even if I did talk about you. Which I won't."

"You're the one they arrested in the nursery a few years back," he said. "You broke in during a blackout. They found you in the middle of a wrecked room with all those babies."

I took a deep breath. "Yeah."

Lamar was silent for a second. Then he said, "You know that the year before, the SIDS rate there was the highest in the nation? They averaged one case every ten days. No one could explain it."

"I didn't know that," I said.

"Since they arrested you there, they haven't lost one," he said. He turned back to me. "You did something."

"Yeah. Do you like ghost stories?"

He snorted out a breath through his nose. "I don't like any of this crap, man. Why do you want me to tell you what I saw?"

"Because what you know might help me keep more people from getting hurt."

He nodded, frowning. "All right," he said after a moment. "But I'm not saying this right now. You understand me? I'm not going to say this again. To anyone. Only reason I'll tell you is that you helped those babies."

I nodded.

He sat down on the edge of the gurney. "We got the call around midnight. Headed over to Wacker. The cops were there already. Found this guy on the street, all busted up. Two hits in the chest and two in the abdomen. He was bleeding bad."

I nodded, listening.

"We tried to stabilize him. But there wasn't much point to it. Simmons and me both knew that. But we tried. It's what you do, you know? He was awake for it. Scared as hell. Screaming some. Kept begging us not to let him die. Said he had a little girl to look after."

"What happened?"

"He died," Lamar said, his voice flat. "I've seen it before. Here in town. In action while I was in the corps. You get to where you can recognize death when he comes knocking." He rubbed his large, rather slender hands together. "We tried to resuscitate, but he was gone. That's when it happened."

"Go on."

"This woman shows up. I don't know from where. We just looked up and she was standing over us looking down."

I leaned forward. "What did she look like?"

"I don't know," Lamar answered. "She was . . . like, wearing this costume, right? Like those people at Renaissance fairs. Big old black robe with a hood over her head. I didn't see much of her face. Just her chin and her throat. She was white."

"What did you do?"

"I figured she was a nut. You get them a lot this time of year. Or maybe going to a costume party or something. Hell, it's almost Halloween. She looks at me and tells me to back up and let her help him."

How many women in a black hooded robe could have been running around town last night? Kumori. That would have been maybe forty-five minutes or an hour before I saw her at Bock's.

Lamar peered at my face. "You know her," he said.

"Not personally. But yeah. What did she do?"

His face grew more remote. "She knelt down over him. Like, straddling the stretcher. Then she leaned down. The robe and the hood fell over them both, right. Like, I couldn't see what she was doing." He licked his lips. "And it got cold. I mean, ice started forming on the sidewalk and the stretcher and on our truck. I swear to you, it happened."

"I believe it," I said.

"And the victim all of a sudden starts coughing. Trying to scream. I mean, it wasn't like the wounds were gone, but . . . I don't know how to describe it. He was holding on." His face twisted with a sickened expression. "He was in agony, and he was stable. It was like . . . like he wasn't being *allowed* to die.

"So the woman stands up. She tells us we've got less than an hour to save him. And then she's gone. Like, poof, gone. Like she was all in my imagination."

I shook my head. "Then?"

"We get him brought in. The docs patched him up and got fresh blood into him. He passed out about an hour later. But he made it."

Lamar was silent for a long moment.

"That couldn't have happened," he said then. "I mean, I've seen people pull through some bad stuff. But not like that. He should have been dead. Everything I know tells me so. But he kept going."

"Sometimes miracles happen," I said quietly.

He shuddered. "This wasn't a miracle. There wasn't any angel choir singing. My skin tried to crawl away and hide." He shook his head. "I don't want to think about it."

"What about your partner?" I asked.

"He drank himself under the table twenty minutes after our shift ended. Hell, only reason I wasn't with him was that I was teaching a CPR class this morning." He looked at me. "That help?"

"It might," I said. "Thank you."

"Sure."

"What are you going to do now?" I asked.

"Gonna go find my own table." Lamar stood up and said, "Good luck, man."

"Thanks."

The big man left, and while I got my prescriptions and filled out the last forms, I thought about what he'd had to say. I got the prescriptions filled at the hospital pharmacy, called a cab, and told him to take me to Mike's to pick up the Blue Beetle.

I sat in the backseat with my eyes closed and thought about what I'd learned. Kumori had saved the gunshot victim's life. If everything Lamar had said was accurate, it meant that she had gone out of her way to do it. And whatever she'd done, it had been an extremely difficult working to leave a mystic impression as intense as it did. That might explain why Kumori had done very little during the altercation with Cowl. I had expected her to be nearly as strong as her partner, but when she tried to take the book from me, her power hadn't been stronger than my own muscles and limbs.

But the Kemmler Alumni Association was in town with some vicious competition in mind. Why would Kumori have expended her strength for a stranger, rather than saving it for battling rival necromancers? Could the shooting victim have been important to her plans in some way?

It didn't track. The victim was just one more thug for the outfit, and he certainly wasn't going to be doing anything useful from his bed in intensive care.

I had to consider the possibility that she'd been trying to do the right thing: using her power to help someone in dire need.

The thought made me uncomfortable as hell. I knew that the necromancers I'd met were deadly dangerous, and that if I wanted to survive a conflict with them, I would have to be ready to hit them fast and hard and without any doubts. That's easy when the enemy is a frothing, psychotic monster. But Kumori's apparently humanitarian act changed things. It made her a person, and people are a hell of a lot harder for me to think about killing.

Even worse, if she'd been acting altruistically, it would mean that the dark energy the necromancers seemed to favor might not be something wholly, inherently evil. It had been used to preserve life, just as the magic I knew could be used either to protect or to destroy.

I'd always considered the line between black magic and white to be sharp and clear. But if that dark power could be employed in whatever fashion its wielder chose, that made it no different from my own.

Dammit. Investigation was supposed to make me certain of what needed to be done. It was not supposed to confuse me even more.

When I opened my eyes, thick clouds had covered the sun and painted the whole world in shades of grey.

Chapter

Twenty

It was past the middle of the afternoon by the time I got the Blue Beetle from Mike's and headed back to my apartment. I tried to be wary of possible tails, but by then the local was wearing off and my leg was hurting again. I don't know if you've ever had a serious physical injury, but there's more to it than simply increasing the amount of discomfort. It's tiring. The pain carries with it a tax of bone-deep weariness that makes you want to crawl into a dark hole and hibernate.

So when I say I tried to be wary, what I mean is that I flicked a glance at my rearview mirror a couple of times whenever I had the presence of mind to remember to do so. As long as the bad guys were restricting themselves to driving brightly painted side-panel vans or maybe nitro-burning funny cars, I was perfectly safe.

I got back to my place, disabled the wards, unlocked the door, and slipped inside. Mister came flying down the stairs at my back, and thumped companionably against my legs. I all but screamed. "Stupid cat," I snarled.

Mister wound around my legs in a pleased fashion, unconcerned with my opinion of him. I limped inside and locked up behind me. Mouse waited until Mister was bored with me, then shambled over to snuffle at my legs and collect a few scratches behind his ears.

"Hey, there," Thomas greeted me quietly. He sat in the chair by the fire, several candles lit on the end table beside it. He had a book open. Sword and shotgun rested near his hand. He glanced at my leg and rose, his face alarmed. "What happened?"

I grimaced, tottered over to the couch, and plopped down on it. "Sticks and stones may break your bones, but Chinese throwing stars get you a dozen stitches." I drew the ghoul's weapon from my pocket by way of illustration and tossed it down on the coffee table. "How's Butters?"

"Fine," Thomas said. "Funny little guy. Made an awful racket with that . . . polka thing of his for about half an hour, babbled for forty minutes straight, and fell asleep eating dinner. I put him on the bed."

"He's had a stressful day," I said.

"He's a coward," Thomas said.

I glared at him and started to snarl something harsh and defensive.

He held up a hand and hurried to speak. "Don't take that wrong, Harry. He's smart enough to understand what's happening. And he's smart enough to know that there's not a damned thing he can do about it. He knows the only reason he's alive is that someone else is protecting him. He isn't kidding himself that he's somehow done it because of his own cleverness or skill." Thomas glanced at the door to the bedroom. "He doesn't know how to deal with the fear. It's strangling him."

I propped my aching leg up on the coffee table. "Thank you for your professional opinion, Counselor."

Thomas gave me a level look. "I've seen it before. I know what I'm talking about."

"Whatever," I said.

"When you were attacked in the morgue last night, he froze. Didn't he."

I shrugged one shoulder. "Not everyone is cut out for the battlefield."

"But he froze," Thomas said. "You had to scream orders into his ear and haul him around like luggage, right?"

"That doesn't make him a coward."

"He lets his fear control him. That's what a coward is, Harry."

"A lot of people would react the same way," I said.

"A lot of people aren't making themselves into excess baggage for my brother," he shot back.

"No one does well their first time out," I said.

"It isn't an isolated incident," Thomas said. "You told me that when he reported on the corpses taken from Bianca's manor, and they locked him up in the nuthouse."

"So?"

"So do you think he got his job back without backing down? Admitting to some shrink that he hadn't really seen what he saw?" Thomas shook his head. "He was afraid to lose his career. He caved."

I sat silently.

"Doesn't make him a bad person," Thomas said. "But he's a coward. He's either going to get you killed or else freeze at a bad moment and die—and you'll torture yourself over how it's all your fault. If we want to survive, we need to get him somewhere safe. Then cut him loose. Better for everyone."

I thought about it for a minute.

"You might be right," I said. "But if we tell him to rabbit, he's never going to be able to get over the fear. We'll be making it worse for him. He has to face it down."

"He doesn't want to."

"No," I said, "but he needs to."

Thomas looked from me to the fire and nodded. "It's your show."

I watched Mouse mosey over to his bucket-sized food bowl. He sat down by it and waited expectantly until Mister prowled over to him. Then he bent down to eat. My cat stalked up to Mouse and promptly swatted him on the muzzle with one paw. Mouse opened his jaws in a doggy grin and walked a couple of steps in the direction Mister had swatted him.

Mister regarded Mouse with lordly disdain, then ate part of a single piece of kibble. Then he slapped at the bowl of food, scattering bits over the kitchen floor, and walked away. Once he was done, Mouse padded back over, patiently ate the spilled food, and then resumed munching on the bowl.

"Remember when Mouse would slide all the way to the wall when Mister did that?" Thomas asked.

"Heh. Yeah."

"Do you think Mister realizes that the dog is about twenty times bigger than he used to be?" Thomas asked.

"Oh, he realizes it, all right," I said. "He just doesn't see how it's relevant."

"One of these days Mouse is going to disabuse him of the notion."

I shook my head. "He won't. Mister made his point when Mouse was tiny. Mouse is the sort to respect tradition."

"Or he's scared to cross the cat." Thomas's eyes drifted to my bandages and he nodded at my leg. "How bad is it?"

"I can walk. I wouldn't want to go dancing."

"Is that your next move, dancing?"

I leaned my head back on the couch and closed my eyes. "I'm not sure what to do next. How are you as a sounding board?"

"I can look interested and nod at appropriate moments," he said.

"Good enough," I said.

I told Thomas everything.

He listened, taking it all in, and the first thing he said was, "You have a *date?*"

I opened my eyes and blinked at him. "What. Is that so hard to conceive?"

"Well, yeah," he said. "Christ, Harry, I thought you were going to spend the rest of your life as a hermit."

"What?"

He rolled his eyes. "It isn't like you've gone looking for women," Thomas said. "I mean, you never hit any clubs. Try to get any phone numbers. I figured you just didn't want to." He mulled it over for a minute and then said, "Good God. You're *shy.*"

"I am not," I said.

"The girl practically had to throw herself into your arms. My sister would laugh herself sick."

I glowered at him. "You are not a spectacularly helpful sounding board."

He stretched out a little and crossed his legs at the ankle. "I'm so pretty, it's hard for me to think of myself as intelligent." He pursed his lips. "There are two things you need to know."

"The book," I said, nodding.

"Yeah. Everyone is hot and bothered over this *Erlking* thing. You read it?"

"Yeah."

"And?"

I raked my fingers through my hair. "And nothing. It's a collection of essays about a particular figure of faerie lore called the Erlking."

"Who is he?"

"He's one of the high sidhe," I said. "And he isn't part of Winter or Summer. He's a wyldfae."

"Powerful?"

"Very," I said. "But just how powerful he is varies depending on who was writing about him. Some of them ranked him among the top faerie nobles. A couple claimed he was on par with one of the Faerie Queens."

"What does he do?"

"He's some kind of hunter spirit," I said. "Associated with all kinds of primal violence. He's apparently one of the beings who can call up and lead the Wild Hunt."

"The what?" Thomas said.

"It's a gathering of some of the more predatory beings of Faerie," I said. "They appear in the autumn and winter usually, usually along with storms and rough weather. A gathering of black hounds the size of horses with glowing red eyes, led by a hunter with the horns of a stag on a black horse."

"The Erlking?" Thomas asked.

"There are several figures who can lead the hunt, apparently," I said. "None of them are particularly friendly. The Hunt will kill anything and anyone it runs across. It's major-league dangerous."

"I think I've heard about it," Thomas said. "Is it true that you can avoid being hunted by joining them?"

I shrugged. "I don't know. I've never heard of anyone who met the Hunt and survived. Could be that they won't hunt what they think of as another predator."

"Like sharks," Thomas said. "It's all about body language."

"I wouldn't count on nonverbal cues to protect you from the Hunt," I said. "Assuming you ever saw them. It appears maybe only once every five or six years, and can show up almost anywhere in the world."

"Is it the Hunt you think the Kemmlerites are interested in?"

"I'm not sure," I said. "I can't think what else it would be. The Erlking has a reputation as a being that preys upon children, or at least one that heralds their deaths. A couple of wizards even peg him as a guardian who ensures that children's souls aren't harmed or diverted as they depart dying bodies."

"Sounds like there is a mixed opinion on this Erlking guy."

"Faeries are like that," I said. "They aren't ever quite what they seem to be. It's hard to pin them down."

"But why would a gang of necromancers be interested in him? Is there anything in the book that makes sense?"

"Not that I saw," I said. "There were stories, songs, lectures, accountings, bad sketches, and worse poetry about the Erlking, but nothing practical."

"Nothing you saw," Thomas said.

"Nothing I saw," I confirmed. "But these lunatics would hardly be this serious about the book if it wasn't there somewhere."

"Do you think it's connected to this Darkhallow that Corpsetaker was talking about?" Thomas asked.

"I don't know," I said. "What's a Darkhallow?"

We listened to the fire crackle for a minute before Thomas said, "I hate to say this, but maybe you should contact the Council."

I grimaced. "I *know* I should," I said. "I don't know what they're doing. And these necromancers are strong, Thomas. Stronger than me. I don't think I can take them in a straight fight."

"Sounds like a good reason to call for help."

"I can't do that," I said. "Mavra would torpedo Murphy."

"I don't think Murphy would want you to get killed over this, Harry," he pointed out. "And what's going to happen if the Council hears that you knew these folk were around and didn't report it to them? They aren't going to be happy."

"I know," I said. "I know. But at the moment it's my choice, and I'm not going to choose for my friend to get hurt. I can't."

He nodded, as if he'd expected the answer.

"Plus there's one more reason not to call in the Council," I said.

"Why?"

"Right now, Cowl, Grevane, and Corpsetaker aren't working together. If I call in the Council it gives them a common enemy and a reason to cooperate."

"They have a common enemy," he pointed out. "You."

I laughed, and it came out a little bitter. "They aren't worried about me. Hell, I can't even figure out what's going on." I rubbed at my eyes. "You said there were two things I need to know. What's the second thing?"

"Your car."

"Oh, I got it back," I said. "It's out front."

"No, dummy," Thomas said. "Whoever trashed your car did it deliberately. They were trying to tell you something."

"It might not even be related to this situation," I said.

He snorted. "Yeah. It just happened now, out of all the times it could have happened."

"Whoever was sending the message, it's a little obscure. You think it's one of the Kemmler crowd?"

"Why not?" he said.

I thought about it for a minute. "It doesn't seem like something Grevane would do. I bet he's more like the kind to send undead minions to deliver his messages. Corpsetaker would send a nightmare or a forced hallucination or something. She's big on the mind magic. Ghouls don't really send messages. They just eat you."

"That leaves Cowl, his buddy, and Grevane's buddy with the liver spots."

"Yeah," I said. "I almost feel like there was something familiar about Liver Spots," I said. "I'm not sure what. I might be grasping at straws."

"What about Cowl and Kumori?"

"I don't know, man," I said. "They were just a couple of people in cloaks. I never saw their faces. If I had to guess from the way they talked, I'd bet that they were Council."

"That would be a very good reason to cover their faces," Thomas agreed.

"There's no point in chewing this over and over," I said. I rubbed at my eyes. "Bony Tony's numbers mean something. They'll lead to the book, somehow. I'm sure of it."

"Maybe a locker number?" Thomas asked.

"Too many digits," I said.

"Maybe it's some kind of cipher. Substituting letters for numbers."

I raised my eyebrows. "That's a thought." I dug the folded piece of paper out of my pocket and passed it over to him. "Stay here and work on it. See if you can make any sense out of it."

He accepted the paper. "Now I feel like James Bond. Suave and intelligent, breaking all the codes while looking fabulous. What are you going to do?"

"I think the Erlking is the key to this," I said. "And the Erlking is a faerie."

He lifted his eyebrows. "Meaning?"

"When you want to know about faeries," I said, "it's best to ask a faerie. I'm going to call up my godmother and see if she knows anything."

"From what you've told me, isn't that kind of dangerous?"

"Very," I said.

"You're hurt. You should have some backup."

I nodded. "Watch the fort," I said. "Mouse."

The big dog lifted his shaggy head from the floor, ears perked forward, serious eyes on me.

"Come on," I told him. "We're going for a ride."

"Oh, Harry," Thomas said.

"Yeah?"

"Before you go . . . would you mind if I, uh, helped Butters out by getting his polka contraption loaded up into your trunk?"

"What. You don't like polka?"

Thomas's expression looked strained. "Please, Harry. I like the little guy, but come *on*."

I rubbed at my mouth with one hand to cover up the smile. "Sure. Probably safest for everyone that way."

"Thank you," he said, and collected the polka suit and brought it up the stairs behind me as I prepared to take a chance on a conversation with one of the more dangerous beings I knew.

Chapter

Twenty-one

Mouse and I took the Beetle out of Chicago proper, following the lake north out of town. For once I wished I had an automatic transmission. Driving stick with only one good hand and one good leg is not fun. In fact, it's the next best thing to impossible, at least for me. I wound up using my wounded leg more than I should have, and the discomfort intensified. I thought about the painkillers in my pocket, and then blew them off. I needed to be sharp. When all of this was over, there would be time to muddle my head with codeine. So I drove, and swore under my breath at anything that made me change gears, while Mouse rode along in the passenger seat with his head usually sticking out the window.

By the time I was far enough from town to start calling out to my godmother, the sun had set, though the cloud-veiled western sky still glowed the color of campfire embers. I pulled off onto a side road that was made of old gravel and stubborn weeds that kept trying to grow up in the road's smooth center. It led down to a little dead end where some kind of construction project never went through. It was a popular spot for local kids to hang out and imbibe illegal substances of one intensity or another, and there were empty beer cans and bottles scattered around in abundance.

Mouse and I left the car up on the road, and walked maybe fifty yards down through trees and heavy undergrowth to the shore of the lake. At one point on the shore, a little spit of land formed a promontory only ten or twelve inches higher than the surface of the water.

"Wait here," I told Mouse, and the dog sat down at the end of the spit of land, watching me with alert eyes, his ears flicking around at all the little sounds. Then I walked out onto the spit to its end, and a cold wind off the lake swept around me, blowing my coat and threatening my balance. I grimaced and leaned on my staff, out at that point of land where earth and water and sky met one another, and focused my thoughts, blocking out the pain of my leg, my fears, my questions. I gathered together my will, then lifted my face to the wind and called out, quietly, "Leanansidhe. An it please thee, come hither and hold discourse with me."

I sent my will, my magic coursing into the words, and they reverberated with power, echoing from the surface of the lake, repeating themselves in whispers in the swirling wind, vibrating the ground upon which I stood.

Then I waited. I could have repeated myself, but my godmother had certainly heard me. If she was going to come, she would. If she wasn't, no amount of repetition was likely to change her mind. The wind blew colder and stronger, throwing cold droplets up from the lake and into my face. One gust of wind brought me the sound of an airliner overhead, and another the lonely whistle of a freight train. Distantly, somewhere on the lake, a bell rang out several times, a solemn sound that made me think of a funeral dirge. Beyond that, nothing stirred.

I waited. In time, the fire faded from the overcast sky, and only the darkest tones of purple were left on the western horizon behind me. Dammit. She wasn't coming.

After I thought that but before I could actually turn around, there was a swirling in the waters near my feet, and a slow spiral of water spray spun up from the surface of the lake, a bizarre sight. The spray rolled up and away from a female form, beginning at the feet, bare and pale, and rolling up over a medieval-style gown of emerald green. The gown was belted with a woven silver rope, and a slightly curved, single-edged knife of some dark, glassy material hung at an angle through it.

When the spray rolled up over the woman's face, I expected my godmother's blazing wealth of copper and scarlet curls, her wide feline eyes of amber, her features that always made her seem smug and somewhat pleased with herself, in absence of the animation of any other emotion.

Instead I saw a long, pale throat, features of heart-stopping, cold beauty, canted eyes greener than any color to be found in the natural world, and long, silken hair of purest white, bound within a circlet of what looked like rose vines surrounded in gleaming ice, beautiful and brittle and cruel.

Behind me, a deep-throated snarl burst forth from Mouse, back on the shore.

"Greetings, mortal," said the faerie woman. Her voice shook water and earth and sky with subtle power. I felt it resonating through the elements around me as much as heard it.

My mouth went dry and my throat got tight. I leaned on my staff to help me balance as I cast a courtly bow in her direction. "Greetings, Queen Mab. I do beg your pardon. It was not my intention to disturb thee."

My head shifted into panicked, quick thought. Queen Mab had come to me, and that absolutely could not be good. Mab, monarch of the Winter Court of the Sidhe, the Queen of Air and Darkness, was not a very nice person. In fact, she was one of the most feared beings of power you'd find short of archangels and ancient gods. I'd once used my wizard's Sight to look upon Mab as she unveiled her true self in a working of power, and it had come perilously close to driving me insane.

Mab was not some paltry mortal being like Grevane or Cowl or the Corpsetaker. She was far older, far crueler, far more deadly than they could ever be.

And I owed her a favor. Two, to be exact.

She stared at me for a long and silent moment, and I didn't look at her face. Then she let out a quiet laugh and said, "Disturb me? Hardly. I am here only to fulfill the duties I have been obliged to take upon myself. It is no fault of thine that this summons reached mine ears."

I straightened up slowly and avoided her eyes. "I had expected my godmother to come."

Mab smiled. Her teeth were small and white and perfect, her canines delicately sharp. "Alas. The Leanansidhe is tied up at the moment."

I drew in a breath. My godmother was a powerful member of the Winter Court, but she couldn't hold a candle to Mab. If Mab wanted to take Lea down, she certainly could do it—and for some reason the thought spurred on a protective instinct, something that made me irrationally angry. Yes, Lea was hardly a benevolent being in her own right. Yes, she'd tried to enslave me several times in the past several years. But for all of that, she was still *my* godmother, and the thought of something happening to her angered me. "For what reason have you detained her?"

"Because I do not tolerate challenges to my authority," she said. One pale hand drifted to the hilt of the knife at her belt. "Certain events had convinced your godmother that she was no longer bound by my word and will. She is now learning otherwise."

"What have you done to her?" I asked. Well. It didn't sound like a question so much as a demand.

Mab laughed, and the sound of it came out silvery and smoother than honey. The laugh bounded around the waves and the earth and the winds, clashing against itself in a manner that made the hairs on my neck stand up and my heart race with a sudden apprehension as I felt an odd kind of pressure settle over me, as if I were closed into a small room. I gritted my teeth and waited the laugh out, trying not to show how harshly it had affected me. "She is bound," Mab said. "She is in some discomfort. But she is in no danger from my hand. Once she acknowledges who rules Winter, she will be restored to her station. I can ill afford the loss of so potent a vassal."

"I need to speak to her now," I said.

"Of course," Mab said. "Yet she languishes in the process of enlightenment. Thus am I here to fulfill her obligation to teach and guide you."

I frowned. "You locked her away somewhere, but you're keeping her promises?"

Something cold and haughty flickered through Mab's eyes. "Promises must be kept," she murmured, and the words made wave, wind, and stone tremble. "My vassal's oaths and bargains are binding upon me, so long as I restrain her from fulfilling them."

"Does that mean that you will help me?" I asked.

"It means that I will give you what she might give you," Mab said, "and speak what knowledge she might have spoken to you were she here in flesh, rather than in proxy." She tilted her head slowly to one side. "You know, wizard, that I may speak no word that is untrue. Thus is my word given to you."

I eyed her warily. It was true that the high Sidhe could not speak words that were untrue—but that wasn't the same thing as *telling* the truth. Most of the Sidhe I had met were past masters of the art of deception, speaking in allusions and riddles and inferences that would undermine the necessary honesty of their words so thoroughly that they might be much stronger lies than if they had simply spoken a direct falsehood. Trusting the word of one of the Sidhe was an enterprise best undertaken with extraordinary caution and exacting care. If I had any choice in the matter, I would avoid it.

But there was nothing I could do but forge ahead. I still had to find out more about what Sergeant Kemmler's Lonely Hearts Club Band was doing in Chicago, and that meant taking the risk of speaking with my godmother. Mab was simply more of the same risk.

A *lot* more of it.

"I seek knowledge," I said, "about the one known as the Erlking."

Mab arched an eyebrow. "*Him*," she said. "Yes. Your godmother knows some little of him. What would you know of him?"

"I want to know why all of Kemmler's disciples are grabbing up all the copies of the White Council's book about him."

Nothing that I could imagine would truly rattle Mab's composure, but that sentence apparently came close. Her expression froze, and with it the wind came to a sudden, dead halt. The waves of the shore abruptly stilled to a sheet of glass beneath her feet, dimly reflecting the glow of the city skyline in the distance and the last shreds of purple light in the leaden sky.

"Kemmler's disciples," she said. Her eyes were deeper than the lake she stood upon. "Could it be?"

"Could what be?" I asked.

"The *Word*," she said. "*The Word of Kemmler*. Has it been found?"

"Um," I said. "Sort of."

Her delicate white brows rose. "Meaning what, pray tell?"

"Meaning that the book was found," I said. "By a local thief. He tried to sell it to a man named Grevane."

"Kemmler's first student," Mab said. "Did he acquire the book?"

"No," I said. "The thief used mortal technology to conceal the book, in order to prevent Grevane from taking it from him without paying."

"Grevane killed him," Mab guessed.

"And how."

"This mortal ferromancy—technology, you called it. Does it yet conceal the book?"

"Yeah."

"Grevane yet seeks it?"

"Yeah. Him and at least two more. Cowl and the Corpsetaker."

Mab lifted a pale hand and tapped a finger to rich, lovely lips the color of frozen mulberries. Her nails were colored with shining opalescence gorgeous to the eye and distracting as hell. I felt a little dizzy until I forced myself not to look at them. "Dangerous," she mused. "You have fallen among deadly company, mortal. Even the Council fears them."

"You don't say."

Mab narrowed her eyes, and a little smile graced her lips. "Impudent," she said. "It's sweet on you."

"Gosh, that's flattering," I said. "But you haven't told me a thing about why they might be interested in the Erlking."

Mab pursed her lips. "The being you ask me about is to goblins as I am to the Sidhe. A ruler. A master of their kind. Devious, cunning, strong, and swift. He wields dominion over the spirits of fallen hunters."

I frowned. "What kind of spirits?"

"The spirits of those who hunt," Mab said. "The energy of the hunt. Of excitement, hunger, bloodlust. Betimes, the Erlking will call those spirits into the form of the great black hounds, and ride the winds and forests as the Wild Hunt. He carries great power with him as he does. Power that calls to the remnants of hunters now passed on from mortal life."

"You're talking about ghosts," I said. "The spirit of hunters."

"Indeed," Mab said. "Shades that lay in quiet rest, beyond the beck of the mortal pale, will rise up to the night and the stars at the sound of his horn, and join the Hunt."

"Powerful shades," I said quietly.

"Specters most potent," Mab said, nodding, her eyes bright and almost merry as they watched me.

I leaned on my staff, trying to get as much weight as I could off of my injured leg, so that it would stop pounding enough to make me think. "So a gaggle of wizards whose stock in trade is enslaving the dead to their will is interested in a being whose presence calls up powerful spirits they couldn't otherwise reach." I followed the chain of logic from there. "There's something in the book that tells them how to get his attention."

"Darling child," Mab said. "So clever for one so young."

"So what is it?" I asked. "Which part of the book?"

"Your godmother," she said, her smile growing wider, "has no idea."

I ground my teeth together. "But you do?"

"I am the Queen of Air and Darkness, wizard. There is little I do not."

"Will you tell me?"

She touched the tip of her tongue to her lips, as if savoring the taste of the words. "You should know us better than that by now, wizard. Nothing given by one of the Sidhe comes without a price."

My foot hurt. I had to hop a little bit on my good leg when my balance wavered. "Great," I muttered. "What is it you want?"

"You," Mab said, folding her hands primly in front of her. "My offer of Knighthood yet stands open to you."

"What's wrong with the new guy?" I asked, "that you'd dump him for me?"

Mab showed me her teeth again. "I have not yet replaced my current Knight, treacherous though he is," she purred.

"He's still alive?" I asked.

"I suppose," Mab said. "Though he very much wishes that he were not. I have taken the time to explain to him at length the error of his ways."

Torture. She'd been torturing him in vengeance for his treachery for more than three years.

I felt a little sick to my stomach.

"If you like, you might consider it an act of mercy," she said. "Accept my offer, and I will forgive your debt to me and answer all your questions freely."

I shuddered. Mab's last Knight had been an abusive, psychotic, drug-addicted, murdering rapist. I was never clear on whether he got the job *because* of those qualities or whether they had been instilled in him on the job. Either way, the title of Winter Knight was a permanent gig. If I accepted Mab's offer, I'd be doing it for life—though there would, of course, be no promises as to how long that life would be.

"I told you once before," I said, "that I'm not interested."

"Things have changed, wizard," Mab said. "You know the kind of power you face in Kemmler's heirs. As the Winter Knight, you would have strength far outweighing even your own considerable gifts. You would have the wherewithal to face your foes, rather than slinking through the night gathering up whispers to use against them."

"No." I paused and then said, "And no means no."

Mab shrugged one shoulder, a liquid motion that drew my eyes toward the curves of her breasts within the silken gown. "You disappoint me, child. But I can wait. I can wait until the sun burns cold."

Thunder rumbled over the lake. Off in the southwest, lightning leapt from cloud to cloud.

Mab turned her head to watch. "Interesting."

"Uh. What's interesting?"

"Powers at work, preparing the way."

"What is that supposed to mean?" I asked.

"That you have little time," Mab said. She turned to face me again. "I must do what I might to preserve your life. Know this, mortal: Should Kemmler's heirs acquire the knowledge bound within the *Word,* they will be in a position to gather up such power as the world has not seen in many thousands of years."

"What? How?"

"Kemmler was"—Mab's eyes grew distant, as if in memory— "a madman. A monster. But brilliant. He learned how to bind to his will not only dead flesh, but shades—to rend them asunder and devour them to feed his own power. It was the secret of the strength that allowed him to defy all the White Council together."

I added two and two and got four. "The heirs want to call up the ancient spirits," I breathed. "And then devour them for power."

Mab's deep-green eyes almost seemed to glow with intensity. "Kemmler himself attempted it, but the Council struck him down before he could finish."

I swallowed. "What happens if one of his heirs is able to do it?"

"The heir would gain power such as has not been wielded by mortal hands in the memory of your race," Mab said.

"The Darkhallow," I said. I rubbed at my eyes. "That's what it is. A ritual, tomorrow night. Halloween. They all want to be the one to make themselves into a junior-league god."

"Power is ever sweet, is it not?"

I thought about it some more. I had to worry about more than just Kemmler's cronies. Mavra wanted the *Word*, too. Hell's bells. If Mavra succeeded in making herself into some kind of dark goddess, there wasn't a chance in hell that she wouldn't obliterate me at the first opportunity. "Can they do it without the *Word?*"

Mab's mouth curled up in a slow smile. "If they could, why would they seek it so desperately?" The wind began to stir again, and the lake began to resume its ebb and flow. "Beware, wizard. You are engaged in a most deadly game. I should be disappointed were I deprived of your service."

"Then get used to it," I said. "I'm never going to be your knight."

Mab tilted back her head and let out that nerve-searing laughter again. "I have time," she said. "And you mortals find life to be very sweet. Two favors you yet owe me, and make no mistake, I will collect. One day you will kneel at my feet."

The lake suddenly surged, dark waters whirling up in a snake-quick spiral, forming a waterspout that stretched from the lake's surface up out of sight into the darkness above me. The wind howled, driving my balance to one side, so that my wounded leg buckled and I fell to one knee.

Then, as suddenly as it began, the gale was gone. The lake was calm again. The wind sighed mournfully through tree branches sparsely covered in dead leaves. There was no sign of Mab.

I grimaced and struggled to my feet. I glanced back at Mouse, who was sitting on the shore, watching me with worried doggy eyes.

"She always has to have the last word," I told him.

Mouse padded over to me, and I scratched his ears a couple of times while he snuffled at me. He looked warily out at the lake.

"One problem at a time," I told him. "We'll handle Mab later. Somehow."

I walked back to the Beetle more slowly than ever, and Mouse stayed within a step or two the entire time. The adrenaline faded and left me wearier than ever. I had to fight to stay awake all the way back to my place. A thin, cold, drizzling rain began to fall.

I had just gotten home and out of the car when Mouse let out a warning snarl. I spun and wavered, then planted my staff hard on the ground to keep from falling over.

Out of the darkness and rain, a dozen or more people suddenly loomed into view. All of them walked toward me, steady and unhurried.

And all of them marched in step with one another.

In the distance I heard the low, rumbling thunder of a drum played on a big bass stereo.

Behind the first group came another. And behind them another. By then I could see the eyes of the nearest—empty, staring eyes in sunken, deathly faces.

My heart lurched in sudden terror as the zombies closed in on me.

I shambled down my stairs and tripped, stumbling against my door. I fumbled at my keys, frantically taking down my wards so that my own security spells didn't kill me on my way in. Mouse stayed at my back, continuous snarls bubbling from between his bared teeth.

"Thomas!" I screamed. "Thomas, open the door!"

I heard a noise, close, and spun around.

Mindless faces appeared at the top of the stairs leading down to my apartment door, and Grevane's killing machines leapt down them, straight at me.

Chapter

Twenty-two

Mouse leapt into the air as the lead zombie flung itself at me, and met it with an ugly sound of impact. The dog and the animate corpse dropped onto the stairs. The zombie swung an arm at Mouse, but the dog rolled, taking the blow on one slab of a shoulder, his snarl sharpening at the impact. The dog surged against the zombie's legs and got his teeth into the corpse's face. He shook his head violently, while the zombie stumbled and reeled under the ferocity of the attack.

The second zombie bypassed the struggling pair, reaching out for me. I barely had time to brandish my staff at the creature and snarl, *"Forzare!"*

Unseen force struck the zombie like an ocean wave, flinging it back up the stairs and out of sight.

Mouse let out a shrieking sound of pain, ripped his fangs once more at the zombie's face, and pushed away from it. The zombie's face had been crushed and torn until it was unrecognizable. Both eyes had been torn out, and the undead thing flailed around wildly, striking blindly with heavy sweeps of its arms. Mouse leaned heavily against me, one paw held lifted from the ground, snarling.

Three more zombies were already most of the way down the stairs, and there was no time to do anything but try my staff again. I raised it, but the nearest zombie was faster than I had guessed, and he batted the wood out of my hand. It smacked against the concrete wall of the stairwell and rebounded onto the blinded zombie, out of my reach. The zombie snatched at my arm and I barely avoided it.

The door opened at my back and Thomas called, "Down!"

I dropped to the ground and did my best to haul Mouse down with me. There was a roar of thunder, and the leading zombie's head vanished into a spray of ugly, rotten gore. The remainder of the being thrashed for a second and then fell drunkenly to one side, collapsing into immobility.

Thomas stood in the doorway, dressed only in a pair of blue jeans. He held the sawed-off shotgun against his shoulder, and his eyes blazed with a cold silver fury. He worked the pump on the gun and fired it three times more, destroying or driving back my nearest attackers for a moment. Then he seized the collar of my duster and dragged me forcibly into the apartment. Mouse came with us, and Thomas slammed the door shut.

"Get the locks," I told him. He started shoving the door's two heavy security bolts shut, while I crawled to the door, laid my hands against it, and with a whisper of will rearmed the wards that protected the apartment. The air hummed with a low buzz as the wards snapped back up into place.

Silence fell over the apartment.

"Okay," I said, panting. "That's it. Safe at home." I looked around the apartment and spotted Butters hovering near the fireplace, poker in hand. "You okay, man?"

"I guess so," Butters said. He looked a little wild around the eyes. "Are they gone?"

"If they aren't yet, they will be. We're safe."

"Are you sure?"

"Definitely," I said. "There's no way they're going to get in here."

The words were hardly off my lips when there was a thunder crack of sound and a heavy thump that knocked scores of books off my bookshelves and sent us all staggering around like the cast of the original *Star Trek*.

"What was that?" Butters screamed.

"The wards," Thomas snapped.

"No," I said. "I mean, come on. Walking right into those wards is suicide."

There was another clap of thunder, and the apartment shook again. A flash of bright blue light bathed the outside of the boardinghouse, and even reflected through the sunken windows near my apartment's ceiling, it was painfully bright.

"Can't commit suicide if you're already dead," Thomas said. "How many of those things were out there?"

"Uh, I'm not sure," I said. "A lot?"

Thomas swallowed, got the box of shells off the mantel, and started loading them into the shotgun. "What happens if he just keeps throwing zombies at the wards?"

"I didn't build them to keep up a continuous discharge," I said. There was another roaring sound and another flash of light, but this time there was barely a tremor on the floor. "They're going to fade and collapse."

"How long?" Thomas asked.

There was a crackling buzz from outside, too slow, this time, to be heard only as a roar of noise. Blue-white light flickered dimly. "Not long. Dammit."

"Oh, God," Butters said. "Oh, God, oh, God. What happens when the wards are gone?"

I grunted. "The door is made of steel. It will take them some time to get through it. And after that, there's the threshold. That should stop them, or at least slow them down." I raked my fingers over my hair. "We've got to come up with something, fast."

"What about the extra defenses?" Thomas asked.

"They're standing right outside," I said.

"Hence the need for extra defenses," Thomas snapped. He pumped a round into the shotgun's chamber and slipped another into the extra slot in its clip.

"Those defenses are meant to stop a magical assault," I said. "Not physical entry."

"Will they keep the zombies out?" Butters asked.

"Yes. But they'll also keep us *in*."

"What's so bad about that?" Butters asked.

"Nothing," I said, "until Grevane sets the building on fire. Once they go up, I can't take them down again. We'll be trapped." I ground my teeth. "We've got to get out of here."

"But the zombies are out there!" Butters said.

"I'm not the only one who lives here," I said. "If he burns down the house to get to me, people will die. Thomas, get dressed and get your shoes on. Butters, there's a ladder under that Navajo rug there. I want you to take a candle and go down it. There's a black nylon backpack on a table, and a white skull on a wooden shelf. Put the skull in the backpack and bring it to me."

"What?" Butters said.

"Do it!" I snapped.

Butters scurried over to the Navajo rug, found the trapdoor down to my lab, and grabbed a candle. He disappeared down the ladder.

Thomas put the shotgun down and opened his trunk. It didn't take him long to get dressed in socks, black combat boots, a white T-shirt, a black leather jacket. Maybe it was part of his supernatural sex-vampire powers—dressing quickly for a hasty getaway.

"You see?" he said while he dressed. "About Butters."

"Shut up, Thomas," I said.

"What is the plan?" he said.

I limped over to the phone and put it to my ear. Nothing.

"They cut the phone."

"We can't call for help," Thomas said.

"Right. Only thing we can do is smash our way out to the car."

Thomas nodded his head with a jerk. "How you want to do it?"

"What do you think?"

"Big old wall of fire would do it. Cover our left flank and keep the bad guys off of us. I'll take the right flank and shoot anything that moves."

Fire magic. A sudden memory of my burned hand flashed through my head so intensely that I felt actual, physical pain in the nerve endings that had been destroyed. I thought about what I would need to do to manage the wall Thomas had suggested, and at the mere *thought* my stomach twisted in revulsion—and worse, with doubt.

For magic to work, you have to believe in it. You have to believe that you can and should perform whatever action you had in mind, or you get zippo. As my hand burned with phantom agony, I realized something I had not admitted, not even to myself.

I wasn't sure I *could* use fire magic again.

Ever.

And if I tried it and failed, it would only make it more difficult to focus my will on it again in the future, each failure building a wall that would only grow more difficult to breach. My belief in my powers might never recover.

I looked down at my maimed hand, and for just a second I actually saw the blackened, cracked flesh, my fingers swollen, the whole of it seeping blood and fluid. The second passed, and there was only my hand in its leather glove again, and I knew that beneath the glove it was scarred in various shades of white and red and pink.

I wasn't ready. God, even to save lives that included my own, I wasn't sure that I would be able to call up fire again. I stood there feeling helpless and angry and afraid and stupid—and most of all, ashamed.

I shook my head at Thomas and avoided meeting his eyes while I gave him an excuse. "I'm all but done," I said quietly. "I've got to save whatever I have left to block Grevane if he throws power at us directly. I don't know how much I'm going to be able to do."

He searched my expression for a second, frowning. Then he shrugged into the jacket, his face grim. He seized the saber in its scabbard and buckled it on with a worn leather belt. He settled it at his hip and picked up the shotgun again. "Guess it's up to me, then."

I nodded.

"I'm not sure how hard I'll be able to push," he said quietly.

"You handled Black Court vampires pretty well last year," I said.

"I'd been feeding on Justine every day," he said. "I had a lot to draw on. Now . . ." He shook his head. "Now I'm not sure."

"We aren't exactly overstaffed here, Thomas."

He closed his eyes for a second, and then nodded. "Right."

"Here's the plan. We get to the Beetle. We drive away."

"And then what? Where do we go after that?" he asked.

"You don't see me nitpicking your plans, do you?"

There was a sudden, heavy thump against the steel security door. It rattled in its frame. Bits of dust descended from my ceiling. Then another. And another. Grevane had thrown enough zombies at the wards to wear them out.

Thomas grimaced and looked at my leg. "Can you get up the stairs on your own?"

"I'll make it," I said.

Butters came panting up the stepladder from the lab, his face pale. He wore my nylon pack, and I could see Bob the skull making one side of it bulge a little.

"Gun," I said to Thomas, and he handed me the shotgun. "Right. Here's how it works. We open the door." I gestured with the shotgun. "I sweep it clear enough to get Thomas clear of the doorway. Then Thomas goes in front. Butters, I'm going to hand you the shotgun."

"I don't like guns," Butters said.

"You don't have to like it," I said. "You just have to carry it. With my leg hurt, I can't get up the stairs without using my staff."

The steel door rattled again, the pace of the blows against it increasing.

"Butters," I snapped. "Butters, you've got to take the gun when I hand it to you and follow Thomas. All right?"

"Yeah," he said.

"Once we get up the stairs, Thomas runs interference while I start the car. Butters, you'll get in the backseat. Thomas gets in and then we leave."

"Um," Butters said, "Grevane trashed my car so I couldn't get away, remember? What if he's done the same thing to yours?"

I stared at Butters for a second and tried not to show him how much that worried me.

"Butters," Thomas said quietly, "if we stay here we're going to die."

"But if they've destroyed the car—" Butters began.

"We'll die," Thomas said. "But we don't have a choice. Whether or not they've destroyed it, our only chance of getting out of this alive is to get to the Beetle and hope it runs."

The little guy got even paler, and then abruptly doubled over and staggered over to the wall beneath one of my high windows. He threw up. He straightened after a minute and leaned back against the wall, shaking. "I hate this," he whispered, and wiped his mouth. "I hate this. I want to go home. I want to wake up."

"Get it together, Butters," I said, my voice tight. "This isn't helping."

He let out a wild laugh. "Nothing I can do would *help,* Harry."

"Butters, you've got to calm down."

"Calm down?" He waved a shaking hand at the door. "They're going to kill us. Just like Phil. They're going to kill us and we're going to die. You, me, Thomas. We're all going to die!"

I forgot my bad leg for a second, crossed the room to Butters, and seized him by the front of his shirt. I hauled up until his heels lifted off of the floor. "Listen to me," I snarled. "We are *not* going to die!"

Butters stared up at me, pale, his eyes terrified. "We're not?"

"No. And do you know why?"

He shook his head.

"Because Thomas is too pretty to die. And because I'm too stubborn to die." I hauled on the shirt even harder. "And most of all because tomorrow is Oktoberfest, Butters, and polka will never die."

He blinked.

"Polka will never die!" I shouted at him. "Say it!"

He swallowed. "Polka will never die?"

"Again!"

"P-p-polka will never die," he stammered.

I shook him a little. "Louder!"

"Polka will never die!" he shrieked.

"We're going to make it!" I shouted.

"Polka will never die!" Butters screamed.

"I can't believe I'm hearing this," Thomas muttered.

I shot my half brother a warning look, released Butters, and said, "Get ready to open the door."

Then the window just over Butters's head exploded into shards of broken glass. I felt a hot, stinging sensation on my nose. I stumbled, my wounded leg gave out, and I fell.

Butters shrieked.

I looked up in time to see dead grey fingers clutching the little guy by the hair. They hauled him off of his feet, and two more zombie hands latched onto him and pulled him up through the broken window and out of the apartment. It happened so fast, before I could get my good leg under me, before Thomas could draw his saber.

There was a terrified scream from outside. It ended abruptly.

"Oh, God," I whispered. "Butters."

Chapter

Twenty-three

I stood staring up at the broken window in stunned silence for a second.

"Harry," Thomas said, quiet urgency in his voice, "we need to go."

"No," I said. "I'm not leaving him."

"He's probably dead already."

"If he is," I said. "It won't protect him from Grevane. I won't leave him there."

"Do we have a chance in a fight?"

I shook my head with a grimace. "Help me up."

He did. I limped over to the window and shouted, "Grevane!"

"Good evening," Grevane said, the rich, cultured tones of his voice a marked contrast to the dull, steady pounding at my front door. "My compliments to your contractor. That door is really quite sturdy."

"I like my privacy," I called back. "Is the mortician alive?"

"That's a somewhat fluid term in my experience," Grevane said. "But he is well enough for the time being."

My knees wobbled a little in relief. Good. If Butters was still all right, I had to keep Grevane talking. Barely five minutes had passed since the attack began. Even if the bad guys had cut the phone lines to the whole boardinghouse, the neighbors would have heard the racket and watched the light show from my wards. Someone was sure to call the authorities. If I could keep Grevane busy long enough, they would arrive, and I was willing to bet money that Grevane would rabbit rather than take chances this close to his goal. "You've got him. I want him."

"As do I," Grevane said. "I presume he found the information in the smuggler's corpse."

"Yes," I said.

"And I take it you also know."

"Yes."

He made a thoughtful sound. He was very near the broken window, though I couldn't see him. "That presents a problem for me," Grevane said. "I have no intention of sharing the *Word* with anyone. I'm afraid it will be necessary for me to silence you."

"I'm the least of your worries," I called back. "Corpsetaker and Li Xian took the information from me this afternoon."

There was a silence, broken only by the slow, steady pounding on my door.

"If that had happened," Grevane said, "you would not be alive to speak of it."

"I got lucky and got away," I said. "Corpsetaker sounded all hot and bothered about this Darkhallow thing you guys have planned."

I heard the angry sound of someone spitting. "If you are telling the truth," Grevane said, "then it profits me nothing to allow you and the mortician to live."

"That's one way to look at it," I said. "But you could just as easily say that it costs you nothing to do it, either. Last night you wanted to make me a deal. You still willing to talk?"

"To what purpose?" he said.

There was the shrieking sound of steel beginning to bend under stress. One corner of the door, up at the top, bent in, letting in cold evening air.

"Hurry," Thomas urged me. "We have to do something fast."

"Give me Butters," I said to Grevane. "I'll give you the information I found."

"You offer me nothing. I have him already," Grevane said. "I can extract the information from him myself."

"You could," I said, "if he knew it. He doesn't."

Grevane snarled something in a language I didn't understand. I heard scuffing shoes, then the sound of a slap and a dazed exclamation from Butters. "Is that true?" Grevane asked him. "Do you have the information about the *Word?*"

"Dunno what it is," Butters mumbled. "There was a jump drive. Numbers. It was a whole bunch of numbers."

"What numbers?" Grevane snarled.

"Don't know. Whole bunch. Can't remember them all. Harry has them."

"Liar," Grevane said. There was the sound of another blow, and Butters cried out.

"I don't know!" Butters said. "There were too many and I only saw them for a sec—"

Another blow fell, this time with the dull, heavy sound of a closed fist hitting flesh.

I clenched my teeth, rage filling me.

"I don't know, I don't know, I don't know . . ." Butters said. It sounded like he was crying.

"Look at me," Grevane said. *"Look."*

I closed my eyes and turned my face a little from the window. I could imagine what was happening. Butters, probably on his knees, being held by a pair of zombies, Grevane standing over him in his trench coat, pinching Butters's chin between his thumb and forefinger. I could imagine him forcing Butters's eyes up to meet his, to begin a soulgaze. Grevane wanted to see the inside of Butters's head, in a swift and harsh attempt to assess the truth.

And Butters would be exposed to the corruption of a soul steeped in dark magic and a lifetime of murder.

I heard a high-pitched little sound that rose rapidly, growing louder and louder until it was a wail of terror and madness. There was no dignity in the sound. No self-control. I would never have recognized it as Butters's voice if I hadn't known he was out there. But it was him. Butters screamed, and he kept screaming without pausing to take a breath until it wound down to a frozen, gurgling sound and died away.

"Well?" asked another voice, one I did not recognize. It rasped harshly, as if the man speaking had spent a lifetime imbibing cheap Scotch and cheaper cigars.

"He doesn't know," Grevane reported quietly, disgust in his voice.

"You're sure?" said the second voice. I moved a bit to one side and stood up on tiptoe to peer out the window. I could see the second speaker. It was Liver Spots.

"Yes," Grevane said. "He doesn't have any strength to him. If he knew, he'd answer."

"If you kill the mortician, you'll have to kill me," I called. "Of course, I'm the only one with the information, other than Corpsetaker. I'm sure that you psychotic necro-wannabes with delusions of godhood are all about sharing with your fellow maniacs."

There was silence from outside.

"So you should go ahead and take me out," I said. "Of course, when I lay down my death curse on you, it's going to make it that much harder for you to beat out Corpsetaker for the Darkhallow, but what's life without a few challenges to liven things up?" I paused and then said, "Don't be an idiot, Grevane. If you don't deal with me, you'll be cutting your own throat."

"Is that what you think?" Grevane said. "Perhaps I will simply walk away."

"No, you won't," I said. "Because when Corpsetaker gets her membership to the Mount Olympus Country Club, the first thing she's going to do is find her nearest rival—you—and rip your pancreas out through your nose."

The door suddenly bent on a diagonal on the top half, folding it in as if it had been wax paper. The door didn't quite go down, but I could see dead fingers reaching up through it, trying to rip and tear the weakened section.

"Harry," Thomas said, his voice tight with apprehension. He drew his saber and went to the door. He hacked at dead fingers that appeared in the breach. They spun through the air and landed on the floor, still bending and wriggling like bisected earthworms.

"Make up your mind, Grevane!" I called. "If this goes any further, I'm going to do everything in my power to kill you. I can't beat you. We both know that. But you won't get the information out of me against my will. I'm not a pansy. I can push you hard enough to make you kill me."

"You would have me believe that you would simply commit suicide?" Grevane asked.

"To take you down with me?" I replied. "Oh, hell, yeah. Count on it."

"Don't listen to him," Liver Spots hissed. "Kill him. He knows he's finished. He's desperate."

Which was true, dammit, but the last thing I needed was for someone to point that out to Grevane. A zombie finger flew past my head, and another bounced off my duster and fell to the floor at my feet, still twitching, a long and yellowed fingernail making an unsettling scratching sound against my boot. The pounding on the door got louder, the whole thing rattling in its frame.

And then, just like that, it stopped. Silence fell over the apartment.

"What are your terms?" Grevane asked.

"You release Butters to me," I said. "You let us drive off with your sidekick in the car. Once we're away from here, I give him the numbers and drop him off. Mutual truce until sunrise."

"These numbers," Grevane said. "What do they mean?"

"I don't have a clue," I said. "At least not yet. Neither did Corpsetaker."

"Then what value do they have?" he asked.

"Someone is bound to figure it out. But if you don't deal with me now, it sure as hell won't be you."

There was another long pause, and then Grevane said, "Give me your pledge that you will abide by the terms."

"Only in return for yours," I said.

"You have it," Grevane said. "I swear it by my power."

"*No*," hissed Liver Spots. "Don't do this."

I lifted my eyebrows and traded a speculative look with Thomas. Oaths and promises have a certain kind of power all their own—that was one reason they were so highly regarded among the beings of the supernatural community. Whenever someone breaks a promise, some of the energy that went into making it feeds back on the promise breaker. For most people that isn't a really big deal. Maybe it shows up as a little bad luck, or a cold or a headache or something.

But when a more powerful being or a wizard swears an oath by his own power, the effect is magnified significantly. Too many broken oaths and promises can cripple a wizard's use of magic, or even destroy the ability entirely. I've never seen or heard of a wizard breaking an oath sworn by his own power. It was one of the constants of the preternatural world.

"And by my own power, I swear in return to abide by the terms of the agreement," I said.

"Harry," Thomas hissed. "What the hell are you doing?"

"Saving our collective ass, I hope," I said.

"You don't actually think he'll abide by it, do you?" Thomas whispered.

"He will," I said, and as I said it I realized how confident I was that I was right. "If he wants to survive, he doesn't have much choice. Grevane's entire purpose here is gaining power. He won't jeopardize that now by breaking an oath sworn by his magic."

"You hope."

"Even if he decides to screw us, it's good to keep him talking. The longer we delay, the more likely it is the cops are going to show up. He'll back off before he faces that."

"But if the cops don't show, you're giving him what he needs to make himself into a freaking nightmare," Thomas said.

I shook my head. "Might not be a bad thing. I can't beat him. Corpsetaker, either. Throwing Grevane into the mix is going to make it harder for either of them to concentrate on me."

Thomas exhaled slowly. "It's a hell of a risk."

"Oh, no. A risk," I said. "Well, we wouldn't want that, now, would we?"

"No one likes a wiseass, Harry."

"Butters is counting on me," I said. "Right now, I'm all he's got. Do you have any better ideas?"

Thomas grimaced and shook his head.

"Very well," Grevane called. "How shall we proceed?"

"Pull your zombies back," I said. As I did, I found a pen and a piece of paper, pulled out the folded piece of paper from my pocket, and made a copy of the numbers. "You go with them. Liver Spots and Butters wait by the car. We all get in and drive off. Once I'm a few blocks away, I'll drop Liver Spots off with the numbers, unharmed."

"Agreed," Grevane said.

We waited for a minute, and then Thomas said, "You hear anything?"

I went to the door and Listened. I could hear someone breathing fast and heavy. Butters. Nothing else. I shook my head and glanced at Thomas.

He came over to the door, sword still in hand. He opened it slowly. The pounding it had taken had warped it, and he had to haul hard on the door to get it unstuck from its frame. Thomas looked out for a moment. There were a couple of still-twitching pieces of zombie on the stairs, but other than that it was empty. He paced slowly up the stairs, looking around him as he went. My staff still lay at a slant on the floor before the door. Thomas nudged it back into the apartment with his foot. "Looks clear."

I grabbed the shotgun and picked up the staff, holding both awkwardly with my good hand. Mouse fell into place at my side, his hackles still stiff, a low, almost subsonic growl rumbling in his chest every few moments. I hobbled out and up the stairs.

Cold rain fell, light but steady. It was dark. Really dark. No lights were on anywhere in sight. Grevane must have hexed this entire portion of the city power grid when the attack began. I didn't make use of electricity in my apartment, so it hadn't been noticeable to me inside.

I got a sick, sinking little feeling. If the lights were all out and the phones were all down, then there might not *be* any cops on the way. By the time the wards had begun to make noise, the phones were already dead. Without lights, there was an excellent chance that no one had seen anything unusual in the dark, and the rain would have muffled sounds considerably. People tended to stay home in comfortable surroundings in such situations—and if someone had seen or heard a crime going on but had no way to notify the authorities about it, it was unlikely that they would do anything but stay at home and keep their heads down.

Zombie scrap parts littered the top of the stairs, the gravel parking lot, and the little lawn. Some of them looked burned, while others seemed to have melted like wax in the summer sun. There were a number of blank, black spots burned into the ground. I couldn't easily count how many zombies had been destroyed, but there had to have been almost as many down as I had seen in the opening moments of the attack.

Grevane had brought more. The rain almost hid them, but I could see the zombies at the limit of my sight, standing in silence, motionless. There were dozens of them. Hell's bells. If we'd made that run for the car, we wouldn't have had a prayer. That big, booming stereo bass rumbled steadily in the background.

Near the Beetle stood Liver Spots. He wore the same coat, the same broad-brimmed hat, the same sour expression on his wrinkled, spotted face. His fine white hair drifted around in every tiny bit of moving air wherever it wasn't wet from the rain. I studied him for a minute. He was a good two or three inches under average height. His features seemed familiar, I was certain, but I couldn't place them. It bothered me—a lot—but this was no time to start entertaining uncertainties.

Butters lay curled in a fetal position on the muddy, wet gravel at Liver Spots's feet. He was breathing hard and fast, and his eyes stared sightlessly forward.

Liver Spots gestured curtly at Butters. In reply I held up the copy of the numbers, then slipped it back in my pocket. "Put him in the car," I told Liver Spots.

"Do it yourself," the man responded, his voice rough, harsh.

Mouse focused on Liver Spots and let out a low, rumbling growl.

I narrowed my eyes at him, but said, "Thomas."

Thomas sheathed the sword and picked up Butters like a small child, his eyes on Liver Spots. He came back to the car, and Mouse and I watched Liver Spots closely the whole while.

"Put him in the back," I said.

Thomas opened the door and set Butters in the backseat. The little guy leaned his head against the wall and sat all curled up. You could have fit him into a paper grocery sack.

"Mouse," I said. "In."

Mouse prowled into the backseat and sat leaning against Butters, serious dark eyes never leaving Liver Spots.

"All right," I said, passing the shotgun to Thomas. "It works like this. Thomas, you get in the back. Spots, you're riding shotgun. And when I say riding shotgun, I mean that Thomas is going to shove it up your ass and pull the trigger if you try anything funny."

He stared at me, eyes flat.

"Do you understand me?" I said.

He nodded, eyes narrowed.

"Say it," I told him.

Raw hatred dripped from his words. "I understand you."

"Good," I said. "Get in."

Liver Spots walked toward the car. He had to step around me to get to the passenger's-side door, and when he drew even with me he suddenly stopped and stared at me. There was a puzzled frown on his face. He stayed that way for a second, looking at me from soles to scalp.

"What?" I demanded.

"Where is it?" he said. He sounded as if he was speaking for his own benefit rather than for mine. "Why isn't it here?"

"I've had a long day," I told him. "Shut your mouth and get in the car."

For a second I saw his eyes, and at my words they suddenly burned with a manic loathing and scorn. I could see, quite clearly, that Liver Spots wanted me dead. There wasn't anything rational or calm about it. He wanted to hurt me, and he wanted me to die. It was written in his eyes so strongly that it might as well have been tattooed across his face. I needed no soulgaze, no magic, to recognize murderous hate when I saw it.

And he still looked familiar, though for the life of me—maybe literally—I couldn't remember from where.

I avoided his eyes in time to avert a soulgaze of my own and said, "Get into the car."

He said, "I'm going to kill you. Perhaps not tonight. But soon. I'm going to see you die."

"You'll have to wait in line, Spots," I told him. "I hear the only tickets left are in general admission."

He narrowed his eyes and began to speak.

Mouse let out a sudden, warning snarl.

I tensed, watching Liver Spots, but he did the same thing I did. He flinched and then looked warily around. When his eyes got to a spot behind me, they widened.

Thomas had the shotgun on him, so I turned from Liver Spots and looked for myself.

From the rain and the dark came a rising cloud of light. It drew nearer with unsettling speed, and after only a few speeding heartbeats I could see what made the light.

They were ghosts.

Surrounded in a sickly greenish glow, a company of Civil War–era cavalry rushed toward us, dozens of them. There should have been a rumble of thundering hooves accompanying them, but there was only a distant and pale sound of a running herd. The riders wore broad-brimmed Union hats and jackets that looked black rather than blue in the sickly light, and bore pistols and sabers in their semitransparent hands. One of the lead riders lifted a trumpet to his lips as he rode, and ghostly strains of the cavalry charge drifted through the night air.

Behind them, mounted on phantom horses that looked as if they'd been drowned, were Li Xian and the Corpsetaker. The ghoul wore a tom-tom drum at his side, held in place by a heavy leather belt draped sideways from one shoulder. While he rode, he beat out a staccato military rhythm on it with one hand, and it sounded somehow primitive and wild. The Corpsetaker had changed into clothes made of heavy biker leather, complete with a chain gauntlet and spiked fighting bracers on her forearms. She wore a curved sword on her belt, a heavy tulwar that looked ugly and murderous. As she came closer, she sent her ghostly steed racing to the head of the troop and drew her blade. She spun it over her head, laughing in wild abandon, and bore straight down upon us.

"Treachery!" howled Liver Spots. "We are betrayed!"

Grevane appeared in the mist from among the motionless zombies. He stared at the oncoming Corpsetaker and let out a howl of rage. He raised his hands, and every zombie in sight abruptly stiffened and then broke into a charge.

"Kill them!" Grevane howled. Actual, literal foam formed at the corners of his mouth, and his eyes burned beneath the brim of the fedora. "Kill them all!"

Liver Spots whirled toward me, producing a tiny pistol from somewhere in his sleeve, a derringer. From the size of it, it couldn't have held a very heavy bullet, but he wouldn't need it to be heavy to kill me at this range. I dove back and to my right, trying to get the car between Liver Spots and me. There was a startling popping sound and a flash of light. I hit the muddy gravel hard. Liver Spots came around the car after me, evidently determined to use the second bullet in the pistol.

Thomas didn't have time to get out of the car. There was a sudden explosion and my windshield blew outward in a cloud of shot and shattered glass. Both tore into Liver Spots, and he stumbled and went down.

I lifted my staff in my good hand and brought it down hard on his wrist. There was a brittle, snapping sound, and the little gun flew from his grasp.

He went into an utter rage.

Before I knew what was happening, Liver Spots had thrown himself on top of me and had both of his hands fastened on my throat. I felt him shut off my airway, and struggled against him. It didn't do much good. The old man seemed filled with maddened strength.

"It's mine!" he screamed at me. He shook me on each word, slamming my head back against the gravel in precise, separate detonations of pain and bright stars in my vision. "Give it to me! Mine!"

A zombie landed on the gravel near us in a crouch and turned toward me. Its dead eyes regarded me without passion or thought as it formed a fist and drove it at my head.

Before it could land, a flickering saber from one of the spectral cavalry whispered through the night and the rain and struck the zombie on the neck. The corpse's head flew from its shoulders, dribbling a line of sludgy black ichor, and landed with its empty eyes staring into mine.

Thomas screamed, "Down!"

I stopped struggling to get up, and tried to press myself as flat to the ground as I could.

The driver's-side door to the Beetle flew open, swept just over the end of my nose, and struck Liver Spots in the face. He flew back from me.

Thomas leaned out of the driver's side to grab at me, but a second ghostly horseman swept by, sword hissing. Thomas ducked in time to save his neck, but took part of the slash across his temple and ear and scalp, and that side of his head and shoulder was almost immediately covered in a sheet of blood a few shades too pale to be human.

Thomas recovered his balance and pulled me grimly into the car. I fumbled with the keys and shoved them into place. I twisted the key in desperate haste, mashing on the gas as I did. The engine turned over once and then stalled.

"Dammit!" Thomas cried in frustration. A streak of faint green light appeared in the air over the car's hood. A second later another went by, this time ending at the hood. There was a startling sound of impact and the frame of the car rattled. A bullet hole appeared in the hood.

I tried the car again and this time coaxed the old VW to life.

"Hail the mighty Beetle!" I crowed, and slapped the car into reverse. The wheels spun up gravel and mud, and I shot back straight into a crowd of zombies, slamming into them and sending them flying.

I whipped the car's hood toward the street and shifted into drive. As I did, I got a look at the Corpsetaker bearing down on Grevane, tulwar raised. From somewhere in his coat, Grevane produced a length of chain, and as the sword swept toward him he held up the chain, his arms outstretched, and caught the blow on the links between them, sliding the deadly blade away from him.

Corpsetaker howled in fury and whirled the phantom mount around to charge him again, almost absently striking the head from a zombie as she passed it.

I flattened the gas pedal, and the Beetle lurched forward—straight toward a trio of ghostly cavalry troops. They bore down on us, not wavering.

"I hate playing chicken," I muttered, and shifted into second.

Just before I would have hit them, the cavalry leapt, translucent horses and riders rising effortlessly into the air, over the car, to land on the ground behind me. I didn't give them a chance to whirl and try it again. I bounced the Beetle out onto the street, turned left, and charged away at flank speed. I got a few blocks away, then slowed enough to roll down the window.

There were no screams or shrieks of battle. The rain muffled the sound, and in the heavy darkness I couldn't see anything going on behind me. I could dimly hear the whumping bass drum that kept Grevane's zombies going, still somewhere out there in the background. Beyond that, very quiet but getting nearer, I heard sirens.

"Everyone all right?" I asked.

"I'll make it," Thomas said. He had stripped out of his jacket and shirt, and had the latter pressed to the side of his bleeding head.

"Mouse?" I asked.

There was a wet, snuffling sound by my ear, and Mouse licked my cheek.

"Good," I said. "Butters?"

There was silence.

Thomas looked at the backseat, frowning.

"Butters?" I repeated. "Heya, man. Earth to Butters."

Silence.

"Butters?" I asked.

There was a long pause. Then a slow inhalation. Then he said, in a very weak voice, "Polka will never die."

I felt my mouth stretch into a fierce grin. "Damn right it won't," I said.

"True." Thomas sighed. "Where are we going?"

"We can't go back there," I said. "And with the wards torn down, it wouldn't do us too much good anyway."

"Where, then?" Thomas asked.

I stopped at a stop sign and patted at my pockets for a moment. I found one of the two things I was looking for.

Thomas frowned at me. "Harry? What's wrong?"

"The copy of the numbers I made for Grevane," I said. "It's gone. Liver Spots must have grabbed it from me when we were tussling."

"Damn," Thomas said.

I found the key to Murphy's house in another pocket. "Okay. I've got a place we can hole up for a while, until we can figure out our next move. How bad is the cut?"

"Bleeder," Thomas said. "Looks worse than it is."

"Keep pressure on it," I said.

"Thank you, yes," Thomas said, though he sounded more amused than annoyed.

I got the Beetle moving again, frowning out the windows. "Hey," I said. "Do you guys notice something?"

Thomas peered around for a moment. "Not really. Too dark."

Butters drew in a sharp breath. His voice still unsteady, he said, "That's right. It's too dark." He pointed out one window. "That's where the skyline should be."

Thomas stared out. "It's gone dark."

"Lights are out," I said quietly. "Do you see any anywhere?"

Thomas looked around for a moment, then reported, "Looks like a fire off that way. Some headlights. Some police lights. The rest are . . ." He shook his head.

"What happened?" Butters whispered.

"So that's what Mab meant. They did this," I said. "The heirs of Kemmler."

"But why?" Thomas asked.

"They think that one of them is going to become a god tomorrow night. They're creating fear. Chaos. Helplessness."

"Why?"

"They're preparing the way."

Thomas didn't say anything. None of us did.

I can't speak for the others, but I was afraid.

The Beetle's tires whispered over the streets as I drove through the cold, lightless murk that had fallen over Chicago like a funeral shroud.

Chapter

Twenty-four

Murphy's house had belonged to her grandmother. It was a dinky little place, and resided in a neighborhood built before Edison's lights went into vogue, and while some areas like that became ragged and run-down, this particular street looked more like some kind of historical real estate preserve, with well-kept lawns, trimmed trees, and tidy paint jobs on all the homes.

I pulled the Beetle into the driveway, hesitated for half a second, and then continued up onto the lawn and around to the rear of the house, parking beside a little outbuilding that looked like a toolshed as envisioned by the Gingerbread Man. I killed the engine, and sat for a moment listening to the car make those just-stopped clicking sounds. Without the headlights, it was very dark. My leg hurt like hell. It seemed like a really great idea to close my eyes and get some rest.

Instead I fumbled around until I found the cardboard box I keep in the car. Next to a couple of holy-water balloons, an old pair of socks, and a heavy old potato, I found a crinkling plastic package. I tore it open, bent the plastic tube inside sharply, and shook it up. The two chemical liquids inside mixed, and the glow stick began to shine with gold-green light.

I got out of the car and hauled my tired ass toward the back door. Thomas and Mouse and Butters followed me. I unlocked the door with Murphy's key, and led everyone inside.

Murphy's place was . . . dare I say it, really cute. The furniture was old Victorian, worn but well cared for. There were a lot of doilies in its decorating scheme, and all in all it was a very girly sort of place. When Murphy's grandmother passed away and Murphy moved in, she hadn't changed it much. The sole concession to the presence of Chicago's toughest little detective was a simple wooden stand on the fireplace mantel, which held a pair of curved Japanese swords one over the other.

I went from the living room into the kitchen, and opened the drawer where Murphy kept her matches. I lit a couple of candles, then used them to find a pair of old glass kerosene lamps and get them going.

Thomas came in while I was doing that, grabbed the glow stick, and held it in one hand while he opened the refrigerator and rummaged inside.

"Hey," I said. "That's not your fridge."

"Murphy would share, wouldn't she?" Thomas asked.

"That isn't the point," I said. "It's not yours."

"The power's out," Thomas replied, shoulder deep in the fridge. "This stuff is going to spoil anyway. All right, pizza. And beer."

I stared at him for a second. Then I said, "Check the freezer, too. Murphy likes ice cream."

"Right," he said. He glanced up at me and said, "Harry, go sit down. I'll bring you something."

"I'm fine," I said.

"No, you aren't. Your leg is bleeding again."

I blinked at him and looked down. The white bandages had soaked through with fresh, dark red. The bandage wasn't saturated yet, but the stain had covered most of the white. "Damn. That's inconvenient."

Butters appeared in the kitchen doorway, ghostly somehow in his pale blue scrubs. His hair was a mess, all muddy and mussed. His glasses were gone, and he had his eyes squinted up as he looked at us. He had a cut on his lower lip that had closed into a black scab, and he had one hell of a shiner forming over his left cheekbone, presumably where Grevane had struck him.

"Let me wash up," Butters said. "Then I'll see to it. You'll want to make sure that stays clean, Harry."

"Go sit down," Thomas said. "Butters, are you hungry?"

"Yes," Butters said. "Is there a bathroom?"

"Hall, first one on the left," I said. "I think Murphy keeps a first-aid kit under the sink."

Butters moved silently over to one of the candles, took it, and left just as quietly.

"Well," I said. "At least he's clear now."

"Maybe so," Thomas said. He was moving things from the fridge to the kitchen counter. "They know he doesn't know anything. But you risked your life to protect his. That might start them to thinking."

"What do you mean?" I asked.

"You were willing to die to protect him. You think Grevane understands enough about friendship to comprehend why you did it?"

I grimaced. "Probably not."

"So they might start wondering what made him so valuable to you. Wondering what you know that they don't." He rummaged in a cupboard and found some bread, some crackers. "Maybe it won't amount to anything. But it might. He should be careful."

I nodded agreement. "You can keep an eye on him."

Thomas glanced at me. "You think you're going out now?"

"Soon as I eat something," I said.

"Don't be stupid," Thomas said. "Your leg is hurt. You can barely walk straight. Eat. Get some sleep."

"There's no time," I said.

He glared at me for a second, then pressed his mouth into a line and said, "Let's talk about it after we eat something. Everyone's angry when they're hungry. Makes for bad decisions."

"Probably smart," I said.

"Take the coat off. Go sit down. Let Butters look at your leg."

"It just needs a new bandage," I said. "I can do that myself."

"You're missing my point, dummy," Thomas said. "A friend would let Butters deal with a problem that he's capable of handling. He's had plenty of the other kind tonight."

I glared at Thomas, shrugged out of the duster, and limped for the living room. "It's easier to deal with you when you're a simple, selfish asshole."

"I forget how limited you are, brain-wise," Thomas said. "I'll be more careful."

I settled cautiously down onto Murphy's old couch. It creaked as

I did. Murphy isn't large, and I doubt that her grandma was, either. I'm not exactly layered in muscle, but as tall as I am, no one ever mistakes me for a lightweight. I shoved some doilies off the coffee table so that they wouldn't get blood all over them, and propped my throbbing leg up on the table. It took a little bit of the pressure off of the injury, which didn't mean it stopped hurting. It just hurt a little bit less aggressively. Whatever; anything was a relief.

I sat like that until Butters emerged from the hall that went back to the bathroom and the house's two bedrooms. He had Murphy's medical kit in hand. I remembered one of those little standard first-aid kits that would fit into the glove box of a car. Murphy had evidently been planning ahead. She'd replaced the little medical kit with one the size of a contractor's toolbox.

"I don't think I'm quite that hurt," I told Butters.

"Better to have it and not need it," he replied quietly. He set down the kerosene lamp and the toolbox. He rummaged in the box, came out with a pair of safety scissors, and set about stripping the bandage away, his motions smooth and confident. Once he had the bandage clear, he peered at the injury, moved the lamp to get a better look, and winced. "This is a mess. You've popped the two center sutures." He glanced up at me apologetically. "I'll have to replace them, or the others are going to tear out one at a time."

I swallowed. I did not want to do sutures without anesthetics. Hadn't I already experienced enough pain for one day?

"Do it," I told him.

He nodded and set about cleaning the bloodied skin around the injury. He wiped his hands down with a couple of sterilizing wipes, and snapped on some rubber gloves. "There's a topical here. I'll use it, but it's not much stronger than that stuff you get for a toothache."

"Just get it over with," I said.

He nodded, produced a curved needle and surgical thread, adjusted the lamp again, and set to work. He was fairly quick about it. I did my best to hold still. When he was finished, my throat felt raw and rough. I hadn't actually done any yelling, but only by strangling any screams before they came out.

I lay there kind of limply while Butters re-covered the wound. "You started on the antibiotics, right?" he asked.

"Not yet," I said.

He shook his head. "You should take them right away. I don't want to think about what might have gotten into the wound back at your apartment." He swallowed and went a little pale. "I mean, my God."

"That's the worst part about the walking dead," I said. "The stains."

He smiled at me, or at least he tried to. "Harry," he said. "I'm sorry."

"For what?"

"I . . ." He shook his head. "I was useless back there. Worse than useless. You could have been hurt."

Thomas appeared in the doorway to the kitchen, pale and silent. He arched his brow, somehow managing to say, "I told you so," without actually opening his mouth.

I glared back at him, in an effort to convey several uncharitable things. He smiled a little and faded back into the kitchen. Butters missed the whole thing.

"Don't worry about it," I said. "You ever had anything like this happen before?"

"Like zombies and ghosts and necromancers?" Butters asked.

"Like life-threatening and dangerous," I said.

"Oh." He was quiet for a minute. "No. I tried to go into the army, but I couldn't make it through boot. Wound up in the hospital. Same thing when I tried to be a policeman. The spirit was willing, but Butters was weak."

"Some people just aren't cut out for that kind of thing," I told him. "That's nothing to be ashamed of."

"Sure, it isn't," he said, but he wasn't agreeing with me.

"You can do a lot that I can't," I told him. I nodded at my leg.

"But this stuff is . . . hell, it's *simple*," Butters said. "I mean, the words get a little bit long. But all in all, it isn't that complicated."

"Listen to yourself, Butters," I told him. "You're sitting there with a straight face saying that medicine and medical forensics is simple, except for the long words. Do you have any clue what it's like to *not* be as intelligent as you?"

He shook his head impatiently. "I'm not some kind of genius." He frowned. "Okay, well, technically I have a genius IQ, but that isn't the point. A lot of people do. The point is that I've spent most of my adult life doing this. That's why I can do it well."

"And the point is," I told him, "that I've spent most of my adult life doing zombies and ghosts and other things trying to kill me. That's why I can do it well. We've got different specialties. That's all. So don't beat yourself up for not being better at my job than I am."

He started cleaning up the medical detritus, throwing things away and stripping out of the gloves. "Thanks, Harry. But it's more than that. I just . . . I couldn't *think*. When those things grabbed me. When he was hitting me. I knew I should have been doing something, planning something, but my brain wouldn't work." He slammed something down into the trash can with more force than necessary. "I was too afraid."

I was too tired to move, and for the first time I started to notice how cold it was without my coat. I folded my arms and tried not to shiver. I watched Butters quietly for a moment and said, "It gets easier."

"What does?"

"Living with the fear."

"It goes away?" he asked.

"No," I said. "Never. Gets worse, in some ways. But once you face it down, you learn to accommodate it. Even work with it, sometimes."

"I don't understand," he whispered.

"Fear can't hurt you," I said. "It can't kill you."

"Well, technically—"

"Butters," I said. "Don't give me statistics on heart failure. Fear is a part of life. It's a warning mechanism. That's all. It tells you when there's danger around. Its job is to help you survive. Not cripple you into being unable to do it."

"I have empirical evidence to the contrary," he said, bitter humor in his voice.

"That's because you've never thought about it before," I said. "You've reacted to the fear, but you haven't ever faced it and put it into the right perspective. You have to make up your mind to overcome it."

He was quiet for a second. "Just like that?" he said. "Just make up my mind and poof, it's different?"

"No. But it's the first step," I said. "After that, you find other steps to take. Think about it for a while. Maybe you'll never need it again. But at least you'll be ready if it happens sometime down the line."

He closed up the medical toolbox. "You mean it's over?"

"For you," I said. "Grevane knows that you don't have anything he wants. He's got no reason to look for you. Hell, for that matter, I think you were just in the wrong place at the wrong time when he *did* come looking. Anyone with access to the corpse and the ability to find where Bony Tony had hidden the jump drive would have been good enough for Grevane. Your part in this is over."

Butters closed his eyes for a second. "Oh, thank God." He blinked up at me. "Sorry. I mean, it isn't that I don't like being around you, but . . ."

I smiled a little. "I understand. I'm glad you're all right." I glanced down at my leg. "Looks nice and neat again. Thanks, Butters. You're a good friend."

He frowned up at me. "Yeah?"

"Yeah."

I thought I saw him straighten his shoulders a little. "Okay."

Thomas appeared in the door of the kitchen. "Gas stove. Hot food and tea. Sugar?"

"Tons," I said.

"Not for me," Butters said.

Thomas nodded, and slipped back into the kitchen.

"So how come if I'm your friend, you don't tell me important things?" Butters said.

"Like what?" I asked him.

Butters gestured at the kitchen. "Well. That, you know . . . you're gay."

I blinked at him.

"I mean, don't get me wrong. It's the twenty-first century. You can live your life how you want, and it doesn't make you any less cool."

"Butters—" I began.

"And hey, look at the guy. I mean, I'm not even gay, and I think he looks great. Who could blame you?"

Choking sounds came from the kitchen.

"Oh, shut up!" I snarled at Thomas.

He kept on making choking sounds that bubbled with laughter.

"You should have just said something," Butters said. "Don't feel like you have to hide anything, Harry. I won't judge. I owe you too much for that."

"I'm not gay," I stated.

Butters nodded at me, compassion and empathy all over his face. "Oh. Okay, sure."

"I'm not!"

Butters raised his hands. "It wasn't my place to intrude," he said. "Later, some other time, maybe. None of my business."

"Oh, for crying out loud," I muttered.

Thomas came out bearing plates of steaming, reheated pizza, some roast beef sandwiches, and crackers with slices of cheese partly melted on them. He put them down and came back with bottles of cold beer and cups of hot tea. He poured my tea for me, then leaned over and gave me a chaste kiss on the hair. "There you go."

Butters pretended not to notice.

I punched Thomas awkwardly in the ribs. "Give me the damned pizza before I kill you."

Thomas sighed and confided to Butters, "He gets like this sometimes."

I grabbed the pizza from Thomas, and leaned over enough to snag a beer. Mouse, who had been lying by the front windows staring out at the darkness, got up and came nosing over toward the food.

"Oh, here," Thomas said. "The antibiotics." He put a couple of pills down on my plate.

I growled wordlessly at him, washed them down with a swallow of beer, and fell to eating pizza and roast beef sandwiches and crackers with cheese. I shared a bit with Mouse, every third or fourth bite, until Thomas snagged the last roast beef sandwich and put it on the floor for Mouse to have to himself.

I finished the beer and settled back with the tea afterward. I hadn't realized how hungry I was until I'd started eating. The tea was sweet and just barely cool enough to drink. In the wake of the meal and the evening's excitement, I finally started to feel warm and human again. The pain in my leg faded until it was barely noticeable.

I blinked heavily down at my bandaged leg and said, "Hey."

"Hmmm?" Thomas asked.

"You bastard. Those weren't antibiotics."

"No, they weren't," Thomas said, and without a trace of shame. "They were the painkillers. You idiot. You need to rest before you kill yourself."

"Bastard," I said again. The couch really was very comfortable. I finished my tea over the next several moments. "Maybe you have a point."

"Of course I do," Thomas said. "Oh, here's the antibiotic, by the way." He passed me a single horse pill. I swallowed it with the last of my tea. Thomas set the teacup aside and then helped me to my feet. "Come on. Get a few hours of rest. Then you can figure out your next move."

I grunted. Thomas helped me into one of the darkened bedrooms, and I sank onto a soft bed, too tired to be angry. Too tired to be awake. I vaguely remember stripping out of my shirt and shoes before pulling soft and heavy covers over me. Then there was blessed darkness, warmth, and quiet.

The last thing I thought, before I dropped off to sleep, was that the covers smelled faintly of soap and sunlight and strawberries.

They smelled like Murphy.

Chapter

Twenty-five

In the odd dream, I had a hot tub.

I lay back in it, luxuriating, the water churning to a controlled froth by jets that hit it and me from dozens of angles. The water was at that perfect temperature, a little short of scalding my skin, and the heat of it sank into muscle and bone, warming me deliciously and washing away aches and pains.

It was an odd dream, because I have never in my life been in a hot tub.

I opened my eyes and looked slowly around me. The hot tub was set in the floor of what looked like a natural cave. Low, reddish light came from what looked like some kind of moss growing on the stalactites overhead.

That was odd, because I'd never been in a cave like this, either.

"Hello?" I called. My voice bounced around the empty cavern.

I heard the sound of movement, and a woman stepped into sight from behind a rock formation. She was a little taller than average and had hair that fell in a sheet of golden silk to her shoulders. She was dressed in a silken tunic belted with soft rope, both pure white. The outfit neither displayed any impropriety nor allowed anyone looking to ignore the beauty of the body it clothed. Her eyes were of a deep, deep blue, like a sunny October sky, and her skin glowed with wholesome appeal. She was, quite simply, a stunning creature.

"Hello. I thought it was time we had a talk," she said. "You've had a hard day. I thought pleasant surroundings might suit you."

I eyed her for a moment. I was naked, which was good. The surface of the pool had enough in the way of bubbles and froth to be opaque, which was also good. It saved me the embarrassment of my response to her. "Who are you?"

She lifted golden brows in a faint smile, and seated herself beside the hot tub, on the floor of the cave, her legs together and to one side, her hands folded on her lap. "Have you not reasoned it yourself by now?"

I stared at her for a long minute and then said, quietly, "Lasciel."

The woman bowed her head, smiling in acknowledgment. "Indeed."

"You can't be here," I said. "I sealed you into the floor under my lab. I imprisoned you."

"Indeed you did," the woman said. "What you see here is not my true self, as such. Think of me as a reflection of the true Lasciel who resides within your mind."

"As a what?"

"When you chose to touch the coin, you accepted this form of my awareness within you," Lasciel said. "I am an imprint. A copy."

I swallowed. "You live in my head. And you can talk to me?"

"I can now," Lasciel said. "Now that you have chosen to employ what I have offered you."

I took in a deep breath. "Hellfire. I used Hellfire today to empower my magic."

"You made the conscious choice to do so," she said. "And as a result, I can now appear to your conscious mind." She smiled. "Actually, I've been looking forward to meeting you. You are a great deal more interesting than most I have been given to."

"You, uh," I said, "you don't look much like a demon."

"Keep in mind, please, that I was not always a resident of Hell. I relocated there." She looked at herself. "Shall I add the wings? A harp? A golden halo?"

"Why are you asking me?" I asked.

"Because I am something of a guest," she said. "It costs me nothing to take on an appearance that pleases my host."

"Uh-huh," I said. "If you're my guest, then get out."

She laughed, and there was nothing alluring or musical about it.

It was just laughter, warm and genuine. "That isn't possible, I'm afraid. By taking the coin, you invited me in. You cannot simply will me away."

"Fine," I said. "This is a dream. I'll wake up. See ya."

I made the simple effort of will required to wake myself from a dream.

And nothing happened.

"Maybe it's the painkillers," Lasciel suggested. "And you were, after all, very tired. It looks like we'll be spending a little time together."

I glared for a while. I don't usually take the time to glower at things in dreams, either. "What do you want?" I said.

"To make you an offer," she said.

"The answer is no," I said. "We now return me to my regularly scheduled dream."

She pursed her lips, then smiled again. "I think you want to hear me out," she said. "This is your dream, after all. If you truly wished me to begone, don't you think you could make it so?"

"Maybe it's the hot tub," I suggested.

"I saw that you'd never experienced one," Lasciel said. She dipped a toe into the pool and smiled. "I have, often. Do you like it?"

"It's okay," I said, and tried to look like I didn't think it was just about the nicest thing ever for an aching and tired body. "You know what I know, eh?"

"I exist within your mind," she said. "I see what you see. Feel what you feel. I learn what you learn—and quite a bit more besides."

"What is that supposed to mean?" I said.

"That I can do you a great deal of good," she said. "I have the knowledge and memory of two thousand years of life upon this world, and infinite thousands outside it. I know many things that could be of use to you. I can advise you. Teach you secrets of your craft never known to mortalkind. Show you sights no human has ever seen. Share with you memory and image beyond anything you could imagine."

"By any chance does all of this knowledge and power and good advice come for only three easy installments of nineteen ninety-five plus shipping and handling?"

The fallen angel arched a golden brow at me.

"Or maybe it comes with a bonus set of knives tough enough to saw through a nail, yet still cut tomatoes like *this*."

She regarded me steadily and said, "You aren't nearly as funny as you think you are."

"I had to come up with some kind of response to your offer to corrupt and enslave me. Bad jokes seemed perfectly appropriate, because I can only assume that you've got to be kidding."

Lasciel pursed her lips, a thoughtful expression. It made me start thinking about how soft her mouth looked, for example. "Is that what you think I want? A slave?"

"I got a look at how you guys work," I said.

"You're referring to Ursiel's previous host, yes?"

"Yes. He was insane. Broken. I'm not eager to give it a whirl for myself."

Lasciel rolled her eyes. "Oh, please. Ursiel is a mindless thug. He doesn't care what happens to the holder of his coin, provided he gets to taste blood as often as possible. I don't operate that way."

"Sure you don't."

She shrugged. "Your derision will not unmake the truth. Some of my kindred prefer domination in their relationships with mortals. The wiser among us, though, find a mutual partnership to be much more practical, and beneficial for both parties. You saw something of how Nicodemus functions with Anduriel, did you not?"

"No offense, but I would shove a sharpened length of rebar into one ear and out the other if I thought I was going to turn into anything like Nicodemus."

Her expression registered surprise. "Why?"

"Because he's a monster," I said.

Lasciel shook her head. "Perhaps from your perspective. But you know very little of him and his goals."

"I know he did his damnedest, literally, to kill me and two of my friends, and God knows how many innocent people with that plague. And he *did* kill another friend."

"What is your point?" Lasciel asked. She seemed genuinely confused.

"The point is that he crossed the line, and I'm never going to play on his team. He doesn't get understanding or sympathy anymore. Not from me. He's got payback coming."

"You wish to destroy him?"

"In a perfect world he would vanish off the face of the earth and I would never hear of him again," I said. "But I'll take whatever I can get."

She absorbed that for a few moments, and then nodded slowly. "Very well," she said. "I will depart. But let me leave you with a thought?"

"As long as you leave."

She smiled, rising. "I understand your refusal to allow another to control your life. It's a poisonous, repugnant notion to think of someone who would dictate your every move, impose upon you a code of behavior you could not accept, and refuse to allow you choice, expression, and the pursuit of your own heart's purpose."

"Pretty much," I said.

The fallen angel smiled. "Then believe me when I say that I know *precisely* how you feel. All of the Fallen do."

A little cold spot formed in the pit of my stomach, despite the hot tub. I shifted uncomfortably in the water.

"We have that in common, wizard," Lasciel said. "You've no reason to believe me, but consider for a moment the possibility that I am sincere in my offer. I could do a great deal to help you—and you could continue to live your life on your own terms, and in accordance with your own values. I could help you be ten times the force for good that you already are."

"With that power, I should have power too great and terrible. And over me the Ring would gain a power still greater and more deadly," I said.

"Gandalf to Frodo," the demon said, smiling. "But I am not sure the metaphor is applicable. You needn't actually take up the coin, if it did not suit you to do so. The aid I can offer you in this shadow form is far more limited than if you took up the coin, but it is not inconsiderable."

"Ring, coin, whatever. The physical object is only a symbol in any case—a symbol for power."

"I merely offer you the benefit of my knowledge and experience," she said.

"Yes," I said. "Power. I've already got more than I'm comfortable with."

"Which is the foremost reason that you, of all people, are capable of wielding it responsibly."

"Maybe I am," I said. "Maybe not. I know how it works, Lasciel. The first taste is free. The price goes up down the line."

She watched me with luminous blue eyes.

"See, if I start leaning on you now, how long is it going to be before I decide that I need more of your help? How long before I start digging up the concrete in my lab because I think I need your coin in order to survive?"

"And?" she asked quietly. "If you *do* need it to survive?"

I sat in the swirling hot waters and sighed. Then I closed my eyes, made an effort of will, and reshaped the dream we stood within, so that the hot tub was gone and I stood dressed and facing her on a solid cavern floor. "If it comes to that, I hope I die with a little bit of style. Because I'm not going to sign on with Downbelow. Not even in hell's Foreign Legion."

"Fascinating," Lasciel said. She smiled at me.

My God, it was beautiful. It wasn't merely physical loveliness or the appearance of warmth. It was the whole sense of her, the vibrant, glowing *life* of the being before me, a life with energy enough to ignite a star. Seeing her smile was like watching the sun rise on the very first morning, like feeling the caress of the first breeze of the first spring. It made me want to laugh and run and spin around in it, like the sunny days of a childhood I could only dimly remember.

But I held myself back. Beauty can be dangerous, and fire, though lovely, can burn and kill when not treated with respect. I faced the fallen angel cautiously, my posture unthreatening but unbowed. I faced her beauty and felt the radiant warmth of her presence and held myself from reaching out for it.

"I'm not fascinating," I said. "I am what I am. It isn't perfect, but it's mine. I'm not making deals with you."

Lasciel nodded, her expression thoughtful. "You've been burned in bargains past, and you have no desire to repeat the experience. You are wary of dealing with me and those like me—and for good reason. I don't think I would have had any lasting respect for you, had you accepted my offer at face value—even though it is genuine."

"Gee. I would have felt crushed by your lack of respect."

She laughed with a lot of belly in it, genuinely pleased. "I admire your will. Your defiance. As something of a defiant being myself, I think we might forge a strong partnership, given time to develop it."

"That won't happen," I said. "I want you to leave."

"Get thee behind me?" she asked.

"Something like that."

She bowed her head. "As you wish, my host. I request that you merely consider my offer. Should you wish to converse with me again, you have only to call my name."

"I won't," I said.

"As it pleases you," she said.

Then she was gone, and the dream cavern was darker and lonelier for her absence. I relaxed and went back to my sleep and my solitary dreams.

I was too tired to remember if any of them had a hot tub.

I slept hard and didn't wake up until well after sunrise. I heard voices, and after a minute I identified the sharp, crackling edges of tone that told me they were coming out of a radio. I got up and gave myself a washcloth bath at the bathroom sink. It wasn't as nice as a hot tub, and not even as nice as a shower, but I didn't feel like sticking my aching leg into a trash bag and taping it shut so that I could get one without getting my bandages wet.

I couldn't find my clothes anywhere, so I wandered out into the house in my bare feet and mangled pants. The hospital staff had cut the pant leg mostly off of my wounded leg, and the edges were rough and uneven. I passed a mirror in the hallway of the house and stopped to examine myself.

I looked like a joke. A bad joke.

". . . mysterious power outage continues," the radio announcer was saying. "In fact, it's difficult to estimate how long we'll be able to stay on the air, or even how many people are actually receiving this broadcast. Gasoline-powered generators have been encountering odd trouble throughout the city, batteries seem unreliable, and other gasoline-powered engines, including those of vehicles, are behaving unpredictably. The telephone lines have been having all kinds of problems, and cell phones seem to be all but useless. O'Hare is completely shut down, and as you can imagine, it's playing havoc with airline traffic throughout the nation."

Thomas was standing in the kitchen, at the gas stove. He was making pancakes and listening to an old battery-powered radio sitting on Murphy's counter. He nodded to me, put a finger against his lips, and flicked a glance at the radio. I nodded, folded my arms, and leaned against the doorway to listen to the announcer continue.

"National authorities have declined to comment on the matter, though the mayor's office has given a statement blaming the problems on unusual sunspot activity."

Thomas snorted.

The radio prattled on. "That answer doesn't seem to hold much water, given that in cities as near as the south side of Joliet all systems are behaving normally. Other sources have suggested everything from an elaborate Halloween hoax to the detonation of some kind of electromagnetic pulse device, which has disrupted the city's electrical utilities. A press conference has reportedly been scheduled for later this evening. We'll be on the air all through the current crisis, giving you up-to-date information as quickly as we . . ."

The announcer's voice broke up into wild static and sound. Thomas reached over and flicked the radio off. "Had it on for twenty minutes," he said. "Got a clear signal for maybe five of them."

I grunted.

"Do you know what's happened?"

"Maybe," I said. "Where's Butters?"

Thomas tilted his head toward the back door. "Walking Mouse."

I took a seat at the little kitchen table, getting my weight off of my injured leg. "Today's going to be pretty intense," I said.

Thomas flipped a pancake. "Because of the heirs of Kemmler?"

"Yeah," I said. "If Mab is right about what they're trying to do, someone has to stop them before tonight."

"Why?"

"Because after that I'm not sure anyone will be *able* to stop them," I said.

My brother nodded. "Think you can take them?"

"They're fighting among themselves," I said. "They're all going to be more worried about their fellow necromancers than they are about me."

"Uh-huh," Thomas said. "But do you think you can take them?"

"No."

"Then what you're talking about isn't heroism, man. It's suicide."

I shook my head. "I don't need to kill them. I only need to stop them. If I play this right, I won't need to fight anybody."

Thomas flipped another pancake. The cooked side was a uniform shade of perfect light brown. "How are you going to manage that?"

"They need two things to make this godhood thing go," I said. "The Erlking and the knowledge in *The Word of Kemmler.* If I can deny them either, the whole shebang is canceled."

"You figure out those numbers yet?" Thomas asked.

"No."

"So . . . what? You going to put a hit on the Erlking to keep him from showing up?"

I shook my head. "Mab gave me the impression that the Erlking was in the same weight class as her."

"She tough?" Thomas asked.

"Beyond the pale," I said.

"So you can't kill the Erlking. What, then?"

"I summon him myself."

He arched an eyebrow.

"Look, no matter how mighty he is, he can't be in two places at once. If I call him up and keep him busy, then the heirs can't summon him to their ceremony."

He nodded. "How are you going to call him?"

"The book," I said. "It's almost got to be one of those poems or songs. One of them must be an incantation to attract the Erlking's attention."

"But you don't have the book," Thomas said.

"Yeah," I said. "That's the kink I haven't worked out yet."

Thomas nodded, scraping the last of the batter out of a bowl and onto the griddle. "Even if you do figure out how to call the Erlking, it sounds like he might be kinda dangerous."

"Probably. But impersonal. That means not as dangerous as one of the heirs going godly and showing up to give me some payback for annoying them." I shrugged. "And the only one in danger will be me."

"Wrong," Thomas said. "I'll be with you."

I had been sure he would say something like that, but hearing it still felt pretty good. Thomas had a truckload of baggage, and he wasn't always the most pleasant person in the world—but he was my brother. Family. He'd stand with me.

Which made what came next hard to say.

"You can't," I said.

His expression smoothed over into neutrality. "Because of Mavra?"

"No," I said. "Because I'm going to bring in the White Council."

Thomas dropped his spatula onto the kitchen floor.

"I have to," I said. "It took all the Wardens together to take down Kemmler and his students last time. I might not be able to prevent the Erlking's arrival. If that happens, someone has to stop the heirs directly. I can't do it. The Wardens can. It's as simple as that."

"Okay," he said. "But that doesn't explain why I can't stick with you."

"Because to them you're just a White Court vampire, Thomas. With whom I am supposed to be at war. If they learn that you're my brother, it might give the people in the Council who don't like me grounds to question my loyalty. And even if they believe that I'm not acting against the Council or being controlled by you, they'd still be suspicious of you. They'd want assurances that you were on their team."

"They'd use me," he said quietly. "And use me against you."

"They'd use us both against each other. Which is why you can't be around when they show."

Thomas turned and studied my face carefully. "What about Murphy? If you call in the Council, Mavra will screw up her life."

I chewed on my lip a little. "Murphy wouldn't want me to put innocents in danger to protect her. If one of the heirs turns into some kind of dark god, people are going to die. She wouldn't forgive me for protecting her if that was the cost," I said. "Besides. This isn't about recovering the *Word*. This is about stopping the heirs. I can still get the book to Mavra and fulfill our bargain."

Thomas took a deep breath. "Is that wise?"

"I don't know. She's not exactly alive. I doubt Kemmler's techniques would apply to her use of magic."

"If they didn't," Thomas said, "then why would she want the book?"

Which was a damned good question. I rubbed at my eyes. "All I know is that I've got to stop the heirs. And I've got to protect Murphy."

"If the Council finds out that you're planning on using them to defeat the heirs so that you can give Kemmler's book to a vampire of the Black Court, you'll be in trouble."

"Not for long," I said. "The Wardens will execute me on the spot."

"God. And you can accept that? From your own people?"

"I'm acclimated," I said.

We were quiet for a moment.

"You want me to sit this out," Thomas said. "You don't want me to help."

"I don't see that I have much choice," I told him. "Do you?"

"You could just leave this whole thing. We could head for Aruba or something."

I looked at him.

"Okay," he said. "You won't. But a guy can hope. I just don't like the idea of sitting on the sidelines when you might need my help." He frowned. "Hey. You're doing this on purpose. You're trying to keep me out of it to protect me, you . . . sneaky little bitch."

"It works out that way," I said. "Think of it as payback for those painkillers."

He grimaced at me, then nodded.

"And thank you," I said quietly. "You were right. I needed the rest."

"Of course I was right," Thomas said. "You looked like you were about to pass out. You still don't look great."

"I'm hungry. Did you make those pancakes for breakfast, or are they only decorative?"

"Go ahead and mock," Thomas said. He slapped a bunch of pancakes onto a plate and brought it over to the table along with a plastic bottle of maple syrup. "Here. Happy birthday."

I blinked at the pancakes and then up at him.

"I'd have gotten you a present, but . . ." He shrugged.

"No," I said. "I mean, no, that's okay. I'm surprised you remembered at all. No one has remembered my birthday since Susan left town."

Thomas got himself a plate and left the rest on a third plate for Butters. He sat down at the table and started eating them without syrup. "Don't make a big thing of it. I'm sort of surprised I remembered it myself." He nodded at the world in general. "So you think Grevane and the Corpsetaker are the ones who turned the lights out?"

I shook my head. "They were both stretching themselves by keeping so many undead under their control. That's why the Corpsetaker went after Grevane with a sword, and why he defended himself physically."

"Then who did it?"

"Cowl," I said. "He made himself scarce last night. My guess is that he was too busy setting it up to take a swing at Grevane or the Corpsetaker."

"Why Cowl?"

"Because this is a major hex, man. If you'd have asked me yesterday, I wouldn't have thought this was possible. I don't know how he did it, but . . ." I shivered. "His magic is stronger than mine. And from what I saw of his technique, he's a hell of a lot more skilled, too. If he's as good at thaumaturgy as he is at evocation, he's the most dangerous wizard I've ever seen."

"I'm not sure how he did it matters as much as why," Thomas said.

I nodded. "He gets a lot of advantages. Paralyzes human power structures. Keeps cops and so on too busy to interfere with whatever they're doing."

"But that's not the only reason. You said something about preparing the way?"

"Yeah." I finished a large bite of syrupy pancake goodness. "Black magic is tied in pretty closely with a lot of negative emotions—especially fear. So if you do something that scares a whole lot of people, you get an environment that is better for black magic. This stunt is going to cause havoc. Make a lot of people worry. It will help with the heirs' major mojo tonight."

"You're sure it's tonight?"

I nodded. "Pretty much. It's Halloween. The barriers between the mortal world and the spirit world are at their weakest. They'll be able to call up the most spirits to devour tonight. All the acts of black magic they've been working around town were also part of that preparation. Creating spiritual turbulence. Making it easier to use larger and larger amounts of black magic."

Thomas ate several bites while I listened. Then he said, "How are you going to contact the Council with the phones out?"

"Alternative channels," I said. "I'll call up a messenger."

"Meanwhile," Thomas said, his voice a little bitter, "I will stay here and do . . . nothing."

"No, you won't," I said. "Because you're going to be figuring out where they can call up the most old spirits. Not only that, but I'm leaving you a copy of Bony Tony's code numbers. Figure out what they mean."

He toyed with a bit of pancake. "Old spirits would come from a graveyard, right?"

"Probably," I said. "But sometimes they can get attached to possessions instead of a specific location. See what you can find out about Native American burial grounds or ruins. That's the right age bracket for what the heirs want."

"Okay," Thomas said without much confidence. "And you want me to figure out the numbers, too."

"With Butters," I said. "He can help you on both counts. He's damned smart."

"Assuming he wants to help," Thomas said. "He might want to cash in his chips and get out of this game while he's still alive."

"If he does, then you'll be on your own," I said. "But I don't think he will."

Just then the kitchen door opened and Butters came in with a panting Mouse. The big dog padded over to me and nudged my hand with his nose until I scratched him in his favorite spot, just behind one notched ear.

"Don't think who will what?" Butters asked. "Oh, hey, pancakes. Are there any for me?"

"Counter," Thomas said.

"Cool."

"Butters," I said. "Look, I think you're going to be all right on your own now. If you want me to, I'll take you home after breakfast."

He peered owlishly at me and said, "Of course I want to go home. The Oktoberfest polka-off is tonight."

Thomas arched an eyebrow at me.

Butters looked back and forth between us and said, "Do you need me to do something?"

"Maybe," I said. "There's some research to be done. I totally understand if you want to get while the getting's good. But if you're willing, we could use your help."

"Research," Butters said. "What kind of research?"

I told him.

Butters chewed on his lip. "Is it . . . is anything going to try to kill me for doing it?"

"I don't think so," I said. "But I can't lie to you. These are some dangerous people. I can't predict everything they might do."

Butters nodded. "But . . . if you don't get this information, what happens?"

"It gets harder to stop them."

"And if you don't stop them, what happens?"

I put my fork down, suddenly not very hungry. "One of them gets phenomenal cosmic power, and all the living space he can take. I get killed. So will a lot of innocent people. And God only knows what someone could do with power like that over the long term."

Butters looked down at his pancakes.

I waited. Thomas said nothing. His appetite hadn't been affected, and the sound of his knife and fork on the plate was the only one in the kitchen.

"This is bigger than me," he said finally. "It's bigger than polka, even. So I guess I'll help."

I smiled at him. "Appreciate it."

Thomas looked up, studying Butters speculatively. "Yeah?"

Butters nodded, and grimaced. "If I walk away when I know I could lend a hand . . . I'm not sure I could live with that. I mean, if you were asking me to shoot somebody or something, I'd head for the hills. But research is different. I can do research."

I rose and clapped Butters gently on the shoulder. "Thomas will fill you in."

"Where are you going?" he asked.

"I have to figure out how to call up the Erlking," I said.

"Is that why everyone wanted that book?"

"Apparently."

"But you had it. Heck, you *read* it."

I rubbed at my eyes. "Yeah. I know. But I didn't know exactly what I was looking for."

Butters nodded. "Frustrating, huh."

"Just a bit."

"It's too bad you don't have a photographic memory," Butters said. "I knew a guy in college with one of those, the bastard. He could just look at a page, and then read it back to himself in his head a week later."

A thought struck me hard, and I felt my limbs twitch with sudden excitement. "What did you say?"

"Uh. You don't have a photographic memory?" Butters asked.

"*Yes,*" I said. "Butters, you are a genius."

"I am," he said. Then his brow furrowed in puzzlement. "I am?"

"Brilliant," I said. "Certifiably."

"Oh. Good."

I rose and started gathering my things. "Where is that backpack I had you wear?"

"Living room," Butters said. "Why?"

"You might need it." I limped out to the living room and got the backpack. I touched it lightly, and felt the solid curve of Bob the skull within. I got my coat and my car keys and headed for the back door.

"Where are you going?" Thomas asked.

"Gumshoeing," I said.

"You shouldn't go alone."

"Probably not," I agreed. "But I am."

"At least take Mouse," Thomas said.

The big dog tilted his head quizzically, looking back and forth between Thomas and me.

"And hold his leash in my teeth?" I said. "I've only got the one hand to work with."

Thomas frowned and then rolled a shoulder in a shrug. "Okay."

"The phones are apparently unreliable," I said. I tossed the backpack at Thomas. He caught it. "Bob will know how to reach me if you find something. Got that, Bob?"

A muffled voice from the backpack said, "*Jawohl, herr kommandant.*"

Butters jumped halfway out of his chair and made a squeaking sound. "What was that?"

"Explain it to him," I told Thomas. "I'll be in touch as soon as I can."

My brother nodded at me. "Good luck. Be careful."

"You too. Keep your eyes open. Thanks again, Butters."

"Sure, sure. See you soon." Butters poked at the backpack with his fork.

"Hey!" Bob protested from inside the pack. "Stop that! You'll scratch it all up!"

I swung out the door. The night's rest had done me good, and realizing how it might be possible to stop the heirs of Kemmler had given me an electric sense of purpose. I strode to the car, barely feeling my aching leg.

I turned my hand over and regarded Shiela's phone number, written on it in black marker.

I didn't have a photographic memory.

But I knew someone who did.

Chapter

Twenty-seven

I went to my office. Traffic wasn't as bad as it could have been. It looked like the commuters hadn't poured into town in the usual volume. The traffic lights were out, but there were cops at most of the problem intersections, and everyone seemed to be driving slowly and reasonably during the crisis. That's what they were calling it on the radio—the crisis. There were a lot more people than usual out and about on the street, and with far less of the usual brisk, businesslike manner.

All in all, it was about the best reaction to the situation you could hope for. It seemed like people could go one of two ways: Either they freak out and start rioting, or they actually act like human beings in trouble ought to, and look out for one another. When LA blacked out, there had been big-time rioting. In New York, people had pulled together.

It was just as well that people hadn't reacted quite so blindly as they might have. Without even trying, I could feel the slow, sour tension of black magic pulsing and swirling through the city. With the subtle influence of all that dark energy behind it, even a mild panic could have turned ugly, and fast.

Of course, it wasn't dark yet. Nightfall could change things.

As advanced as mankind likes to think it is, we all have that age-old, primal, undeniable dread of darkness. Of being unable to see danger coming. We don't like to think that we're afraid of the dark anymore, but if that's true, then why do we work so hard to make sure our cities are constantly lit? We cloak ourselves in so much light that we can barely see the stars at night.

Fear is a funny thing. In the right light, even tiny and insignificant fears can suddenly grow, swelling up to monstrous proportions. With the black magic rolling around the way it was, that instinctive fear of the dark would feed upon itself, doubling and redoubling, and with no explanation to tell them why the lights hadn't come on, people would start to forget their carefully rational reasons not to be afraid in favor of panic.

Even assuming I prevented a brand-spanking-new dark godling from arising, tonight could be bad. It could be very bad.

I got to my office and tried to call Shiela's number. The phones weren't cooperating with me, which hardly came as a surprise. They rarely worked perfectly on the best of days. I kept a copy of a reverse phone book at my office, though, and I found the address of her Cabrini-Green apartment. While it wasn't as bad as it had been in the past, it wasn't exactly the best part of town, either. I had a brief pang of longing for the gun I'd lost in the alley behind Bock's place. It wasn't that the gun was more effective than other things I could do to defend myself, but it was a hell of a lot more of a deterrent to the average Chicago thug than a carved stick.

Just for fun, I tried the phones again, dialing my contact number for the nearest outpost of the Wardens.

So help me God, the phone rang.

"Yes," answered a woman with a low, roughened voice.

I fumbled my little notebook of security phrases out of my duster's pocket. "One second," I said. "I didn't think the call would go through." I flipped the little notebook open to the last page and said, "Uh, chartreuse sirocco."

"Rabbit," answered the voice. I checked the notebook. It was the countersign.

"This is Wizard Dresden," I said. "I have a Code Wolf situation here. Repeat, Code Wolf."

The woman on the other end of the phone hissed. "This is Warden Luccio, wizard."

Holy crap, the boss herself. Anastasia Luccio was one of the next in line for a seat on the Senior Council, and was the commander of the Wardens. She was one tough old bird, and she was the field commander of the Council's forces in the war with the Red Court.

"Warden Luccio," I said respectfully—both because she probably deserved it and because I needed to get along with her as well as I possibly could.

"What is the situation?" she asked.

"At least three apprentices to the necromancer Kemmler are here in Chicago," I said. "They found the fourth book. They're going to use it tonight."

There was a stunned silence from the other end of the phone.

"Hello?" I said.

"Are you sure?" Luccio asked. Her voice had a faint Italian accent. "How do you know who they are?"

"All those zombies and ghosts were sort of a giveaway," I said. "I confronted them. They identified themselves as Grevane, Cowl, and Capiorcorpus, and they each had a drummer with them."

"*Dio,*" Luccio said. "Do you know where they are?"

"Not yet, but I'm working on it," I said. "Can you help?"

"Affirmative," Luccio said. "We will dispatch Wardens to Chicago immediately. They will arrive at your apartment within six hours."

"Might not be the best place," I said. "I was attacked there last night, and my wards got torn apart. The apartment may be under surveillance."

"Understood. Then we will rendezvous at the alternate location."

I checked the notebook. I'd have to meet them at McAnally's. "Gotcha," I said.

"Che cosa?" she asked.

"Uh, understood, Warden," I said. "Six hours, alternate location. Don't skimp on the personnel, either. These folks are serious."

"I am familiar with Kemmler's disciples," she said, though her tone was more one of agreement than reprimand. "I will lead the team myself. Six hours."

"Right. Six hours."

She hung up the phone.

I settled it back onto its cradle, lips pursed in thought. Hell's bells, the war captain of the White Council herself was to take the field. That meant that this situation was being regarded as an emergency tantamount to a terrorist with an armed nuclear bomb. If the head Warden was coming out to battle, it meant that the Wardens were going to pull out all the stops.

I was going to have a lot of help for a change. Help that held me in deadly suspicion, and who might execute me if they learned some of my secrets, but help nonetheless. I felt an odd sense of comfort. The Wardens had been one of my biggest fears practically since I had learned about their existence. There was something deeply satisfying about seeing the object of that fear take a hostile interest in Grevane and company. Like when Darth Vader turns against the emperor and throws him down the shaft. There's nothing quite so cool as seeing someone who scares the hell out of you go at an enemy.

And then a disturbing thought occurred to me: Why in hell was the war captain of the White Council answering the freaking phones? Why wasn't a junior member of the Wardens doing the receptionist work?

I could think of only a couple or three reasons.

None of them were pleasant.

My brief flash of relief and confidence melted away. Good thing it did, too. I'm sure the world would come to an end if I were allowed to feel a sense of relief and well-being for any length of time.

I shoved my worry out of my head. It wasn't going to help anything. The only one I could count on to ride to my rescue was me. If the Wardens managed to do it anyway, it would be a nice surprise, but I had to get myself moving before the problem started looking too big. It was the same principle as cleaning a really messy room. You don't think about everything you have to do. You focus on one thing and get it done, then move on to the next.

I needed the summons that was hidden in *Der Erlking.* To get that, I had to talk to Shiela. *Right, Harry. Get a move on.* I tried the phone once more, but I guess I'd already won the functional tech lottery: All circuits were busy.

I hadn't been sitting down very long, but it was long enough for my leg to make it clear to the rest of my body that it didn't want to be walked on any more today.

"Get with the program," I told my leg severely. "You don't have to be happy about it, but I need you functional."

My leg sat there in sullen silence and throbbed, which I took as assent. I reached for my keys, and then heard a soft sound at my office door.

I whirled my staff into my hand, calling up my will, and the runes were already smoldering with sullen orange light when the door opened.

Billy stood in the doorway, his expression frozen in surprise, his mouth open. He was wearing jeans, cowboy boots, and an old leather jacket. He hadn't worn his glasses much over the past several years, but he had them on today. His hair had been mussed by the wind, which sighed against my office windows. I heard a few drops of rain begin to fall, striking with dull taps on the glass.

"Um," he said after a minute. "Hi, Harry."

I scowled at him and lowered the staff, letting the power ease out of it. The warmed wood felt good under my hand, and the faint scent of wood smoke lay on the air. "Bad time to be appearing suddenly in my office door," I said.

"Next time I'll whistle or something," Billy replied.

"How'd you find me?"

"It's your office." He looked around the place. "You talking to someone?"

"Not really," I said. "What do you need?"

He opened his coat. The handle of a gun protruded from his belt—my revolver. "Artemis Bock came by my place. He said there was some trouble at his store."

"Yeah," I said. "Bad guys were trying to rough him up. I argued with them about it."

Billy nodded. "That's what he said. He found this in the alley outside. He said there was blood."

"One of them clipped my leg," I said. "I got it taken care of."

Billy nodded, worried. "Um. He was worried about you."

"I'm fine." I stood up, careful about my leg. "Bock okay?"

"Um," Billy said. He looked at me, his expression clearly concerned. "Yeah. Not hurt, I mean. Some damage to the store, which he said he didn't mind. He wanted me to thank you for him." He pulled the gun out of his belt and said, "And I thought you might need this."

"Shouldn't carry it in your pants like that," I said. "Good way to sing soprano."

"It's empty," he said, and offered me the handle of the gun.

I took it, flipped the cylinder open, and checked it. The gun wasn't loaded. I slid it into the pocket of my duster, then opened the drawer of my desk and took out a small box of ammunition I kept there. I put it in the pocket along with the gun. "Thanks for bringing that by," I said. "Why'd you come looking here?"

"You didn't answer the phone at your place. I went by there. It looked like someone tried to tear the door off."

"Someone did," I said.

"But you're all right?" There was a little more weight on the question than I would have expected.

"I'm fine," I said, getting impatient. "Hell's bells, Billy. If you've got something to say, go ahead and say it."

He inhaled deeply. "Um. Well. I'm sort of afraid to."

I arched a brow at him, and scowled again.

"Look. You . . . aren't acting right, Harry."

"Meaning?" I asked.

"Meaning not like yourself," Billy said. "People have been noticing."

"People?" I asked. My leg pounded. I had no time for this kind of psychological patty-cake. "What people?"

"People who respect you," he said carefully. "Maybe who are even a little bit afraid of you."

I just stared at him.

"I don't know if you know this, Harry. But you can be a really scary guy. I mean, I've seen what you can do. And even the people who haven't seen themselves have heard stories. Believe me, we're all glad you're one of the good guys, but if you weren't . . ."

"What?" I said, suddenly feeling more tired. "If I wasn't, then what?"

"You'd be scary. Really scary."

"Get to your damned point," I said quietly.

He nodded. "You've been talking to things."

"Excuse me?"

He lifted his hands. "Talking to things. I mean, you were talking to things when I was outside your door."

"That was nothing," I said.

"Okay," Billy said, though his tone suggested that he was placating me rather than agreeing.

"What is this talking-to-things crap? Did Bock say I was doing that?"

"Harry—" Billy said.

"Because I wasn't," I said. "Good God, I do some crazy crap, but it's usually the 'this is never going to work but I have to try it' variety of crazy. I'm not insane."

Billy folded his arms, his eyes searching my face. "See, that's the thing. If you were truly insane, would you be able to realize it?"

I rubbed at the bridge of my nose. "So let me get this straight. Because Bock said something about me, and because you heard me talking to myself, suddenly I'm ready for the room with rubber walls."

"No," he said. "Sort of. Harry, look, it isn't like I'm trying to accuse—"

"That's funny, because it sounds like an accusation from this end," I said.

"I only—"

I slammed my staff down on the floor, and Billy flinched.

He tried to cover it, but I had seen the motion. Billy flinched like he was genuinely afraid that I was going to hurt him.

What the hell?

"Billy," I said quietly. "There is some bad business going on. I don't have time for this. I don't know what Bock told you, but he's had a bad couple of days. He's rattled. I'm not going to hold anything against him."

"All right," he said quietly.

"I want you to go home," I told him. "And I want you to start sending out word around to the in crowd. Everyone wants to be behind a threshold tonight."

He frowned and took off his glasses, scrubbing at them with a corner of his shirt. "Why?"

"Because the White Council is sending a war party to town. You don't want anyone you know to get caught in the backwash."

Billy swallowed. "This is big, then?"

"And I have to get moving. I don't have time for distractions." I stepped forward and put my hand on his shoulder. "Hey, it's me. Harry. I'm as sane as I ever am, and I need you to trust me for a little while. Tell people to keep their heads down. Okay?"

He took a deep breath and then nodded sharply. "I'll do it, man."

"Good. I don't know why you're so worried about me. But we'll sit down and talk after the dust settles. Figure out what's up. Make sure I haven't stripped a gear when I wasn't looking. I promise you."

"Right," he said, nodding. "Thank you. I'm sorry if this is . . . aw, hell, man."

"Enough with sharing the emotions," I said. "We're gonna turn into women as we stand here. Get a move on."

He chucked my arm with a mostly closed fist, and left.

I waited for him to go. I didn't feel like riding down in the elevator with him, wondering if he was afraid of me suddenly turning on him with an ax or a butcher knife or something.

I leaned on my staff and thought about it for a second. Billy was really worried about me. Worried enough that he was afraid that I might do something to him. What the hell had I done to set that off?

And an even better question, which I had to ask myself, followed on the heels of that first one.

What if he was right?

I poked at my skull with a finger. It didn't *feel* soft or anything. I didn't feel insane. But if you'd really lost it, would you have enough left upstairs to know? Crazy people never *thought* they were crazy.

"I've always talked to things," I said. "And to myself."

"Good point," myself agreed with me. "Unless that means you've been nuts all along."

"I don't need wiseass remarks," I told myself severely. "There's work to do. So shut up."

All I could think was that it had been Georgia's idea. She was always buried to the ears in her psych textbooks. Maybe she had fallen victim to some kind of inverted psychological hypochondria or something.

Thunder rumbled outside, and the rain started coming down harder.

I didn't need any doubts distracting me right now. I shrugged off the whole conversation with Billy, tabling it for later. I loaded my gun, since not loading it would have been almost as good as not having it, then slipped it back into my pocket, locked up my office behind me, and headed for the car.

I had to get to Shiela and see if her remarkable memory could call up the poems and stanzas from that stupid book. And then I had to figure out how to call up a wild and deadly lord of the darker realms of Faerie and sidetrack him so that the heirs of Kemmler couldn't use him to promote themselves to demigod status. And along the way, I had to find *The Word of Kemmler* and get it to Mavra, somehow, without the White Council learning what I was up to.

Easy as breathing.

As I rode down in the elevator, I had to admit that Billy might have a point.

Chapter

Twenty-eight

The Cabrini-Green tenement Shiela lived in had seen better days—but it had seen worse, too. The city had dumped a lot of money into urban renewal projects there, and it was an ongoing process. Shiela's building was still undergoing renovation, and the lobby and many of the floors were only half-finished. No workmen were in the building when I went into the lobby, but there were dozens of tarps, stacks of drywall and raw lumber, heavy tool lockers that had been bolted to the floor, and other evidence of the contractors who would doubtless have been working had the city's lights not been out.

I walked over to the elevators and to the security panel there, and found the button of Shiela's apartment on the ninth floor. I pressed it and held it down for a minute before I realized that, duh, the power was out and I wasn't going to be able to ring her apartment.

I grimaced and looked around for the stairs. Nine flights up on my leg wasn't going to feel nice, but it wasn't as though I had an infinite number of options.

The door to the stairs was locked, but it was a standard fire door with a push bar on the other side. I lifted my staff, looked around the lobby to make sure no one had wandered in to see me, and then gestured with the staff and murmured, *"Forzare."*

I sent a bare whisper of my power through the door and then drew it back toward me with a sharp gesture. I caught the push bar on the other side with it, and the door trembled and then swung open by an inch or two. I thrust the end of my staff into it to hold it open, then grabbed on and heaved. I stared at the stairs for a second, but they didn't get any shorter or turn into an escalator or anything, so I sighed and started painfully hauling myself up them, one step at a time.

Nine floors and 162 steps later, I paused to catch my breath, and then opened the door to the ninth-floor hallway in the same manner I had the one in the lobby. The ninth-floor hallway was still under construction, and several of the apartments in it were missing doors, and even walls. I limped along until I found Shiela's apartment and then knocked on the door.

I felt a tingling tension over the door as I touched it—a magical ward of some kind. It was nowhere near as strong as the ones on my apartment had been, but it was stable. That was fairly impressive. Shiela might not have a ton of inborn talent, but she evidently had enough discipline to offset the lack. I held my hand out lightly, just over the surface of the door, sending my senses running over the ward, getting more of a feel for its strength. It couldn't have stopped me if I used my power to force my way in, but it felt strong enough to give me a solid kick in the teeth if I tried it physically. It would certainly scare the hell out of a would-be burglar. Not bad.

After a minute I heard footsteps and the door opened a little. I could see a security chain and a slender stripe of her face that included one of Shiela's dark, sparkling eyes. She let out a surprised little sound and then said, "Harry. Just a minute."

I waited while she shut the door and took off the security chain. Then she opened the door again, smiling at me. She had an infectious smile, and I found myself answering it with one of my own.

She was dressed in a scarlet sequined bodice that made her chest into something very difficult not to stare at, nearly translucent baggy leggings, leather sandals that wrapped around her calves, and 6.5 million pounds of bangles on her arms and ankles. Her hair had been caught up in a high ponytail fixed into place to rise over some kind of mesh headdress, and her smooth, bare shoulders looked lovely and strong.

"Hi," she said.

"Hi," I said back. "Is your roommate Shiela in, Genie?"

She laughed. "You caught me in the nick of time. I was just about to leave to get together with some people I know."

"Costume party?" I asked.

"No, I dress like this all the time." Her eyes sparkled. "It *is* Halloween."

"Even with the lights out?"

She bobbed her brows, her smile wicked for a second. "Who knows. That might make it more fun."

I had been right about the curves that had been hidden under her loose clothing back at Bock's. They were awfully pleasant ones. It was an effort of will to stay focused on her face—especially when she laughed. Her laugh made all sorts of interesting little quivers run over her. "Do you have a minute?" I asked.

"Maybe even two," she said. "What did you have in mind?"

"I need your help with something," I said. I looked up and down the hallway. As far as I knew I hadn't been followed, and I'd been watching my back—but that didn't mean that no one was there. I was pretty good at noticing such things, but there were plenty of people (and nonpeople) who were better than me. "If you don't mind, can we talk about it inside?"

Her expression became a little wary, and she looked up and down the hall herself. "Are you in trouble? Is this about the people at the store?"

"Pretty much," I said. "May I come in?"

"Of course, of course," she said, and stepped back inside, holding the door open for me. I limped in. "Oh, my God," she said, staring at me as I came in. "What happened?"

"A ghoul threw a knife into my leg," I told her.

She blinked at me. "You mean . . . a real ghoul? An actual ghoul?"

"Yeah."

Her face twisted up with dismay. "Oh. Wow. I've heard stories, but I never thought . . . you know. It's hard to believe they're really out there. Does that make me an idiot?"

"No," I said. "It makes you lucky. If I never see another ghoul, it will be too soon."

Her apartment was pretty typical of the kind: small, worn, run-down, but clean. She had mostly secondhand furniture, an ancient old fridge, mismatched bookshelves that overflowed with paperbacks and textbooks, and a tiny, aged television that looked as if it didn't get much use.

"Sit down," she said, picking up a couple of blankets and a throw pillow from the couch, clearing off a space for me. I tottered over to the couch and sat, which felt entirely too good. I grunted and got my leg elevated onto the coffee table, and it felt even better.

"Thanks," I said.

She shook her head, staring at me. "You look frightful."

"Been a tough couple of days."

She studied me with serious eyes. "I suppose it must have been. What are you doing here?"

"The book," I said. "The one on the Erlking that I got from Bock."

"I remember," she said.

"Exactly."

"Um. What?"

"That's why I'm here," I said. "You remember but I don't, and the bad guys stole my copy. I need you to remember it for me."

She frowned. "The whole thing?"

"I don't think so," I said. "There were several poems and stanzas in there. I think what I need is in one of them."

"What do you need?" she said.

I stared at her for a second. Then I said, "It might be better if you don't know."

She lifted her chin and regarded me for a moment, as if I'd just said something bad about her mother. "Excuse me?"

"This is some bad business," I said. "It might be safer for you if I don't tell you much about it."

"Well," she said. "That's quite patronizing of you, Harry. Thank you."

I held up a hand. "It isn't like that."

"Yes," she said. "It is. You want me to give you information, but you won't tell me why or what you are going to do with it."

"It's for your own protection," I said.

"Perhaps," she replied. "But if I give you this information, I'm going to bear some responsibility for what you do with it. We don't know each other very well. What if you took the information I gave you and used it to hurt someone?"

"I won't."

"And maybe that's true," she said. "But maybe it isn't. Don't you see? I have an obligation in this matter," she said, "to use my talent responsibly. That means not using it blindly or recklessly. Can you understand that?"

"Actually," I said, "I can."

She pursed her lips and then nodded. "Then if you want me to help you, tell me why you need it."

"You could be put at risk if you become involved in this," I said. "It could be very dangerous." I left a clear silence between the last two words for emphasis.

"I understand," she said. "I accept that. So tell me."

I stared at her for a second, and then sighed, a little frustrated. She had a point, after all. But dammit, I didn't want to see anyone else get hurt because of Kemmler's disciples. Particularly not anyone with such lovely breasts.

I jerked my eyes away from them and said, "The people you've seen around the store are going to use the book to call up the Erlking."

She frowned. "But . . . he's an extremely powerful faerie, yes? Can they do that?"

"Do you mean is it possible?" I asked. "Sure. I whistled up Queen Mab a few hours ago, myself." Which was technically the truth.

"Oh," she said, her tone mild. "Why?"

"Because I needed information," I said.

"No, not that. Why are these people calling up the Erlking?"

"They're going to use his presence on Halloween night to call up an extra-large helping of ancient spirits. Then they're going to bind and devour those spirits in order to give themselves a Valhalla-sized portion of supernatural power."

She stared at me, her mouth opening a little. "It's . . . a rite of ascension?" she whispered. "A real one?"

"Yeah," I said.

"But that's . . . that's insane."

"So are these people," I said. "What you tell me could stop it from happening. It could save a lot of lives—not least of which is my own."

She folded her arms over her stomach as if chilled. Her face looked pale and worried. "I need the poems because I'm going to summon the Erlking before they can do it and to make sure that I sidetrack him long enough to ruin their plans."

"Isn't that dangerous?" she asked.

"Not as dangerous as doing nothing," I said. "So now you know why. Will you help me?"

She fretted her lower lip, as though mulling it over, but her eyes were sparkling. "Say please."

"Please," I said.

Her smile widened. "Pretty please?"

"Don't push me," I half growled, but I doubt it came out very intimidating.

She smiled at me. "It might take me few minutes. I haven't looked at that book in some time. I'll have to prepare. Meditate."

"Is it that complicated?" I asked.

She sighed, the smile fading. "There's so much of it, sometimes my head feels like a library. I don't have a problem remembering. It's finding where I've put it that's a challenge. And not all of it is very pleasant to remember."

"I know what that's like," I said. "I've seen some things I would rather weren't in my head."

She nodded, and paced over to settle down on the couch next to me. She drew her feet up underneath her and wriggled a bit to get comfortable. The wriggling part was intriguing. I tried not to be too obviously interested, and fumbled my notebook and trusty pencil from my duster's pocket.

"All right," she said, and closed her eyes. "Give me a moment. I'll speak it to you."

"Okay," I said.

"And don't stare at me."

I moved my eyes. "I wasn't."

She snorted delicately. "Haven't you ever seen breasts before?"

"I wasn't staring," I protested.

"Of course." She opened one eye and gave me a sly oblique glance. Then she closed her eyes with a little smile and inhaled deeply.

"That's cheating," I said.

She smiled again, and then her expression changed, her features growing remote. Her shoulders eased into relaxation, and then her eyes opened, dark, distant, and unfocused. She stared into the far distance for several moments, her breathing slowing, and her eyes started moving as if she were reading a book.

"Here it is," she said, her voice slow, quiet, and dreamy. "Peabody. He was the one to compile the various essays."

"I just need the poems," I said. "No need for the cover plate."

"Hush," she said. "This isn't as easy as it looks." Her fingers and hands twitched now and then while her eyes swept over the unseen book. I realized after a moment that she was turning the pages of the book in her memory. "All right," she said a minute later. "Ready?"

I poised my pencil over my notepad. "Ready."

She started quoting poetry to me, and I started writing it down. It wasn't in the first poem or the second, but in the third one I recognized the rhythms and patterns of a phrase of summoning, each line innocent on its own, but each building on the ones preceding it. With the proper focus, intent, and strength of will, the simple poem could reach out beyond the borders of the mortal world and draw the notice of the deadly faerie hunter known as the Erlking, the lord of goblins.

"That's the one," I said quietly. "I need you to be completely sure of your accuracy of recollection."

Shiela nodded, her eyes faraway. Her hand made a reverse of the page-turning motion she used and she spoke the poem to me again, more slowly. I double-checked that I'd written it all down correctly.

It doesn't do to mangle a summoning. If you get the words wrong, it can have all kinds of bad effects. Best-case scenario, the summoning doesn't work, and you pour all the effort into it for nothing. One step worse, a bungled summoning could call up the wrong being—maybe one that would be happy to rip off your face with its tentacle-laden, extendable maw. Finally, at the extreme end of negative consequences, the failed summons might call up the being you wanted—in this case the Erlking—only it would be insulted that you hadn't bothered to get it right. Uber-powerful beings of the spirit world had the kind of power and tempers that horror movies are made of, and it was a bad idea to get one of them mad at you.

If you called up a being incorrectly, there was very little you could do to protect yourself from them. That was the job hazard of summoning. If I chanted the Erlking to Chicago, I had to be damned sure I did it correctly, or it would be worth as much as my life.

"Once more," I told Shiela quietly when she was finished. I had to be sure.

She nodded and began again. I checked my written version. They all came out the same for the third time in a row, so I was as sure as I reasonably could be that it was accurate.

I stared at the notepad for a moment, trying to absorb the summoning, to remember its rhythm, the rolling sound of consonant and verb that were only incidentally related to language. This wasn't a poem—it was simply a frequency, a signal of sound and timing, and I committed it with methodical precision to memory, the same way I stored the precise inflections required to call upon a spirit being using its true name. In a sense, the poem *was* a name for the Erlking. He would respond to it in the same way.

When I looked up again a few moments later, I felt the gentle pressure of Shiela's gaze. She was watching me, her eyes worried. "You're either incredibly stupid or one of the most courageous men I've ever seen."

"Go with stupid," I said lightly. "In my experience, you can't go wrong assuming stupid."

"If you use the summoning," she said quietly, not smiling at my tone, "and something bad happens to you, I will be to blame."

I shook my head. "No," I said. "I know what I'm doing. It will be my own damned fault."

"I'm not sure that your acceptance can absolve me of responsibility," she said, frowning. "Is there anything else I can do to help you?"

"There's no need to offer," I said.

"Yes," she said earnestly. "There is. I need to know that I've done whatever I can. That if something happens to you, it won't be because of something I didn't do."

I studied her face for a moment, and found myself smiling. "You take this whole responsibility thing very seriously," I said.

"Is there some reason I shouldn't?" she asked.

"None at all," I said. "It's just unusual from someone . . . well, don't take this the wrong way, but it's unusual from someone so far down the ladder, when it comes to raw power."

She smiled a little. "It doesn't take much power to hurt someone," she said. "It's far easier than healing the damage. It's always like that, for everything. Not just magic."

"Yeah. But not many people seem to get that." I reached over and put my right hand on hers. She had very soft, very warm hands. "Thank you for helping me. If there's anything I can ever do to pay you back . . ."

She smiled at me and said, "There is one thing."

"Oh?" I asked.

She nodded. "A friend told me once that you can tell a lot about a person from how they do things the first time."

I blinked a couple of times and then said, "Uh. Like what?"

"Like this," she said, and came to me. She moved beautifully—fluid and graceful and elegantly feminine. She was all warm curves and soft flesh scented of wildflowers as she slid one leg over mine, straddling my thighs. Her gentle hands lightly framed my face as she leaned down to kiss me, her eyes rolling back and closing in anticipation as her mouth met mine.

The kiss began slowly, quietly—sensuous but not impassioned, patience without hesitance. Her lips were a warm and gentle contact on mine, and there was a sense of exploration to her mouth, as she felt her way around the kiss. Maybe I was just too tired, or too injured, or too worried about my prospects for immediate survival, but it felt good. It felt really good. Shiela's mouth wasn't inflamed with need. She demanded nothing with the kiss. All she wanted was to taste my mouth, to feel my skin under her hands.

And then without warning, a desperate yearning for more of that simple contact, that human warmth, roared through me in a flash fire of need.

Nearly everyone underestimates how powerful the touch of another person's hand can be. The need to be touched is something so primal, so fundamentally a part of our existence as human beings that its true impact upon us can be difficult to put into words. That power doesn't necessarily have anything to do with sex, either. From the time we are infants, we learn to associate the touch of a human hand with safety, with comfort, with love.

I hadn't been touched much for . . . well, a long damned time. Thomas may have been my brother, but he avoided physical contact, even casual and incidental contact, like the plague. I hadn't exactly been overwhelmed with romantic interests, either. The closest thing to it I'd had of late had been the advances of a neophyte succubus—and that contact had been anything but loving.

When sex becomes part of the equation, the impact of another's touch can be even more urgent and profound—so much so that good sense, even basic logical deduction, can go right out the window, washed away in a flood of needs that simply *must* be met.

I hadn't been touched in a long time. I hadn't been kissed in even longer. Given how likely it was that I was going to die before my next sunrise, Shiela's presence, her warmth, the simple fact that she *wanted* to be touching me crowded out every worry and fear, and I was glad to see them go. Shiela's kiss freed me from pain and from fear—even if only for a moment. And I wanted to hold on to that moment for as long as I possibly could.

I tightened my grip on the kiss, and my good arm rose, sliding deliberately around the small of her back, pulling her toward me.

Shiela let out a hiss of sudden excitement, but her kiss grew no deeper, no swifter. Her mouth stayed in its gentle rhythm, and I leaned harder into it. Her breath quickened still more, but her kiss deepened only slowly, maddeningly patient, torturously gentle. Her hips shifted in slow tension against mine, and I could feel the heat of her against me.

What I wanted to do was to reach up and haul down the sequined top. I wanted my mouth to explore every sinuous curve of her. I wanted to drive her mad with need, to fill my senses with her warmth, her cries, her scent. I wanted to forget everything arrayed against me, even if it was just for a little while, and bare her an inch at a time. The emptiness that her warmth had begun to fill howled at me to let go.

But what I did was open my mouth and brush my tongue over her lips, gently and slowly, and only once. She shivered at that touch, and her teeth tugged delicately at my lower lip. I drew the kiss to a slow, quiet close, and bowed my head, so that my forehead rested against hers. Both of us remained like that for a minute, breathing a little fast.

"Did you want to stop?" she whispered.

"No," I answered. "But I needed to."

"Why?"

"Because you don't know me," I said. "Did you want me to stop?"

"No," she said. "But I needed you to. You don't know me, either."

"Then why kiss me?" I asked.

"I . . ." I heard a touch of something like embarrassment in her voice. "It's been a long time for me. Since I've kissed anyone. I didn't realize how much I've missed it."

"Same here."

Her fingers stirred lightly, touching the sides of my face. "You seem so alone. I just . . . wanted to know what it was like. Just the kiss. Before anything else gets involved."

"That's reason enough," I agreed. "What did you think of it?"

She made a low sound in her throat. "I think I want more."

"Mmmm," I said, agreeing. "That works for me."

She let out a quiet, wicked little laugh. "Good." She shivered again and then drew away from me, dark eyes bright, still breathing fast enough to make her chest absolutely mesmerizing. She stood up, smiling. "Is there anything else I can do to help you?"

"Grab my staff for me?"

She arched a brow.

I felt my cheeks flush. "Uh. The literal staff."

"Oh," she said, and passed it to me.

She watched me with quiet concern as I heaved myself to my feet, but she made no move to help me, for which my ego was entirely grateful. I hobbled over to her door, and she walked beside me.

I turned to her and touched her cheek with my right hand. She leaned her face against my palm, just a little, and smiled up at me.

"Thank you," I told her. "You're a lifesaver. Probably literally."

She looked down and nodded. "All right. Be careful?"

"I'll try," I told her.

"Try hard," she said. "I'd like to see you again soon."

"Okay. I'll survive. But only because you asked."

She laughed, and I smiled, and then I left her in her apartment and started back down the stairs to the street.

Going down was a lot harder than going up had been. I made it to the third floor before I had to stop for a breather, and I sat down to rest my aching leg for a moment.

So I was panting and sitting flat on my ass when the air in front of me wavered, and a dark, hooded figure stepped forward from out of nowhere, one hand extended, some sort of fine mesh that covered her outstretched palm flickering with ugly purple light.

"Be very still, Dresden," Kumori said, her voice soft. "If you try to move, I'll kill you."

Chapter

Twenty-nine

Kumori stood about four feet from me—easily within reach of my staff, if I wanted to strike at her. But since I was sitting down and had only one strong hand to swing the staff, I wouldn't be able to hit hard enough to disable her, even if I somehow managed to hit her before she unleashed the power she was holding in her hand.

And besides. She was a girl.

Unless she proved herself to be some kind of monstrous thing that just looked like a girl, I wasn't going to hit her. On some rational level, I knew my attitude was dangerously illogical, but that didn't change anything. I don't hit girls.

I had the feeling she was quick enough to beat me, as she stood over me with the magical equivalent of a cocked and readied gun sparkling through the metal mesh over her right palm. I could feel the air vibrating with a low, steady note of power, and her stance was both confident and wary.

One thing I was pretty sure of—she was here to talk. If she'd wanted to kill me, she could have done it already. So I stayed sitting, set my staff aside, very slowly, and mildly raised both hands. "Take it easy there, cowgirl," I said. "You got me dead to rights."

I couldn't see her face within the depths of the hood, but I heard a dry note of amusement in her voice. "Take off the bracelet, please. And the ring on your right hand."

I arched a brow. The ring was spent, and probably didn't have enough juice left in it to push her back a step, but I'd never run into anyone who had noticed it before. Whoever she was, Kumori knew how wizards operated, and it made me even more sure that she was hiding her face because she was someone I might recognize—someone on the White Council.

I slipped the bracelet off my left hand and lowered it slowly to the stair beside me, but getting that ring off was going to be problematic. "I can't get the ring off," I said.

"Why not?" Kumori asked.

"Fingers on my left hand don't work anymore," I said.

"What happened?"

I blinked at her for a second. The question had been polite. In fact, if I didn't know any better, I'd have taken her tone for actual interest.

"What happened to your left hand?" she asked, her tone patient.

I answered her as politely as I could while staring at her, trying to figure her out. "I was fighting vampires. There was a fire. Burned my hand so bad the doctors wanted to take it off. There's no way I can get the ring off unless you want to come over here and take it yourself."

She was still for a moment. Then she said, "It might be easier if you would agree to a truce for the duration of this conversation. Are you willing to give your word on it?"

She wanted a truce, which meant that she had indeed come to talk, rather than to execute me. There sure as hell wouldn't be any harm in agreeing to a truce, and it might prevent hostilities that could be triggered by raw nerves. "In exchange for yours," I said. "This conversation and half an hour after its conclusion."

"Done," Kumori said. "You have my word."

"And you have mine," I said.

She lowered her hand at once, taking the odd mesh over it and its sparkling energies into the deep sleeves of her robe. I didn't take my eyes off her as I reclaimed my shield bracelet and fixed it back onto my wrist. "All right," I said. "What did you want to talk about?"

"The book," she said. "We still want your copy."

"You'll have to talk to the Corpsetaker," I said. "He and his ghoul took it from me last night. But if you go looking, he looks like a girl in her early twenties. Great dimples."

The hood shifted, as though Kumori had tilted her head to one side. "You know of the source of the Corpsetaker's name?"

"I figure he's a body switcher," I said. "I've heard necromancers can do that kind of thing. Move their consciousness from one body to another. Exchange with some poor sucker who can't protect themselves. Corpsetaker was in that old professor's body. I figure he swapped with his assistant, and then killed the old man's body with the girl's mind inside."

The hood nodded, conceding me the point. "But I have difficulty believing your story. Had the Corpsetaker taken the book from you, he would have killed you as well."

"Wasn't for lack of trying," I said, and gestured at my leg. "He was overconfident, and I was a little bit lucky. He got the book, but I got away."

She was silent for a moment and then said, her voice thoughtful, "You're telling me the truth."

"I'm bad at lying. Lies get all confusing. Can't keep them straight."

Kumori nodded. "Then let me make you this offer."

"Join or die?" I guessed.

She exhaled softly through her nose. "Hardly. Cowl has a certain amount of respect for you, but he believes you too raw to make some sort of alliance feasible."

"Ah," I said. "Then you'll probably go to the second offer I always get. Go away and you won't kill me."

"Something like that," Kumori said. "You have no real idea of what is going on here. Your ignorance is more dangerous than you know, and your continued involvement in this matter could cause disastrous consequences."

"What do you want me to do?" I asked.

"Withdraw from the field," she said.

"Or what?"

"Or you will regret it," she said. "That isn't a threat. Simply a fact. As I said, Cowl has a certain respect for you, but he will not be able to protect you or treat you gently should you continue to involve yourself. If you stand in his way, he *will* kill you. He would prefer it if you stood clear."

"Gosh. That's so altruistic of him." I shook my head. "If he kills me, he'll have my death curse to contend with."

"He has already contended with such curses," Kumori said. "Many times. I advise you to retire from the field."

"I can't do that," I said. "I know what you people are doing. I know about the Darkhallow. I know why you're doing it."

"And?"

"And I can't let that happen," I said. "Insurance in Chicago is expensive enough without adding in a petulant new deity tearing up the real estate."

"Our goals are not so different," Kumori said. "Grevane and the Corpsetaker are madmen. They must be stopped."

"From what I've seen of old Cowl, he's a couple of french fries short of a Happy Meal too."

"And you would do what?" Kumori asked. "Prevent them from reaping the bounty of the Darkhallow? Take the power for yourself?"

"I want to make sure *nobody* takes it," I said. "I don't particularly care how I get it done."

"Truly?" she asked.

I nodded. "Now here's where I make you an offer."

She hesitated, clearly taken off guard. "Very well."

"Bail," I told her. "Leave Cowl and the Sociopath Squad to their squabbling. Give me what information I need to stop them."

"He'd kill me in a day," she said.

"No," I told her. "I'd take you to the White Council. I'd get you protection."

She stared at me from within her hood, utterly silent.

"See, Kumori, you're sort of a puzzle," I said. "Because you're working with these necromancers. In fact, I'm willing to bet you aren't bad at necromancy yourself. But you went out of your way to save someone's life the other night, and that just doesn't jive with that crowd."

"Doesn't it?" she said.

"No. They're killers. Good at it, but they're just killers. They wouldn't take a step out of their way to help someone else. But you went way the hell out of your way to help a stranger. It says that you aren't like them."

She was silent for a moment more. Then she said, "Do you know why Cowl has made a study of necromancy? And why I have joined him?"

"No."

"Because necromancy embraces the power of death, just as magic embraces the power of life. And as magic can be twisted and perverted to cruel and destructive ends, necromancy can be turned upon its nature as well. Death can be warded off, as I did for the wounded man that night. Life can be served by that dark power, if one's will and purpose are strong."

"Uh-huh," I said. "You got involved with the darkest and most corruptive, insanity-causing forces in the universe so that you could jump-start wounded bodies to life."

She moved her hand, a sudden, slashing motion. "No. No, you idiot. Don't you see the potential here? The possibility to end *death*."

"Uh. End death?"

"You will die," she said. "I will die. Cowl will die. Everyone now walking this tired old world knows but one solid, immutable fact. Their life will end. Yours. Mine. Everyone's."

"Yeah," I said. "That's why they call us 'mortals.' Because of the mortality."

"Why?" she asked.

"What?"

"Why?" she repeated. "Why must we die?"

"Because that's the way it is," I said.

"Why must that be the way it is?" she said. "Why must we all live with that pain of separation? With horrible grief? With rage and loss and sorrow and vengeance ruling the lives of every soul beneath the sky? What if we could change it?"

"Change it," I said, my skepticism clear in my voice. "Change death."

"Yes," she said.

"Just . . . poof. Make it go away."

"What if we could?" she said. "Can you imagine what it would mean? If mere age would not lay mankind low after his threescore and ten, how much better would the world be? Can you imagine if da Vinci had continued to live, to study, to paint, to invent? That the remarkable accomplishments of his lifetime could have continued through the centuries rather than dying in the dim past? Can you imagine going to see Beethoven in concert? Taking a theology class taught by Martin Luther? Attending a symposium hosted by Albert Einstein? *Think,* Dresden. It boggles the *mind.*"

I thought about it.

And she was right.

Supposing for half a second that what she said might be possible, it would mean . . . Hell. It would change *everything.* There would be so much more time, and for everyone. Wizards lived for three or even four centuries, and to them even their own lives seemed short. What Kumori was talking about, the end of death itself, would give everyone else the same chance to better themselves that wizards enjoyed. It would, in a single stroke, create more parity between wizards and the rest of mankind than any single event in history.

But that was insane. Setting out to conquer *death?* People died. That was a fact of life.

But what if they didn't have to?

What if my mother hadn't died? Or my father? How different would my life be today?

Impossible. You couldn't just drive death away.

Could you?

Maybe that wasn't the point. Maybe this was one of those things in which the effort meant more than the outcome. I mean, if there was a chance, even a tiny, teeny chance that Kumori was right, and that the world could be so radically changed, wouldn't I be obliged to try? Even if I never reached the goal, never finished the quest, wouldn't the attempt to vanquish death itself be a worthy pursuit?

Wow.

This question was a big one. Way bigger than me.

I shook my head and told Kumori, "I don't know about that. What I know is that I've seen the fruits of that kind of path. I saw Cowl try to murder me when I got in his way. I've seen what Grevane and the Corpsetaker have done. I've heard about the suffering and misery Kemmler caused—and is still causing today, thanks to his stupid book.

"I don't know about something as big as trying to murder death.

But I know that you can tell a tree from what kind of fruit falls off it. And the necromancy tree doesn't drop anything that isn't rotten."

"Ours is a calling," Kumori said, her voice flat. "A noble road."

"I might be willing to believe you if so much of that road wasn't paved in the corpses of innocents."

I saw her head shake slowly beneath the hood. "You sound like them. The Council. You do not understand."

"Or maybe I'm just not quite arrogant enough to start rearranging the universe on the assumption that I know better than God how long life should last. And there's a downside to what you're saying, too. How about trying to topple the regime of an immortal Napoleon, or Attila, or Chairman Mao? You could as easily preserve the monsters as the intellectual all-stars. It can be horribly abused, and that makes it dangerous."

I faced her down for a long and silent second. Then she let out a sigh and said, "I think we have exhausted the possibilities of this conversation."

"You sure?" I asked her. "The offer is still open. If you want to get out, I'll get the Council to protect you."

"Our offer is open as well. Stand aside, and no rancor will follow you."

"I can't," I said.

"Nor can I," she said. "Understand that I do not wish you any particular harm. But I will not hesitate to strike you down should you place yourself in our path."

I stared at her for a second. Then I said, "I'm going to stop you. I'm going to stop you and Cowl and Grevane and Corpsetaker, and your little drummers too. None of you are going to promote yourself to godhood. No one is."

"I think you will die," she said, her tone even, without inflection.

"Maybe," I said. "But I'm going to stop you all before I go. Tell Cowl to get out of the way now, and I won't hunt him down after all of this is over. He can walk. You too."

She shook her head again and said, "I'm sorry we could not work something out."

"Yeah," I said.

She hesitated. Then she asked me, her voice soft and genuinely curious, "Why?"

"Because this is what I have to do," I said. "I'm sorry you aren't going to let me help you."

"We all act as we think we must," she said. "I will see you by and by, Dresden."

"Count on it," I said.

Kumori left without another word, gliding silently down the stairs and out of sight.

I sat there for a moment, aching and tired and more scared than I had sounded a minute before.

Then I got up, shoved my pain and my fear aside, and hobbled out to the Blue Beetle.

I had work to do.

•

Chapter

Thirty

I went back to my car, got in, and headed out to find a few things I would need to make the summoning of the Erlking marginally less suicidal. Serious summoning spells have to be personalized both to the entity to be summoned and to the summoner, and it took me a little while to find enough open businesses to get it all. Traffic on the streets grew steadily worse as the afternoon wore on, slowing me down even further.

More ominous than that, the tenor of the city had begun to slowly, steadily change. What had been an atmosphere of bemused enjoyment of an unanticipated holiday from the daily grind had turned into annoyance. As the sun tracked across the sky and the power still hadn't come back on, annoyance started turning into anger. By high noon, there were police visible on every street in cars, on motorcycles, on bicycles, and on foot.

"That all for ya?" asked an enterprising vendor. He was a pot-bellied, balding gardener selling fresh fruit and vegetables from the back of a pickup on a corner, and he was the only one I'd seen who wasn't trying to gouge Chicagoans in their moment of trial. He put the pumpkin I'd chosen in a thin plastic bag as he did, and took the money I offered him.

"That's everything," I said. "Thanks."

Shouting broke out somewhere nearby, and I looked up to see a whip-thin young man sprinting down the sidewalk across the street. A pair of cops chased him, one of them shouting at his use-lessly squealing radio.

"Christ, look at that," the vendor said. "Cops everywhere.

Why do they need the cops everywhere if this is just a power outage?"

"They're probably just worried about someone starting a riot," I said.

"Maybe," the vendor said. "But I hear some crazy things."

"Like what?" I asked.

He shook his head. "That terrorists blew up the power plant. Or maybe set off some kind of nuke. They can disrupt electronics and stuff, you know."

"I think someone might have noticed a nuclear explosion," I said.

"Oh, sure," he said. "But hell, maybe somebody did. Practically no phones, radio is damned near useless. How would we know?"

"I dunno. The big boom? The vaporized city?"

The vendor snorted. "True, true. But something happened."

"Yeah," I said. "Something happened."

"And the whole damned city is getting scared." The vendor shook his head as more shouting broke out farther down the block. A police car, lights and sirens wailing, tried to bull through the traffic to move toward the disturbance, without much success.

"Getting worse," the vendor observed. "This morning it was all smiles. But people are getting afraid."

"Halloween," I said.

The vendor glanced at me and shivered. "Maybe that's part of it. Maybe just because it's getting darker. Clouding over. People get spooked sometimes. Just like cattle. If they don't get the lights on, tonight might be bad here."

"Maybe," I said. I juggled the bag with my staff, trying to work out how to carry them both back down the street to the Beetle.

"Here," said the vendor. "I'll help you, son."

"Thank you," I told him, though to be honest I felt embarrassed that I actually wanted his help, much less needed it. "That old Bug there."

He walked the fifty feet down the sidewalk with me. He dropped off the sack in the front-end trunk of the VW, nodded at me, and said, "About time I got my old self out of here anyway, I think. Getting tense around here. Thunderstorm's coming in."

"Newspaper weatherman said it was supposed to be clear," I said.

The vendor snorted and tapped his nose. "I lived around this old lake all my life. There's a storm coming."

Boy was there. In spades.

He nodded to me. "You should get home. Good night to stay in and read a book."

"That sounds nice," I agreed. "Thanks again."

I nudged the Beetle out into traffic by virtue of being more willing to accept a fender-bender than anyone else on the road. I had everything I needed to try to whistle up the Erlking, but it had eaten up a lot of my day. I'd tried to call Murphy's place every time I'd stopped the car, but I never got a line through to Thomas and Butters, and now, with the afternoon sun burning its way down toward the horizon, I had run out of daylight.

It was time to rendezvous with the Wardens, so I headed for McAnally's.

Mac's tavern was tucked in neatly beneath one tall building and surrounded by others. You had to go down an alley to get to the tavern, but at least it had its own dinky parking lot. I managed to find a spot in the lot and then limped down the alley to the tavern, taking the short flight of steps down to the heavy wooden door.

I opened the door onto a quiet buzz of activity. In times of supernatural crisis, McAnally's became a sort of functional headquarters for gossip and congregation. I understood why. The tavern was old, lit by a dozen candles and kerosene lamps, and smelled of wood smoke and the steaks Mac cooked for his heavenly steak sandwiches. There was a sense of security and permanence to the place. Thirteen wooden pillars, each one hand-carved with all manner of supernatural scenes and creatures, held up the low ceiling. Ceiling fans that normally turned in lazy circles were not moving now, thanks to the power outage, but the actual temperature of the bar was unchanged. There were thirteen tables scattered out irregularly around the room, and thirteen stools at the long bar.

The whole layout of the place was meant to disperse and divert dangerous or destructive energies that might accompany any grouchy wizard types into the tavern—nothing major. It was just a kind of well-planned feng shui that cut down on the number of accidents bad-tempered practitioners of the arts might inadvertently inspire. But that dispersal of energies did a little something to ward off larger magical forces as well. It wasn't going to protect the place from a concentrated magical attack: McAnally's wasn't a bomb shelter. It was more like a big beach umbrella, and when I came through the door I felt a sudden relief of pressure I hadn't realized had built up. The minute I shut the door behind me, some of the fear and tension faded, the dark energies Cowl had stirred up sliding around the tavern like a stream pouring around a small, heavy stone.

A sign on the wall just inside the door proclaimed, ACCORDED NEUTRAL TERRITORY. That meant that the signatories of the Unseelie Accords, including the White Council and the Red Court, had agreed that this place would be treated with respect. No one was supposed to start any kind of conflict inside the tavern, and would be bound by honor to take outside any fight that did come up, as rapidly as possible. That kind of agreement was only as good as the honor of anyone involved, but if I broke the Accords in the building, the White Council would hang me out to dry. From past experience, I assumed that the Red Court would come down on any of their folk who violated the tavern's neutrality in the same way.

The tavern was crowded with members of the supernatural community of Chicago. They weren't wizards. Most of them had only a pocketful of ability. One dark-bearded man had enough skill at kinetomancy to alter the spin on any dice he happened to throw. An elderly woman at another table had an unusually strong rapport with animals, and was active in municipal animal shelter charities. A pair of dark-haired sisters who shared an uncanny mental bond played chess at one of the tables, which seemed kind of masturbatory, somehow. In one of the corners, five or six wizened old practitioners—not strong enough to have joined the Council, but competent enough in their own right—huddled together over mugs of ale, speaking in low tones.

Mac himself glanced over his shoulder. He was a tall, spare man in a spotless white shirt and apron. Bald and good at it, Mac could have been any age between thirty-five and fifty. He pursed his lips upon seeing me, turned back to his wood-burning stove, and quickly finished up a pair of steaks he'd been cooking.

I started limping over to the bar, and as I went the room grew quiet. By the time I was there, the uneven thump of my staff on the floor and the sizzling of the steaks were the only sounds.

"Mac," I said. Someone vacated a stool, and I nodded my thanks and sat down with a wince.

"Harry," Mac drawled. He slipped his frying pan off the stove, slapped both steaks onto plates, and with a couple of gestures and brief movements made fried potatoes and fresh vegetables appear on the plates, too. It wasn't magic. Mac was just a damned good cook.

I glanced around the room and spoke in a voice loud enough for everyone to hear. "I need some space, Mac. Some people are meeting me here shortly. I'll need several tables."

A round of nervous whispers and quiet comments went through the crowd. The old practitioners in the corner rose from their table without further ado. Several of them nodded at me, and one grizzled old man growled, "Good luck."

The less experienced members of the supernatural crowd looked from me back to the departing seniors, uncertainty on every face.

"Folks," I said, in general. "I can't tell you what to do. But I would like to request that you all think about getting home before dark. Come nightfall, you want to be behind a threshold."

"What's happening?" blurted one of the youngest men in the room. He still had pimples.

Mac eyed him and snorted.

"Come on. I'm a wizard. We have union rules against telling anybody anything," I said. There was a round of muted chuckles. "Seriously. I can't say any more for now," I said. And I couldn't. Odds were better than good that one or more spies lurked among the patrons of the tavern, and the less information they had about White Council plans and activities, the better. "Take this seriously, guys. You don't want to be outside come nightfall."

Mac turned around to the bar and swept his eyes over it, his expression polite and pointed. He grunted and flicked his chin at the door, and the noise from the room rose again as people began speaking quietly to one another, getting up, and leaving money on the tables as they left.

Two minutes later, Mac and I were the only people left in the tavern. Mac walked around the edge of the bar and sat down next to me. He put one steak-laden dinner plate on the bar in front of me, kept the other for himself, and added a couple of bottles of his home-brewed dark ale. Mac flipped the tops off with a thumbnail.

"Bless your soul, Mac," I said, and picked up one bottle. I held it up. Mac clinked his bottle of ale against mine, and then we both took a long drink and fell to on the steaks.

We ate in silence. After a while, Mac asked, "Bad?"

"Pretty bad," I said. I debated how much I could tell him. Mac was a good guy and a long-term acquaintance and friend, but he wasn't Council. Screw it. The man gave me steak and a beer. He deserved to know something more than that there was a threat he probably couldn't do anything about. "Necromancers."

Mac's fork froze on the way to his mouth. He shook his head, put his last bite of steak into his mouth, and chewed slowly. Mac never used a sentence when one word would do. "Wardens?"

"Yeah. A lot of them."

He pursed his lips with a frown. "Kemmler," he said.

I arched an eyebrow, but I wasn't really surprised that he knew the infamous necromancer's name. Mac always seemed to have a pretty darned good idea about what was going on. "Not Kemmler. His leftovers. But that's bad enough."

"Ungh." Mac finished up his plate in rapid order, then rose and started collecting money and clearing the tables in the corner farthest from the door. At some point he collected my barren plate and empty bottle and put a fresh ale down in front of me.

I sipped at it, watching him. He didn't make a production of it, but he checked the short-barreled shotgun he kept on a clip behind the bar, and put a pair of 1911s in unobtrusive spots behind the bar, so that no matter where he stood, one of the weapons would be within easy reach. He handled them like he knew exactly what he was doing.

I sipped at the ale and mused. I knew little of Mac's background. He'd opened the tavern a few years before I'd moved to Chicago. No one I'd talked to knew where he'd been before that, or what he had done. I wasn't surprised that he knew something about weapons. He'd always moved like someone who could handle himself. But since he wasn't exactly a chatterbox, most of what I knew came from observation. I hadn't the faintest idea of why or where he'd learned the business of violence.

I could respect that. I had run through a few bad patches that were just as well left behind and forgotten.

Mac looked up abruptly, and started polishing the bar near the shotgun's clip. A second later the door opened, and a Warden of the White Council came in.

He was a tall man, six feet and then some, and built with the solidity of an aging soldier. His lank hair had more grey in it than I remembered, and was drawn back into a ponytail. His face was narrow, almost pinched, and in the absence of any other expression, he looked like he had just taken a big bite of alum-sprinkled lemon rind. The Warden wore the grey cloak of his office over black fatigues. He carried a carved staff in his right hand, and bore a long-bladed sword on his left hip.

That much I had expected.

What surprised me was how battered he looked.

The Warden's cloak was ripped in several spots, and stained with what could have been mud, blood, and greenish motor oil. There were burn marks along the hem, and several raw, ragged holes in it that might have been the results of corrosive burns. His staff looked similarly nicked and stained—and the man himself looked like a boxer after a tough tenth round. He had bruises on one cheek. His nose had been broken sometime in the past several weeks. There was an ugly line of fresh, scarlet scar tissue running from his hairline to one eyebrow, and I could see white bandages through a hole in his jacket, over his left biceps.

For all of that, he came through the door like a man who knew he could clear out a bar full of marines if he needed to, and his eyes settled on me at once. His mouth twisted into an even more sour frown.

"Wizard Dresden," he said quietly.

"Warden Morgan," I responded. I figured Morgan would be along with any Wardens sent to Chicago. It was in his area of responsibility, and he didn't like me. He'd spent a few years following me around, hoping to catch me performing black magic so that he could execute me. It hadn't happened, and the Council had lifted my probation. I don't think he had ever forgiven me for that. He blamed me for other things too, I think, but I had always figured they were just excuses. Some people don't get along, ever. Morgan and I were two of them.

"McAnally," Morgan said to the tavern keeper.

"Donald," Mac replied.

Interesting. Hell, I'd been on the Council for years, and I hadn't known Morgan's first name.

"Dresden," Morgan said. "Have you checked for veils?"

"If I told you I had, you'd check it yourself anyway, Morgan," I said. "So I didn't bother."

"Of course you didn't," he said. I saw him frown a little in concentration, and then his eyes went a bit out of focus. He swept his gaze around the room, using his Sight, that odd, half-surreal sense that lets wizards observe the forces of magic moving around them. A wizard's Sight cuts through all kinds of veils and spells meant to disguise and distract. It's a potent ability, but it comes at a price. Anything you see through the Sight stays with you, never fading in your memory, always right there for recall, as if you'd just seen it. You can't just forget something that you See. It's there for life.

Morgan didn't let his gaze linger too long near Mac or myself, and then he nodded to himself, and called out, "Clear."

The door opened and Warden Luccio came in. She was a solid old matriarch of a woman, as tall as most men and built like someone who did plenty of physical labor. Her hair was a solid shade of iron grey, cropped into a neat, military cut. She too wore a Warden's grey cloak, though she wore clothes suitable for hiking or camping beneath that: jeans, cotton, flannel, boots, all in muted tones of grey and brown. She too carried a staff and bore a sword at her side, though hers was a slender scimitar, light and elegant. Though not as worn as Morgan's, her gear also showed evidence of recent action.

"Warden Luccio," I said, and rose from the barstool to incline my head to her.

"Wizard," she said quietly. I would have needed a high-speed camera to take in the details of her smile, but at least it was there. She nodded to me and then a little more deeply to Mac.

Behind her came three more Wardens. The first was a young man I vaguely recognized from a Council meeting a few years back. He had naturally tanned skin, dark hair, dark eyes, and sharp-edged, classically Spanish features. I remembered him in an apprentice's brown robe back then, and covering his mouth with one hand to conceal a grin inspired by some of my dialogue with the Council's bigwigs.

The brown robe was gone, and he looked like he had filled in a little since I'd first seen him, but good Lord, he was younger than Billy the werewolf. He wore a grey cloak that looked reasonably clean and not at all damaged, and black fatigues beneath that. A simple, straight sword hung from one hip, and was balanced on the other side by a holstered Glock and, I kid you not, three round fragmentation grenades. His staff was fairly new-looking, but there were enough dents and nicks in it to make me think he had kept things from hitting him with it, and he walked with a kind of arrogant confidence you see only in people who have not yet realized their own mortality.

"This is Warden Ramirez," Luccio said. "Ramirez, Dresden."

"How's it going?" Ramirez said, flashing me a grin.

I shrugged. "You know. Pretty much the usual."

Two more Wardens came in behind him, and they looked even younger and greener. Their cloaks and staves were immaculate, and they wore clothes and equipment so similar to Ramirez's that they qualified as a uniform. Luccio introduced the blocky young man with distant, haunted eyes as Kowalski. The sweet-faced young Asian girl's name was Yoshimo.

I limped over to Luccio and nodded at the tables Mac had set up. "I hope there's room enough. When are the other Wardens arriving?"

Luccio fixed me with a quiet, weary gaze. Then she drew her hands from beneath her cloak and held out a folded bundle wrapped in brown paper, offering it to me. "Take it."

I took the bundle and unwrapped it.

It was a folded grey cloak.

"Put it on," said Luccio in her quiet, steady voice. "And then every available Warden will be here."

Chapter

Thirty-one

I stared at Luccio for a second.

"That's a joke," I said. "Right?"

She gave me a brief, bitter smile. "Master McAnally," she said to Mac. "I think we could use a round. Do you have anything decent to drink?"

Mac grunted and said, "Got a new dark."

"Is it worth drinking?" Luccio asked. She sounded tired, but there was a teasing tone to her voice.

Mac glowered at her in answer, and she gave him a smile that was part challenge and part apology, and took a seat at one of the tables. She gestured at the table and said, "Wardens, please join me."

Morgan took the seat to Luccio's right, and the look he gave me could have burned holes in sheet metal. I did what I always did when Morgan did that: I eyed him right back, then dismissed him as if he weren't even there. I pulled out the chair opposite Luccio and sat. The two youngest Wardens sat down, but Ramirez stayed standing until Mac had brought over bottles of his dark ale and left them on the table. He headed back over to the bar.

Ramirez glanced at Luccio, and she nodded. "Close the circle, please, Warden."

The young man drew a piece of chalk from his pocket, and quickly drew a heavy line on the floor all the way around the table. He finished the circle, then touched it lightly with the forefinger of his right hand and spoke a quiet word. I felt a flicker of his will as he released a tiny bit of power into the circle. The circle closed around us in a sudden, silent tension, raising a thin barrier around us that was almost entirely impregnable to magical forces. If anyone had been trying to spy on the meeting with magic, the circle would prevent it. If anyone had left some kind of listening device nearby, the magic-saturated air within the circle would be certain to fry it within a minute.

Ramirez nodded to himself and then reversed the last open chair at the table and straddled it, resting one arm on the back. Morgan slid him the last bottle of ale, and he took it in one hand.

"Absent friends," Luccio murmured, holding up her bottle.

I could get behind that toast. The rest of us muttered, "Absent friends," and we had a drink, and Luccio stared at her bottle for a moment.

I waited in the pregnant silence and then said, "So. Making me a Warden. That's a joke, right?"

Luccio took a second, slower taste of the ale and then arched an eyebrow at the bottle.

Behind the bar again, Mac smiled.

"It's no joke, Warden Dresden," Luccio said.

"As much as we all would like it to be," Morgan added.

Luccio gave him a look of very gentle reproof, and Morgan subsided into silence. "How much have you heard about recent events in the war?"

"Nothing in the past several days," I said. "Not since my last check-in."

She nodded. "I thought as much. The Red Court has begun a heavy offensive. This is the first time that they've concentrated their efforts on disrupting our communications. We suspect that a great many wizards never received word through our usual messengers."

"Then they found weaknesses in the communications lines," I said. "But they waited to exploit them until it would hurt us the most."

Luccio nodded. "Precisely. The first attack came in Cairo, at our operations center there. Several Wardens were taken, including the senior commander of the region."

"Alive?" I asked.

She nodded. "Yes. Which was an unacceptable threat."

When vampires take you alive, it isn't so that they can treat you to ice cream. That was one of the really nightmarish facets of the war with the Red Court. If the enemy got you, they could do worse than kill you.

They could make you one of their own.

If they managed to turn a Warden, especially one of the senior commanders, it would give them access to a treasury of knowledge and secrets—to say nothing of the fact that they would effectively gain, in many ways, a wizard of their own. Vampires didn't use magic in the same way that mortal wizards did. They tapped into the same nauseating well of power that Kemmler and those like him used. But from what I understood of it, the skills carried over. A turned wizard would be a deadly threat to the Wardens, the Council, and mortals alike. We never talked about it, but there was a sort of silent understanding among wizards that we would never be taken alive. And an equally silent fear that we might be.

"You went after them," I guessed.

Luccio nodded. "A major assault. Madrid, São Paolo, Acapulco, Athens. We struck at enemy strongholds there to acquire intelligence to the whereabouts of the prisoners. Our people were being held in Belize." She waved a hand vaguely at Morgan.

"Our intelligence indicated the presence of the highest-ranking members of the Red Court, including the Red King himself. The Merlin and the rest of the Senior Council took the field with us," Morgan said quietly.

That made me raise my brows. The Merlin, the leader of the Senior Council, was as defensive-minded as it was possible to be. He'd guided the White Council into the equivalent of a cold war with the Red Court, with everyone moving carefully and unwilling to commit, in the hopes that it would give the war time to settle away into negotiations and some kind of diplomatic resolution. An offensive action like a full assault from the Senior Council, the seven oldest and strongest wizards on the planet, had been long overdue.

"What changed the Merlin's mind?" I asked quietly.

"Wizard McCoy," Luccio said. "When our people were taken,

he persuaded most of the Senior Council to take action, including Ancient Mai and the Gatekeeper."

That made sense. My old mentor, Ebenezar McCoy, was a member of the Senior Council. He had a couple of longtime friends on the Council, but that didn't give him a majority vote. If he wanted to get anything done, he had to talk someone from the Merlin's bloc into casting their vote with him—either that, or convince the Gatekeeper, a wizard who habitually abstained from voting, to take a stand with him. If Ebenezar had convinced Ancient Mai *and* the Gatekeeper to vote with him in favor of action, the Merlin would have little choice but to move.

And just because the Merlin was a master of wards and defensive magic did not mean that he couldn't kick some ass if he needed to. You don't get to be the Merlin of the White Council by collecting bottle caps, and Arthur Langtry, the current Merlin, was generally considered to be the most powerful wizard on earth.

I had seen for myself what Ebenezar McCoy was capable of. A couple of years ago he had pulled an old Soviet satellite out of orbit and brought it down into the lap of Duke Ortega, the warlord of the Red Court. He'd killed a ton of vampires in doing it.

He'd also killed people. He'd taken the force of life and creation and used it to wipe out the lives of mortals—victims of the Red Court's power. And it wasn't the first time he'd done it. Ebenezar, I'd learned, held an office that did not officially exist—that of the White Council's assassin. Known as the Blackstaff, he had a license to kill, as well as to break the other Laws of Magic when he deemed it necessary. When I learned that he was violating and undermining the same laws he'd taught me to obey, to *believe* in, it had wounded me so deeply that in some ways I was still bleeding.

Ebenezar had betrayed what I believed in. But that didn't change the fact that the old man was the strongest wizard I'd ever seen in action. And he was the youngest and least powerful of the Senior Council.

"What happened?" I asked quietly.

"There was no evidence of the presence of the Red King or his entourage, but other than that the attack went as planned," Morgan said. "We assaulted the vampires' stronghold and took our people back with us."

Luccio's face twisted in sudden and bitter grief.

"It was a lure," I said quietly. "Wasn't it?"

"Yes," she said quietly. "We moved out and took our wounded to the hospice in Sicily."

"What happened?"

"We were betrayed," she said, and her words carried more sharp edges than a sack of broken glass. "Someone within our ranks must have reported our position to the Red Court. They attacked us that night."

"When was that?" I asked.

Luccio frowned, then glanced across the table at Ramirez.

"Three days ago, Zulu time," Ramirez provided quietly.

"I've not slept," Luccio said. "Between that and all the travel, I lose track." She took another drink of ale and said, "The attack was vicious. They were coming for the Senior Council, and their sorcerers managed to cut us off from escaping into the Nevernever for nearly a day. We lost thirty-eight Wardens that day, in fighting all over Sicily."

I sat there for a moment, stunned. Thirty-eight. Stars and stones, there were only about two hundred Wardens on the Council. Not every wizard had the kind of talent that made them dangerous in a face-to-face confrontation. Most of those who did were Wardens. In a single day, the Red Court had killed nearly 20 percent of our fighting force.

"They paid for it," Morgan rumbled quietly. "But . . . they seemed almost mad to die in order to kill us. Driven. I saw four different death curses unleashed that day. I saw vampires climb over mounds of their own dead without so much as slowing down. We must have taken twenty of their warriors for every loss of our own." He closed his eyes and his sour face was suddenly masked with very real and very human grief. "They kept coming."

"We had many wounded," Luccio said. "So many wounded. As soon as the Senior Council was able to open the ways into the Nevernever, we retreated to the paths through Faerie. And we were pursued."

I sat up straight. "What?"

Morgan nodded. "The Red Court followed us into the territory of the Sidhe," he said.

"They had to know," I said quietly. "They had to know that by pressing the attack in Faerie itself they would anger the Sidhe. They've just declared war on Summer and Winter alike."

"Yes," Morgan said in a flat voice. "But it didn't stop them. They attacked us as we retreated. And . . ." He glanced at Luccio as if in appeal.

She gave him a firm look and said to me, "They had called demons to assist them." She inhaled slowly. "Not simply beasts from the Nevernever. They had gone to the Netherworld. They had called Outsiders."

I took a longer drink of Mac's ale. Outsiders. Demons were bad enough, but they were at least something I was fairly familiar with. The reaches of the Nevernever, the world of spirit and magic that surrounds the mortal world, are filled with all kinds of beings. Most of them really don't give a damn about mortal affairs, and we are nothing but a remote and unimportant curiosity to them. When beings of the spirit world are interested in mortal business, it's for a good reason. The ones who like to eat us, hurt us, or generally terrify us are what wizards commonly refer to as demons, as a general term. They're bad enough.

Outsiders, though, were so rarely spoken of that they were all but a rumor. I wasn't really clear on all of the details, but the Outsiders had been the servants and foot soldiers of the Old Ones, an ancient race of demons or gods who had once ruled the mortal world, but who had apparently been cast out and locked away from our reality.

There was a specific Law of Magic against contacting them—Thou Shalt Not Open the Outer Gates. No one wanted to be the one suddenly suspected of opening ways for the Outsiders to enter the mortal world. The Wardens absolutely did not play around with violations of the Laws of Magic. Their entire purpose in life was to protect the Council—first from violators of the seven Laws, and then from everyone else.

I eyed the folded grey cloak on the table in front of me.

"I thought only mortal magic could call up Outsiders," I said quietly.

Luccio said quietly, "You are correct."

My stomach lurched a little. Someone had told the Red Court where to find the Council. Someone had blocked off their escape route to the Nevernever so strongly that the most powerful wizards on the planet had required a full day to open them again. And someone had begun calling up Outsiders in numbers, sending them to attack the White Council.

The Council is not what it was, Cowl had said. *It has rotted from the inside. It will fall. Soon.*

"The Wardens fell back to fight a holding action against the Red Court so that our wounded could escape to safety," Luccio reported, her crisp voice at odds with her weary eyes. "That was when they loosed the Outsiders upon us. We lost another twenty-three Wardens in the first moments of combat, and many more were wounded." There was silence while she took a long pull from her bottle, emptying it, then setting it down sharply on the table, anger flickering in her eyes. "If Senior Council members McCoy and Liberty had not come to our aid, we might have all died there. Even with them, we managed to hold them only long enough for the Gatekeeper and the Merlin to raise a ward behind us, to give us time to escape."

"A *ward?*" I blurted. "Are you telling me that they stonewalled an entire *army* of vampires and demons? With *one* ward?"

"You don't get to be Merlin of the White Council by collecting bottle caps," Ramirez said, his voice dry.

I glanced aside at Ramirez. He grinned at me and swigged beer.

"McCoy was injured," Luccio continued.

Ramirez snorted. "Who *wasn't?*"

Luccio snapped, "Carlos."

He lifted a hand in surrender and settled back onto his chair again, but his grin never faded.

"There were many injuries," Luccio continued. "But as the hospice in Sicily had been taken, we diverted the worst cases to a hospital we control in the Congo." She stared at her bottle for a moment. Her mouth opened, and then she closed it again. She closed her eyes.

Morgan frowned at her. Then he put a hand on Luccio's shoulder, looked at me, and said, "The vampires knew."

I got a sick, twisting feeling in my stomach. "Oh, God."

"It was daylight there," Morgan said. "And the place was a fortress of the Merlin's wards. There was no way for the vampires to breach it from the Nevernever, and nothing short of a demon lord could have broken through them." His mouth twisted, and his eyes glittered with rage and hate. "They sent mortals against us. Against men and women lying injured, unconscious, helpless in their beds." The anger in his voice seemed to strangle him for a moment.

"But . . ." I said. "Look, I know what it's like going up against mortals you don't want to kill. It's difficult, but they can be stopped. Fought. Bullets and explosives can be defended against."

"Which is why they used gas," Ramirez said quietly, stepping in where Morgan's and Luccio's voices had failed. His own tone was serious. His grin had vanished. "A nerve agent, probably sarin. They deployed it against the entire hospital, the people we had protecting it, and six square blocks of city around it." He put his own bottle down and said, "No one survived."

"My God . . ." I whispered.

There was dead silence.

"Ebenezar?" I asked in a whisper. "You said he was wounded. Was he . . ."

Ramirez shook his head. "Stubborn old bastard wouldn't go to the hospital," the young Warden said. "He went with one of the teams staging a counteroffensive with the Fellowship of Saint Giles."

"Thousands of innocent mortals died," Luccio said, and there was a slow, low snarl in her voice. She kept it tightly leashed and under control, but I heard it. I recognized it, and I knew what it was like to feel it permeating my words. "Women. Children. Thousands. And today I buried one hundred and forty-three Wardens."

I sat there, stunned.

In a single, vicious stroke, the Red Court had very nearly destroyed the White Council.

"They have crossed every line," Luccio said, her voice quiet and precise. "Violated every principle of war of our world and the mortal world alike. Madness. They have gone mad."

"They've committed suicide," I said quietly. "They don't have a prayer against the Council and the Faerie Courts alike."

"The Sidhe were taken by surprise," Morgan rumbled. "They aren't prepared for a fight. And we're holding on by our fingernails. We've got less than fifty Wardens capable of combat. Without our communications network in order, members of the Council have been attacked individually and by surprise. We don't know how many more wizards have died."

"And it gets even better," Ramirez said. "Agents of the Red Court are haunting the ways through Faerie. We were attacked on the way here, twice."

"Our priority," Luccio said, voice crisp, "is to consolidate our forces and to draw upon every available resource to restore the Wardens as a fighting force. We must draw the members of the Council together and make sure that they are protected. We're reorganizing our security." She shook her head. "And frankly, we must protect the lives of the Senior Council. So long as they are concealed from the enemy and still able to take action, they are a dangerous force. Together they wield more power than any hundred members of the Council, and it can be concentrated with deadly effect, as the Merlin showed in the Nevernever. So long as they stand ready to strike, the enemy cannot openly unveil his full strength."

"More important," Morgan growled, "the mortal wizards who betrayed us, whoever they are, fear the Senior Council. That is why their first move was an attempt to destroy them."

Luccio nodded. "If we can hold on until the Faerie Courts mobilize for action, we can recover from this attack. Which brings us to today," Luccio said, and studied me, tired and frank. "Every other Warden able to fight is currently either engaged against the enemy or safeguarding the Senior Council. Our lines of support and communication are tenuous." She gestured at those seated at the table. "This is every resource the White Council has to spare."

I looked at the weary captain of the Wardens. At the battered Morgan. At Ramirez, who had reclaimed his cocky smile, and at Yoshimo and Kowalski, untried, quiet, and frightened.

"Warden Luccio," I said. "May I speak to you privately?"

Morgan scowled and said in a hot voice, "Anything you have to say to her you can say to all—"

Luccio put her hand on Morgan's arm, a gentle gesture, but it cut him off. "Morgan. Perhaps you would be so kind as to get me another bottle. And I'm sure McAnally would be willing to provide us all with some dinner."

Morgan stared at her for a second, then at me. Then he rose, smudged the chalk circle with a boot, and broke the circle around the table, releasing the buzzing tension from the air.

"Come on, kids," Ramirez told the other two younger wardens, rising. "We have to go sit with Uncle Morgan while the other adults have a serious talk." He put a hand on my shoulder on the way past and squeezed. "Hey, bartender! Are those onion rings I smell?"

I waited until they had all settled down at the far end of the bar and Mac began to bring them some food. Then I turned to Luccio and said, "I can't be a Warden."

She studied me for a second and then asked, in a very precise, very polite voice, "And why not?"

"Because you people have been threatening to kill me for doing something I didn't do since I was sixteen years old," I said. "You're all convinced I'm some sort of hideous threat, and every time you get the chance you try to make my life miserable."

Luccio listened attentively and then said, "Yes. And?"

"And?" I said. "I've spent my entire adult life with the Wardens looking over my shoulder waiting for a chance to accuse me of things I didn't do, and trying to set me up and entrap me when you never found me doing anything."

Luccio's eyebrows shot up. "What?"

"Don't give me that," I said. "You know damned well that Morgan tried to provoke me into attacking him just before we got the treaty with Winter, so he and the Merlin would have an excuse to throw me to the vampires."

Luccio's eyes widened, and her voice came out harder. *"What?"* She shot a look at Morgan, and then back at me. "Are you telling me the truth?"

There was some kind of cadence to the question that her words didn't usually have, and on pure instinct I reached out with my senses. I could feel a light tension in the air, humming like the space between the tines of a tuning fork.

"Yes," I told her. The humming chime continued unabated. "I'm telling you the truth."

She stared at me for a long second and then settled back onto her chair. The humming tension faded. She folded her hands on the table, frowning down at them. "Then . . . There were rumors. Of how Morgan behaved around you. But I thought that they were only that."

"They weren't," I said. "Morgan has threatened and persecuted me every time he got the chance." I clenched my right hand into a fist. "And I have done *nothing*. I won't become a part of that, Warden Luccio. So keep the cape. I wouldn't polish my car with it."

She regarded her folded hands, eyes narrow. "Dresden," she said quietly. "The White Council is at war. Would you simply abandon your own people to the mercies of the Red Court? Would you stand aside and let Kemmler's disciples have their way?"

"Of course not," I said. "And I never said I wouldn't fight. But I won't be wearing *this*." I shoved the cloak across the table. "Keep it."

She shoved it back to the table before me. "Put it on."

"Thank you, no."

"Dresden," Luccio said, and her voice was calm and agate-hard. "It is not a request."

"I don't respond well to threats," I said.

"Then respond to reality," she snapped. "Dresden, the Wardens are all but shattered. We need every battle-capable wizard we can recruit, train, or conscript."

"A lot of wizards can fight," I growled.

"And they *aren't* Harry Dresden," she said. "You idiot. Don't you know what I am offering you?"

"Yeah. The chance to hunt down teenage kids who were never told the Laws of Magic and execute them for breaking them. The chance to badger and intimidate and interrogate anyone who doesn't suit me. Neither of which I want anything to do with."

"Ebenezar said you were stubborn, but not that you were a fool.

The Council has been betrayed, Dresden. And *you* are the most in-famous wizard in it. There are many who have spoken out against you. Many who say that you began the war with the Red Court intentionally so that you could create an opportunity to bring about the fall of the Council."

I burst out in bitter laughter. "*Me*? That's *insane.* For crying out loud, I can't even balance my stupid checkbook!"

Luccio's eyes softened a little, and she sighed. "I believe you." She shook her head. "But you have a reputation, and the members of the Council will be badly unsettled by this loss. Their fear could easily turn upon you. That is why you are going to join the Wardens."

I scowled. "I don't get it."

"It is time to set our past differences aside. If you wear the cloak of a Warden and step in to fight when the Council is in its hour of need, it will make our people look at you differently."

I took a deep breath. "Oh. Vader syndrome."

"Excuse me?"

"Vader syndrome," I said. "There's no ally so impressive, en-couraging, and well loved as an ally who was an enemy that made you shake in your boots a couple of minutes ago."

"There's more to it than that," Luccio said. "I think that you do not realize your own reputation. You have overcome more enemies and battled more evils than most wizards a century your senior. And times are changing. There are more young wizards attaining membership to the Council than ever before—like Ramirez and his companions, there. To them, you are a symbol of defiance to the conservative elements of the Council, and a hero who will risk his life when his principles demand it."

"I am?"

"You are," Luccio said. "I can't say that I approve of it. But right now the Council will need every scrap of courage and faith we can muster. Your presence and support in the face of a greater danger will appease your detractors, and the presence of a wizard who has experience in battle will encourage the younger members of the Council." She grimaced. "Put simply, Dresden, we need you. And you need us."

I rubbed at my eyes for a moment. Then I said, "Let's say I do sign on. I'm willing to wear the cloak. I'm willing to fight for as long as the war is on. But I won't move away from Chicago. There are people here who depend on me." I glowered. "And I won't bow my head to Morgan. I don't want him within a hundred miles of my town."

Luccio rubbed at her jaw, and then nodded slowly, her eyes thoughtful. "I have to reassign Morgan in any case." She nodded again, more sharply. "Then I'm conscripting you into the Wardens as a regional commander."

I blinked.

"You'll be in charge of security and operations in this region, and coordinate with the other three American regional commanders."

"Uh," I said. "What does that mean?"

"That it will be your job to protect mortals in this area. To be vigilant against supernatural threats in your region, and represent the Council in matters of diplomacy. To aid and assist other wizards who come to you for aid and protection, and, when required, to strike out at the enemies of the Council, such as the Red Court and their allies."

I frowned. "Uh, I pretty much do that anyway."

Luccio's face broke into the first genuinely warm smile I'd ever seen on her, the care lines vanishing, replaced with crow's-feet at the corners of her eyes. "So now you'll do it in a grey cloak." Her expression sobered. "You're a fighter, Dresden. If the White Council is to survive, we need more like you."

She pushed away from the table and walked over to the bar, carrying our empty bottles with her.

When she came back, I had just finished getting the cloak pin settled and draping the heavy, soft grey fabric around my shoulders. She stopped in front of me and looked me up and down for a moment. Ramirez glanced at me, and his grin widened. Morgan looked, and from his expression you would think someone had just shoved a knife into his testicles. Mac's brow furrowed, and he studied me in the cloak, his lips quietly pursed.

"Thank you," Luccio said quietly, and offered me an ale.

I accepted it with a nod. We touched bottles and took a drink.

"Very well then, Commander," Luccio said, her tone turning brisk and businesslike. "This is your territory, and you have the most recent intelligence on Kemmler's disciples. What is our next step?"

I shoved my hair back from my eyes and said, "Okay, Warden Lucc—uh, Captain Luccio. Let's sit down and get to work. It's getting dark, and we don't have much time."

Chapter

Thirty-two

When I walked through the door of Murphy's house, it was raining and I was still wearing the grey cloak. I limped into the kitchen, where Thomas and Butters and Bob were sitting at a table with a bunch of candles, paper, pencils, and empty cans of Coors.

Thomas's jaw dropped open. "Holy crap," he said.

Butters blinked at Thomas and then at me. "Uh. What?"

"Harry!" Bob said, orange eye lights glowing brightly. "You *stole* a Warden's cloak?"

I scowled at them and took the cloak off. It dripped all over the kitchen floor. "I didn't steal it." Mouse came padding into the room, tail wagging, and I rubbed briefly at his ears.

"Oh," Bob said. "So you took it off a body?"

"No," I said, annoyed, and settled onto a chair at the table. "I got drafted."

"Holy crap," Thomas said again.

"I don't get it," Butters said.

"Harry's joined the wizard secret police!" Bob burbled. "He gets to convict on suspicion and take justice into his own hands! How cool is that!"

Thomas looked at me steadily and then at the door behind me. Then back to me.

"I'm alone," I said quietly. "Relax."

He nodded. "What happened?"

"A lot," I said. "There isn't time to cover it all now. But the

Wardens are in town, and I'm not so worried about them crawling all over and finding out everyone's secrets."

"Why not?" Thomas asked.

"Because at the moment all five of them are at a hotel downtown, getting showers and changing bandages while I try to come up with more information about the heirs of Kemmler."

Thomas blinked slowly. "All *five* . . . and they have wounded?"

I nodded, my lips pressed hard together.

"Wow," Thomas said quietly. "How bad is it?"

"They drafted *me*," I said.

"That's bad, all right," Bob said cheerfully.

I looked at the scattered papers and books on the table. "Tell me you guys came up with something."

Butters blinked a few times and then started fumbling at the papers on the table, peering at them in the candlelight. "Uh, well, there's good news and bad news."

"Bad first," I said. "I'm going to need the pick-me-up afterward."

"We've got nothing on those numbers," Butters said. "I mean, they aren't a code. They're too short. They could be an address or an account number, but none of the banks we could get on the phone use that number of digits." He coughed apologetically. "If I could have gotten on the Net I could have gotten you a lot more, but . . ." He gestured uselessly around the room. "We couldn't get one call in fifty to go through, and at most of the places we called, no one answered. And in the past hour the phones have gone out altogether."

I shook my head. "Yeah. City's going insane, too. There were two fires between here and McAnally's. Some kind of riot going in Bucktown, I heard on a police radio."

"The governor has asked for help from the National Guard," Thomas said quietly. "They're sending troops in to keep order on the streets."

I blinked. "How did you find that out?"

"I called my sister," he said.

I frowned. "I thought Lara wasn't speaking with you."

Thomas's voice went dry. "Just because she cut me off from the family's money, kicked me out of any of our holdings, made it clear that I no longer have their protection, and she's holding the woman I love as a virtual prisoner, don't think she doesn't still like me, personally."

"So she did you a little favor," I said.

"Technically," Thomas said, "she did *you* a little favor."

"Why did she do that?" I asked.

"Well, I hinted about how since her entire power base depended on a certain secret being kept, and since you were awfully irrational about protecting the good citizens of Chicago, that you might develop loose lips to sink her ship if she didn't help you in your moment of need."

"Um," I said. "So you're telling me that I just engaged in blackmail against the ruler of the White Court. By proxy."

"Yeah," Thomas said. "You've got some great big brass balls on you to do something like that, Harry."

"I guess I do." I shook my head. "Why did I do that?"

"Because we needed help," Thomas said. "We were getting nowhere fast. Lara's got a ton of resources available to her, and a lot of manpower. She was able to come up with some of the other information we needed."

"Which is the good news," Butters said. "She wasn't blacked out and cut off from the Internet like we are, and she was able to get a bunch of information we couldn't." He passed me a piece of paper. "Not on the numbers—but one of her people was able to find out about Native American artifacts and weapons here in Chicago."

I looked up sharply at Butters. "Yeah?"

He nodded at the paper and I read over it. "Yep," he said. "The Native American Center is using their facility to host this big display on tribal hunting and warfare before all of us palefaces showed up with guns and smallpox. The History Channel is using it as a part of some history-of-warfare special, and they were filming there all last week."

"Yeah," I said. "That could have some old hunter spirits attached to it." I read over the list. "Dammit, I should have remembered this myself. The Field Museum has that big Cahokian artifacts exhibit that Professor Bartlesby was in charge of. Hell, it was a bunch of Indian artifacts that Corpsetaker helped assemble himself. Probably with tonight in mind."

Butters nodded. "And the Mitchell Museum up in Evanston has got more Native American artifacts than either one put together."

"Crap," I said. "That's it."

"How do you know that?" Butters asked.

"It only stands to reason," Bob supplied. "The whole point is to summon up as many old spirits as possible and then consume them. The most spirits are going to be attracted to wherever there is the most old junk."

I nodded. "I remember this place now. That museum's on a college campus, right?"

"Kendall College," Butters confirmed.

"College campus on Halloween night," Thomas said. "Hell of a place for a gang of necromancers to slug it out. There's going to be collateral damage."

"No, there isn't," I said, and I was surprised how vicious my own voice sounded. "Because we're going to stop this stupid summoning. And then we're going to hunt those murderous bastards down and kill them."

There was dead silence in the kitchen.

Thomas and Butters both stared at me, expressions apprehensive.

"Maybe it's the cloak," Bob suggested brightly. "Harry, do you feel any more judgmental and self-righteous than you did this morning?"

I took a slow and deep breath. "Sorry," I said. "Sorry. That came out kinda harsh."

"Maybe a little," Butters said, his voice all but a whisper.

I rubbed at my face and glanced at the battery-powered clock on the wall of Murphy's kitchen. "Okay. Sundown's in just over an hour. I have to be ready to call up the Erlking by then."

"Um," Thomas said. "Harry, if it's the Erlking's presence that's going to attract all of these old spirits to their old tools and stuff, then won't it do the same thing no matter *who* calls him up?"

"Yeah," I said. "Unless the one who calls him traps him in a circle to contain his power and leaves him there."

Bob made a spluttering sound. "Harry, that's a dangerous proposition. No, scratch that, it's an *insane* proposition. Even assuming you have the will to trap something like the Erlking in a circle, and even if you keep him there all night, he is *not* going to let that kind of insult go. He'll come back the next night and kill you. If you're lucky."

"I can worry about that after I've done it," I said.

"Wait," Butters said. "Wait, wait. I mean, will it really matter? These guys don't have the bad magic book, right? Without that book, all they can do is call up the spirits. They can't, you know, eat them. Right?"

"We can't assume that they don't have it," I said. "Grevane might have found it."

"But the other two couldn't, right?" Butters said.

"Even if they haven't, they'll still be there," I said. "They can't afford to assume that their rivals haven't gotten the book. So they're going to show up with everything they have to try to prevent one of the others from going through with the ritual."

"Why?" Butters asked.

"Because they hate each other," I said. "And if one of them goes all godly, he's going to enjoy crushing the others. It will probably be the first thing he does."

"Oh," Butters said.

"That's why I need you to do something for me, Thomas."

My brother nodded. "Name it."

I grabbed a blank piece of paper and a pencil and started writing. "This is a note. I want you to take it down to the address I'm writing down and get it to the Wardens."

"I'm not going anywhere close to the Wardens," Thomas said.

"You don't have to," I said. "They're at a hotel. You'll leave it at the desk and ask the clerk to take it to them. Then clear out fast."

"Are they going to trust a note?" Thomas asked, skeptical.

"I told them to expect a messenger if I couldn't get there myself. They know about the Erlking. That I'm trying to sidetrack him. They need to know where the heirs of Kemmler are going to be so that they can take them down."

"Five of them," Thomas said quietly. "They'll be outnumbered by one."

I grimaced. It would be worse than that. Ramirez had looked like he could handle himself, but the two rookies couldn't have stood up to any of the heirs or their companions, from what I'd seen. "Once I've secured the Erlking, I'll be along as quick as I can. Besides that, they're Wardens," I said. "They'll take down Kemmler's flunkies."

"Or die trying," Thomas said. He grimaced. "How should I get down there?"

I went to another kitchen drawer and rummaged in it until I found Murphy's spare keys. I tossed them to Thomas. "Here. Her motorcycle is in the shed."

"Right," he said, but his expression was wary. "She going to mind me stealing her bike?"

"It's in a good cause," I told him. "The streets are bad, and the Wardens need to get moving soonest. Go."

Thomas nodded, pocketed the keys, and shrugged into his leather jacket. "I'll get back here as soon as I'm done."

"Yeah," I said quietly. "Thomas. To the Wardens you're nothing but a White Court vampire. If they see you, they'll be out for blood."

"I understand," he said. His voice was a little bitter. "If I'm not back in time, Harry . . . good luck."

He offered his hand, and we traded grips, hard. My hand must have been cold with nerves, because his felt warm. Then he let go of my hand, nodded to Bob and Butters, and headed out into the rain. A minute later Murphy's Harley grumbled in the backyard, and then purred off into the rain and gloom.

I sat there in silence for a minute, then got up and went to the stove. I got the teapot out, filled it up, and put it on the gas burner to boil. It took me a minute to find Murphy's collection of teas, and it was gratuitously complex. I mean, come on, how many different types of tea do you really need? Maybe I'm prejudiced, because I take my tea with so much sugar that the actual flavor is sort of an aftertaste.

I found some in instant bags that smelled vaguely minty. "Tea?" I asked Butters.

"Sure," he said.

I got out two cups.

"What's next?" he asked.

"Hot tea," I said. "Staying warm. Then I go out in the rain and call up the Erlking. You're staying inside while I do."

"Why?" he asked.

"Because it's going to be dangerous."

"Well, yeah," he said. "But why inside the house? I mean, this supergoblin can just rip the walls apart, right?"

"Strong enough to do it, probably," I said. "But it can't. The house is protected by its threshold."

Butters looked at me blankly. "Which means what?"

I leaned a hip on the counter and explained. "A threshold is a kind of energy that surrounds a home. It's . . ." I frowned, thinking how to explain it. "It's sort of like the home has a positive charge to it. If outside magic wants to come in, it has to neutralize that charge first. Big, tough things from the Nevernever need a lot of power just to stay in our world. They don't usually have enough to take out a threshold and still have enough juice to be dangerous."

"It's like that vampire thing?" he asked. "They can't come in if you don't invite them?"

"Pretty much, yeah. If you invite something in, your threshold won't affect it. But other magical beings and energy have trouble with it. It's a solid defense."

"Didn't help your place much," Butters observed.

"My place is a rental apartment," I said. "And except for the past several months, it's been just me living there. Doesn't give it the same kind of energy as you'd find in a long-established home."

"Oh. Is that what they mean by 'safe as houses,' then?"

I smiled a little. "A house doesn't make a home. When the place has got history, family, emotions, worries, joys worked into the wood, that's when it gets a solid threshold. This house has been in the Murphy clan for better than a hundred years, and lived in for every one of them. It's solid. You'll be safe in here."

"But it's not going to get loose once you call it up," Butters said. "Right?"

"That's the plan. But even if it did, *you* aren't the one who is going to piss it off. There won't be any reason for it to come after you."

"Oh, good," he said. He blinked at me and said apologetically, "Not that I want it to come after *you*, Harry."

"I don't blame you," I said.

Butters nodded. "Why zombies?" he asked.

"Huh?"

"Sorry. Changing topics. New question. Why do all these necromancer types use zombies?"

"Not all of them do," I pointed out. "Corpsetaker had called up a bunch of semicorporeal ghosts. Specters."

"But human," Butters said. "Zombies look human. Specters look human. Why not whistle up a pack of decayed rats? Or maybe semicorporeal mosquitos? Why use people?"

"Oh," I said. "It's got to do with a kind of metaphysical impression that any given creature leaves upon its death. Sort of like a footprint. Human beings leave larger footprints than most animals, which means that you can pour more energy into reanimating them."

"They make stronger goons," Butters clarified.

"Yes."

"How come Grevane had fresh corpses when he came to get me, but he attacked your house with old ones? I mean, I saw those things up close." He shivered. "Some of them must have dated back to the beginning of the twentieth century."

"Same reason they animate humans instead of animals," I said. "Older corpses leave a deeper metaphysical imprint. They're harder to call up, but once you get them here they're easier to control, stronger, more difficult to damage."

"Old corpses get you stronger undead flunkies," he said.

"Right," I said. I could see the wheels turning in Butters's head as he processed the information. He looked like he was busy lining up dozens more questions spawned by the answers to the first few, and I had a feeling he would pursue them with relentless curiosity.

"Okay. But what if—"

"Butters," I said as gently as I could. "Not now. All I want to do is have a quiet cup of tea." An inspiration hit me. "Ask Bob," I told him. "Bob knows a hell of a lot more than I do, anyway."

"Oh," Butters said. He looked from me to the skull. "Um. Yeah, I guess Thomas was talking to it."

"He!" Bob said indignantly. "I am very much a he! I'm not some kind of freaking animatronic Tinkertoy!"

"Right," Butters said. "Um. Sorry. Bob. Do you mind if I ask you some questions?"

"It's a waste of my vast intellect and talent," Bob sneered.

"Do it, Bob," I told him.

"Oh, man." The orange lights in the skull's eye sockets rolled. "Fine. I haven't got anything better to do than to teach kindergarten."

"Great!" Butters bubbled, and sat down at the table. He grabbed some more paper and a pencil. "Well, how about we start with . . ."

I fixed myself a cup of tea and one for Butters. I put the cup down near him, but he took little notice of it. He was deeply involved in a conversation with Bob.

I slipped out into the living room and put my aching leg up on the table, then settled back onto the couch with my tea. I sat in the gloom, sipping hot, sweet mint something-or-other and tried to order my thoughts. I was tired enough that it didn't take too long.

I was about to call up a peer of Queen Mab and try to trap it for an entire night. A garden spider had about as much chance of trapping a Bengal tiger. Except that the Bengal tiger probably wouldn't bother to squash the spider for daring to make the attempt. The Erlking would.

That made the whole notion more stupid than most of my plans, but I didn't have too much choice in the matter. The presence of the Erlking in the area would drastically increase the number and the potency of the undead that the Kemmlerites were planning to summon tonight. If I could block the Erlking's presence from Chicago, it would take a big chunk out of the powers the necromancers would summon. Grevane and company were formidable enough without calling up an army of superzombies and über-ghosts. If I could stop that from happening, it might give Luccio and her Wardens a real chance to defeat them.

If I wasn't fast enough to call the Erlking before one of the Kemmlerites, or if he escaped my hold and ran loose through Chicago, people would die. The Erlking would summon the Wild Hunt into a lightless Chicago Halloween night, and anyone they caught in the open would be torn to shreds.

Lightning flickered outside, somehow too dark and dull to be natural. A beat later, thunder ripped through the evening air, shaking the little house. The wind started to pick up, and the steady beat of rain on the windows surged and retreated with its restless gusting.

I didn't feel like a wizard. I didn't feel like a deadly and powerful Warden. I didn't feel like the supernatural champion of Chicago, or a fearless foe of evil, a daring summoner able to cast his defiance into the teeth of a supernatural titan, or an enlightened sage of the mystic arts. I felt like a scarred, battered, aching, one-handed man with few pleasant prospects for the future and a ridiculous pair of pants with one leg slashed off.

Mouse padded over to me through the dimness. He chuffed softly at me, and then laid his head down on my leg. My eyes were closed, but I could hear his tail thumping softly against the couch. I rested my bad hand on Mouse's head and petted him awkwardly. Mouse didn't mind. He just leaned against me, loaning me the warmth of his fur and the silent faithfulness of his presence.

It made me feel better. Mouse might not have been the smartest creature on earth, but he was steady, kind, loyal, and was possessed of the uncanny wisdom of beasts for knowing whom to trust. I might not have been a superhero, but Mouse thought that I was pretty darned cool. That meant something. It would have to be enough.

I set my teacup down, took my foot off Murphy's coffee table, and rose. I picked up my staff without looking at it, took a deep breath, and clenched my jaw.

Then I marched into the kitchen in a lopsided stalk. "Butters," I said. "Stay here with Bob and Mouse. Watch my back. If you see anyone trying to sneak up on me, give a yell."

"Right," he said. "Will do."

I nodded to him and went out into the rain to test my will against the legendary lord of the Wild Hunt.

Chapter

Thirty-three

The rain had plastered my hair to my head by the time I got all the material for the summoning out of the Beetle's trunk. I stuffed it all into a gym bag and then walked out to the middle of the backyard. It wasn't quite too dark to see—not yet. But I didn't want to make any mistakes, so I used the last of the chemical light sticks Kincaid had given me before our raid on Mavra's scourge the year before. I snapped it and shook it up, and green-yellow light spread out in a little pool around me. The rain limited how much it could spread, and it created the illusion that the entire world had shrunk to a ten-foot circle rain and grass and green-golden light.

I started with the circle where I intended to trap the Erlking. The coil of barbed wire still gleamed with its factory finish. I uncoiled enough of it to give me several small holes in my fingers and to join into a circle about seven feet across. Though it wasn't cold iron in the technical sense, it was very much what the faeries meant when they said "cold iron"—the wire had plenty of iron in it, and cold iron was the bane of the faerie world.

I laid the barbed wire out, straightening it slightly as I went, and tacked it down into the damp earth with horseshoe-shaped metal staples as long as my little finger. I double-checked every staple, and then clipped the barbed wire from the larger roll and used a pair of pliers to twist the loose ends together. After that, I marked out the points of an invisible five-pointed star within the circle, and placed several articles with an affinity for the Erlking; a heavy collar one might place on a hunting hound, a whetstone, a small bowie knife, flint and steel, and several steel arrowheads.

Then I placed my own affinity items opposite those of the Erl-king's, outside the circle; a used copy of *The Hobbit,* the splintered end of my last blasting rod, my .44, a parking ticket I hadn't paid yet, and finally my mother's silver pentacle amulet. I stepped back and went over the circle again, making sure that it was fixed solidly and that nothing had fallen across it.

In the back of my mind somewhere, I was aware of the ap-proach of sunset. I don't know how I knew it, really. It was already darker than most nights, and I certainly couldn't judge when the sun would be down with all those rain clouds in the way—but that didn't seem to matter. I could feel the sunlight still gliding down to be trapped in the overcast, could feel its presence and warmth with some part of my mind that wasn't entirely beholden to mere physics. I could feel it fading, and felt the concurrent stirring of the magical forces of night as it did.

The energy of night was far different than that of the daylight—not inherently evil, but wilder, more dangerous, more unpre-dictable. Night was a time of endings, and this night, Samhain, All Hallow's Eve, was particularly so. On this night, the forces of the spirit world, the wild things that haunted the Nevernever, drawn to death and decay, would flit freely back and forth. Spirits would turn restless in their graves and wander the world, mostly unseen by mortal eyes. The wild beasts could feel the night coming, and their metropolitan cousins could sense the knife-edge of danger and energy in the air. Dogs began to howl in the neighborhood around me, first one, then two, then dozens, and their long, low, mournful howls rose up in a haunting tide.

Dark was only moments away, and I stripped the black leather glove from my bad hand and knelt by the barbed-wire circle. Then I leaned down and pressed my left palm, all scarred but for the shape of Lasciel's sigil like a living brand on my skin, against the nearest tine of barbed wire, pressing my flesh down with careful deliberation. I didn't feel the wire cut me, but there was a trickle of warmth over a portion of the sigil, and my blood—black in the greenish chemical light—slipped down over the barbed wire, mix-ing with my will to send energy coursing into the cold-iron prison I had built.

The prison was built and the trap was set. I wished that there had been more time to assemble the articles I'd needed. If there had been months to prepare, I could have worked with Bob to figure out the best way to do the job. The materials might have been rare and expensive and difficult to attain, but it was within the realm of possibility to build a circle from which even a being like the Erlking could not lightly escape.

But there hadn't been time, and if my quickie-mart Alcatraz was going to do the job, it would need all of my focus and determination.

So I shut my doubts into a closet in the back of my mind, along with my fears. I knelt in my coat in the rain, staff still in my right hand, and took slow, deep breaths. I envisioned myself drawing in power with each breath, and exhaling weakness and distraction. I felt the magic stirring around me and within me as I did, and I started building up my will, gathering my strength for use, until the wet grass seemed to sparkle with too many points of green-gold light and the hairs on my neck rose up on end.

I took in a final deep breath, and on the exhale night fell.

I opened my mouth and began to call out in the steady cadence of the summoning. My voice rang hollow in the wind and rain, muffled but strong, and I poured some of my will into the words, until the power in them began to make the air ripple around them as they flowed from my lips. There, in the darkness, I reached into the spirit world to call up one of the deadliest beings of Faerie.

And the Erlking answered.

One moment the circle was empty. Then there was a flash of lightning, a crash of thunder, and a disembodied black shadow appeared on the grass within the circle—the shadow of a tall, standing figure with no physical presence to cast it.

I barely stopped myself from flinching and breaking off the summoning chant—a mistake that would have freed the Erlking to leave at best, and freed it to kill me at worst. But I recovered myself and kept up the litany all the way through to the end. When I finished it, my voice had risen to a strident, silvery clarion, and on the last word lightning flashed down from the storm, green and white and eye-searing. It struck down upon the circle, slammed against it, and then scattered out around the circle in a hissing

matrix of electricity and steam and magic, defining the cylinder of
the magic circle in a sparkle of greenish light that rose up into the
night for a moment, and then faded away.

When it was gone, the shadow within my circle was no longer
alone.

The Erlking stood better than eight feet high. Other than that it
looked more or less like a human dressed in close-fitting leathers
and mail of some dark, matte black substance. It wore a bucket-
shaped helmet that covered its face, and the horns of an enormous
stag rose up and away from the helm. Within the slit of the helmet's visor, I could see twin gleams of amber fire, and as those terrible eyes settled upon me, I could feel the presence of the being
behind them like a sudden raw and wild hunger that pressed
against the *outside* of my skin. I could feel the Erlking's lust for the
wild night, for the hunt, and for the kill. Lightning flashed again
and the rain came down harder, and he raised his arms slowly, dismissing me and stretching his body up to glory in the storm.

It is time, mortal. Release me.

The words suddenly appeared in my head without going
through my ears, scarlet and glowing and scalding. This time I did
flinch as the Erlking's will sent meaning into my thoughts like a
well-thrown spear. I tore my attention away from that lance of
thought and spoke aloud in reply.

"I will not release you."

The glowing eyes within the helm snapped back to me, flaring
larger and brighter. *I am no beast to be lured and trapped, mortal.
Set me free and join me in the hunt.*

Images came with the thoughts this time—the rush of rain and
wind in my face, raw hunger in my belly that I was about to sate,
the strength and power of my body and that of the mount beneath
me, and the glorious thrill of the chase as the prey fled as it was
created to do, testing my strength, speed, endurance, and will while
the night called and the storm raged around me. To my surprise,
there was no sense of hate in it, no twisting bitterness of despair.
There was only a wild and ferocious joy, an adrenaline sense of excitement, of passion, of savage harmony red in tooth and claw.

I barely managed to pull my thoughts back into my own control, grinding my teeth and reminding myself that I was kneeling in Murphy's backyard, not pursuing game through the forest primeval. The Erlking might not be evil incarnate, but that didn't mean that he wasn't far too dangerous to be allowed to go free. "No," I growled. "I will not release you."

His amber-flame eyes narrowed, and he dropped slowly into a crouch, knees bent, his fingers resting lightly on the grass just inside the barbed wire. Those eyes were barely three feet from mine, and he considered me in silence that swiftly became a torment of suspense.

You are he, the Erlking cast at me. *He who defied Queen Winter. He who slew Lady Summer.*

In those thoughts, I saw Mab standing over me as I lay stunned beside the Summer Lady's corpse, offering me her hand. I felt Aurora's blood drying on my skin, tasted it, harsh and sweet, in my mouth. I had to force myself not to try to spit the phantom taste from my tongue.

"I am he," I said.

We are not foes, came his thoughts. And . . . he was curious about it. Even baffled. In sending me his thoughts, I also got flashes of emotion from him. *You are part of the hunt. A predator. Why do you call me if not to join me?*

"To prevent another from setting you free this night."

The Erlking tilted its head. There was no sending of thought, but I read the gesture clearly enough to interpret it as if he had. *Why?*

"Because your presence would mean suffering and death for those people I would protect."

Man suffers. Man dies. It is how things are.

"Not tonight it isn't," I growled.

Hunter, cast the Erlking. *You are not strong enough to hold me. Release me, lest I turn the hunt upon you.*

And suddenly I felt the other side of the hunt. I felt my legs singing with the strength of terror. I felt my lungs burning, felt my body moving with the power and grace that only the approach of death can summon from it. I fled over the rough ground, bounding like a deer, and knew the whole while that there was no escape.

"Thrice I say and done." I gasped, forcing the words out in a defiant scream. "I will. Not. Release you."

And the Erlking rose, an unearthly scream piercing the night. The chorus of howling dogs rose with it, louder and louder, and the storm lashed at the air with sabers of wind and lances of lightning. The sound was deafening, the light searing, and the freaking ground started to tremble as the Erlking lashed out against my circle with his will.

I stood my ground, facing the Erlking and casting my will into the circle, forcing it against his own power, struggling to contain him while he sought to burst free from my enchantment. It was an enormous struggle, and almost hopeless. I felt like a man straining to push a car up a hill. Not only was it a difficult weight to begin to move, but a greater force was working against me, and if I allowed it to move even an inch it would begin to gain momentum and crush me beneath it.

So I fought for that inch, refusing to give it to him. The Erlking wasn't an evil being—but he was a force of nature, power, and violence without conscience or restraint.

He screamed again, and the howling wind and rain and the call of beasts grew even louder. Again he surged against the circle of my will, and again I held him in. Wild, the Erlking shook his head like a maddened beast, and his antlers slammed against the confining wall of the circle that imprisoned him, sending ripples of greenish light out through the circle. Then he reached to his side and drew a black sword from its scabbard. He lifted the blade, and a lance of green lightning flashed down from the storm, touching upon its tip and wreathing it in blinding light. Then he took the sword in both hands and brought it down upon the barrier.

I have little memory of what the third blow was like. I remember it in much the same way I do the burning of my left hand. There was too much light, too much energy, a tide of agony, and I was terrified. My vision faded to a blind field of white, and I thrust my staff hard against the ground to keep from falling.

And then my vision began to clear. The tide began to recede. And within the circle, whirling in a frenzy of frustration and need, was the Erlking. His power was fading, and the circle I'd built had been good enough to give me enough leverage to hold him.

I thought I heard a muffled voice somewhere amid all the wind and rain and thunder and the swift pounding of my own heart. I started to look around for the source of the noise.

And then someone hit me on the back of the head.

I remember *that* part, because I'd been through it before. A flash of light, pain, a sickening whirling sensation as I fell, and a disjointed looseness to limbs that had suddenly gone useless. I fell to one side, shocked that the whole world had suddenly tilted on end. The grass suddenly felt cold and wet against my cheek.

With a shriek of triumph, the Erlking shattered my circle into a cloud of golden light that faded and vanished. There was a roar of wind, and then an enormous horse landed in Murphy's yard as if it had just vaulted over the whole of her house. The Erlking flung himself up onto the black steed's back and let loose an eerie cry. When he did, all the howling music of the dogs, primitive and fierce, seemed to congeal into flashes of lightning that leapt *up* from the ground and into the clouds. For a second there was silence, and then the screaming winds warbled and whistled into deeper, more terrifying howls than any dog had ever uttered. From the shadows rushed a great hound, a beast the size of a pony with dark fur, gleaming white teeth, and the flaming amber eyes of the Erlking himself. More hounds came leaping from the shadows, bounding in bloodthirsty joy around the Erlking's horse.

The Erlking whirled his steed, lifted his black sword in a mocking salute to me, and then cried out to his steed and his hounds. The black horse gathered itself and leapt into the air, then started churning its legs as if running up a hill—and kept going up. The hounds leapt and followed their master up into the teeth of the storm. Lightning flashed in my eyes, and when it died again, they were gone.

The Wild Hunt was loose in Chicago.

And I had been the one to call them here.

I struggled until I began to move. I wasn't able to get enough balance to rise, but I managed to roll over onto my back. Cold raindrops slapped against my face.

Cowl put the barrel of my own .44 to the end of my nose and said, "An impressive display, Dresden. It's always such a pity when someone with such talent dies so young."

Thirty-four

I looked at the cavernous barrel and thought to myself that a .44 really was a ridiculously big gun. Then I looked past it to Cowl and said, "But you aren't planning on doing it yourself, are you? Otherwise you'd have just shot me in the back of the head and had done with it. With me groggy like that, you might not even have had a death curse to worry about."

"Very good," Cowl said approvingly. "Your reason, at least, seems sound. Provided you remain very still and give me no reason to think you a threat, I'll be glad to let you live until the Erlking returns for you."

I held still, partly because I didn't want to get shot, and partly because I thought I might throw up if I moved my head too much. "How'd you find me?" I asked.

"Kumori and I have been taking turns tailing you most of the day," he said.

"When do you people sleep?" I asked.

"No rest for the wicked," Cowl said. His tone was amused from within his heavy hood, but the gun never wavered.

"Someone had to keep an eye on me," I said. "You and Grevane and Corpsetaker all wanted the Erlking to be in town. It didn't matter to you who called him as long as someone did."

"And you were the only one with an interest in keeping him away," Cowl said. "All I needed to do was watch you and ensure that you did not actually trap the Erlking."

"And that's why you followed me," I said.

"It's one reason," he replied. "I think you might actually have done it, you know, had I not interrupted you. I was the only one of the three of us who thought you might succeed."

"I don't get it," I said. "I thought that you guys hated one another's guts."

"Oh, yes."

"Then are you working together or trying to kill each other?" I asked.

"Why, yes," Cowl said, and what sounded like a genuine laugh bubbled in his voice. "We smile at one another and play nicely all in the name of Kemmler's greater glory, of course. But we are all planning on killing one another as soon as it's convenient. I take it that Corpsetaker tried to remove Grevane last night?"

"Yeah. It was a real party."

"Pity. I would have enjoyed watching them in action again. But I was busy with the actual work. That's how it usually works out."

"Taking out the city's power grid."

"And phone lines, radio communications, and quite a few other, subtler things," Cowl said. "It was difficult, but someone had to do it. Naturally it fell to me. But we'll see how things settle out before morning."

"Heh," I said. "They think they're using you to get the serious technical magic done, while they save up their juice for the fight. And you think you're lulling them off guard, so that when the Darkhallow goes down, you get the power."

"There's no real reason to practice my swordplay and summoning of the dead when I have no intention of entering a tactical contest with them."

"You really intend to make yourself into a god?" I asked.

"I intend to take power," Cowl said. "I regard myself as the least of the possible evils."

"Uh-huh," I said. "Someone is going to get the power. Might as well be you. Something like that?"

"Something like that," Cowl said.

"What if no one got it?" I said.

"I don't really see that happening," he said. "Grevane and the Corpsetaker are determined. I intend to beat them to the prize and use it to destroy them. It's the only way to be sure one of those madmen does not become something more terrible than the earth has ever seen."

"Right," I said. "You're the correct madman for the job."

Cowl was silent for a long moment in the rain. Drops fell off the end of my pistol in his gloved hand. Then he said, his voice pensive, "I do not perceive myself to be mad. But if I were truly mad, would I be able to tell?"

I shivered. Probably from the rain and the cold.

Cowl took a step back from me and said, voice firm and confident again, "Did you find him?"

I looked behind me and saw Kumori glide out the back door of Murphy's house. "Yes."

I stared hard at Kumori, and my heart lurched in my chest.

She left the door open behind her. There was no candlelight in the kitchen. There was no movement inside the house.

"Excellent," Cowl said. He took a step back from me. "I have already warned you to stay clear of my path, Dresden. I now suspect that you are too proud to back down. I know of the Wardens now in the city. They pose no serious obstacle to my plans."

"You think you can take them in a fight?" I said.

"I have no intention of *fighting* them, Dresden," Cowl replied. "I'm simply going to kill them. Join them if it suits you to do so instead of waiting for the Erlking. It makes no difference to me how you die."

His voice was steady and absolutely confident. It scared me. My heart lurched in my chest, fear for Butters and a dawning understanding of Cowl's quiet madness competing to see which could make it race faster.

"There's one problem, Cowl," I said.

Cowl began to turn away, but then paused. "Oh?"

"You still don't have the *Word*. How are you going to manage the Darkhallow without it?"

For an answer, Cowl carefully lowered the hammer on my revolver and turned away. And he laughed, quietly, under his breath. He started walking, and Kumori hurried to his side. Then Cowl tossed my gun into the grass, raised his hand, and flicked it at the air before him. I felt a surge of power as he parted the veil between the material world and the Nevernever and they both stepped through it, vanishing from Murphy's backyard. The rift sealed behind Cowl, so quietly and smoothly that I would never have been able to tell it had opened at all.

I was left alone in the wind and the darkness and the cold rain. Somewhere in the distance there was an echoing howl that came from above me and very far away.

It should have frightened me, but I was so woozy that I mostly wanted to lie down and close my eyes for a minute. I knew that if I did I might not open them for a while. Maybe not ever.

I had to check on Butters and Mouse. I rolled over and picked up my staff, then crawled a couple of feet and got my mother's pentacle. Then I stood up. My head pounded with a dull, throbbing beat of pain, and I bowed my head forward for a moment, letting cold rain fall onto the lump forming on the back of my skull. The worst of it passed after a minute, and I got the pain under control. I'd taken harder shots to the head than that one had been, and I didn't have time to coddle myself. I blew out a harsh breath and shambled into the house.

I found it dark, all the candles that had been lit now extinguished. I lifted my mother's pentacle and ran my will through it, causing it to pulse and then glow with silver-blue light. I lifted the pentacle over my head and surveyed the kitchen.

It was empty. There was no sign of Mouse or Butters—and no evidence of a struggle, either. My fear subsided a little. If Kumori had found them, there would be signs of violence—blood, scattered furnishings. Butters's papers were still stacked up neatly on the kitchen table.

Murphy's house wasn't a large one, and there were only so many places Butters could be. I limped into the living room and then down the short hall to the bedrooms and the bathroom.

"Butters?" I called softly. "It's Harry. Mouse?"

There was a sudden rough scratching at the door of the linen closet beside me, and I almost jumped through the ceiling. I swallowed in an effort to force my heart back down into my chest, then opened the closet door.

Butters and Mouse crouched on the floor of the closet. Butters was at the rear, and though Mouse looked cramped, he crouched solidly between Butters and the door. His tail began to thump against the inside of the closet when he saw me, and he wriggled his way clear to come to me.

"Oh, thank God," Butters said. He squirmed out of the closet after Mouse. "Harry. Are you all right?"

"Been worse," I told him. "Are you okay? What happened?"

"Um," Butters said, "I saw you out there. And then . . . there was something inside that ring of barbed wire. And I was . . . I couldn't see it very well, but then the wind kicked up and I thought I saw something moving outside and . . . I yelled and sort of panicked." His face flushed. "Sorry. I was just . . . much shorter than that thing. I panicked."

He'd rabbited. All in all, probably not a stupid reaction to the presence of an angry lord of Faerie. "Don't worry about it," I said. "Mouse stayed with you?"

"Yeah," Butters said. "I guess so. He started to try to get outside when that thing in the circle screamed. I was holding him back. I didn't realize I still had his collar when I, uh . . ."

Butters's face turned greenish and he said, "Excuse me." Then he sprinted for the bathroom.

I heard him throwing up inside and frowned down at Mouse.

"You know what?" I told the dog. "I don't care if Butters had been chock-full of gamma radiation and had green skin and purple pants. There's no way he could haul you into a closet with him."

Mouse looked up at me and tilted his head to one side, doggy expression enigmatic.

"But that would mean that it was the other way around. That you were the one hauling Butters to a hiding place."

Mouse's jaw dropped open into a grin.

"But *that* would mean that you knew you couldn't handle Kumori, and that she was dangerous to Butters. And you knew that I wanted you to protect him. And that instead of fighting or running away, you formulated a plan to hide him." I frowned. "And dogs aren't supposed to be that smart."

Mouse snorted out a little sneeze, shook his fuzzy head, and then flopped over onto his back, eyes begging me to scratch his tummy.

"What the hell," I said, and started scratching. "Looks to me like you earned it."

Butters emerged from the bathroom a couple of minutes later. "Sorry," he said. "Nerves. I, uh . . . Harry, I'm sorry I ran away like that."

"Took cover," I provided. "In the action business, when you don't want to say you ran like a mouse, you call it 'taking cover.' It's more heroic."

"Right," Butters said, flushing. "I took cover."

"It's fun, taking cover," I said. "I take cover all the time."

"What happened?" Butters asked.

"I called the Erlking, but someone kept me from keeping him penned up. They came in the house for a minute, and . . ." I felt my voice trail off. My relief that Butters and Mouse were all right began to fade, as I realized that they had never been what Kumori had been searching for.

"What?" Butters said quietly. "Harry, what is it?"

"Son of a *bitch*," I swore, and my voice was a sulfurous snarl. "How could I be so *stupid?*"

I whirled and stalked back down the hall, through the living room, and into the kitchen, lifting my light.

On the kitchen table there were only empty cups of tea, empty cans, unlit candles, paper, and pens.

In the spot where Bob the skull had sat, there was nothing.

"Oh, man," Butters said quietly at my elbow. "Oh, man. They took him."

"They took him," I spat.

"Why?" Butters whispered. "Why would they do that?"

"Because Bob the skull hasn't always been mine," I growled. "He used to belong to my old teacher, Justin. And before that he belonged to the necromancer, Kemmler." I whirled in a fury and slammed my fist into Murphy's refrigerator so hard that it dented the side and split my middle knuckle open.

"I . . . I don't get it," Butters said, his voice very quiet.

"Bob did for Kemmler what he did for me. He was a consultant.

A research assistant. A sounding board for magical theory," I said. "That's why Cowl took him."

"Cowl's doing research?" Butters asked.

"No," I spat. "Cowl knew that Bob used to be Kemmler's. Somewhere in there, Bob knows everything about the theory that Kemmler did."

"What does that mean?"

"It means that Cowl doesn't need *The Word of Kemmler* now. He doesn't need the stupid book to enact the Darkhallow because he's got the spirit that helped Kemmler *write* it." I shook my head, bitter regret a metallic taste in my mouth. "And I practically gave it to him."

Chapter

Thirty-five

I gave the blood on my torn knuckle a disdainful glance, then snapped, "Get your things and hold on to Mouse. We're going."

"Going?" Butters asked.

"It isn't safe for you here now," I said. "They know about this place. I can't leave you behind."

Butters swallowed. "Where are we going?"

"They tailed me all day. I've got to make sure the people I've seen today are all right." I paused, thoughts tearing through my head. "And . . . I've got to find the book."

"The necromancer's book?" Butters asked. "Why?"

I got out my keys and headed for the Beetle. "Because I have no freaking clue what's supposed to be happening at this Darkhallow. The only part that I understood enough to stop was the summoning of the Erlking, and that's been blown to hell. I keep getting burned because I don't know enough about what's going on. I've got to figure out how to throw a wrench into Cowl's gears during the Darkhallow."

"Why?"

"Because the only other thing I can do is try to kick my way through a crowd of necromancers and undead and try to punch his ticket face-to-face."

"Wouldn't that work?"

"If I could pull it off," I said, and went out into the rain. "But I'm a featherweight fighting in the heavyweight division. Nose-to-nose, I think Cowl would probably kick my eldritch ass. My only real chance is to fight smart, and that means I've got to know more about what's going on. For that, I need the book."

Butters hurried after me, a couple of fingers through Mouse's collar. We got into the Beetle and I revved it up. "But we still haven't figured out those numbers," he said.

"That has to change," I said. "Now."

"Um," said Butters as I got the Beetle moving, "you can say 'now' all you want, but I still don't know."

"Could it be a combination?" I said. "Like to a safe?"

"The older safe combinations need some kind of designation for left and right. The newer ones might use some kind of digital code, sure, but unless you find a safe with a password sixteen numerals long, that won't help us much."

"A credit card," I said. "That's sixteen digits, right?"

"Can be," Butters said. "You think that's what the number was? Maybe a credit card or debit card account that Bony Tony wanted his fee to get paid to?"

I grimaced. "Doesn't make any sense," I said. "Something like that would be in his pocket. Not hidden in a balloon hanging from a string down his throat."

"Good point," Butters said.

We rode in silence for a while. Except for the headlights of other cars, the streets were dark. Between the total lack of lighting, the dark, and the heavy rain, it was like driving through a cave. Traffic was tight and snarled anywhere near the highways, but it had thinned out considerably since the afternoon. The people of Chicago seemed to mostly be staying home for the night, which was a mercy in more ways than one.

Butters looked around nervously a few minutes later. "Harry. This isn't exactly the best neighborhood."

"I know," I said, and pulled over in front of a hydrant, the only open space in sight.

He swallowed. "Why are you stopping the car?"

"I need to check on someone," I said. "Stay here with Mouse. I'll be right back."

"But—"

"Butters," I said impatiently. "There's a girl here who helped me out earlier today. I have to make sure Cowl and his sidekick haven't harmed her."

"But . . . can't you do this after you stop the bad guys?"

I shook my head. "I'm doing my best, here. I don't know what might happen in the next few hours, but dammit, this girl helped me because I asked her to. *I* dragged her into this. Cowl and Kumori were going to considerable lengths to destroy every copy of *Der Erlking* that they could find, and if they guessed that I got it from her memory she'll be in danger. I need to be sure she's all right."

"Oooooh," Butters said. "This is the girl who asked you out, right?"

I blinked. "How did you know that?"

"Thomas told me."

I growled under my breath and said, "Remind me to punch his lights out sometime soon."

"Hey," Butters said. "At least he didn't let me keep thinking you were gay."

I gave Butters a flat look and got out of the car. "Stay in the driver's seat," I told him. "If there's trouble, run. Try to circle back for me."

"Right," Butters said. "Got it."

I hurried through the rain and the darkness into Shiela's building. I drew out my pentacle and willed light from it, and went up the stairs to her floor as I had that morning. The stairs and the hallway had that illusory unfamiliarity that darkness can give a place you've seen only once or twice, but I found my way to Shiela's door easily enough.

I paused for a moment and tried to sense the wards she'd woven, and found that they were still in place. That was good. If anyone had come in after her for some reason, they'd have either torn the ward down or set it off on the way through.

Unless, of course, someone had gone to the trouble to get invited in first. Shiela didn't seem to be the kind to turn folks away out of a sense of general paranoia. I knocked several times.

There wasn't an answer.

She had said she was going out, earlier. She was probably at some costume party somewhere. Talking with friends. Eating good food. Having fun.

Probably.

I knocked again and said, "Shiela? It's Harry."

I heard a couple of soft steps, the creak of a floorboard, and then the door opened to the length of its security chain. Shiela stood in the opening. There was soft candlelight coming from her apartment. "Harry," she said quietly, her mouth curling into a smile. "What are you doing here? Hang on." She closed the door, the security chain rattled, and then she opened it again. "Come in."

"I really can't stick around," I said, but I stepped through the door anyway. She had half a dozen candles lit on the end table beside her couch, and there was a mussed blanket on the couch next to a paperback novel.

Shiela's long, dark hair was piled up into bun and held in place with a couple of chopsticks, leaving her ears and the smooth skin of her neck intriguingly bare. She was wearing a Bears football jersey made of soft cotton that hung to her knees, and she wore pink slippers on her feet. The jersey was loose on her, but she had the curves to make it look more appealing than it had any right to be. I could see her calves, and they did a wonderful job of blending softness and strength.

Shiela saw me looking, and her cheeks turned a little pink. "Hi," she said, her voice quiet.

"Hi," I said back, and smiled at her. "Hey, I thought you had a party tonight?"

She shook her head. "I was walking. I didn't want to walk in the rain, and I couldn't call anyone to get me a ride, so I'm home." She tilted her head to one side and frowned at me. "You seem . . . I'm not sure. Tense. Angry."

"Both," I said. "There are some things happening."

She nodded, her dark eyes serious. "I've heard that there's something bad brewing. It's what you're working on, isn't it?"

"Yes."

She fretted at her lower lip. "Then why are you here?"

She looked beautiful like that, in a sleepshirt in the candlelight. She wasn't wearing any makeup, but she looked deliciously soft and feminine. I thought about kissing her again, just to make sure that the first one hadn't been some sort of anomaly. Then I shook my head and reminded myself that tonight was about business. "I just needed to make sure that you were all right."

Her eyes widened. "Am I in some kind of danger?"

I lifted my hand placatingly. "I don't think you are now. But I was followed today. I had to be sure that you were safe. Have you seen anyone? Maybe felt nervous or anxious for no reason?"

"No more than any other day," she said. Thunder rumbled, and the rain kept drumming on her windows. "Honestly."

I let out my breath and felt myself relax a little. "Okay, good. I'm glad."

Thunder rumbled again and we both just stood there, staring at each other. Both of us glanced, just for a second, at the other's eyes, then pulled away before anything could happen.

"Harry," she said quietly. "Is there anything I can do to help you?"

"You already have," I said.

She took a step closer, and her dark eyes looked huge. "Are you sure?"

My heart sped up again, but I took a little step back from her. "Yeah. Shiela, I knew I wouldn't be able to focus on the rest of tonight if I didn't look in on you first."

She nodded then, and folded her arms. "All right. But when you're finished with this, there's something I'd like to talk to you about."

"What?" I asked.

She shook her head and put her hand on my arm. "It would take some time to explain it. If you think you need your focus for tonight, I don't want to distract you with anything."

I looked at her, and then deliberately down her, and said, "That's probably best. I'm finding you very distracting right now."

She flushed brighter. "No. That's just you reacting to being in danger. You're afraid that you're going to die, and sex is very life affirming."

"Is that what it is?" I drawled.

"Among other things," she said.

For a few seconds my hormones did their best to lobby for overcoming distraction by means of indulgence, but I reined them in. Shiela was right: I was in pain and in fear and in danger, and those kinds of circumstances have a tendency to make you pay attention to different things—the soft shine of candlelight on Shiela's hair, for example, or the soft scent of rose oil and flowered soap on her skin—and Shiela had been in danger for part of that time as well.

I didn't want to take advantage of that. And I didn't want to start anything with her that I wasn't going to be able to finish. For all I knew I'd be dead before another day was out, and it wouldn't be right to allow things to go any further just because I was afraid.

On the other hand, though, there was nothing wrong with savoring life while you still had it.

I leaned down to her, lifted her chin gently with my right hand, and kissed her mouth again. She quivered and returned it with a slow, hesitant shyness. I stayed like that for a moment, tasting her lips, my fingertips light on her chin, and then straightened, breaking it off very slowly.

She opened her eyes a moment later, her breathing a little fast.

I touched her cheek with my fingertips and smiled at her. "I'll call you soon."

She nodded, her eyes clouding with concern. "Be careful."

"Harry?" called a voice.

I blinked and looked around.

"Harry!" he called again, and I recognized Butters's voice. There was a curious quality to the acoustics of his voice—as if he were standing in an empty room, with no furniture or carpeting to absorb any sound.

Shiela froze, looking toward her door, and then said, "Dammit."

I blinked at her. "What?"

"I didn't want this to distract you," she said, and her tone was enigmatic.

I frowned at her for a moment and then opened the door to the apartment. Butters stood in the hall. He'd improvised a lead for Mouse out of what looked like the torn hem of his scrubs tunic, and my big shaggy dog headed for me, nose to the ground, pulling Butters along the way. Butters, for his part, stumbled along uncertainly, as if he'd had a little too much to drink and couldn't get his balance.

"Butters?" I said. "What's up?"

"The car died," he said. "And there were some guys who looked like they didn't like me on the street, so I came to find you."

Butters stopped, or tried to. Mouse chuffed out a breath in greeting and headed straight for me. I leaned down to scratch at Mouse's ears. "Hey, Mouse. Shiela, this is my dog, Mouse. And this is Waldo Butters. He's a friend of mine."

Shiela blinked her eyes closed slowly and looked away.

Butters peered and squinted, looking around him. "What?"

I frowned at him and touched his arm. "Are you okay?"

He flinched a little when I touched him, then clapped a hand down on my arm as if using it to orient on me. "Harry?" he asked. "Don't you have a light?"

I lifted my eyebrows at him and lifted my pentacle, willing it to light. "Here," I said. "Shiela, I hope you don't mind if they come in?"

Butters peered up at me and then around him.

"Harry?" he asked.

"Yeah?"

"Um, who are you talking to?"

I stared at him for a silent second.

And then a few details floated together in my mind, and the bottom dropped all the way out of my stomach.

I closed my eyes for a moment, and opened my inner vision, my wizard's Sight, and turned to face Shiela.

The little apartment simply dissolved, sliding away like paint being washed away by a stream of falling water. In its place I could see a dimly lit, gutted building. Studs stood naked where the drywall had been removed. There were piles of scrap wiring, half-rotted-looking ducts, and similar refuse, which had been removed from the building and thrown aside into refuse piles. The place had been prepared for renovation—but it was empty. The only window I could see was broken. Thunder rumbled, the sound slightly different than it had been a moment before. The driving rain gained a couple of notches of volume, beating hollowly on the old apartment building.

I stared at Shiela with my Sight, and she stood there unchanged—except that I could see a faint tint of light around her, subtle but definite. It meant that she was either a noncorporeal presence or an illusion of thought and energy rather than a reality. But if she'd been an illusion, she should have faded away entirely, as the apartment had done.

I released my Sight again. My stomach twisted on itself, a burning, bitter feeling. "Shiela," I said quietly. "Stars and stones, it's all but your real name, isn't it? Lasciel."

"It's close," Shiela agreed quietly.

"Harry?" Butters whispered. His eyes were very wide. "Who are you talking to?"

"Shut up a minute, Butters," I said, staring at her. She regarded me quietly, her eyes now steady on mine. "That's what Billy was talking about. Bock started looking awfully odd when I was speaking to you at the bookstore. And you never interacted with anyone else. Never opened any doors in the store. Didn't pick up the book when I was looking for it." I glanced down at my hand, where she'd written her number in permanent ink. It was now gone. "Illusions," I said.

"Yes," she said calmly. "Some of appearance only. Some of seeming."

"Why?"

"To *help* you," she said. "I told you that I could not make open contact with your conscious mind. That is why I created Shiela." She gestured down at herself. "I wanted to help you, but I couldn't do it directly. So I tried to do it this way."

"So you lied to me," I said.

She arched a brow. "I had little choice in the matter."

"What about after you made contact with me?" I said, and my voice was bitter too. "I used the Hellfire and you came to me in a dream."

"That was after you met Shiela, if you will recall," she said.

"But you didn't *need* Shiela anymore."

"No," she said. "I didn't. But I found that I . . ." She rolled her shoulders in a shrug. "That I enjoyed being Shiela. That I enjoyed interacting with you as one person to another. Without being regarded with fear and suspicion. I know that you understand what it is like. You've felt it often enough in your own life."

"But oddly enough," I said, "I haven't gone off and pretended to be someone else to gain another's trust."

"You've felt that isolation for less than two score years, my host. I've lived with it for millennia."

"Yeah? How long were you planning on stringing me along?"

Her soft mouth turned into a firm line. "I was going to tell you once the night's business was done—assuming you lived through it."

"Sure you were," I said.

"I told you," she said. "I didn't want it to become a distraction for you."

I barked out a harsh little laugh. "And why should I believe that?"

"Because your death would mean the death of this part of me," she said, gesturing down at herself again. "The thought shadow of Lasciel would not survive your death—and the true Lasciel, my true self, would remain trapped for who knows how long. You have no idea of what it is to be trapped without sound, sight, or senses, waiting for someone to bring you forth from oblivion."

I stared hard at her. "I don't believe you."

"You need not, my host," she said, and gave me a little bow. "But that makes it no less true."

"You *kissed* me," I said.

Shiela-Lasciel's eyebrows lifted and she gave me an almost whimsical smile. "When I said that it has been a long time since I was close to anyone, I meant it. I enjoyed that contact, my host. As, I think, did you."

"Oh, let me guess," I said. "You did that for me, too. Because you wanted to help me."

"I kissed you because I desired it and because it was pleasurable. If you will recall, my host, I *did* help you. I gave you the summons to call the Erlking, did I not?"

I opened my mouth and then closed it again, struggling to find something to say.

"I have never wished you ill, my host," she said. "In fact, I have done all that I can to assist you."

I suddenly felt very tired and rubbed at my forehead. I reminded myself that Lasciel was a fallen angel. That she was one of the thirty demons of the Order of the Blackened Denarius. That she was known as the Temptress and the Webweaver, and that she was ancient, powerful, and deadly dangerous at the art of manipulation.

She could not be trusted; nor could her little carbon copy that had taken up residence in my head.

But she had helped me. And she had kissed me. Sure, a kiss was just a kiss, but her desire for it, her hesitation, the sense of yearning to her had been genuine. She had wanted to do it. She had enjoyed it. She was one hell of a good kisser.

Hell *being the operative word,* I reminded myself.

"I can still help you, my host," she said. "You are a powerful mortal, but your foes are more formidable still. They will kill you." Her face took on an expression of frustrated protest. "Let me help you survive. Give me the chance to preserve myself. Please."

I stared at her for a moment. She looked lovely and sincere and afraid.

She looked exactly like the kind of woman in trouble whom I could never turn away.

"I have no intention of dying," I said quietly. "But you aren't going to be part of the equation."

"If you don't—"

"Save it," I told her quietly. "I know how this works. First I allow you to help with this problem. Then with the next one. Then with the one after that. And at some point I'll need more power for what will probably look like a very good reason and dig up the coin. And then you'll be able to do pretty much anything you want with me." I shook my head. "That's one big, long, slippery slope. No."

She clenched her jaw, her expression frustrated. "But I do not wish you any harm."

"Maybe," I said. "But there's no way for me to know that."

She arched one dark eyebrow at me.

Then, as quickly as blinking, the building was on fire. It rose up in a sudden explosion of heat and flame that engulfed the bare studs on the walls and chewed at the floor. Vicious heat assaulted my back, a searing pain that left me with no choice but to move forward. Behind me the fire roared up higher, and I looked around frantically, suddenly panicked. The only portion of the building that wasn't being swallowed by rising, hungry flame led to the broken window. I sprinted to it, spotted the old iron of a fire escape lattice beneath it, and ducked down to go through onto the fire escape before I was burned to charcoal.

And then the flames vanished, the air became cool once more, and the beat of rain replaced the roar of flame. I stood at the window, one leg raised onto the sill, the rain soaking my chest and my jeans.

And there was no fire escape outside the window.

There was only a long, long drop to the sidewalk beneath.

I swallowed and drew back from the window, shaking. The whole thing had happened so *fast*. My reaction to the fire had been sheer and naked terror, and even now my hand throbbed with the pain of illusory burns. Ever since that fire I'd had nightmares of more. The illusion of fire had cut straight through to my pain and terror and utterly bypassed my brain.

Which was exactly what Lasciel meant it to do.

"Harry?" Butters called, his voice high and thready. I couldn't see him. He stood back in the darkness of the empty building, and in my mindless panic I had allowed the light of my mother's pentacle to go out.

"I'm okay," I told him. "Just stay where you are. I'm coming."

I lit the pentacle again, and found Lasciel standing next to me, one eyebrow still raised. "That is how you know," she said. "If I wished to kill you, my host, your blood would be seeping from your broken corpse and mixing with the rain on the sidewalk."

There wasn't much I could say to that.

"Let me help you," she urged me. "I can help you defend yourself against the disciples of Kemmler. I can teach you magics you have never considered. I can show you how to make yourself stronger, swifter. I can show you how you might heal the damage to your hand, if you have enough discipline. There wouldn't even be a scar."

I turned my back on her. My heart pounded against my chest as I walked back to Butters.

She was lying to me. She had to be. That's what the Denarians did. They lied and manipulated their way into a mortal's good graces, gradually giving them more power while they fell more deeply under their demonic influence.

But she was telling the truth about one thing, for sure: She could make me stronger. Even the weakest Denarian I had seen, Quintus "Snakeboy" Cassius, had been a certifiable nightmare. With Hellfire to supplement my magic and an enormously powerful being to serve as a tutor and consultant, my abilities could grow to epic proportions.

If I had power like that, I could protect my friends—Murphy, Billy, and the others. I could turn my power against the Red Court and help save the lives of the Wardens and the Council. I could do a lot of things.

And her kiss . . . The illusion had all been in my head, but it had been so utterly *real.* Every detail. Shiela herself had been so thoroughly genuine that I would never have guessed she was an illusion. Indeed, there was little difference, from my own perspective, between that complex an illusion and reality. The feel of her, the scent, everything had been there.

And she had been just as convincingly real in her blond-goddess form beside the hot tub in my dream. Her appearance had to be malleable. She could appear to me as anything.

As anyone.

Some darker, baser part of my nature toyed with *that* notion for a moment. But only for a moment. I didn't dare let that thought flow through my head for long. Her touch had been too soft, too gentle, too warm. Too good. I'd been without female company for years, and more of that warmth, that pleasing contact, was a temptation too great to allow myself to dwell upon.

I turned slowly and faced Lasciel.

She lifted her eyebrows, leaning a little forward in anticipation of my answer.

I knew how to manipulate and control my dreams—and this manifestation of Lasciel's shadow was nothing more than a waking dream.

"This is my mind," I told her quietly. "Get thee behind me."

I focused my thoughts and my power and brought forth my own illusion of imagination and thought. Silver manacles appeared from nowhere, manifested from my focus and desire, and locked themselves around Lasciel's wrists and ankles. I gestured sharply and visualized her being lifted through the air. Then I opened my hand, my spread fingers out, palm to the floor, and she fell into an iron cage that appeared from my concentrated effort. The door slammed and locked behind her.

"Fool," she said in a quiet voice. "We will die."

I closed my eyes and with a last effort of imagination and will summoned a heavy tarp that fell over the cage, covering it and blocking Lasciel from sight and sound.

"Maybe we will," I muttered to myself. "But I'll do it on my own."

I turned around to find Butters staring at me, his expression almost sick with fear. Mouse sat beside him, also staring at me, somehow managing to look worried.

"Harry?" he asked.

"I'm okay," I told him quietly.

"Um. What happened?"

"A demon," I told him. "It got into my head a while back. It was causing me to experience . . . hallucinations, I guess you could call them. I thought I was talking to people. But it was the demon, pretending to be them."

He nodded slowly. "And . . . and it's gone now? You did, like, some kind of autoexorcism?"

"Not gone," I said quietly. "But it's under control. Once I knew what it was doing, I was able to lock it away."

He peered at me. "Are you crying?"

I turned my face away, trying to make it look like I was staring at the window while I wiped a hand over my eyes. "No."

"Harry. Are you sure you're all right? Not, you know . . . insane?"

I looked back up at Butters and suddenly laughed. "Look who's talking, polka boy."

He blinked for a moment and then smiled a little. "I just have better taste than most."

I walked to him and rested my hand on his shoulder. "I'm all right. Or at least no crazier than I usually am."

He looked at me for a moment and then nodded. "Okay."

"Good thing you came along when you did," I said. "You tipped the demon's hand when you came up here. There was no way it could fit you into the illusion."

"I helped?" he said.

"Big-time," I said. "I think I'm just too used to knowing more than most people about magic. The demon was using some of my expectations against me. It knew exactly how to hide things from a wizard."

An idle thought flicked through my brain at the words. And suddenly I froze with my mouth open.

"Hell's bells," I swore. "That's it."

"It is?" Butters asked. "Er, *what* is?"

Mouse tilted his head to one side, ears perked inquisitively.

"How to hide things from a wizard," I said, and I felt my mouth stretching into a wide, half-crazy grin. I dug in my memory until I found the string of mystery numbers and recited them. "Ha!" I said, and threw my hand up in the air in triumph. "Hah! Ha-ha! Eureka."

Butters looked distressed.

"Let's go," I told him, rising excitement making tingles of nervous energy shoot through my limbs. I started walking to give some of it an outlet. "Come on, let's hurry."

"Why?" Butters asked, bewildered.

"Because I know what those numbers mean," I said. "I know how to find *The Word of Kemmler.* And to do it, I need your help."

Chapter

Thirty-six

The lights of Chicago were still out and the night was growing even darker. The storm had driven most people from the streets, and now headlights appeared only intermittently. The National Guard had set up around Cook County Hospital, bringing in generators and laboring to keep them running while providing a shelter of some sort and a presence of authority on some of the streets—but they were as badly hampered by the lack of reliable telephone and radio communications as anyone else, and rain and darkness had cast them into the same morass of confusion as the rest of the city.

The net result of it was that some streets were bright with the headlights of military trucks and patrolled by National Guardsmen, and some of them were as black and empty as a crooked politician's heart. One section of State Street was sunken in blackness, and I pulled the Beetle up onto the sidewalk in front of a darkened Radio Shack.

"Stay, Mouse," I told the dog, and got out of the car. I walked to the glass door and considered it and the bars on it. Then I leaned my staff against it, drew in my will, and muttered, *"Forzare."*

There was no flash of light with the release of energy—I'd kept the spell tidy enough to avoid that. Instead it all went into kinetic force, snapping the plate glass as cleanly as if I'd used a cutter, and bending the center bars out into a neat bow shape, large enough to slip through.

"Holy crap," Butters said, his voice a hushed shout. "You're breaking in?"

"No one's minding the store," I said. I nudged a few pieces of door that hadn't fallen out of the frame, then carefully slid into the building. "Come on."

"Now you're entering," Butters informed me. "You're breaking. *And* entering. We're going to jail."

I stuck my head out between the bars and said, "It's in a good cause, Butters. We're the secret champions of the city. Justice and truth are on our side."

He looked at the front of the store uncertainly. "They are?"

"They are if you *hurry* up before someone in a uniform spots us," I said. "Move it."

I went back into the store, lifting up my amulet and willing it to light. I stared around me at all the technological things, only a very few of which I could readily identify. I turned in a circle, looking for one particular gadget, but I had no idea where in the store it would be.

Butters came in and looked around. The blue light of my pentacle gleamed on his glasses. Then he nodded decisively at a section of counter and walked over to it.

"Is this it?" I asked him.

"Something wrong with your eyes?" he asked me.

I grimaced at him. "I don't get in here a lot, Butters. Remember?"

"Oh. Oh, yeah, right. The Murphyonic technology thing."

"Murphyonic?"

"Sure," Butters said. "You exude a Murphyonic field. Anything that can go wrong does."

"Don't let Murph hear you say that."

"Heh," Butters said. "Bring the light." I lifted it higher and stepped up behind him. "Yeah, yeah," he said. "They're right here under the glass." He peered around behind the counter. "There must be a key here somewhere."

I lifted up my staff and drove it bodily down through the glass, shattering it.

Butters looked a little wild around the eyes, but he said, "Oh, right, I forgot. Burglary." One hand darted in and plucked up an orange box. Then he looked around and picked up a couple of packs of batteries from a rack on the wall. He hadn't touched a thing but what he had taken with him, and neither had I. Without security systems, the only way we would get caught would be by finger-prints or direct apprehension, and I was glad we didn't have to take the time to wipe anything for prints before commencing the get-away.

I led Butters back to the car, and away we got.

"I can't see anything," Butters said. "Can you make the light again?"

"Not this close to the gadget," I told him. "A minute or two wouldn't be a problem, but the longer I work forces near it, the more likely it is to give out."

"I need some light," he said.

"All right, hang on." I found a spot near an alley and parked with the Beetle's headlights pointing at the overhanging awning of a restaurant. I left the car running and got out with Butters. He opened the box and took out the batteries and did gadgety things with them while I kept an eye out for bad guys, or possibly the cops.

"Tell me why you think this is it again?" Butters said. He had drawn a little plastic device the size of a small walkie-talkie from the box and fumbled with it until he found the battery cover.

"The numbers in Bony Tony's code are just longitude and lati-tude," I said. "He hides the book, see. He records the coordinates with one of those global satellite thingies all those soldiers raved about during Desert Storm."

"Global positioning system," Butters corrected me.

"Whatever. The point is that you need a GPS to find those spe-cific coordinates. They're accurate to what? Ten or twelve yards?"

"More like ten feet," Butters said.

"Wow. So Bony Tony figures that most wizards wouldn't have a clue about what a GPS device is—and the ones who do can't *use* one because they're high-tech, and running one even close to a wizard will short it out. It's his insurance, to make sure that Gre-vane can't screw him."

"But Grevane did," Butters said.

"Grevane did," I echoed. "The idiot. He never considered that Bony Tony might have been able to outfox him. So he knows that Bony Tony has got the key to finding *The Word of Kemmler* on him, but Grevane never even considers that it might be something he can't access. He just blunders along doing as he pleases, which he's used to."

"Whereas you," Butters said, "read books at the library."

"And magazines, 'cause they're free there," I said. "Though I have to give most of the credit to Georgia's SUV. I might not have thought of this if it hadn't had the same system."

"Note the past tense on that," Butters said. "Had." He glanced up at me pointedly. "I'm about to turn it on. Do you need to move off?"

I nodded at him and backed off all the way to the car and tried to think technologically friendly thoughts. Butters stood in the headlights for a minute, frowning down at the gadget and then peering up at the sky.

"What's wrong?" I asked.

"Signal isn't coming through very well. Maybe it's the storm."

"Storm isn't helping," I said back. "There's magic at work too." I chewed on my lip for a second. "Turn it off."

Butters did and then nodded at me. I hurried over to him and said, "Now hold still." Then I drew a piece of chalk from my duster pocket and marked out a quick circle around him on the concrete.

Butters frowned down at the chalk and said, "Is this . . . some kind of mime training? Do you want me to press my fingers against an invisible wall?"

"No," I said. "You're going to throw up a circle around you—an outwardly directed barrier. It should put a screen between you and any outside magical influence."

"I am, huh?" he said. "How do I do that?"

I completed the circle, reached for my penknife, and passed it to him. "You need to put a drop of your blood on the circle, and picture a wall going up in your head."

"Harry. I don't know magic."

"Anyone can do this," I said. "Butters, there isn't any time. The circle should hold out Cowl's working and give you a chance to get a signal normally."

"An anti-Murphyonic field, huh?"

"You've watched too many *Trek* reruns, Butters. But basically, yeah."

He pressed his lips together and then nodded at me. I backed away to the Beetle again. Butters grimaced and then touched the penknife to the base of his left thumbnail, where the skin is thin and fragile. Then he leaned over self-consciously and squeezed his thumb until a drop of blood fell on the chalk circle.

The circle barrier snapped up immediately, invisibly. Butters looked around for a second and then said, "It didn't work."

"It worked," I told him. "It's there. I can feel it. Try again."

Butters nodded and went back to his gizmo. Five seconds later, his face brightened. "Hey, whaddya know. It worked. So this circle keeps out magic?"

"And only magic," I said. "Anything physical can cross it and disrupt the barrier. Handy for hedging out demons and such, though."

"I'll remember that," Butters said. He peered down at the gadget. "Harry!" he exclaimed. "You were right! The numbers match up to coordinates right here in Chicago."

"Where?" I demanded.

"Hang on." The little guy punched buttons and frowned. "I have to get it to calculate distance and heading from here."

"It can do that?" I asked.

"Oh, yeah," he said. "Plus AM/FM radio, weather reports, fish and game reports, maps of major cities, locations of restaurants and hotels for travelers, all kinds of stuff."

"That," I said, "is really cool."

"Yeah. You really get a lot for the five hundred bucks on this model." The whole time his fingers flicked back and forth on the gadget. "Right," he said. "Uh, northwest of us and maybe a mile off."

I frowned at him. "Doesn't it tell you the address or something?"

"Yeah," Butters said, pushing more buttons. "Oh, wait. No, you have to buy the expansion card for that." He looked up thoughtfully. "Maybe we could go back and get it?"

"One little burglary and you've gone habitual," I said. "No, it's a bad idea. If a patrol car spotted the broken window there will be police there. I doubt anyone saw us, but there's no reason to take chances."

"Well, how do we find it then?" he asked.

"Turn it off. Then break the circle with your foot and get in the car. We'll head that way and stop in a bit and you can check again. Rinse and repeat."

"Right, good idea." He turned the gizmo off and smudged the chalk circle with his foot. "Like that?"

"Like that. Let's go."

Butters got in the Beetle and we started through the dark, dank streets. After several long blocks I stopped with my lights shining into the awning in front of an apartment building, and Butters got out to repeat the process. He took my chalk with him, dribbled a bit of his blood on the circle he drew, and tried the GPS gadget again. Then he hurried through the rain back into the car.

"More north," he said.

I peered at the darkness as I got moving, going through my mental map of Chicago. "Soldier's Field?"

"Maybe," he said. "I can't see anything."

We drove north and cruised past the home of da Bears. I stopped just on the other side and Butters checked again, facing the stadium. Then he blinked and turned around. His eyes widened and he came running back to the car. "We're really close. I think it's the Field Museum."

I got the car moving. "Makes sense," I said. "Bony Tony had plenty of contacts there. He did some trading in discretionary antiquities."

"You mean stolen artifacts?"

"What did I just say? He probably has some kind of arrangement with security there. Maybe he stashed it in a staff locker or something."

I parked in front of the Field Museum under a NO PARKING sign. There were a couple of actual spots I could have used, but the drive was even closer. Besides, I found it aesthetically satisfying to defy municipal code.

I put the Beetle's parking brake on and got out into the rain. "Stay, Mouse," I said. "Come on, Butters. Can that thing get us close to the book?"

"Within ten feet or so," he said. "But Harry, the museum is closed. How are we going to—"

I blew out the glass of the front door with my staff, just as I had at Radio Shack.

"Oh," he said. "Right."

I strode into the main hall, Butters walking on my heels. Lightning flashed, abruptly illuminating Sue the Tyrannosaurus in all her bony Jurassic glory. Butters hadn't been expecting it, and let out a strangled little cry.

Thunder rolled and I got out my amulet for light, lifting an eyebrow at Butters.

"Sorry," he said. "I, uh . . . I'm a little nervous."

"Don't worry about it," I told him, my own heart pounding wildly. The sudden reveal of that monstrous skeleton had shaken me, too.

Don't look at me like that. It was a tense sort of evening.

I looked slowly around the place, and Listened for a moment. I couldn't sense anyone's presence. I opened my Sight again, just for a quick glance around, but I didn't see anyone hiding behind a veil of magic. I backed off. "Check again."

He did so, though the shining floor of the museum didn't take the chalk as readily as concrete. A few minutes later he nodded toward Sue and said, "Over that way."

He broke the circle and we hurried across the enormous floor. "Try to keep quiet," I told him. "Security might still be around."

We stopped at Sue's feet and checked again. Butters frowned, peering around. "This can't be right," he said. "According to the GPS, these coordinates are inside that wall. Could Bony Tony have hidden it in the wall?"

"It's stone," I said. "And I think someone might have noticed if he'd torn out a wall in the entry hall and replaced it."

He shook the GPS a little. "I don't get it, then."

I chewed on my lip and looked up at Sue.

"Elevation," I said.

"What?"

"Come on." I pointed up. "There's a gallery overlooking the main hall. It must be either up there or on a floor below us."

"How do we know which?"

"We look. Starting with the upstairs. The levels below us are like some kind of gerbil maze from hell." I started for the stairs, and Butters came after me. Going up them was a pain, but my instincts were screaming that I was right, and my excitement made the discomfort unremarkable.

Once on the gallery, we went past a display of articles from

Buffalo Bill's Wild West Show—saddles, wooden rifles that had
been carried by the show's cowboys and Indians alike, cavalry bu-
gles, feathered war bonnets, beaded vests, moccasins, ancient old
boots, several worn old tom-toms, and about a million old photographs. Beyond that was some kind of interactive ecology display,
and just past that there was a table bearing the weight of an enormous, malformed-looking dinosaur skull.

Butters checked again and nodded toward the skull. "I think it's
there."

I went down to the skull. The display proclaimed that it was
Sue's actual skull, but that geological shifts and pressures had
warped it, so the museum had created an artificial skull for the display. Holding my light up, I walked slowly around the skull—an
enormous block of rock now. I peered into darkened crevices in the
rock, and when I didn't find a book I got down on the floor and
started checking under the heavy platform that supported the skull.

I found a manila envelope duct-taped to the underside of the
platform, and snatched it. I got out from under the platform and
tore the envelope open, my fingers shaking.

An old, slender black volume not much larger than a calendar
notebook fell from the envelope.

I held it in my bare right hand for a moment. There was no tin-
gle of arcane energies to the book, no sense of lurking evil or im-
minent danger. It was simply a book—but nonetheless I was sure I
had found *The Word of Kemmler.* My fingers shook harder, and I
opened it.

The front bore a spidery scrawl of cursive writing: *The Word of
Heinrich Kemmler.*

"Hey, that was kind of fun!" Butters said. "Is that it?"

"This is it," I said. "We found it." I glanced up at Butters and
said, "Actually, *you* found it, Butters. I couldn't have done it without your help. Thank you."

Butters beamed. "Glad I could help."

I thought I heard a noise.

I lifted a hand, forestalling whatever Butters was about to say.

The sound didn't repeat itself. There was only thunder and rain.

I put a finger to my lips and Butters nodded. Then I closed my eyes and reached out with my senses, slow and careful. For the barest second I felt my thoughts brush against a stirring of cold energy.

Necromancy.

I drew back from it with panicked haste. "Butters, get out."

The little ME blinked up at me. "What?"

"Get out," I said, my voice harsher. "There's a fire exit at the far side of the gallery. Go out it. Run. Get out of here and don't stop until you're someplace safe. Don't look back. Don't slow down."

He stared at me, his eyes huge, his face deathly pale.

"Now!" I snarled.

Butters bolted. I could hear terrified little sounds escaping his throat as he sprinted toward the far end of the gallery.

I closed my eyes and concentrated again, drawing in my will and power as I did so, casting my senses about in an effort to find the source of the dark power. I touched the necromantic working again, and this time I didn't even try to hide my presence by pulling away.

Whoever it was had come in through the door I'd broken open. I could feel a slithering sort of power there, mixed in with a cold kind of lust, a passion for despair.

I walked to the railing of the gallery and looked down into the entry hall.

Grevane stood below, trench coat wet and swaying, water dripping from the brim of his fedora. There was a half circle of dead men standing behind him, and he beat a slow rhythm on his leg with one hand.

I wanted to cut and run, but I couldn't. I had to hold things up here until Butters had a chance to get away. And besides, if I ran away, toward the back exit and nowhere near my car, Grevane's zombies would catch me and tear me apart.

I licked my lips, struggling to weigh my options.

Then I had an idea. Holding my pentacle's chain in my teeth for light, I opened the book and started flipping through it, one page after another. I didn't read it. I didn't even try to read it. I just opened the pages, fixed my gaze at a couple of points on each, and moved on.

It wasn't a long book. I was finished less than two minutes later.

There was a sound from the stairway, and I rose, readying my shield bracelet.

Grevane came onto the gallery floor, zombies marching behind him. He stood and stared at me for a moment, his expression impossible to read.

"Stay back," I said quietly.

He blinked at me very slowly. "Why?"

I held up the book in one hand. "Because I've got the *Word* here, Grevane. And if you don't back off, I'll burn it to ash."

His eyes widened, and he lurched a half step closer to me, licking his lips. "No, you won't," he said. "You know that. You want the power as much as I do."

"God, you people are dysfunctional," I said. "But just to save time I'll give you a reason that you're capable of understanding. I've read the book. I don't need it anymore. So if you push me, I'll be glad to flash-fry it for you."

"You didn't read it," Grevane spat. "You haven't had it for ten minutes."

"Speed-reading," I lied. "I can do *War and Peace* in thirty minutes."

"Give me the book," Grevane said. "I will allow you to live."

"Get out of my way. Or I will allow it to burn."

Grevane smiled.

And suddenly a weight fell on me, like someone had dropped a lead-lined blanket on my shoulders. My ears filled with rushing, hissing whispers. I stumbled and felt a dozen flashes of burning, needle-fine pain, and between that and the extra weight I fell to my knees. It took me a second to realize what was happening.

Snakes.

I was covered in snakes.

There were too many of them to count or identify, and they were all furious. Some dark green reptile as long as my arm struck at my face, sinking fangs into my left cheek and holding on. More of them struck at my neck, my shoulders, my hands, and I screamed in panic and pain. My duster took several hits, but the enspelled leather held out against them. I tore at my neck and shoulders and head, ripping snakes free of me by main strength, their fangs tearing at my flesh as I did.

I struggled to order my thoughts and rise, because I knew Grevane would be coming. I tried to gather my shield as I pushed myself to my hands and knees, but I saw a flash of a heavy boot driving toward me and light exploded in my eyes and I flopped back to the floor, briefly stunned.

I blinked slowly, waiting for my eyes to focus.

Liver Spots appeared in my vision, weathered and strange, white hair wiry and stiff beneath his hat, his loose skin somehow reptilian in the dim light.

"I know you," I slurred, the words tumbling out without checking in with my brain. "I know who you are now."

Liver Spots knelt down over me. He took my wrists and clamped something around them.

While he did, Grevane came up and took *The Word of Kemmler* from my limp fingers. He opened it and began scanning through pages until he found the passage he'd been looking for. He read it, stared at it for a long moment, and then opened his mouth in a slow, wheezing cackle.

"By the night," he said, his voice dusty and amused. "It's so simple. How could I not have seen it before?"

"You are satisfied?" Liver Spots asked Grevane.

"Entirely," Grevane said.

"And you will stand by our bargain."

"Of course," Grevane answered. He read another page of the book. "A pleasure working with you. He's all yours." Grevane turned, still beating a slow rhythm on his leg, and the shambling zombies followed him.

"Well, Dresden," Liver Spots said once they were gone. His voice was a rich, rough purr. "I believe you were saying you recognized me?"

I stared up at him blankly.

"Let me help your memory," he said. He took an olive-drab duffel bag from his shoulder and set it on the ground. Then, mostly with one hand, he opened it.

And he drew out a Louisville Slugger.

Oh, my God. I tried to move, but I couldn't. The metal bindings burned cold on my wrists.

"You," I said. "You busted up my car."

"Mmmm. Much as *you* broke my ankles. My knees. My wrists and my hands. With a Louisville Slugger baseball bat. While I lay helpless on the floor."

Quintus Cassius, the Snakeboy, the serpent-summoning sorcerer and former Knight of the Order of the Blackened Denarius, smiled down at me. He leaned over, kneeling and far too close to me for comfort, and whispered to me as if to a lover.

"I have dreamed of this night, boy," he purred, and gently stroked the side of my face with the baseball bat. "In my day, we would say that revenge is sweet. But times have changed. How do you say? Payback is a bitch."

Chapter

Thirty-seven

I stared up at the withered old man I'd called Liver Spots, and behind the loose skin, the wrinkles, the white wiry hair, I could see the man who had been one of the Order of the Blackened Denarius.

"How?" I asked him. "How did you find me?"

"I didn't," he said. "The coroner's apartment was easy enough to find. I took hairs from his brush. Since you were so eager to keep him sheltered under your wing, it wasn't too terribly difficult to keep track of him—and you—once we had destroyed your wards."

"Oh," I said. My voice shook a little.

"Are you afraid, boy?" Cassius whispered.

"You're about the fifth-scariest person I've met today," I said.

His eyes became very cold.

"Don't knock it," I said. "That's really better than it sounds."

He rose slowly, looking down at me. The fingers of his right hand tightened and loosened on the handle of the bat. Hatred burned there as well, mindless and irrational and howling to be slaked. Cassius hadn't exactly been stable when I'd faced him two years before. From the look of him now, he was preparing a campaign for the presidency of the World Psychosis Association.

I knew that Cassius was a killer, like few I'd ever seen. He had spent what might have been fifteen or sixteen centuries bound to a different fallen angel within his own silver coin, working hand in hand with the head of the Order. He had, I was sure, personally done away with hundreds of foes who had done far less to him than I had.

He would kill me. If a flash of rage took him, he'd cave my head in with that bat, screaming the whole time.

I shuddered at the image and reached out for my magic, seeing if I could draw in enough to try to sucker punch him. But when I tried, the manacles on my wrists suddenly *writhed,* moving, and dozens of sharp points suddenly pricked into my wrists, as if I had swept my hand through a rosebush. I winced in pain, my breath frozen in my chest for a second.

Cassius smiled at me. "Don't bother. We've used those manacles on wizards and witches for centuries. Nicodemus himself designed them."

"Yeah. Ouch." I winced, but no amount of writhing would move my arms very much, and I couldn't move to try to make the thorny manacles hurt less.

Cassius stared down at me, his eyes bright. He stood there, watching me try to writhe, enjoying my helplessness and pain.

An image flashed through my mind—an old man of faith and courage who had willingly given himself into the hands of the Order in exchange for my freedom. Shiro had died after sustaining the most hideous torments I had ever seen visited upon a human body—and some of them had come at the hands of Cassius. I closed my eyes. I knew what he wanted. He wanted to hurt me. He wanted to see how much pain he could deliver before I died. And there was nothing I could do to prevent it.

Unless . . .

I thought of what Shiro had told me about having faith. For him it was a theological and moral truth upon which he had based his life. I didn't have the same kind of belief, but I had seen how forces of light and darkness came into conflict, how imbalances were redressed. Cassius was in the service of some of the darkest forces on the planet. Shiro would have said that nothing he did could have prevented a balancing force of light—such as Shiro and his brother Knights—from being placed in his way. In my own experience, I had noticed that when something truly, deeply evil arose, one of the Knights tended to show up.

Maybe one would show up to face Cassius.

Hell's bells. That was mighty thin.

But it was technically possible. And it was all I had.

I almost laughed. What I needed to survive this lunatic was something I had never had much of: faith. I had to believe that some other factor would intervene. I had no other option.

But that didn't mean I couldn't try to help intervention along. The longer I kept breathing, the more likely it was that someone would happen across the scene—maybe even someone who could help. Maybe even someone like my friend Michael.

I had to keep Cassius talking.

"What happened to you?" I asked him a moment later, opening my eyes. I'd read somewhere that people love to talk about themselves. "The last time I saw you, you could have passed for forty."

Cassius stared at me for a moment more, and then leaned his bat on the floor. "It was the result of losing my coin to you and your friends," he said, voice creaking. "While I held my coin, Saluriel prevented age from ravaging my body. Now nature is collecting her due from me. Plus interest." He waved his stiff-fingered right hand, wrinkled, spotted, swollen with what looked like bad arthritis. "If she has her way, I will be dead within the year."

"Why?" I asked him. "Isn't your new demon stopping the clock for you?"

His eyes narrowed, unsteady and cold. "I have no Denarius now," he said, his voice low and very polite. "When I eventually left the hospital and rejoined Nicodemus, he had no coin being held as a spare." Mad fire flickered through his gaze. "You see, he'd given it to you."

I swallowed. "That's what you were looking for, outside my apartment. You wanted the Denarius."

"Lasciel wouldn't be my first choice, but I must be content with what is available."

"Uh-huh. So where's Nicodemus? He's helping you, I take it."

Cassius's eyes closed almost all the way. "Nicodemus cast me out. He said that if I was too much a fool to keep possession of my coin that I deserved whatever befell me."

"What a guy."

Cassius shrugged. "He is a man of power, with no tolerance for fools. Once you are dead and Lasciel's coin is mine, he will take me back."

"You sound pretty confident there," I said.

"Is there some reason I should not be?" He moved stiffly over to his duffel bag. "You should make this simpler for both of us. I'm willing to make you an offer. Give it to me now, and I will make your death quick."

"I don't have it," I told him.

He let out a rough cackle. "There are only so many places one can hide it," he said. "If you are holding it as part of you, enough pain will make you drop it." He drew out a slender little coping saw from the bag and set it on the floor. "I once knew a man who swallowed his Denarius, and would swallow it again when it came through."

"Yuck," I said.

Cassius put a standard-head screwdriver down next to the saw. "And one who cut himself open and placed the coin in his abdominal cavity." He drew a vicious-looking hooked linoleum knife from the bag and held it thoughtfully. "If you tell me, I'll take your throat."

"And if I don't?" I asked.

He pared a yellowed fingernail with the knife. "I go on a treasure hunt."

I studied him for a minute, then said, "I don't have it with me. That's the truth. I bound Lasciel and buried the coin."

He let out a snarl and snatched at my left hand. He tore my glove from it, and then twisted my hand to show me my own horribly scarred palm, and the name-sigil of the demon Lasciel upon it, the only skin that wasn't layered in scar tissue. "You *have* it," he spat. "And it is *mine*."

I took a deep breath and tried to embrace an optimistic conviction in the moral rectitude of my cause; to think positive.

Hey, hideous torture would draw things out. It wasn't the way I would have chosen to stall Cassius, but again, I wasn't spoiled for choice.

"I'm telling you the truth," I said. "Besides, you wouldn't have made it quick, even if I did give it to you."

He smiled. It looked grandfatherly. "Probably," he agreed. He reached into the duffel bag again and pulled out a three-foot length of heavy chain, the kind they used to use for bicycle locks. He held it in one hand while he moved my wrists, lifting them so that I lay flat on my back, my arms outstretched over my head. "I'm a winner either way."

I wasn't strong enough to move them. The damned manacles made me weaker than a newborn kitten.

"Surrender your coin," Cassius said pleasantly. Then he gave me a hard kick in the ribs.

It drove the breath from me and hurt like hell. I managed to choke out the words, "Don't have it."

"Surrender your coin," he said again. And this time he swung the chain and lashed it down hard over my stomach. My duster was open and the chain tore through my shirt and ripped at the flesh of my belly. My vision went red with a sudden haze of agony. "I d-d-don't . . ." I began.

"Surrender your coin," he purred. And he hit me again with the chain.

Rinse and repeat. I don't know how many times.

An eternity later, Cassius touched his tongue to some of the blood on the chain and regarded me thoughtfully. "I hope you aren't too impatient for me to get the bat," he said. "You see, my balance is quite unsteady these days. I'm told it's a result of all the damage to my knees and ankles."

I lay there hurting. My belly and chest were on fire. Blood from one of the snakebites had trickled into my left eye, and had crusted my eyelashes together so that I couldn't open it again.

"You see, I've only got this one good hand to swing the bat with. My other was badly broken by multiple blunt-impact traumas. One-handed, I'm afraid it's difficult to aim properly or judge the power of my swing."

I tried to look around me, but I couldn't get my right eye to move properly.

"As a result," Cassius continued, "once I start paying you back for what you did to me, I'm afraid it's quite likely that I might hit you too hard and too many times. And I want to savor this."

Where was Michael? Where was . . . anyone?

Cassius leaned down and said, "And when I start, Dresden, I

want to be free to indulge myself. To really let go and live the moment. I'm sure you understand."

No one is coming to save you, Harry.

I rasped, "I told you."

He paused, eyebrows lifted, and rolled a hand. "Pray continue."

"Told you," I said, and it was marred with a groan. "Told you if I ever saw you again I would kill you."

He let out a low, amused little chuckle and put the chain down.

He picked up the linoleum knife. Then he knelt stiffly down beside me, and calmly cut my shirt open and spread it and my duster away from my abdomen. "I remember," he said. "One should never make promises one cannot keep."

"I didn't," I told him quietly.

"Best you hurry then," he told me. "I can't imagine you have more than a few moments to make good." He prodded my belly with his finger, drawing a gasp of pain from me. "Mmmm. Nice and tender now. The better to cut through."

I watched the knife move, slow and bright and beautiful. Time seemed to slow down as it did.

Dammit, I was *not* going to die. I was not going to let this murderous bastard kill me. I was going to survive. I didn't know how I would do it, but my will locked onto the notion and I found myself grinding my teeth. I had shown him mercy before. He'd had his chance to walk away. I was going to live. And I was going to kill him.

The knife bit into the muscle of my stomach. He moved it very slowly, staring at the inner edge of the hooked blade as he drew it toward my groin in a gradually deepening incision. It hurt almost as much as the chain, but it left me with enough breath to scream.

I did. I howled at him at the top of my lungs. I shrieked profanities at him. I even managed to twitch my body a little, and I began calling up my will again, bringing fresh agony from the manacles.

He finished his first long, shallow, almost delicate cut, lifted the knife from my flesh, and repositioned it beside the first. The whole while I never stopped ranting at the top of my lungs. I doubted it was coherent enough to understand—but it described my feelings perfectly. I screamed and I kept on screaming.

And because I did, Cassius never heard Mouse's claws on the marble floor.

The air suddenly shook with a bellowing, damned near leonine roar. Cassius's head whipped around in time to see my dog leap from twenty feet away and hurtle forward like a grey-furred wrecking ball.

Mouse's front paws hit Cassius squarely on the sternum, and a bloodcurdling snarl exploded from the huge dog's chest as they both went down. Mouse snapped his jaws at Cassius's throat, but he had too much momentum remaining from his charge. His paws slid on the smooth floor, carrying him past Cassius before his teeth could do more than lightly rip at one shoulder.

Cassius screamed in rage, crouching, and flicked his hand at Mouse. There was a surge of dark magic, a shimmering blur, and suddenly a serpent coalesced from the shadows lying upon the gallery. It reared up for a second, and I could see the deadly outline of a cobra's hood rising a good five feet from the floor. Then the serpent launched itself at Mouse.

My dog saw it coming, sprang back from the serpent's first strike, and then leapt forward, jaws trying to latch on behind the shadow serpent's head. Lashing loops of reptilian darkness whipped into coils that tried to trap the big dog, and the pair of them rolled along the floor, each seeking to grasp and kill the other.

Cassius stared at Mouse for a second, eyes wide, and then turned to me. There was actual, literal foam at the corner of his mouth, and his face was stretched into a grotesque grimace of fury. He lurched over to my side, speaking a language I didn't recognize in a half-hysterical shriek. Then he seized my hair, jerked my head back to bare my throat, and swept the knife down toward my jugular.

Before his arm was halfway down, there was a thin, high-pitched, tinny-sounding wail. Butters threw himself onto Cassius's back, carrying them both over me and to the floor. The knife missed me entirely, and went skittering away on impact.

Cassius snarled another oath and tried to crawl for the knife. Butters tried to pull Cassius away, his face deathly pale. The little guy had all the fighting prowess of a leatherback turtle, but he got his arms and legs around Cassius's torso and clung like a wild-haired monkey.

Cassius's body may have been weakened, but he'd had more than a millennium to learn about infighting. He twisted his shoulders and then slammed the side of his head into Butters's nose with a crunching sound of impact. Butters reeled from the blow, and blood spattered his face and upper lip.

Cassius then twisted again and escaped Butters's grip. He heaved himself toward the knife.

"Butters!" I screamed, helpless to move and furious and terrified. "Don't let him get the weapon!"

The little medical examiner shook his head once, then let out that tinny wail of challenge again and threw himself at Cassius. Butters caught him around one leg. Cassius kicked at his face, but Butters ducked his head down and the blows rolled off his shoulders. Cassius pushed himself a little closer to the knife.

Butters lifted his head with a squeak of defiance and sank his teeth into Cassius's leg.

The former Denarian howled in sudden, startled pain.

Another bellowing roar shook the gallery, and I looked up to see Mouse gripping the shadow serpent's neck in his heavy jaws. Mouse shook his head violently. There was a burst of crunching sounds, and suddenly the shadow serpent stiffened and then abruptly dissolved into gallons and gallons of translucent, gelatinous ectoplasm.

Butters yelped and I looked up to see Cassius holding the knife, sweeping it clumsily at his opponent. Butters skittered away from the knife, eyes wide with terror.

But he skittered directly between Cassius and me.

And held his ground.

Mouse didn't skip a beat after killing the serpent. This time he rushed forward low, his snarls in chorus with the growling of thunder outside. He hit Cassius at the knees with the full power of his body, and Cassius went down like a tenpin before a bowling ball.

Butters rushed forward and kicked at Cassius's knife hand. The weapon skittered away again, over the edge of the gallery and into the great hall below. Cassius kicked at Butters and got him in the shins, sending Butters to the floor.

Cassius got out from under Mouse and lurched for me, his eyes mad, his hands outstretched in strangling claws.

Mouse landed on his back, and the huge dog's jaws closed on the man's neck.

Cassius froze in place in sudden terror, his eyes very wide. He stared at me.

For a second there was total silence.

"I gave you a chance," I told him, my voice quiet.

Quintus Cassius's liver-spotted face went pale with horrified comprehension. "Wait."

"Mouse," I said. "Kill him."

I had only one open eye with which to watch Cassius meet his end. But in that final second, rage and terror and horrified realization flashed through his eyes. And just as Mouse's jaws crushed the delicate bones of his neck, there was a flare of ugly energies, a flash of unholy purplish light around him, and he spoke words that rang in echoes totally out of proportion to their volume.

"DIE ALONE," he spat.

A flood of power hit me and my vision went black.

The last thing I heard was the snapping of bone.

Chapter

Thirty-eight

I didn't wake up.

It was more like I felt myself putting together some kind of awareness, the way a stagehand constructs a set. Evidently I was a minimalist, because the reality I awoke to was a bare black floor, a single hanging lamp overhead, and three chairs.

I walked forward into the light and stared at the chairs.

In one sat Lasciel, again in her angelic, blond, wholesome form. She wasn't wearing the white tunic, though. Instead, she was clothed in an Illinois Department of Corrections prison jumpsuit. The orange suited her hair and complexion quite well. She wore prison shackles, wrists and feet, and sat primly in her chair.

In the second chair was me. Well. It was a version of me, some kind of subconscious alter ego of mine. His hair was clipped shorter and neater than mine, and he wore a dark beard that was kept in similar fastidious order. He wore a black silk shirt, black trousers, and his hands (both of them) were unmarred, his fingertips held together in a steeple that rested on his chin.

"Another dream," I said, and sighed. I slumped down into the third chair. I looked more or less as I had when I woke up that morning. My shirt was slashed open, though there wasn't any blood on my torso, and my skin hadn't been pounded and ripped with a chain. Wishful thinking.

"Not precisely a dream," the subconscious me said. "Call it a meeting of the minds."

Lasciel smiled, very slightly.

"No," I said, and pointed at Lasciel. "I've said everything I intend to say to her." I turned to my alter ego—though on thinking about it, maybe alter id was more accurate. "As for you, you're sort of a jerk. And the whole look you've got going there says 'evil wizard,' which I am now professionally opposed to."

Alterna-Harry sighed. "I've told you before. I'm not some sort of dark demon. I'm simply the more primal essence of yourself. The one most concerned with such matters as food. Survival." His dark eyes flickered idly over Lasciel. "Mating," he said, a lazy growl to the tone. He looked back to me. "The important things in life."

"That I am even having this dream probably means that I need a good therapist," I said. I stared at my other self and said, "It was you, wasn't it? You wanted to pick up the coin."

"Make sure you remember that I am a part of you before you point any fingers," he said. "And yes. The potential for power in an alliance with Lasciel"—he inclined his head to her, a courtly, gentlemanly gesture, damn his chivalrous eyes—"was too great to simply ignore. There are too many things out there determined to kill you. So long as you keep Lasciel's coin, you both have the option to seek more power if necessary to protect yourself or others, *and* you prevent the coin from being used by unscrupulous sorts like Cassius."

I grimaced. "So?"

"So," he said. "This is a time to consider employing a portion of that power."

I stared at him and said, "You've been talking to her behind my back."

"For months," he said calmly. "It was only polite. After all, you wanted nothing to do with her."

"You asshole," I said. "The whole reason I wasn't talking was that I didn't want the temptation."

"I did," my subconscious said. "Honestly, you should listen to me more often. If you'd taken my advice about Murphy, she wouldn't be in Hawaii. In bed with Kincaid."

Lasciel coughed gently and said, "Gentlemen. If I might offer a suggest—"

Both I and my alternative self said, at the same time and in exactly the same voice, "Shut up."

Lasciel blinked, but did.

My double and I eyed each other, and I nodded slowly. "We're in agreement, then, that her presence and her influence are dangerous."

"We are," my double said. "She must not be allowed to dictate actions or to direct our choices through suggestion or manipulation." My double looked at her and said, "But she can and should be used as a resource, under careful control. She can offer us enormous amounts of information." He eyed her again and said, "And amusement."

Lasciel left her eyes down and smiled, very slightly.

"No," I said. "I've got Bob when I want information. And if I want sex, I'll . . . figure out something."

"You don't have Bob now," my double said. "And you've wanted sex since about twenty minutes after the last time you had it."

"That's beside the point," I told him sullenly. "I'm not quite insane enough to let a fallen angel give me virtual nooky, just for kicks."

"Listen to me," he said, and his voice became sharp, commanding. "Here's the cold truth. You are determined to take us into battle against forces you cannot possibly overcome through main strength. Not only that, but your source of assistance, the Wardens, may also turn against you if they learn the truth about what you're attempting. You are wounded. You are out of contact with your other allies."

"It's the right thing to do," I said, setting my jaw.

My double rolled his eyes. "Tell me, is it morally necessary for you to die in the process?"

I glowered at him.

"This meeting is just a formality, you know," he said. "You are already planning on asking Lasciel's shadow for her help. That's why you read through the book as you did before it was taken from you. You wanted it to go through your mind so that she could see it, and provide you with the text as she did for the summoning of the Erlking."

I lifted a finger. "I only did that in case I wasn't able to pry enough out of Grevane to figure out exactly what Kemmler's disciples are doing."

My double arched a brow. "How'd that work out for you?"

"Don't be a wiseass," I said.

"The point," he said, "is that you have little or no chance to prevail if you blindly rush in. You must know how they intend to manipulate these energies. You *must* know if there is a weak time or place at which to assault them. You must know the details of the Darkhallow, or you might as well cut your own wrists."

"Don't have to," I told him. "I could just sit and wait for the Erlking to come by."

"Six of one, half a dozen of another," my double agreed. "In addition, your body is in no condition to do *anything* at the moment." He leaned forward. "Free her to help us."

I inhaled slowly and stared at Lasciel for a moment. Then I said, "After I killed Justin and got my head together at Ebenezar's place, I promised myself something. I promised that I would live my life on my own terms. That I knew the difference between right and wrong and that I wouldn't cross the line. I wouldn't allow myself to become like Justin DuMorne."

"Don't you want to survive?" my double asked.

I rose from the chair and started walking into the darkness outside the light. "Of course I do. But some things are more important than survival."

"Yeah," my double said. "Like the people who are going to get killed when you die and don't stop Kemmler's disciples."

I froze at the edge of the darkness.

"Take the high road if you want to," my double said. "Choose to walk away from this strength in the name of principle. But after your noble death, everyone you no longer protect, everyone who might one day have come to you for help, everyone who is killed in the aftermath of the Darkhallow—*every* life you might have protected in the future will be on your head."

I stared at the darkness and then closed my eyes.

"Regardless of where it came from, Lasciel offers you the power of knowledge. If you turn aside from that power—power only *you* can take up—then you abandon your commitment to protect and defend those who are not strong enough to do it themselves."

"No," I said. "That isn't . . . that isn't my responsibility."

"Of course it is," my subconscious said, voice clear and sharp. "You coward."

I stopped and turned, staring at him.

"If you go to your death rather than do everything you might to prevent what is happening, you are merely committing suicide and trying to make yourself feel better about it. That is the act of a coward. It is beneath contempt."

I went through the logic of his argument and didn't make any headway against it—of course. While my double might look like another person, he wasn't. He was me.

"If I open this door now," I said slowly. "I might not be able to close it again."

"Or you might," my double said. "I have no intention of allowing her any control. So you will be the one who determines it."

"What if I can't contain her again once she is freed?"

"Why shouldn't you be able to? It's your mind. Your will. Your choice. You still believe in free will, do you not?"

"It's dangerous," I said.

"Of course it is. And now you must choose. Will you face that danger? Or will you run from it, and so condemn those who need your strength to their deaths?"

I stared at him for a minute. Then I looked at Lasciel. She waited, her eyes steady, her expression calm.

"Can you do it?" I asked her bluntly. "Can you show me what was on those pages?"

"Of course," she answered, her manner one of subservience without a trace of resentment. "I would be pleased to offer you whatever assistance you permit."

She looked humble. She looked cooperative. But I knew better. The mere shadow of the fallen angel Lasciel was a vital and powerful force. She might look humble and cooperative, but if that was her true nature she wouldn't have fallen to begin with. I didn't think she was harboring murderous impulses or anything—my instincts told me that she was genuinely pleased to help me.

After all, that was the first step. And she had patience. She could afford to wait.

Dangerous indeed. Lasciel represented nothing less than the intrinsic allure of power itself. I had never sought to become a wizard. Hell, a lot of the time I thought about how nice things might be if I hadn't been one. The power had been a birthright, and if it had grown since then, it had done so by the necessity of survival. But I'd tasted a darker side to the possession of power—the searing satisfaction of seeing an enemy fall to my strength. The lust to test myself against another, to challenge them and see who was the strongest. The mindless hunger for more that, if once indulged, might never be slaked.

One of the coldest, most evil souls I have ever encountered once told me that the reason I fought so hard to do what seemed right was that I was terrified to look within me and see the desire to cease the fight and do as I would, free of conscience or remorse.

And now I could see that he had been right.

I looked at the fallen angel, patiently waiting, and was terrified.

But there were innocent lives at stake: men and women and children who needed protection.

If I didn't give it to them, who would?

I took a deep breath, reached into my pocket, and found a silver key there. I threw it to my double.

He caught it and rose. Then he unlocked Lasciel's shackles.

Lasciel inclined her head to him respectfully. Then she walked over to me, gorgeous and warm in the harsh light, her eyes lowered. Without a trace of self-consciousness, she sank down to her knees, bowed her head, and said, "How may I serve you, my host?"

I opened my eyes and found myself on my back. There was a candle burning nearby. Mouse had curled himself protectively around my head, and his tongue was flicking over my face, rough and wet and warm.

I hurt absolutely everywhere. I'd learned to block out pain under the harsh lessons of Justin DuMorne, but it went only so far.

Lasciel had shown me a different technique.

I couldn't have explained to anyone what I did. I wasn't sure that I understood it myself, at least on a conscious level. I simply knew. I gathered the pain together and fed it into a burning fire of determination in my thoughts, and it began to steadily recede.

I exhaled slowly and began to sit up. My brain registered the screaming torture of the muscles in my stomach—it just wasn't horribly important, and took up little of my attention.

"My God, Harry," Butters said. His voice was thick and slurred, as if he were holding his nose. His hand pushed on my shoulder. "Don't sit up."

I let him push me back down. I needed a couple of minutes to let the pain continue to fade. "How bad is it?"

He exhaled. "It's pretty hideous, but I don't think he actually perforated the abdominal wall. Skin and tissue damage, but you did some bleeding." He swallowed and looked a little green around the gills. "That's my best guess, anyway."

"You okay?"

"Yeah. Yeah, fine. It's just . . . I work with corpses because I just couldn't handle . . . you know . . . actual living people."

"Heh. You can eat lunch while looking at a three-month-old corpse, but first aid on my stomach is too much to handle?"

"Yeah. I mean, you're still alive. That's just weird."

I shook my head. "How long was I out?" I was surprised at how calm and steady my voice sounded.

"It's been about fifteen minutes," Butters said. "I found some bandages and alcohol in the old man's duffel bag. I've got your belly cleaned and covered, but I don't have much of an idea of how much trouble you're in. You need a hospital."

"Maybe later," I said. I lay on my back, poring over what Lasciel had given me about the writings in the book. Hell, the thing had been written in German. I didn't know German, but Lasciel had translated the text about the Darkhallow. It felt like we had talked about it for an hour or more, but dream time and real time aren't always lockstepped.

Butters's nose had swollen up. There was still some blood on his face, and he already had a matched set of gorgeously colorful black eyes. He leaned over and fussed with the bandages on my stomach.

"Hey," I said quietly. "I told you to run. I was doing that heroic rear-guard thing. You screwed it all up."

"Sorry," he answered, his voice serious. "But . . . I got outside and I couldn't run. I mean, I wanted to. I *really* wanted to. But after all you've done for me . . ." He shook his head. "I just couldn't do that."

"What did you do?"

"I ran around the outside of the museum. I tried to find help, but with all the rain and the dark there wasn't anyone around. So I ran to the car and got Mouse. I thought that maybe he could help you."

"He could," I agreed. "He did."

Mouse's tail thumped on the floor, and he kept on licking at my head. I realized, dully, that he was cleaning the dozens of tiny snakebites.

"But he couldn't have done it without you, Butters," I said. "You saved my life. Another five minutes and I'd have been history."

He blinked down at me for a moment and then said, "I did, didn't I?"

"Damned brave of you," I said.

His spine straightened a little. "You think?"

"Yeah."

"And check it out," he said, gesturing at his face, his mouth opening into a toothy smile. "I have a broken nose, don't I?"

"Absolutely," I said.

"Like I'm a boxer. Or maybe a tough-as-nails gumshoe."

"You earned it," I said. "Hurt?"

"Like hell," he said, but he was still smiling. He blinked a few times, the gears almost visibly spinning in his head, and said, "I didn't run away. And I fought him. I jumped on him."

I kept quiet and let him process it.

"My God," he said. "That was . . . that was so *stupid*."

"Actually, when you survive it gets reclassified as 'coura-geous.'" I reached out my right hand. Butters shook it, gripping hard.

He looked at Cassius's body, and his smile faded. "What about him?" he asked.

"He's done," I said.

"That's not what I mean."

"Oh," I said. "We'll leave the body here. No time to move it. He'll be a John Doe on the public records, and there probably won't be a heavy investigation. If we get out quick it shouldn't be an issue."

"No. I mean . . . I mean, my God, he's dead. We killed him."

"Don't kid yourself," I told him. "I'm the one who killed him. All you did was try to help me."

His brow furrowed and he shook his head. "That's not what I mean either. I feel sorry for him."

"Don't," I said. "He was a monster."

Butters frowned and nodded. "But he was also a man. Or was once. He was so bitter. So much hate. He had a horrible life."

"Note the past tense," I said. "Had."

Butters looked away from the corpse. "What happened there at the very end? There was a light, and his voice sounded . . . weird. I thought he'd killed you."

"He hit me with his death curse," I said.

Butters swallowed. "I guess it didn't work? I mean, because you're breathing."

"It worked," I told him. I'd felt that vicious magic grab hold of me and sink in. "I don't think he was strong enough to kill me outright. So he went for something else."

" 'Die alone'?" Butters asked quietly. "What does that mean?"

"I don't know," I said. "Not sure I want to." I took a deep breath and then exhaled. I didn't have enough time to lie there waiting to recover. "Butters, I don't have any right to ask this of you. I'm already in your debt. But I need your help."

"You have it," he said.

"I haven't even told you what it is," I said.

Butters smiled a little and nodded. "I know. But you have it."

I felt my lips peel back from my teeth in a fierce grin. "One little assault and you've gone habitual. Next thing I know you'll be forming a fight club. Help me up."

"You shouldn't," he said seriously.

"No choice," I said.

He nodded and then stood up and offered me his hand. I took it and rose, waiting to sway or pass out or throw up from the pain. I did none of those things. The pain was there, but it didn't stop me from moving or thinking. Butters just stared at me and then shook his head.

I found my staff, picked it up, and walked to the Buffalo Bill exhibit. Butters got the candle, and then he and Mouse kept pace. I looked around for a second, then picked up a long, heavy-duty extension cord running from an outlet on the wall to power some lights on an exhibit in the center of the room. I jerked it clear at both ends and gathered it into a neat loop. Once I had it, I passed it to Butters.

"What are you doing?" he asked.

"Preparing," I said. "I found out about the Darkhallow."

Butters blinked. "You did? How?"

I grunted. "Magic."

"Okay," he said. "What did you learn?"

"That this isn't a rite. It's a big spell," I said. "It all depends on drawing together a ton of dark spiritual energy."

"Like what?" he asked.

"Like a lot of things. The necromantic energy around animated corpses and manifested shades. The predatory spirits of ancient hunters. All the fear that's been growing since last night. Plus, the past several years have seen some serious magical turbulence around Chicago. Kemmler's disciples can put that turbulence to work for them, too."

"Then what?"

"They gather it together and get it going in a big circle. It creates a kind of vortex, which then funnels down into whoever is trying to consume the energy. Poof. Insta-god."

He frowned. "I'm not very clued in on this magic stuff, but that sounds kind of dangerous."

"Hell, yeah," I said, and crossed the room to a rack of riding equipment. "It's like trying to inhale a tornado."

"Holy crap," Butters said. "But how does that help us?"

"First of all, I found out that the vortex itself is deadly. It's going to draw off the life of every living thing around it."

Butters gulped. "It will kill everything?"

"Not at first. But when the wizard at the vortex draws down the power, it's going to create a kind of vacuum where all that power used to be. The vacuum will rip away the life energy of everything within a mile."

"Dear God. That will kill thousands of people."

"Only if they finish the spell," I said. "Until then, the farther back you are from it, the less it will do," I said. "But to get near the vortex, the only way to survive it is to surround yourself with necromantic energy of your own."

"Only those with ghosts or zombies need apply?" he asked.

"Exactly." I lifted a saddle from the rack. Then I got a second one. I hung both over opposite ends of my staff, and picked it up like a plowman's yoke, the saddles hanging. I started walking down the stairs.

"But wait," Butters said. "What are you going to do?"

"Get to the center of the vortex," I said. "The effort it will take to work this spell is incredible. I don't care how good Cowl is. If I hit him as he tries to draw down the vortex, it's going to shake his concentration. The spell will be ruined. The backlash will kill him."

"And everyone will be all right?" he asked.

"That's the plan."

He nodded and then stopped abruptly in his tracks. I felt his stare burning into my back.

"But, Harry. To get there you'll have to call up the dead yourself."

I stopped and looked over my shoulder at him.

Comprehension dawned in his eyes. "And you need a drummer."

"Yeah."

He swallowed. "Could . . . could you get in trouble with your people for doing this?"

"It's possible," I said. "But there's a technicality I can exploit."

"What do you mean?"

"The Laws of Magic specifically refer to the abuse of magic when used against our fellow human beings. Technically it only counts if you call up human corpses."

"But you told me that everyone only calls humans."

"Right. So while the Laws of Magic only address necromancy as used on human corpses, there usually isn't any need for a distinction. Nutty necromancers only call up humans. Sane wizards don't touch necromancy at all. I don't think anyone has tried something like this."

We reached the main level of the museum.

"It's going to be dangerous," I told him. "I think we can do it, but I can't make you any promises. I don't know if I can protect you."

Butters walked beside me for several steps, his expression serious. "You can't try it without someone's help. And if you don't stop it, the spell will kill thousands of people."

"Yes," I said. "But I can't order you to help me. I can only ask."

He licked his lips. "I can keep a beat," he said.

I nodded and reached my destination. I slipped my improvised yoke off my shoulders and dropped both saddles to the floor. My breathing was a little harsh from the effort, even though I barely noticed the pain and strain. "You'll need a drum."

Butters nodded. "There were some tom-toms upstairs. I'll go get one."

I shook my head. "Too high-pitched. Your polka suit is still in the Beetle's trunk, right?"

"Yes."

I nodded. Then I looked up. And up. And up. Another flash of lightning illuminated the pale, towering terror of Sue, the most complete Tyrannosaurus skeleton mankind has ever discovered.

"Okay, Butters," I told him. "Go get it."

Chapter

Thirty-nine

By the time we got outside, the storm had turned into something with its own vicious will. Rain lashed down in blinding, cold sheets. Wind howled like a starving beast, lightning burned almost continually across the sky, and the accompanying thunder was a constant, rumbling snarl. This was the kind of storm that came only once or twice in a century, and I had never seen its equal.

That said, the entire thing was nothing but a side effect of the magical forces now at work over the city. The apprehension, tension, fear, and anger of its people had coalesced into dark power that rode over Chicago in the storm. The Erlking's presence—I could still hear the occasional shrieking howl amidst the storm's angry roaring—stirred that energy even more.

I shielded my eyes from the rain as best I could with one hand, staring up at the lightning-threaded skies. There, a few miles to the north, I found what I had expected—a slow and massive rotation in the storm clouds, a spiral of fire and air and water that rolled with ponderous grace through its cycle.

"There!" I called back to Butters, and pointed. "You see it?"

"My God," he said. He clutched at my shoulders with both hands to hold himself steady, and his bass drum pulsed steadily behind me. "Is that it?"

"That's it," I growled. I shook the water from my eyes and clutched at the saddlehorn to keep my balance. "It's starting."

"What a mess," Butters said. He glanced behind us, at the broken brick and debris and wreckage of the museum's front doors. "Is she all right?"

"One way to find out," I growled. "Hah, mule!"

I laid my left hand on the rough, pebbled skin of my steed and willed it forward. The saddle lurched, and I clutched hard with my other hand to stay on.

The first few steps were the worst. The saddle sat at a sharp incline not too unlike that on a rearing horse. But as my mount gathered speed, the length of her body tilted forward, until her spine was almost parallel with the ground.

I didn't know this before, but as it turns out, Tyrannosaurs can *really* haul ass.

She might have been as long as a city bus, but Sue, despite her weight, moved with power and grace. As I'd called forth energy-charged ectoplasm to clothe the ancient bones, they had become covered in sheets of muscle and a hide of heavy, surprisingly supple quasi-flesh. She was dark grey, and there was a ripple pattern of black along her head, back, and flanks, almost like that of a jaguar. And once I had shaped the vessel, I had reached out and found the ancient spirit of the predator that had animated it in life.

Animals might not have the potential power of human remains. But the older the remains, the more magic can be drawn to fill them—and Sue was sixty-five *million* years old.

She had power. She had power in spades.

I had rigged the saddles to straddle her spine, just at the bend where neck joined body. I'd had to improvise to get them around her, using the long extension cords to tie them into place, and it had been ticklish as hell to get Butters on board without his losing the beat and destroying my control of the dinozombie. But Butters had pulled through.

Sue bellowed out a basso shriek that rattled nearby buildings and broke a few windows as she hurtled forward down the streets of the city. The blinding rain and savage storm had left the streets all but deserted, but even so, there were earthquakes less noticeable than a freaking Tyrannosaur. The streets literally shook under her feet. In fact, we left acres of strained, cracked asphalt behind us.

Here's something else I bet you didn't know about Tyrannosaurs: they don't corner well. The first time I tried to take a left, Sue swung wide, the enormous momentum of her body simply too much for even her muscles to lightly command. She swung up onto the sidewalk, crushed three parked cars under her feet, knocked over two light poles, kicked a compact car end over end to land on its roof, and broke every window on the first two floors of the building beside us as her tail lashed back and forth in an effort to counterbalance her body.

"Oh, my God!" Butters screamed. He kept hanging on to me with his arms, stabbing his legs out alternately to either side in order to operate the bass drum strapped on his back.

"They're probably insured!" I shouted. Thank God the streets weren't crowded that night. I made a note to be sure to have Sue slow down a little before we turned again, and kept the focus of my will on her, her attention on the task at hand.

Just before we turned onto Lake Shore Drive we hit a National Guard checkpoint. There were a couple of army Hummers there, their headlights casting useless cones of light into the night and storm, wooden roadblocks, and two luckless GIs in rain ponchos. As Sue bore down on them, the two men stared, their faces white. One of them simply dropped his assault rifle from numb hands.

"Get out of the way, fools!" I screamed.

The two men dove for cover. Sue's foot crashed down onto the hood of one Hummer, crushing it to the asphalt, and then we were past the checkpoint and pounding our way down the street toward Evanston.

"Heh," I said, looking back over my shoulder. "I'd love to hear how they explain *that* to their CO."

"You *crushed* that truck!" Butters shouted. "You're like a human wrecking ball!" There was a thoughtful pause, and then he said, "Hey, are we going anywhere near my boss's place? Because he just won't shut up about his new Jaguar."

"Maybe later. For now, look sharp," I told him. "She's a lot faster than I thought. We'll be there in just a minute." I ducked under the corner of a billboard as Sue went by it. "Whatever you do, keep that drumbeat going. Do you understand?"

"Right," Butters said. "If I stop, no more dinosaur."

"No," I called back. "If you stop, the dinosaur does whatever the hell it wants to."

Shouts rose up from a side street where a couple more

guardsmen saw us go by. Sue turned her head toward them and let out another challenging bellow that broke more windows and startled the guardsmen so much that they fell down. I felt a surge of simple, enormous hunger run through the beast I'd called up, as though the ancient animus I'd summoned from the spirit world was beginning to remember the finer things in life. I touched Sue's neck again, sending a surge of my will down into her, jerking her head back around with a rumbling cough of protest.

My ears rang in the wake of that vast sound, and I glanced over my shoulder to make sure Butters was okay. His face was pale.

"If this thing gets loose," he said. "That would be bad."

"Which is why you shouldn't stop the drum," I told him. If Sue went wild, I could scarcely imagine the potential carnage she could inflict. I mean, good grief. Look at all the senseless victims in *Jurassic Park II*.

We hit Evanston, the first suburb of Chicago proper, which is mainly separated from Chicago by the presence of trees on the streets and a few more homes than high-rises. But given that it's only a block or two away from the heart of Second City, the addition of trees and homes made it feel more like a park nestled down at the feet of the city.

I guided Sue into a gentler left turn onto Sheridan, slowing down enough to be sure that we wouldn't swerve off the street. As Sue headed in, I was suddenly struck with the realization of how fragile those homes seemed. Good Lord, another driving accident like the one back in town would result in a home being crushed, and not just some dents and broken windows. We would be moving among precisely the people I was trying to protect—families, homes with children and parents and pets and grandparents. Decent folks, for the most part, who just wanted to make their homes peaceful and secure and go about their lives.

Of course, if I didn't hurry up and stop the Darkhallow, every house I was now passing would be filled with its dead.

I checked the sky during the next long flicker of lightning and didn't like what I saw. The clouds were spinning faster, more broadly, and unnatural colors and striations had appeared in their formation. And we were almost under its center.

I guided Sue down another side street, and that's when I felt the cloud of power gathering before me. It swirled and writhed against my wizard's senses, sending tingling shafts of heat and cold and other, less recognizable sensations running through me. I shuddered at the disorienting strength of it.

There was magic being wrought ahead. A lot of it.

"There!" Butters shouted, pointing. "Down that way, that whole block is the campus!"

Lightning flashed again as I turned Sue down the street, and it was over the dinosaur's broad head that I saw Wardens battling for their lives in the street ahead.

They were in trouble. Luccio had them moving in a tight group around a cluster of . . . Hell's bells, around a group of children in colorful Halloween costumes. Morgan was at the head of the group, Luccio brought up the rear, and Yoshimo, Kowalski, and Ramirez were on the flanks.

Even as I watched, I saw dozens of rotting forms lurch out of the shadows ahead of them and charge. More came running in behind them, letting out wails of mad anger.

Luccio whirled to deal with them. And dear God, I suddenly saw the difference between a strong but somewhat clumsy young wizard and a master of the magic of battle.

Fire lashed from her left hand—not a gout of flame like I could call up, but a slender *needle* of fire so bright that it hurt the eyes to see. She swept it in an arc at thigh level, and every one of the zombies coming behind went tumbling to the ground amidst crackling sounds of shattering muscle and singeing meat. Another wave surged up behind the first. Luccio caught one of them in a grip of invisible power and hurled the undead into the ones behind, sending more of them to the ground, but a pair of the zombies got through.

Luccio ducked the grasping arms of the first, caught the thing by a wrist, and sent it stumbling aside with a twist of her body that reminded me of one of Murphy's moves. The second zombie drove a hammer-heavy blow at her head, but that slender blade she wore at her side swept up out of its scabbard and took off its arm at the elbow. Another move brought a chiming surge of some power I could feel even from half a block away singing through the silver steel of her sword, and she flicked it lightly at the zombie's head. The blade touched, there was a flash of light, and the zombie abruptly fell limp to the ground, the magic that had animated it disrupted and gone.

In less than five seconds, Luccio had simply wiped out thirty undead, and it hadn't even been a contest.

I guess you don't get to be commander of the Wardens by collecting bottle caps, either.

My eyes flickered back to the front of the group, where Morgan met the shock of another wave. His style was rougher and more brutal than Luccio's, but he got similar results. A heavy stomp of his foot sent a ripple through the earth that knocked undead to the ground like bowling pins. A gesture of his hand and wrist and a cry of effort drew grasping waves of concrete and earth up to clamp down on the fallen zombies. He closed his fist, and the earth tightened, drawing back down into the ground, cutting and tearing its way through undead flesh and ripping the zombies to shreds. One of the creatures was still mobile, and with a look of contemptuous impatience on his face, Morgan drew the broadsword at his hip—the one used for executions of wizards guilty of breaking one of the Laws of Magic—paused a beat to get the timing right, and then swung, once, twice, *snicker-snack,* and the zombie fell apart into a number of wriggling bits.

Several others got through here and there. Kowalski hammered one to the ground with unseen force, while beside him Yoshimo twisted a hand and the branches of a nearby tree reached down of their own accord, wrapped around the undead's throat, and hauled it up off the ground. Ramirez, a fighter's grin on his face, lashed out with some kind of bright green energy I had never seen before, and the zombie nearest him simply fell apart into what looked like grains of sand. As an afterthought, he drew his sidearm as a second creature charged him, and calmly put two rounds into its head from less than ten feet away. He must have been loaded up with hollow points or something, because the creature's head exploded like rotten fruit and the rest fell twitching to the ground.

None of the zombies got within ten feet of the terrified children.

More of them materialized out of the rain and the night, but Luccio and the Wardens kept moving steadily forward, burning and crushing and slicing and dicing their way across the street, furiously determined to get the children clear.

Which is probably why they didn't see the sucker punch coming.

Out of nowhere there was the roar of an engine, and an old Chrysler shot forward along the street. The driver pulled it into a sharp left turn as it got close to the Wardens and their charges, and the wet rain turned it into a broadside slide. The car swept forward like an enormous broom of iron and steel, and none of the Wardens were looking that way.

I cried out to Sue and hung on to the saddlehorn.

The car slid, sending out a bow wave of sheeting water from the wet street.

Ramirez's head snapped around toward the car and he shrieked a warning. But it was too late to get out of the way. The group was still under attack, and the mindless creatures that assaulted them cared nothing for self-preservation. They would continue the fight, and even if the Wardens could have run from the car, they would never survive being mobbed by the undead in the chaos. In a flash of insight, I realized that these were the same tactics Grevane had used at my apartment—ruthlessly sacrificing minions in order to defeat the enemy.

Everyone else's head turned toward the oncoming car.

The muscles of Sue's legs tensed, and the saddle lurched.

One of the little girls screamed.

And then the Tyrannosaur came down from the leap that had carried her over the besieged Wardens. Sue landed with one clawed foot on the street, and the other came down squarely on the Caddy's hood, like a falcon descending upon a rabbit. There was an enormous sound of shrieking metal and breaking glass, and the saddle lurched wildly again.

I leaned over to see what had happened. The car's hood and engine block had been compacted into a two-foot-thick section of twisted metal. Even as I looked, Sue leaned over the car in a curiously birdlike movement, opened her enormous jaws, and ripped the roof off.

Inside was Li Xian, dressed in a black shirt and trousers. The ghoul's forehead had a nasty gash in it, and green-black blood had sheeted over one side of his face. His eyes were blank and a little vague, and I figured he'd clipped his head on the steering wheel or window when Sue brought his sliding car to an abrupt halt.

Li Xian shook his head and then started to scramble out of the car. Sue roared again, and the sound must have terrified Li Xian, because all of his limbs jerked in spasm and he fell on his face to the street. Sue leaned down again, her jaws gaping, but the ghoul rolled under the car to get away from them. So Sue kicked the car, and sent it tumbling end over end three or four times down the street.

The ghoul let out a scream and stared up at Sue in naked terror, covering his head with his arms.

Sue ate him. Snap. Gulp. No more ghoul.

"What's with that?" Butters screamed, his voice high and frightened. "Just covering his head with his arms? Didn't he see the lawyer in the movie?"

"Those who do not learn the lessons of history are doomed to repeat them," I replied, turning Sue around. "Hang on!"

I rode the dinosaur into the stream of zombies following in the Wardens' wake and let her go to town. Sue chomped and stomped and smacked zombies fifty feet through the air with swinging blows of her snout. Her tail batted one particularly vile-looking zombie into the brick wall of the nearest building, and the zombie hit so hard and so squishily that it just stuck to the wall like a refrigerator magnet, arms and legs spread in a sprawl.

In a couple of minutes there wasn't much in the way of zombies to keep on demolishing, so I swung Sue around to pace after the Wardens. They had gotten clear of the street while I covered their retreat, and I saw Warden Luccio at the door of the nearest building, waving the last two children and Ramirez through the door while she watched out behind.

I guided Sue up to the building, and had her settle down to the ground. "Come on. But keep the drum going," I told Butters.

We slid out of our saddles and ran a couple of steps through the heavy rain to where Luccio stood at the door.

"Hey, there," I said. "Sorry I'm late."

Luccio stared at me for a moment and then at the dinosaur. Her eyes held a mixture of wonder, anger, gratitude, and revulsion. "I . . . *Dio,* Dresden. What have you done?"

"It isn't a mortal," I said. "It's an animal. You know the laws are there to protect our fellow wizards and mortals."

"It's . . ." She looked like she might throw up. "It's *necromancy,*" she said.

"It's necessary," I said, and my voice sounded harsh. I hooked a thumb up. "You've seen the vortex forming?"

"Yes. What is it?"

"Dark power. Kemmler's people are going to call it down and devour it along with all the shades they could get to show up, and if they go through with it and turn one of themselves into a god . . ."

Luccio's eyes widened as she figured it out and caught on. "There will be a vacuum," she said. "It will draw in magic to replace it. It will draw in *life.*"

"Right," I said. "And they're going to be over there, directly under the vortex," I said. "But if anyone tries to go in without a field of necromantic energy around them, the vortex will suck them dry before they get there. We need to get in there to stop them. That's why I borrowed Tiny, here. So don't give me any crap about the Laws of Magic, or at least wait for later, because there are too many lives at stake."

Anger flickered over her face and she opened her mouth. Then she frowned and closed it again. "Where did you get this information?"

"Kemmler's book," I said.

"You found it?"

I grimaced. "Briefly. Grevane jumped me and took it."

Butters looked back and forth between us, marching in place to make the polka suit's drumbeat.

Luccio blinked at him, took a deep breath, then said, "And who is this?"

"The drummer I needed to pull this off," I told her. "And a good friend. He saved my life tonight. Butters, this is Ms. Luccio. Captain, this is Butters."

Luccio gave Butters a courtly little bow, and he ducked his head sheepishly in reply.

"Where did you find those kids?" I asked.

She grimaced. "This building is an apartment complex. We got here just as the first of the undead arose. One of the parents was screaming about the children being at some sort of Halloween party in a building on campus. We were too late to save the women taking care of them, but at least we got the children out."

I chewed on my lip, studying the Warden. "You had evil wizards to gun down. And you stopped to get some kids out of the line of fire? I figured Wardens would have melted the bad guys first, tried to get the civilians clear later."

She lifted her chin and regarded me with an arched brow. "Is that how you think of us?"

"Yes," I said.

She frowned, and looked down at the hilt of her sword. "Dresden . . . the Wardens are not, as a rule, concerned with compassion or empathy. But they were *children*. I am not proud of my every act as a Warden. But I would sooner hurl myself to the demons than leave a child to die."

I frowned at her. "You would," I said thoughtfully. "Wouldn't you?"

She smiled a little, her iron-grey hair plastered to her head with the rain, and it made many wrinkles at the corners of her eyes. "Not all of us share Morgan's attitudes. But even he would never have turned aside from children in danger. He is an enormous ass at times. But a brilliant soldier. And beneath all his flaws, a decent man."

The door to the building slammed open and Morgan came through, sword gripped in both hands. "I told you," he said viciously to Luccio. "I *told* you he would turn on us. This latest violation of the laws only proves what I've said all along. . . ." His voice trailed off slowly as he caught me from the corner of his eye and turned to see me standing there, and Sue crouched a couple of yards behind me.

"Yeah," I told Luccio, and my voice was the only dry thing about me. "I see what you mean."

"Morgan, he found the book." She looked at me. "Tell him."

I relayed everything I had learned to Morgan. He glowered at me with enormous suspicion, but by the time I got to the part where thousands of people would die if we failed to stop the spell, his face became drawn with anxiety and then hardened with determination. He listened without interrupting.

"We need to get to the center of the spell," I finished. "Attack them just as they try to draw it down."

"It's impossible," Morgan said. "I got close enough to see them when we went in for the children. They're in a little patch of grass and picnic tables between the buildings. There are several hundred animated corpses in our way."

"As it happens," I said, jerking my head at Sue, "I brought an animated corpse countermeasure along with me tonight. I'll get us through."

Morgan stared at me for a second and then nodded, the idea clearly gathering momentum in his thoughts. "Yes, then. We try to hit them as they complete the spell. That gives them the most time to backstab one another, and if we disrupt a working that powerful, the backlash will probably kill them."

"Agreed," Luccio said. "How's Yoshimo?"

"Ramirez says her thigh is broken," Morgan growled. "She's not in danger but she won't be doing any more fighting tonight."

"Dammit," Luccio said. "I should have caught that one before it went through."

"No, Captain," Morgan said implacably. "She should never have tried her sword on it. She was an unremarkable fencer, at best."

"Gosh you're a sweetheart, Morgan," I said.

He glared at me, and the sword quivered in his hands.

Luccio brought her hand down between us in a gesture of absolute authority. "Gentlemen," she said quietly. "Later. We've no time."

Morgan took a deep breath in and then nodded.

I folded my arms and kept up my glower, but I hadn't been the one near violence. Point, Dresden.

"I've done for Grevane's drummer, and Sue just ate Corpse-taker's sidekick," I said. "That leaves us with those two and Cowl, plus Cowl's assistant."

"Four of them and five of us," Morgan said.

Luccio grimaced. "It could be worse," she admitted. "But only you and I have any experience with this kind of fight." She glanced at me. "No offense, Dresden, but you're young, and you haven't seen this kind of duel very often—but even you have more experience than Ramirez or Kowalski."

"None taken," I said, beginning to shiver in the rain. "I'd rather be home in bed."

"Morgan, please get the other Wardens and fill them in. Then put Yoshimo where she can see the front door and defend the building. If things don't go well, we may need somewhere to fall back."

"If things don't go well," I said, "we really won't have to worry about that."

Morgan shook his head at me. "I'll be right back."

I stood there for a moment. A mangled zombie wandered up the sidewalk. I walked back to Sue and touched her flank and her thoughts, and she flicked her tail, batting the thing away into the darkness. Then I walked back over to Luccio.

"Incredible," she said quietly, looking at Sue. "Dresden, this . . . this kind of magic is an abomination. Perhaps a necessary one this night, but hideous all the same. And yet look at it. It's amazing."

"Pretty good for zombie crushing too," I said.

"Indeed." She looked up at the sky again. "How will we know when they begin drawing down the power?"

I started to say, "Your guess is as good as mine," but I didn't get any of it out of my mouth before the clouds rolled and stirred and suddenly began to spin in a single enormous spiral. More lightning showed me the dim form of what looked like a thin, almost spidery tornado that dropped from the cloud and began to descend to the ground.

I stiffened and nodded at it. "There you go," I said. "They're starting now."

"Very well," Luccio said. "Then we must move at once. I want you to—"

Luccio didn't get to tell me what she wanted me to do, because

the earth suddenly boiled with writhing masses of pale green light
that came surging up out of the ground. They took on form as they
came, first vaguely human, then over the next instants resolving
into clearer images of what looked like Amerind tribesmen. As
they came, their mouths opened in shrieks and wails of excitement
and rage, and ghostly weapons appeared in their hands—spears
and hatchets, clubs and bows.

One of them turned and threw a translucent, shimmering
spear at my chest. I barely had time to think, but my left arm
swept up, my charred shield bracelet exploded into a cloud of
blue and white sparks, and the hurled spear shattered into angry
green flames against my shield. I heard a short cry beside me
and ducked, narrowly avoiding a swing from a spectral hatchet
whose wielder floated over me. I threw myself forward and
rolled, coming up with my shield ready and my will gathering in
my staff, making the sigils carved along its length glow with
sullen fire.

A specter swung a club at Luccio, and she rolled with the blow,
but even so took a hit to her jaw and mouth that staggered her. She
recovered her balance, ducked to avoid a second swing, and once
more drew the silver sword of a Warden from her hip. Again the
blade sang with that buzzing power I'd sensed before, and Luccio
made a clean lunge at the specter that thrust the blade through its
heart. The specter arched as if in agony and then simply exploded
into flashes of sickly light and falling globs of ectoplasm. Luccio
swept her sword back and spun on a heel to face two more of the
quasi-solid spirits.

I blocked a second blow of the hatchet on my shield, looking
wildly around for Butters. I spotted the little guy five yards away,
on his hands and knees on the crosswalk, his legs still kicking
wildly to keep the drum going. Three of the deadly specters were
closing in on him with wails of madness and rage.

"Butters!" I shouted, and rose to go to him, but two more
specters dove at me and forced me to crouch behind my shield. I
could only watch what happened as the three undead swarmed Butters and attacked him.

Butters spun around wildly, his eyes down, evidently not even
aware that they were coming. One of them swung a great two-

handed club back, as Butters put one hand to his mouth and then slammed it back down on the ground again. The specter's weapon swept down with a clean and lethal grace, heading directly for the back of Butters's head.

And suddenly shattered against the curving curtain of an empowered circle.

Butters looked up at the specters as they flailed uselessly against the circle. He had the piece of chalk I'd given him in one hand, and he'd torn the little cut he'd used before open once more with his teeth. He stood up, the drum still thumping, and gave me a shaky thumbs-up.

"Good, Butters!" I shouted at him. "Stay in there!"

He nodded, his face pale, and marched in place to keep the drum going.

I swung my staff at a specter and hit it, and the ghostly warrior reacted as if struck by a heavy brick. It was a curious kind of impact—not the thudding *thump* of hitting something solid, but *some* kind of impact nonetheless. I knew from the way that the specters had come up through the earth that they were only partially material. A material impact would have little enough effect on them, and the strength of my arm behind the swing meant nothing to them. But the power of my will that I had called up and held ready in my staff—that was something else. That energy was what the specter reacted to, and I pressed my advantage, whipping my staff through the specter's head and belly on two separate swings, driving the apparition away with howls of pain.

In the time it took me to do that, Luccio had simply dispatched three more of the specters with the humming power of her Warden's blade. She looked at me, her eyes wide, and lifted a pointing finger. She snarled a word, and another searing thread of flame shot over my shoulder about eight inches from my right ear. There was a howl, and I turned my head to see another specter that had been charging my back fall, consumed in scarlet flame.

I felt a fierce grin on my face and I turned around to nod my thanks to Luccio—and saw the Corpsetaker come out from under a veil of magic and swing her drawn tulwar at Luccio's back.

"Captain!" I shouted.

Luccio's sword arm swept up and around, blade parallel to her spine as she drew it around her shoulders in a circle, and caught Corpsetaker's attack without even turning to face it. Luccio sprang forward like a cat and spun in place, only to have Corpsetaker press her attack and drive the captain of the Wardens back on her heels.

Corpsetaker's young face was set in a wide and manic smile, cheeks dimpled, her curly hair flying wildly around her head as she charged. She wore a small skin drum of some kind on a rig at her hip, and she beat a swift tattoo on it with one hand while fighting with the other. A fresh cloud of specters swirled up in support of her, and a flying arrow drew a line of scarlet on Luccio's cheek.

I roared out a challenge, brandished my staff, and bellowed, "*Forzare!*" A lance of unseen force lashed out at Corpsetaker, but the necromancer leapt back and away from it. She cried out words in an unknown tongue, and half a dozen specters darted toward me.

I brought up my shield, but was soon hard-pressed to even hold it up against repeated attacks from the specters, and they kept trying to circle around me. If I'd stood my ground they would have killed me, and as much as I wanted to help Luccio, I had no choice but to take one step back after another, until I found my shoulders pressed against Sue's enormous flank.

But my attack on the Corpsetaker had bought Luccio what she needed to make a fight of things—time to recover from the surprise attack. She cut down two more specters with needles of flame, contemptuously slapped aside another cut from Corpsetaker's tulwar, and then took the battle to the necromancer, grey cloak flying in the storm's wind, pressing her hard with the silver rapier and driving Corpsetaker back one step after another.

I dropped the staff and slapped my bare hand on Sue's hide. Though the dinosaur looked like a living beast, that was only appearance. Her own flesh was made of the same ectoplasm that the specters were—I had just poured enough energy into it to make it seem more solid. She was of the same stuff as the specters—and that meant that she could hurt them.

The Tyrannosaur stirred and then snapped her jaws to one side, closing on a specter and tearing it into fading light and globs of goo. She heaved herself to her feet, eyes sweeping around the ground in front of her for the next specter. It lifted a bow and loosed a glowing green arrow that sank into the muscle of her neck, and she bellowed in pain, but the arrow was no more than a bee's sting. One clawed foot came up and down and destroyed a second specter. The others let out wails and shouts of fear and anger and spread out to attack Sue, while the dinosaur lashed her tail around and looked for the next victim.

I saw Luccio drive Corpsetaker forward and around the corner of the building out of sight. I'd given the specters a bigger problem to worry about, and I went after Luccio.

"Harry!" Butters shouted, pointing.

I looked up at the building. I heard children screaming inside. Someone—Ramirez, I thought—screamed, "Get down, get down!" There were flashes of luminous green light swirling here and there in the windows. I heard Morgan shout a challenge, and I heard a raucous booming sound from within. The Wardens there were under attack as well.

"Stay put!" I told him, and ran after Luccio.

It was too thick with shadow to see easily around the side of the building, but in a flash of lightning I saw Luccio make another lunge—her technique gorgeous, back leg stretched forward, spine straight, the sword extended and taking the full weight of her body behind its vicious tip. Luccio knew what she was doing. She dipped the tip of her blade under Corpsetaker's tulwar, and the point sank into the necromancer just under the floating ribs. Corpsetaker's mad smile never faltered.

The lightning died away and I heard a short, gasping cry.

I took my mother's pentacle in hand and lifted it, willing light from it. Silver-blue light filled the little space between buildings. I saw Luccio plant her feet, twist the blade viciously, and whip it back out again.

Corpsetaker fell to her knees. She stared down at her chest and then pressed her hands tightly to the wound. She looked up again, staring at Luccio and then at me. Her eyes clouded over with confusion, and she slowly toppled to her side on the grass.

"Excellent," said Luccio, turning around. She flicked blood from the silver blade and regarded it for a moment, then strode with purposeful steps for the front of the building again. "Come, wizard. We have no time to waste."

"You're going to leave her there?"

"She's finished," Luccio said harshly. "Come."

"Are you all right?" I said.

She shot a hard look at me. "Perfectly. Grevane and Cowl remain. We must find them and kill them." Her eyes flicked to the spiraling clouds overhead. "And quickly. We have only moments. Hurry, fool."

I stood there for a second, staring at Luccio's back. I lifted the pentacle and looked at Corpsetaker's body, lying on its side in the rain. She twitched a little, her dark eyes wide and staring blindly, her face pale.

And my stomach twisted in sudden fear.

I stepped around the corner of the building with my .44 in my hand, aimed it at the back of Luccio's head, drew back the hammer, and shouted, my voice harsh and hard, "Corpsetaker!"

Luccio's steps faltered. Her head snapped around to look at me, and in her eyes I saw a brutal cruelty that could never have belonged to the captain of the Wardens.

I felt the first tug of a soulgaze, but I made my decision in the moment that my voice caused her steps to falter. She opened her mouth, and I saw the Corpsetaker's madness twist Luccio's eyes, felt the sudden, dark tension as she began to gather power.

She never got it. In that single second of uncertainty, Corpsetaker had been relying upon her disguise to defend her, and had her mind bent upon planning her next step—not preparing her death curse. The bullet from my .44 hit her just over her right cheekbone.

Her head snapped back and then forward. It might have been Luccio's body, but it was the Corpsetaker's expression of shock and surprise as the stolen body fell to the ground in a loose tangle of dead limbs.

I heard a low, strangled sound.

I looked up to see Morgan standing in the building's doorway, sword in hand. He stared at Luccio's corpse and rasped, "Captain."

I stared at him for a second, and then fumbled for words. "Morgan. This isn't what it looks like."

Morgan's dark eyes rose to focus on me, and his face twisted with rage. "You." His voice was deadly quiet. The sword rose to a guard and he stalked out into the rain, and his voice rose to a wrathful roar as the ground—the freaking *ground*—began to literally shake. "Murderer! Traitor!"

Oh, shit.

Chapter

Forty

Morgan lashed his fist out at me, shouting something that sounded vaguely Greek, and the very rocks of the earth rippled up in a wave that flew toward me with incredible speed.

I had never fought against earth magic in earnest before, but I knew enough about it to not want to be in the way when it got to me. The gun went back in my pocket, and I took my staff in hand and ran for the nearest tree. I thrust the staff back at the earth as I ran, gathered in my will, and shouted, "*Forzare!*"

Unseen force lashed out at the ground behind me and flung me up at an angle. I hit the branches of the tree maybe ten feet up and scrambled wildly to grab one. I did it, and though it shook the tree like a blow from a giant ax, the wave of power went by under me without, oh, sucking me under the ground or crushing me or anything like that. I can't imagine that whatever Morgan had in mind was less than horribly violent.

Morgan bellowed in rage and charged toward me, sword in hand. I jerked my legs up and he missed my ankles, if not by much. He snarled in rage, whirled with the silver sword of the Wardens abruptly emitting a low howling sound, and struck at the trunk of the tree in a motion of focus and power that reminded me of way too many Kurosawa movies. There was a flash of light as the blade cut all the way through the tree's trunk, the heat of all that force setting both sides of the cut on fire as the tree started to fall.

I dropped clear and rolled as the tree fell out toward the street, and Morgan darted to one side, trying to get around the fallen tree to kill me.

"Morgan!" I shouted. "For God's sake, man! That wasn't Luccio!"

"Lies!" Morgan snarled. He abandoned chasing me around the tree in favor of simply hacking his way through it, and the sword in his hands howled again and again as he struck, cutting trunk and branches like bits of straw.

"It was the Corpsetaker!" I shouted. "The body thief! She let Luccio gut her and then switched places with her!"

His answer was an almost incoherent snarl. He came the last several feet faster than I could have believed and lashed at me with the sword. I brought my shield up and deflected the blow, but the impact of it slammed painfully against the whole left side of my body. There was more than simply physics behind that blade. I backpedaled out into the street, where several more zombies saw me and headed my way. Specters darted or looped lazily about now, with no sense of purpose in them at all, now that their drum was silent and the Corpsetaker was dead.

"Morgan!" I screamed. "Luccio might still be alive! But not if she doesn't get help, and soon! We can't do this!"

"More lies!" He murmured something, the blade in his hands hummed as Luccio's had, and he flicked it lightly out against my shield.

There was a shrieking scream—in my head, rather than in my ears. I don't know how to describe it, except to say that bad audio feedback is musical and soothing by comparison. The power in the silver sword hit my defensive shield and simply undid it, unraveled it, so that all the energy in it went flying apart in all directions, while a hot, tingling pain flashed through my left arm where I wore the bracelet.

Morgan attacked in earnest after that little flick of the blade had destroyed my defense, but his first swing was an overhand one, aimed at my temple. I knocked the blade aside with a sweep of my staff, and saw a flash of surprise cross his face at the speed of the parry. He recovered his balance, but I simply ran from him, taking that vital second to get moving again. Morgan cursed and followed me, but I can move, especially for a man my size, and Morgan wasn't exactly a spring chicken.

I gained ten or twelve feet on him before my legs suddenly

became unsteady and I faltered and nearly fell. I wanted to scream in frustration. Though I didn't feel how much pain my body was in, it was battered and weak. There was no way I could simply outrun him, but I made it back over to where my dinosaur stood, restlessly idle after driving away the specters. I got close enough to touch her and slapped at her flank, desperately willing my intentions to her tiny brain. Doubtless, savvy necromancers had ways of conveying their orders over a distance, but I was new at this, and I had no intentions of refining my technique anytime soon.

Sue spun around as Morgan charged, leaned down low, and opened her vast jaws in a bellow of challenge.

Say what you will about Morgan, the man was no coward. But the bellow of an angry Tyrannosaur is enough to give any mammal a moment or two of doubt. He slid to a halt on his heels, still grasping the sword in his left hand, and stared at Sue and then at me. He took a deep breath and then reached out his right hand, where there was a low, yawning, humming sound that shook the air around his fingers.

"No," he said quietly. "Not even this creature will keep you from justice this time, Dresden. Even if I have to die doing it."

I stared at Morgan, the same old frustration and fear suddenly yielding to a realization. I had always assumed that Morgan's irrational hatred was something personal, reserved for me and me alone. I had assumed that for whatever reason, Morgan's persecution was the result of the political and philosophical enmity of certain members of the White Council, that he was nothing but a pawn for someone higher up in the game.

But politicians don't make good kamikazes. That kind of dedication is reserved for zealots of principle and lunatics. For the first time I considered the notion that perhaps Morgan's hate was not directed at me personally, but at those that he truly believed to be violators of the Laws of Magic, murderers and traitors. I knew people who would face death, even embrace it, rather than surrender their principles. Karrin Murphy was one of them, and I was friends with most of the rest.

At the end of the day, Morgan was a cop. He worked for a different body of law, of course, and under a different set of guidelines, but his duties were the same: Pursue, combat, and apprehend those who violated the laws put in place to protect people from harm. He'd spent more than a century as a policeman dealing with some of the more nightmarish things on the planet. Thinking of him in that light suddenly gave me a different understanding of Morgan's character.

I'd seen burned-out cops before. They'd labored long and hard in the face of danger and uncertainty to uphold the law and protect the victims of crimes, only to see both the law and the victims it should have protected broken, beaten, and abused again and again. It mostly happened to the cops who genuinely cared, who believed in what they were doing, who passionately wanted to make a difference in the world. Somewhere along the way, their passion had become bottled anger. The anger had fermented into bitter hatred. Then the hatred had fed upon itself, gnawing away at them over years, even decades, until only a shell of cold iron and colder hate remained.

I didn't feel contempt for burned-out cops. I didn't feel anger toward them. All I ever felt was sadness and empathy for their pain. They'd seen too much in their daily battle against criminals. Ten or twenty or thirty years of witnessing the most monstrous aspects of humanity had slowly turned them into walking casualties of war.

And Morgan had been on his beat for more than a century.

Morgan didn't hate me. He hated the bad guys. He hated the wizards who abused the power he had dedicated his life to using to protect others. When he looked at me, he didn't see Harry Dresden. He could see only the atrocities and tragedies that had burned themselves into his mind and heart. I understood him. It didn't make me like him, but I could understand the pain that drove him to persecute me.

Of course, my sensitivity and empathy were completely irrelevant, because they wouldn't do a damned thing to stop him. If he charged me, I wouldn't have any options.

"Morgan," I rasped. "Please don't. We can't let Corpsetaker divide us like this. Can't you see that? That was her intention when she took Luccio."

"Traitor," he snarled. "Liar."

I ground my teeth in frustration. "My God, man, thousands of people are about to die!"

His mouth twisted, baring his teeth all the way to the gums. "And you will be the first."

If he charged me again, I wouldn't have any choice but to fight, and he was at least as strong as me, and far more experienced—not to mention the enchantment-breaking silver sword in his hand. If I didn't kill him fast, he would kill me. It was as simple as that. And even if I did kill him, he would spend his death curse on me—and it wouldn't be like the feeble thing Cassius had thrown. Morgan would obliterate me.

I couldn't run. I couldn't survive fighting him, regardless of whether or not I beat him. The best I could hope for would be to take him with me. If I died, Sue would go wild, reverting to the instincts of her ancient spirit. She would hunt. People would die.

But, if Morgan died, it would leave only Kowalski and Ramirez to stop Cowl and Grevane. Even if they could manage to pull off some kind of necromancy to shield them from the vortex as they went in, they would never be able to beat the necromancers within. They would certainly die, and not long after that the Darkhallow would annihilate thousands of innocent lives.

With Morgan leading them, they might have a chance. Not a good one, but at least there was a chance.

Which meant that if I wanted to stop the Darkhallow and save all those lives, I had only one choice. I leaned my suddenly trembling hand against Sue's leg, and she sank back into a passive crouch.

Morgan let out a bellow of defiance and determination and rushed me.

I lowered my shield. My heart pounded with a fear so strong that I nearly threw up.

The lightning gleamed on the silver blade of his sword.

I dropped my staff to the ground and faced him, arms at my sides, my hands clenched into terrified fists. I readied my will, my own death curse, picturing Grevane in my thoughts. At least I could give the Wardens a better chance for victory if I could kill or cripple one of the bastards on my way out.

Time stretched out into an endless moment. I watched Morgan's sword sweep up to the vertical, the blade a gorgeous silver that reflected the lightning ripping apart the spinning vortex behind me.

"Harry!" Butters screamed, his voice horrified, the drum pounding frantically.

As Morgan struck, I took the coward's way out and closed my eyes.

I knew that it was inevitable that one day I would die.

But I didn't want to watch it coming.

Chapter

Forty-one

A gunshot rang out.

Morgan jerked at the hips, suddenly thrown off balance. He spun gracelessly and fell to the ground.

I stared at him in shock.

Morgan let out a snarl, fixed his eyes on me, and lifted his right hand, deep and terrifying power gathering in it.

"Morgan!" snapped a woman's voice. That voice rang with authority and confidence, with command. The speaker damned well *knew* that when she gave an order that it would be obeyed, and imbued the command with a power that had nothing to do with magic. "Stand down!"

Morgan froze for an instant and glanced over his shoulder.

Ramirez stood twenty feet away, his pistol smoking in his hand. The other arm was supporting the weight of the girl I had known as the Corpsetaker. The girl's face was as pale as death, and she could not possibly have been standing on her own, but though her features were exactly the same as when Corpsetaker had been in the body, she did not look like the same person. Her eyes were narrowed and hard, and her expression was filled with a stern, almost regal confidence.

"You heard me," the girl snapped. "Stand *down!*"

"Who are you?" Morgan asked.

"Morgan," Ramirez said. "Dresden was telling the truth. This is Captain Luccio."

"No," Morgan said, shaking his head, but his voice lacked his usual absolute conviction. "No, it's a lie."

"It's no lie," Ramirez said. "I soulgazed her. It's the captain."

Morgan's lips worked soundlessly, but he didn't release the strike he held ready in his hand.

"Morgan," the girl said, quietly this time. "It's all right. Stand down."

"You aren't the captain," Morgan mumbled. "You can't be. It's a trick."

The girl, Luccio, abruptly put on a lopsided smile. "Donald," she said. "Dear idiot. I'm the one who trained you. I am fairly certain that you do not know as much as I do about who I am." Luccio lifted her arm and showed Morgan the silver rapier she'd carried before. She took it in her hand and whipped it in a circle, eliciting a steady, humming power, as I'd felt before. "There. Could another so employ my own blade?"

Morgan stared at her for a moment. Then his hand dropped, suddenly limp, the power he'd held draining away.

My heart started beating again, and I leaned heavily against Sue's flank.

Ramirez holstered his gun and helped the new Luccio over to Morgan's side, then lowered her gently to the ground beside him.

"You're hurt," Morgan said. His own face had gone white with pain. "How bad is it?"

Luccio tried a small smile. "I'm afraid I aimed too well. The wound has done for me. It may take some time, that's all."

"My God," Morgan said. "I'm sorry. I'm so sorry. I saw Dresden shoot you and . . . while you were bleeding. Needed help."

Luccio raised a weak hand. "No time," she said gently.

Ramirez had bent over Morgan, meanwhile, and was examining the gunshot wound. The bullet had caught Morgan in the back of one leg, and it looked messy. "Dammit," Ramirez said. "It hit his knee. It's shattered." He placed his fingers lightly over Morgan's knee, and the older Warden abruptly twisted in pain, his face gone bloodless. "He can't walk."

Luccio nodded. "Then it's up to you." She looked over at me. "And you, Warden Dresden."

"What about Kowalski?" I said.

Ramirez paled. He glanced back at the apartment building and shook his head. "He was sitting on the floor when the specters rose out of it. He never had a chance."

"No time," Luccio said weakly. "You must go."

Butters came marching over to us, drum still beating, his face pale. "Okay," he said. "I'm ready. Let's do it."

"Not you, Butters," I said. "Sue just needs to be able to hear the drum. She'll hear it over there just as well as if you were on her back. I want you to stay here."

"But—"

"I can't afford to spare effort to protect you," I told him. "And I don't want to leave the wounded here alone. Just keep the drum beating."

"But I want to go with you. I want to help. I'm not afraid to"— he swallowed, face pale—"die fighting beside you."

"Look at it this way," I said. "If we blow it, you get to die anyhow."

Butters stared at me for a second, and then said, "Gee. Now I feel better."

"I believe that there's a cloud for every silver lining," I said. "Come on, Ramirez."

Ramirez's grin returned. "Everyone else who lets me ride on their dinosaur calls me Carlos."

I climbed back up into the first saddle, and Ramirez settled into the second.

"God be with you, Harry," Butters said, marching in place on the ground, his face worried.

Given whom I had chosen as my ally, I sort of doubted that if God went with me it would be to assist me. "I'll take whatever help I can get," I said aloud, and laid my hand on Sue's hide. She lurched up from her crouch, and I turned her toward the site of the vortex.

"You're hurt," Ramirez said. He kept his voice pitched very low.

"I can't feel it," I said. "I'll worry about the rest if there's a later. You've got great timing, by the way. Thank you."

"*De nada*," he said. "I was right behind Morgan. I heard you trying to talk to him about Luccio."

"You believed me?" I started Sue forward. It would take her several steps to pick up speed.

Rodriguez sighed. "I've heard a lot about you. Watched you at that Council meeting. My gut says you're okay. It was worth checking out."

"And you soulgazed her. That was some fast thinking. And good shooting."

"I'm brilliant as well as skilled," he said modestly. "It's a great burden, all of that on top of my angelic good looks. But I try to soldier on as best I can."

I let out a short, rough laugh. "I see. I hope I won't embarrass you, then."

"Did I not mention my nearly godlike sense of tolerance and forgiveness?" Sue gathered speed and I turned her down the street. "Hey," he said. "The bad guys are back that way."

"I know," I said. "But they're expecting an attack from that direction. I'm going to circle the block, try to come in behind them."

"Is there time?"

"My baby can move," I told him. Sue broke into her run, and the ride smoothed out.

Ramirez let out a whoop of pure enjoyment. "Now this is cool," he said. "I can't even imagine how complicated this must have been."

"Wasn't complicated," I told him.

"Oh. So summoning up dinosaurs is actually very easy, is it?"

I snorted. "Any other night, any other place, I don't think I could have done it. But it wasn't complicated, either. Lifting up an engine block isn't complicated. It's just a lot of work."

Ramirez was silent for a moment. "I'm impressed," he said.

I didn't know Ramirez very well, but my sense of him told me that those were words he was not in the habit of uttering. "When you do something stupid and die, it's pathetic," I said. "When you do something stupid and survive it, then you get to call it impressive or heroic."

He let out a rueful chuckle. "What we're doing right now . . ." he said. His voice softened and lost its edge of brash arrogance. "It's pathetic. Isn't it?"

"Probably," I said.

"On the other hand," he said, recovering. "If we survive it, we're heroes. Medals. Girls. Endorsements. Cars. Maybe they put us on a cereal box."

"Seems the least they could do," I said.

"So we've got two of them left to take down. Who do we hit first?"

"Grevane," I said. "If he's holding a bunch of zombies as guard dogs, he isn't going to have a lot of attention to spare for defensive spells, or for throwing anything else at us. We hit him fast, hopefully put him down before he can try anything. He handled a chain like he knew how to use it when I saw him fight Corpsetaker."

"Ugh," Ramirez said. "Nasty. Anyone who knows their way around a kusari is a tough customer."

"Yeah. So we shoot him."

"Damn right, we shoot him," Ramirez said. "This is why so many of the younger members of the Council like the way you do things, Dresden."

I blinked. "They do?"

"Oh, hell, yes," Ramirez said. "A lot of them, like me, were apprentices when you were first tried after Justin DuMorne's death. A lot of them are still apprentices. But there are people who think highly of what you've done."

"Like you?"

"I would have done a lot of those things," he said. "Only with a lot more style than you."

I snorted. "Second one we'll hit calls himself Cowl. He's good. I've never seen a wizard stronger than he is, and that includes Ebenezar McCoy."

"A lot of guys who hit hard have a glass jaw. Bet he's all offense."

I shook my head. "No. He's just as good at protecting himself. I flipped a car over on top of him and it barely slowed him down."

Ramirez frowned and nodded. "How do we take him down then?"

I shook my head. "Haven't thought of anything good. Hit him with everything and hope something gets through. And if that wasn't enough, he's got an apprentice with him, called Kumori, who seems personally loyal. She's probably strong enough to be on the Council herself."

"Damn," Ramirez said quietly. "She pretty?"

"She keeps her face covered," I said. "No idea."

"If she was pretty, I'd just turn on the Ramirez charm and have her eating out of my hand," he said. "But I can't take chances with that kind of power if I'm not sure she's pretty. Used recklessly, it could endanger innocent bystanders or land me in bed with an ugly girl."

"Can't have that," I said, turning Sue around another corner. I checked the vortex. The slender, spinning psuedo-tornado was more than halfway to the ground.

"All right then," Ramirez said. "Once we're past Grevane, I'll take on the apprentice. You go for Cowl."

I glanced back at him with an arched eyebrow.

"If we ignore Kumori she'll be free to take us both out. One of us has to counter her. You're stronger than me," he said, his tone matter-of-fact. "Don't get me wrong. I'm so damned good that I make it look easy, but I'm not stupid. You have the best shot at taking Cowl down. If I can drop the apprentice, I'll help. Sound like a plan?"

"Sounds like a plan," I said. "I just wish it sounded like a winning plan."

"You got a better idea?" Ramirez asked me cheerfully.

"No," I said, and I turned Sue down the street that would hopefully let us attack the necromancers from the rear.

"Well, then," he said, his smile ferocious. "Shut up and dance."

Chapter

Forty-two

The campus of the college consisted of only a few buildings—a couple of dorms, a couple of buildings with classrooms, the Mitchell Museum, and an administrative office. The area between them was a nicely kept lawn, too small to look like a park, but larger than you'd want to mow every week. At the center of the area, directly in front of the museum, picnic tables had been over-turned onto their sides around a large circle open to the skies above. I slowed Sue's steps for a moment, to try to get some kind of idea of what we had to contend with.

Standing in silent ranks around that circle were Grevane's style of undead—very solid, very physical, though there were relatively few of them in the half-rotted or desiccated condition of the corpses that had attacked my place. These undead looked like they might still have been saved by a snappy EMT. They all looked like Native American tribesmen, just as Corpsetaker's specters had, though the styles of clothing and weaponry were slightly different.

One other thing was different, too: These undead radiated a kind of hideous, ephemeral cold, and their skin almost seemed to glow with its own pale, horrible light. I could sense the raw power that lay within them, even from a hundred yards away. These undead were different from those that had attacked the Wardens, as different as an old pickup truck was from a modern battle tank. These zombies would not be so easily destroyed as those others, and were likely to be far stronger, far faster.

They stood in ranks around the inner circle, facing outward, but they ranked thicker between the circle and the last location of the Wardens than on the side nearest us. I had managed to outflank the thinking of whoever had those undead in position, and the thought cheered me somewhat. Spirits and specters and formless masses of luminescent light darted and flowed around the circle like strands of kelp and bits of algae caught in a whirlpool. They were all the same unpleasant colors as the lightning in the storm, and even as I watched their numbers visibly grew. Sue paced a restless step forward, and I felt a horrible sensation of cold on the skin of my face and forehead, as if the hovering vortex above was casting out some kind of perverted inversion of sunlight. I crouched a little lower on Sue's back and the feeling faded.

Lightning flashes from different directions cast a web of shadows over the whole place, trees and buildings collaborating with the storm to conceal much of the open circle continually clothed in shifting blocks and threads of darkness. I could see that there was *someone* within the circle of picnic tables, but not who, and I couldn't even be sure of how many.

"That," I said in a low voice, "is a lot of badass zombies."

"And ghosts," Ramirez said.

"And ghosts."

"Look at it this way," he said. "With that many of them, how can we miss?"

"Yeah," I said. "Cool."

I didn't want to do it. I wanted to go find myself a hole and crawl into it. But instead I put my hand on Sue's neck, drew her attention to the zombies, and willed her forward into battle.

Sue leapt forward and hit the nearest rank of zombies before any of them had the chance to notice her. She tore one apart with her vast jaws, smashed several others flat, crushed some with her flailing tail, and generally went to town. After her devastating initial charge, I heard a frantic man's voice shout from within the circle, and the zombies turned to attack.

The zombies whipped out bows and spears and clubs, or else tore at Sue with their bare hands. It wasn't pretty. Arrows streaked through the air with unnatural speed, and when they struck the Tyrannosaur's hide they sounded almost like gunshots. One zombie rammed a spear cleanly through the massive muscle of Sue's right thigh. A swinging club shattered several of her teeth, and even as I watched, an unarmed zombie leapt up onto her flank, got a hold of the heavy extension cord that held the saddles in place, then drove his fist into her flesh up to the elbow, and started raking out gobbets of tissue by the handful.

I brought up the sparkling blue cloud of my shield bracelet in time to intercept an arrow, and others smashed against it with the force of bullets even as I held it in place. Without being told, I felt Ramirez turn to our right, his own left hand extended, and a concave disk of green light expanded weblike from his outstretched fingertips, covering that flank from still more of them.

But as vicious and as strong and as swift and deadly as the zombies were, they couldn't hold a candle to Sue.

The injuries that might have terrified a living beast only infuriated her, and as that rage swelled, her own grey-and-black hide gained a silvery sheen of power. She roared so loudly that my chest and belly shook and my ears screamed with pain. She caught one zombie in her jaws and flung it away. It sailed up over the nearest five-story building and out of sight in the darkness and rain. When she stomped down with her foot, she shattered the concrete of a walkway and drove a footprint more than a foot deep into the earth around it. The zombie assault turned into one enormous exercise in suicidal tactics, for whenever one of the undead warriors managed to get through to harm Sue, the Tyrannosaur not only crushed the unlife out of them, but grew that much more angry and powerful and unstoppable.

It was like riding a carnivorous earthquake.

"Look!" Ramirez screamed. "Look there!"

I followed his nod and spotted Grevane in the circle in his trench coat and fedora. The necromancer was keeping a steady beat on a drum hung from his belt, and he gripped a staff of gnarled, twisted black wood with the other. He stared at us, his face twisted in hatred, and his eyes glittered with insane malice.

I willed Sue to head for the circle, but the Tyrannosaur's will was suddenly no longer pliable or easily led. The blood rage and fury of battle had overloaded what little mind she actually possessed, and now she was nothing but several rampaging tons of killing machine.

"Hurry!" Ramirez shouted.

"She's not listening!" I told him. I applied my will even more forcefully, but it was like one man struggling to hold back a bulldozer. I gritted my teeth, desperately trying to figure a way to get Sue where I wanted her, and hit on one idea. Instead of trying to stop her battle rage, I encouraged it, and then I pointed her at the zombies nearer to the circle.

Sue responded with bloodlust and glee, swerving to charge toward the zombies nearest the circle, crushing and rekilling them as she went.

"We have to jump!" I shouted.

"Wahoo!" Ramirez cried, his smile blazing white.

Sue pursued a dodging zombie to within ten feet of one of the fallen picnic tables, and I let out a scream of fear and excitement as I jumped. It was like falling from a little bit higher than a second-story window, but I managed to land feet-first and well enough to absorb most of the shock of impact, though the flash of pain told me that my knees and ankles were going to be sore for days.

I rose and lifted my shield at once, in time to intercept the deadly flash of Grevane's whirling chain.

"Fool," he snarled. "You should have joined me when you had the chance." His eyes flicked up and glittered. I followed the line of his gaze. The vortex wasn't more than ten feet from the ground.

"You can't draw it in if I'm standing right here," I shouted back, retreating and circling to get into the circle of picnic tables. When I did, that horrible, sickly sense of cold faded. This near, the vortex wasn't drawing the life off of me. It was the eye of the metaphysical hurricane. "One distraction and the backlash will kill you. It's *over.*"

"It is *not* over!" he howled, and the chain whipped out again, striking my shield. "It is *mine!* My birthright! I was his favored child!"

I barely heard a footstep behind me, and whirled in time to lift my shield against another zombie with a spear. The weapon shattered against my upraised shield, but even as it did, I felt a burning impact as Grevane's chain wrapped around my wounded leg and jerked hard. My balance went out from under me, and I fell to the ground.

Grevane's zombie piled onto my back and started *biting* me. I felt hot, horrible pain on my trapezius muscles left of my neck, even through my cloak and spellworked duster. The zombie let out a vicious cry and let go, then went for the unprotected nape of my neck. I struggled to throw it off of me, to get away, but my battered body was weakened and it was incredibly strong.

"Die!" Grevane screamed, wild laughter in his unsteady voice. "Die, die, die—"

His howls broke off into a single quiet, choking noise, and the zombie on my back abruptly froze.

I struggled out from under it in time to see Grevane standing a few feet away, the chain discarded upon the ground, his hand held to his neck. Blood, black in the night, sprayed from between his fingers. His expression became enraged and he turned toward me, extending a hand to the zombie near me. The zombie turned, once more with purpose.

But then Grevane's expression became puzzled. His eyes rolled back in his head, and I saw the long, straight, smooth cut that had opened his neck from one side to the other, cutting all the way to his spine.

Ramirez stepped into my line of vision, his silver sword in hand and coated with blood. In his other hand he held his pistol. Without hesitation or hurry, he raised the gun and aimed at Grevane's head from five feet away.

Then he executed the stunned necromancer.

The body went loose, fell, and lay there in the grass and rain, one leg twitching.

Around us, the zombies had suddenly lost their vibrant animation, and most of them simply stood passively still, staring at nothing. Tyrannosaur Sue couldn't have cared less, and carried on with her killing spree.

Ramirez came to me and helped me to my feet. "Sorry it took me so long. I had to dodge some bad guys."

"You got here," I said, panting.

He nodded once, grimacing. "Couldn't shoot with you that close, in this light. Had to do it the old-fashioned way. You were one hell of a good distraction, though."

"You did fine," I said. I could feel hot wetness trickling down my back. "Thank God he was insane."

"How's that?" Ramirez asked.

"At the end there. You'd opened his throat but he still thought he could keep going. He tried to hang on to his control of the zombies. It was like he didn't think death counted when it came to him."

"And that's lucky why?"

"He refused to believe he was dying," I said. "No death curse."

Ramirez nodded. "Yeah, you're right. Lucky us."

Then a man's voice said, "I don't know if I'd say *that,* gentlemen."

I whirled as one of the passive zombies still standing nearby turned, lifting its spear—and then shimmered into the form of Cowl. He lifted one hand from the folds of his dark cloak, and there was no warning surge of gathering power when a wave of vicious force flickered out from his palm and took Ramirez full in the chest.

The young Warden hadn't been ready for it. The magical blow lifted him from his feet and threw him backward like a rag doll. He hit the ground twenty feet later, limbs already flopping limply, and lay there without moving.

"No!" I shouted, and I whirled on Cowl, Hellfire erupting from the runes of my staff. I lifted the staff, snarled, "*Forzare!*" and sent a lance of vicious energy at the dark figure.

Cowl swiftly crossed his hands at the wrists, forming an X shape with his arms, aligning defensive energy before him—but he hadn't been quite swift enough, or else he hadn't reckoned on how much energy he had to deal with. The lash of raw, scarlet force hammered him hard on the right side of his body, spinning him around and stealing his balance. He stumbled in a corkscrewing motion, and went to the ground.

I drew back the staff for another blow—but then someone pressed against my back, fingers tightened in my hair, and I felt the cold, deadly edge of a knife at my throat.

"Don't move," Kumori's quiet voice said. She was stretched out quite a bit to pulling my hair and holding the knife, but she'd done it right. There was no way I could try to escape her without her opening an artery. I ground my teeth, my power still ready to lash out again, and debated doing exactly that. Kumori would probably kill me, but it might be worth it to finish Cowl.

I looked up at the writhing vortex. Its tip was now barely above the height of my own head.

Cowl recovered his feet by slow degrees, shaken more than hurt, and anger radiated from him in nearly palpable waves. "Idiot," he said, voice harsh. "You have lost. Can you not see? This game is over."

"Don't do this," I growled. "It isn't worth it. You're going to kill thousands of innocent people."

Cowl's hood tilted up toward the descending vortex, and he marched over the grass until he stood directly beneath it. "Keep him still," he snapped to Kumori.

"Yes, lord," Kumori replied. The steel at my throat never wavered.

Cowl's hand dipped into a pouch at his side, and came out holding Bob the skull. The lights in the skull's eye sockets burned a cold shade of blue and violet.

"There, spirit," Cowl said, holding the skull up to see the vortex. "Do you see it?"

"Of course," said the skull, his voice just as cold and empty. "It is precisely as the master described. Proceed." The eye lights swiveled and came to rest on me. "Ah. The White Council's black sheep. I recommend that you kill him immediately."

"No," Kumori said firmly. "His death curse could destroy the working."

"I know that," the skull replied, his voice contemptuous. "But if he lives when Cowl draws down the power he might disrupt it. Kill him now."

"Silence, spirit," Cowl said in a harsh voice. "You are not the master here. Challenge me again at your own peril."

The skull's eye sockets burned colder yet, but he said nothing.

I swallowed. Bob . . . wasn't Bob anymore. I'd known that he was bound and beholden to whoever possessed the skull he resided within, and that their personality would strongly influence his own—but I'd never really imagined what that might be like. Bob wasn't precisely a friend to me but . . . I was used to him. In a way he was family, the mouthy, annoying, irritable cousin who was always insulting you but who was definitely at Thanksgiving dinner. I had never considered the possibility that one day he might be something else.

Something murderous.

The worst part was that Bob had given Cowl good advice. My

death curse might well mess up this spell, but on the other hand, Cowl did not seem one to be afraid of death curses. If he gave me the chance to wait until he was actually at the delicate moment of drawing down the power, I wouldn't need anything as strong as a death curse to upset his balance.

Of course, it would kill me. Kumori's blade would see to that. But I could stop him if I was alive when it went down.

Cowl set the skull aside on the grass, then raised his hands above his head and let the sleeves fall back from his long, weathered arms covered in old scars. He began a chant in a low voice, steady and strong.

The vortex quivered. And then, almost delicately, it began to descend to Cowl, drifting toward him as lightly and slowly as a drifting feather of down.

Power rolled through the heavens, the clouds, the whirling vortex. Spirits and swirling apparitions screamed and wailed their tormented replies. Kumori's hands never weakened or wavered, but I could sense that almost every fiber of her attention was directed toward Cowl.

I might have one chance.

"Bob," I said. *"Bob."*

The blue eye lights turned toward me.

"Think," I said quietly. "Think, Bob. You know me. You've worked with me for years."

The blue eye lights narrowed.

"Bob," I said quietly. "You've got to remember me. I gave you a name."

The skull quivered a little, as if a shudder had run through it, but the eyes continued to burn cold and blue.

And then one of them flickered into a shade of its usual orange, then immediately back to cold blue.

My heart thudded in sudden excitement. Bob the skull, *my* Bob, had just winked at me.

Cowl continued his chant, and the clouds spun more and more rapidly. The rain abruptly stopped, as swiftly as if someone had turned off a faucet, and the air filled with spirits, ghosts, apparitions and specters, caught in some vast and unseen whirlpool that dragged them in accelerating circles. The power in the air made it hard to breathe, and the roar of wailing spirits, vast wind, and an earth-deep rumble grew steadily louder.

"Bob," I shouted into the cacophony, "you have my permission!"

Orange light streaked from the eye sockets of the skull and blazed away from the circle of overturned picnic tables—but even so, I saw Bob's glowing body of energy pulled by the whirling currents of magic. He fought against that horrible vortex, and I suddenly realized that without the shelter of the skull or some other kind of physical body, Bob was no different from any of the other spirit beings trapped in that vast maelstrom. If the Darkhallow was completed, he too would be trapped and devoured.

I thought I saw Bob's form sucked up into the clouds of trapped spirits, but there was too much light and noise for me to be sure of anything.

Cowl kept on chanting, and I saw his body arch with tension. Over the next minute or so, he actually, physically rose above the ground, until his boots were three or four inches in the air. His voice had become part of the wild storm, part of the dark energy, and it rolled and boomed and echoed all around us. I began to understand the kind of power we were dealing with. It was power as deep as an ocean, and as broad as the sky. It was dark and lethal and horrible and beautiful, and Cowl was about to take it all in. The strength it would give him would not make him a match for the entire White Council. It would put him in a league so far beyond them that their strength would mean virtually nothing.

It was power enough to change the world. To reshape it after one's own liking.

The tip of the vortex spun down, danced lightly upon Cowl's lips, and then slipped gently between them. Cowl howled out the last repetition of his chant, his mouth opening wide.

I ground my teeth. Bob hadn't been able to help me, and I couldn't let Cowl complete the spell. Even if it killed me.

I drew in my magic for the last spell I would ever throw, a blast to slam into Cowl, disrupt the spell, let that vast energy tear him to bits.

Kumori sensed it and I heard her let out a short cry. The knife burned hot on my throat.

And then the dinosaur I'd summoned plunged through the clouds of wild spirits and headed directly for Kumori, her eyes blazing with brilliant orange flames. Tyrannosaur Bob let out a bellow and swiped one enormous talon at Kumori.

Cowl's apprentice was tough and competent, but no amount of training or forethought can prepare you for the sight of an angry dinosaur coming to eat your ass. She froze for the briefest second, and I turned, shoving away from her. The knife whipped against my throat, and I felt a hot sting. I wondered if that was what Grevane had felt.

There was no more time. I flung myself across the grass, gripped my staff in both hands, and swung it like a baseball bat at Cowl's head.

The blow connected, right on what felt like the tip of his upturned jaw, snapping his mouth shut and knocking him to the ground. The vortex abruptly screamed and filled with a furious red light. I choked out a cry and fell down on my right side to the ground, bringing up my shield bracelet and holding it over me in an effort to protect myself from the vast forces now flying free from the botched spell.

There was more sound, so loud that no word could accurately describe it, incandescent lightning, screaming faces, and forms of spirits and ghosts, and trembling earth beneath me.

And blackness fell.

Chapter

Forty-three

When I came to my senses there was darkness and steady, cold rain, and I had sunk up to my neck in a deep well of aching pain. Neither lightning nor thunder played through the skies. I lay there for a moment, gathering my wits, and as I did the lights of the city began to come on, bit by bit, as the power grids went back online.

A booted foot pressed into the ground beside my face, and I followed it up, up and up, until I saw the horned helmet of the Erlking outlined against the brightening Chicago skyline.

"Wizard. Called you forth a mighty hunter tonight. One that has not walked this earth since time gone and forgotten."

"Yeah," I said. "Pretty nifty, huh?"

There was a low, wild laugh from that helmet. "Daring. Arrogant. It pleases me." He tilted his head. "And you are poor game at the moment. Because of that, and because you pleased me with your calling of the old hunter, this night you may go free. But beware, mortal. The next time our paths cross, it shall be my very great pleasure to run you down."

There was a gust of cold autumn wind, and the Erlking was gone.

I looked around blearily. Every tree in the area was gone, torn off about a foot from the earth. The picnic tables had been torn to splinters. The buildings of the college, especially the museum, looked as if they had been ravaged by a tornado that had torn out great chunks and sections of them.

My ribs hurt. I looked down and saw that I had fallen around Bob the skull and curled my body around him as I had shielded myself. Orange flame flickered to life in the eye sockets.

"Some show, huh?" Bob said. He sounded exhausted.

"You had to go get the dinosaur, eh?" I said. "I figured you'd just grab a handy zombie."

"Why settle for wieners when you can have steak?" the skull said brightly. "Pretty good idea, Harry, talking to me once Cowl sat me on the ground. I didn't want to work for him anyway, but as long as he had the skull . . . well. You know how it is."

I grunted. "Yeah. What happened?"

"The spell backlashed when you slugged Cowl," Bob said. "Did just a bit of property damage."

I coughed out a little laugh, looking around me. "Yeah. Cowl?"

"Most likely there are little pieces of him still filtering down," Bob said brightly. "And his little dog, too."

"You see them die?" I asked.

"Well. No. Once that backlash came down, it tore apart every enchantment within a hundred miles. Your dinosaur sort of fell apart."

I grunted uneasily.

"Oh," Bob said. "I think that Warden over there is alive."

I blinked. "Ramirez?"

"Yeah," Bob said. "I figured that you were a Warden now and stuff, and that you would probably want me to help out some other Warden. So just before the big bang, I had the dinosaur stand over him, soak up the blast."

I grunted. "Okay," I said. "We've got to help him. But one thing first."

"What's that?" Bob asked.

I squinted around until I found Grevane's battered corpse. Then I crawled over to it. I fumbled in the trench coat's pockets until I found Kemmler's slender little book. I squinted around me, but there was no one to look as I put it in my pocket.

"Okay," I said. "Come on. Watch my back while I help Ramirez."

"You betcha, boss," Bob said, and his voice was very smug. "Hey, you know what? Size really *does* matter."

Ramirez made it out of that evening alive. He had four broken ribs and two dislocated shoulders, but he came through. With Butters's help, I was able to get him, Luccio, and Morgan back to my place. At some point in the evening, Butters had taken off his drum and let Morgan take over the drumming duties while he tried to help Luccio, and as a result her wound hadn't been quite as fatal as she had thought it would be. They were far too badly hurt to stay at my place, though, and Senior Council member "Injun Joe" Listens-to-Wind himself showed up with half a dozen more stay-at-home wizards who knew something about medicine and healing to move them to a more secure location.

"Just don't get it," Morgan was telling Listens-to-Wind. "All of these things happening at once. It can't be a coincidence."

"It wasn't," I heard myself say.

Morgan looked at me. The resentment in his eyes hadn't changed, but there was something else there that hadn't been before—dare I hope it, some modicum of respect.

"Think about it," I said. "All those heavy vampire attacks just when Cowl and his buddies most needed the White Council not to be involved."

"Are you saying that you think Cowl was using the vampires as a tool?" Morgan asked.

"I think they had a deal," I said. "The vampires throw their first major offensive at the right time to let Cowl pull off this Darkhallow."

"But what do they get out of it?" Morgan asked.

I glanced at Listens-to-Wind and said, "The Senior Council."

"Impossible," Morgan said. "By that time, they had to know that the Senior Council was back at Edinburgh. The defenses there have been built over thousands of years. It would take . . ." Morgan paused, frowning.

I finished the sentence for him. "It would take a god to break through them and kill the Senior Council."

Morgan stared at me for a long time, but didn't say anything. It wasn't long before they left, pulling out the wounded Wardens and leaving.

It left me with only about half an hour to meet Mavra's deadline, but since the phones were up again, I left a message at her number and headed for our rendezvous.

I turned up at my grave again, standing over the open hole in the ground as Mavra approached me, this time openly and without melodrama. She faced me over my grave, and said nothing. I took the book out of my pocket and tossed it to her. She picked it up, regarded it, and then drew an envelope from her jacket and tossed it at my feet. I picked it up and found the negatives of the incriminating pictures of Murphy inside.

Mavra turned to leave.

I said, "Wait."

She paused.

"This never happens again," I said quietly. "You try to get to me through other mortals again and I'll kill you."

Mavra's rotted lips turned up at one corner. "No, you won't," she said in her dusty voice. "You don't have that kind of power."

"I can get it," I said.

"But you won't," she responded, mockery in her tone. "It wouldn't be right."

I stared at her for a full ten seconds before I said, in a very quiet voice, "I've got a fallen angel tripping all over herself to give me more power. Queen Mab has asked me to take the mantle of Winter Knight twice now. I've read Kemmler's book. I know how the Darkhallow works. And I know how to turn necromancy against the Black Court."

Mavra's filmed eyes flashed with anger.

I continued to speak quietly, never raising my voice. "So once again, let me be perfectly clear. If anything happens to Murphy and I even *think* you had a hand in it, fuck right and wrong. If you touch her, I'm declaring war on you. Personally. I'm picking up every weapon I can get. And I'm using them to kill you. Horribly."

There was utter silence for a moment.

"Do you understand me?" I whispered.

She nodded.

"Say it," I snarled, and my voice came out so harsh and cold that Mavra twitched and took half a step back from me.

"I understand," she rasped.

"Get out of my town," I told her.

And Mavra retreated into the shadows.

I stood there over my grave for a minute more, just feeling the pain of my battered body, and bitterly considering the inevitability of death. After a moment I felt another presence near me. I looked up and found the dream image of my father regarding my tombstone speculatively.

" 'He died doing the right thing,' " my father read.

"Maybe I can change it to, 'he died alone,' " I said back.

My father smiled a little. "Thinking about the death curse, eh?"

"Yeah. 'Die alone.' " I stared down at my open grave. "Maybe it means I'll never be with anybody. Have love. A wife. Children. No one who is really close. Really there."

"Maybe," my father said. "What do you think?"

"I think that's what he wanted to do to me. I think I'm so tired that I'm hallucinating. And that I hurt. And that I want someone to be holding my hand when it's my time. I don't want to do it alone."

"Harry," my dad said, and his voice was very gentle, "can I tell you something?"

"Sure."

He walked around the grave and put his hand on my shoulder. "Son. Everyone dies alone. That's what it is. It's a door. It's one person wide. When you go through it, you do it alone." His fingers squeezed me tight. "But it doesn't mean you've got to be alone before you go through the door. And believe me, you aren't alone on the other side."

I frowned and looked up at my father's image, searching his eyes. "Really?"

He smiled and drew his finger in an X on his chest. "Cross my heart."

I looked away from him. "I did things. I made a deal I shouldn't have made. I crossed a line."

"I know," he said. "It only means what you decide it means."

I looked up at him. "What?"

"Harry, life isn't simple. There is such a thing as black and white. Right and wrong. But when you're in the thick of things, sometimes it's hard for us to tell. You didn't do what you did for your own benefit. You did it so that you could protect others. That doesn't make it right—but it doesn't make you a monster, either. You still have free will. You still get to choose what you will do and what you will be and what you will become." He clapped my shoulder and turned to walk away. "As long as you believe you are responsible for your choices, you still are. You've got a good heart, son. Listen to it."

He vanished into the night, and somewhere in the city, bells started tolling midnight.

I stared at my waiting grave, and I suddenly realized that death was really not my biggest worry.

He died doing the right thing.

God, I hope so.

Thomas was waiting back at my apartment when I returned, and Mouse came loping in not long after. Murphy's bike had failed him completely, and by the time he'd reached the college campus, the fur had flown and the whole show was over. I crashed hard, and slept for more than a day. When I woke up, I found that my injuries had all been dressed again, and that an IV was hanging beside my bed. Butters showed up every day to check on me, and he had me on antibiotics and had imposed a ferociously healthy diet on me that Thomas made me stick to. I grumbled a lot, and slept a lot, and after several days was feeling almost human again.

Murphy showed up to chew me out for the wreck she found where her house used to be. We'd left the place sort of trashed. But when she saw me in bed, covered in bandages, she stopped in her tracks.

"What happened?" she asked.

"Oh. Things," I said. "Chicago was interesting for a couple of days there." I peered at her. She had a cast on her left arm, as if for a broken wrist, and I thought I saw the edge of a bruise on her neck. "Hey," I said. "What happened?"

Her cheeks turned pink. "Oh. Things. Hawaii was interesting for a couple of days there."

"I'll trade you my story for yours," I said.

She got pinker. "Um. I'll . . . have to think about it."

Then we both looked at each other and laughed, and we left it at that.

Chicago reacted to the events of that Halloween predictably. It was all attributed to the worst storm in fifty years, rioting, a minor earth tremor, a large load of bread produced by a local bakery that had been contaminated with ergot, and similar Halloween-fueled hysteria. In the blackout, some reprehensible types had vandalized the museum and relocated Sue's skeleton to a local campus as some kind of bizarre practical joke. There had been dozens of break-ins, robberies, murders, and other crimes during the blackout, but any other reports and wild stories were automatically put down to hysteria and/or ergot poisoning. Life went on.

Captain Luccio survived her injuries, but not without serious long-term damage that would take a lot of rehabilitation. Between that and the uncertainty of what would happen in her shiny new body, she had been relieved of command as the captain of the Wardens until such time as her health and state of mind were judged to be sound and reliable.

Morgan took her place.

He came to visit me at my place, maybe two weeks later, and gave me the news.

"Dresden," he said. "I was against inducting you in the first place. But Captain Luccio had the right to ignore my recommendation. She made you a Warden and she made you a regional commander, and there's nothing I can do about that." He took a deep breath. "But I don't like you. I think you are dangerous."

His mouth twisted. "But I am no longer convinced you do these things out of malice. I think you lack discipline and judgment. You have repeatedly demonstrated your willingness to put yourself in harm's way to protect others. As much as it galls me to admit it, I don't think you have any evil intentions. I think your questionable actions are the result of arrogance and poor judgment. In the end, it matters little why you do it. But I cannot in good conscience condemn you for it without giving you some sort of chance to prove me wrong."

From Morgan, this was the equivalent of Emperor Constantine converting to Christianity. He was almost admitting that he had been *wrong*. I reached into my pocket, pulled out a penny, and dropped it to the floor.

"What was that for?" he asked.

"I'm just making sure gravity is still online," I said.

He frowned at me, then shrugged and said, "I don't trust you. I'm not committing any Wardens to your command, and, truth be told, we don't have them to spare in any case. But you may be required to participate in missions from time to time, and I will expect you to work with the other regional commander in America. He operates out of Los Angeles. He specifically requested the assignment, and given his role in recent events, he could hardly be gainsaid."

"Ramirez," I guessed.

Morgan nodded. Then he reached into his coat and produced an envelope. He handed it to me.

"What's this?" I asked.

"Your first paycheck," Morgan said, and he didn't look happy to be saying it. "Monthly."

I opened the envelope and blinked. It wasn't a fortune, but it sure as hell would be a nice little addition to my earnings in the investigation business. "I never thought I would hear myself say this," I said as he started to leave, "but thank you, Morgan."

His face twisted up into something bitter, and he managed to spit out the words: "You're welcome." I think he fled before he started to puke.

Several weeks later Butters showed up at my door with a big box wrapped in Christmas paper. I let him in, and he carried it to the living room and presented me with it. "Go ahead. Open it."

I did. Inside the box was a guitar case, and inside that an old wooden guitar. "Uh," I said. "What's this for?"

"Therapy," Butters said. He'd been having me practice squeezing a squishy ball with my left hand, and, just as he'd predicted, I had slowly gained a little more control of it. "You're going to learn to play."

"Uh, my hand doesn't work that well," I said.

"Not yet," Butters replied. "But we'll start slow like everything else, and you can work up to it. Just do the lessons. Look, there's a book in the bottom of the case."

I opened the case and found a book entitled *Guitar for Total Idiots,* while Butters went on about tendons and metacarpal something-or-other and flexibility. I opened the book, but night had fallen and the fire was too low to let me read it. I absently waved a hand at the candles on the table beside the couch and muttered,

"Flickum bicus." They puffed to light with a little whoosh of magic.

I stopped and blinked—first at the candles and then at my burned hand.

"What?" Butters asked.

"Nothing," I said, and opened the book to look over it. "You know, Butters, for a mortician you're a pretty good healer."

"You think so?"

I glanced at the warm, steady flame of the candles and smiled. "Yeah."

AUTHOR'S NOTE

When I was seven years old, I got a bad case of strep throat and was out of school for a whole week. During that time, my sisters bought me my first fantasy and sci-fi novels: the boxed set of *Lord of the Rings* and the boxed set of the Han Solo adventure novels by Brian Daley. I devoured them all during that week.

From that point on, I was pretty much doomed to join SF&F fandom. From there, it was only one more step to decide I wanted to be a writer of my favorite fiction material, and here we are.

I blame my sisters.

My first love as a fan is swords-and-horses fantasy. After Tolkien I went after C. S. Lewis. After Lewis, it was Lloyd Alexander. After them came Fritz Leiber, Roger Zelazny, Robert Howard, John Norman, Poul Anderson, David Eddings, Weis and Hickman, Terry Brooks, Elizabeth Moon, Glen Cook, and before I knew it I was a dual citizen of the United States and Lankhmar, Narnia, Gor, Cimmeria, Krynn, Amber—you get the picture.

When I set out to become a writer, I spent years writing swords-and-horses fantasy novels—and seemed to have little innate talent for it. But I worked at my writing, branching out into other areas, including SF, mystery, and contemporary fantasy, as experiments. That's how the Dresden Files initially came about—as a happy accident while trying to accomplish something else. Sort of like penicillin.

But I never forgot my first love, and to my immense delight and excitement, one day I got a call from my agent and found out that I was going to get to share my newest swords-and-horses fantasy novel with other fans.

The Codex Alera is a fantasy series set within the savage world of Carna, where spirits of the elements, known as furies, lurk in every facet of life, and where many intelligent races vie for security and survival. The realm of Alera is the monolithic civilization of humanity, and its unique ability to harness and command the furies is all that enables its survival in the face of the enormous, sometimes hostile elemental powers of Carna, and against savage creatures who would lay Alera in waste and ruin.

Yet even a realm as powerful as Alera is not immune to destruction from within, and the death of the heir apparent to the Crown has triggered a frenzy of ambitious political maneuvering and infighting amongst the High Lords, those who wield the most powerful furies known to man. Plots are afoot, traitors and spies abound, and a civil war seems inevitable—all while the enemies of the realm watch, ready to strike at the first sign of weakness.

Tavi is a young man living on the frontier of Aleran civilization—because, let's face it, swords-and-horses fantasies start there. Born a freak, unable to utilize any powers of furycrafting whatsoever, Tavi has grown up relying upon his own wits, speed, and courage to survive. When an ambitious plot to discredit the Crown lays Tavi's home, the Calderon Valley, naked and defenseless before a horde of the barbarian Marat, the boy and his family find themselves directly in harm's way.

There are no titanic High Lords to protect them, no Legions, no Knights with their mighty furies to take the field. Tavi and the free frontiersmen of the Calderon Valley must find some way to uncover the plot and to defend their homes against a merciless horde of Marat and their beasts.

It is a desperate hour where the fate of all Alera hangs in the balance, where a handful of ordinary steadholders must find the courage and strength to defy an overwhelming foe, and where the courage and intelligence of one young man will save the Realm—or destroy it.

Thank you, readers and fellow fans, for all of your support and kindess. I hope that you enjoy reading the first book of the

Codex Alera, *Furies of Calderon*, as much as I enjoyed creating it for you.

—Jim

Furies of Calderon is available now in paperback
from Ace Books.

Read on for an exciting preview of
another novel of the Dresden Files

PROVEN GUILTY

by Jim Butcher

Available from Roc

Blood leaves no stain on a Warden's grey cloak.

I didn't know that until the day I watched Morgan, second in command of the White Council's Wardens, lift his sword over the kneeling form of a young man guilty of the practice of black magic. The boy, sixteen years old at the most, screamed and ranted in Korean underneath his black hood, his mouth spilling hatred and rage, convinced by his youth and power of his own immortality. He never knew it when the blade came down.

Which I guess was a small mercy. Microscopic, really.

His blood flew in a scarlet arc. I wasn't ten feet away. I felt hot droplets strike one cheek, and more blood covered the left side of the cloak in blotches of angry red. The head fell to the ground, and I saw the cloth over it moving, as if the boy's mouth was still screaming imprecations.

The body fell onto its side. One calf muscle twitched spasmodically and then stopped. After maybe five seconds, the head did too.

Morgan stood over the still form for a moment, the bright silver sword of the White Council of Wizards' justice in his hands. Besides him and me, there were a dozen Wardens present, and two members of the Senior Council—the Merlin and my one-time mentor, Ebenezar McCoy.

The covered head stopped its feeble movements. Morgan glanced up at the Merlin and nodded once. The Merlin returned the nod. "May he find peace."

"Peace," the Wardens all replied together.

Except me. I turned my back on them and made it two steps away before I threw up on the warehouse floor.

I stood there shaking for a moment until I was sure I was finished, then straightened slowly. I felt a presence draw near me and looked up to see Ebenezar standing there.

He was an old man, bald but for wisps of white hair, short, stocky, his face half covered in a ferocious-looking grey beard. His nose and cheeks and bald scalp were all ruddy, except for a recent, purplish scar on his pate. Though he was centuries old, he carried himself with vibrant energy, and his eyes were alert and pensive behind gold-rimmed spectacles. He wore the formal black robes of a meeting of the Council, along with the deep purple stole of a member of the Senior Council.

"Harry," he said quietly. "You all right?"

"After that?" I snarled, loudly enough to make sure everyone there heard me. "No one in this damned building should be all right."

I felt a sudden tension in the air behind me.

"No, they shouldn't," Ebenezar said. I saw him look back at the other wizards there, his jaw setting stubbornly.

The Merlin, also in his formal robes and stole, came over to us. He looked like a wizard should look—tall, long white hair, long white beard, piercing blue eyes, his face seamed with age and wisdom.

Well. With age, anyway.

"Warden Dresden," he said. He had the sonorous voice of a trained speaker and spoke English with a high-class British accent. "If you had some evidence that you felt would prove the boy's innocence, you should have presented it during the trial."

"I didn't have anything like that, and you know it," I replied.

"He was proven guilty," the Merlin said. "I soulgazed him myself. I examined more than two dozen mortals whose minds he had altered. Three of them might eventually recover their sanity. He forced four others to commit suicide and had hidden nine corpses from the local authorities, as well. And every one of them was a blood relation." The Merlin stepped toward me, and the air in the room suddenly felt hot. His eyes flashed with azure anger, and his voice rumbled with deep, unyielding power. "The powers he used had already broken his mind. We did what was necessary."

I turned and faced the Merlin. I didn't push out my jaw and try to stare him down. I didn't put anything belligerent or challenging into my posture. I didn't show any anger on my face or slur any disrespect into my tone when I spoke. The past several months had taught me that the Merlin hadn't gotten his job through an ad on a matchbook. He was, quite simply, the strongest wizard on the planet. And he had talent, skill, and experience to go along with that strength. If I ever came to magical blows with him, there wouldn't be enough left of me to fill a lunch sack. I did *not* want a fight.

But I didn't back down, either.

"He was a kid," I said. "We all have been. He made a mistake. We've all done that too."

The Merlin regarded me with an expression somewhere between irritation and contempt. "You know what the use of black magic can do to a person," he said. Marvelously subtle shading and emphasis over his words added a perfectly clear, unspoken thought: *You know it because you've done it. Sooner or later, you'll slip up, and then it will be your turn.* "One use leads to another. And another."

"That's what I keep hearing, Merlin," I answered. "Just say no to black magic. But that boy had no one to tell him the rules, to teach him. If someone had known about his gift and *done* something in time—"

He lifted a hand, and the simple gesture had such absolute authority to it that I stopped to let him speak. "The point you are missing, Warden Dresden," he said, "is that the boy who made that foolish mistake died long before we discovered the damage he'd done. What was left of him was nothing more or less than a monster who would have spent his life inflicting horror and death on anyone near him."

"I *know* that," I said, and I couldn't keep the anger and frustration out of my voice. "And I *know* what had to be done. I *know* it was the only measure that could stop him." I thought I was going to throw up again, and I closed my eyes and leaned on the solid oak length of my carved staff. I got my stomach under control and opened my eyes to face the Merlin. "But it doesn't change the fact that we've just *murdered* a boy who probably never knew enough to understand what was happening to him."

"Accusing someone else of murder is hardly a stone you are in a position to cast, Warden Dresden." The Merlin arched a silver brow at me. "Did you not discharge a firearm into the back of the head of a woman you merely *believed* to be the Corpsetaker from a distance of a few feet away, fatally wounding her?"

I swallowed. I sure as hell had, last year. It had been one of the bigger coin tosses of my life. Had I incorrectly judged that a body-transferring wizard known as the Corpsetaker had jumped into the original body of Warden Luccio, I would have murdered an innocent woman and law-enforcing member of the White Council.

I hadn't been wrong—but I'd never . . . never just *killed* anyone before. I've killed things in the heat of battle, yes. I've killed people by less direct means. But Corpsetaker's death had been intimate and coldly calculated and not at all indirect. Just me, the gun, and the limp corpse. I could still vividly remember the decision to shoot, the feel of the cold metal in my hands, the stiff pull of my revolver's trigger, the thunder of the gun's report, and the way the body had settled into a limp bundle of limbs on the ground, the motion somehow too simple for the horrible significance of the event.

I'd killed. Deliberately, rationally ended another's life.

And it still haunted my dreams at night.

I'd had little choice. Given the smallest amount of time, the Corpsetaker could have called up lethal magic, and the best I could have hoped for was a death curse that killed me as I struck down the necromancer. It had been a bad day or two, and I was pretty strung out. Even if I hadn't been, I had a feeling that Corpsetaker could have taken me in a fair fight. So I hadn't given Corpsetaker anything like a fair fight. I shot the necromancer in the back of the head because the Corpsetaker had to be stopped, and I'd had no other option.

I had executed her on suspicion.

No trial. No soulgaze. No judgment from a dispassionate arbiter. Hell, I hadn't even taken the chance to get in a good insult. Bang. Thump. One live wizard, one dead bad guy.

I'd done it to prevent future harm to myself and others. It hadn't been the best solution—but it had been the *only* solution. I hadn't hesitated for a heartbeat. I'd done it, no questions, and gone on to face the further perils of that night.

Just like a Warden is supposed to do. Sorta took the wind out of my holier-than-thou sails.

Bottomless blue eyes watched my face and he nodded slowly. "You executed her," the Merlin said quietly. "Because it was necessary."

"That was different," I said.

"Indeed. Your action required far deeper commitment. It was dark, cold, and you were alone. The suspect was a great deal stronger than you. Had you struck and missed, you would have died. Yet you did what had to be done."

"Necessary isn't the same as *right*," I said.

"Perhaps not," he said. "But the Laws of Magic are all that prevent wizards from abusing their power over mortals. There is no room for compromise. You are a Warden now, Dresden. You must focus on your duty to both mortals and the Council."

"Which sometimes means killing children?" This time I didn't hide the contempt, but there wasn't much life to it.

"Which means always enforcing the Laws," the Merlin said, and his eyes bored into mine, flickering with sparks of rigid anger. "It is your duty. Now more than ever."

I broke the stare first, looking away before anything bad could happen. Ebenezar stood a couple of steps from me, studying my expression.

"Granted, you've seen much for a man your age," the Merlin said, and there was a slight softening in his tone. "But you haven't seen how horrible such things can become. Not nearly. The Laws exist for a reason. They *must* stand as written."

I turned my head and stared at the small pool of scarlet on the warehouse floor beside the kid's corpse. I hadn't been told his name before they'd ended his life.

"Right," I said tiredly, and wiped a clean corner of the grey cloak over my blood-sprinkled face. "I can see what they're written in."

THE
DRESDEN FILES
By
Jim Butcher

"Fans of Laurell K. Hamilton and Tanya Huff will love this new fantasy series."
—*Midwest Book Review*

STORM FRONT

FOOL MOON

GRAVE PERIL

SUMMER KNIGHT

DEATH MASKS

BLOOD RITES

DEAD BEAT

PROVEN GUILTY

WHITE NIGHT

SMALL FAVOR

Available wherever books are sold or at
penguin.com